Praise for *Depraved In...*

"With trademark exuberance and venom, Indiana . . . spins a dizzying tale."

—*Kirkus Reviews* (starred)

"Misanthropic, funny, and razor-sharp . . . this cameo of boredom, calculation, narcissism, and emptiness is not only masterful writing, it also exemplifies Indiana's larger focus: a society whose appetite for dysfunctional celebrity spawns ever more of the same. Praise be to Indiana for writing a novel the way Diane Arbus took photographs: He shines cleansing, deadpan light on corners that allure us against what we hope is our better nature."

—*Kansas City Star*

"Indiana chronicles a fascinating slice of American lowlife with his customary satirical touch. . . . A high-end page-turner with genuine staying power."

—*San Diego Union-Tribune*

"Amphetamine fiction is alive and writhing . . . a hyperkinetic depiction of American greed, the American dream's septic tank."

—*Publishers Weekly*

"Acidly satiric."

—*Library Journal*

"The shocks Indiana delivers, both in crime and its coverage and handling, are more horrible for being grounded in reality. Repellent and fascinating."

—*Booklist*

"A sardonic, thermonuclear course into the heart of American darkness."

—*The Memphis Commercial Appeal*

Praise for *Three Month Fever*

"A legitimate heir to the crime-related nonfiction novel: Capote on peyote."

—*Chicago Reader*

"In Indiana's ingenious hands, what a bewitching, rollicking folly *Three Month Fever* becomes. In a book packed with sharp insight, clever writing, and emotional verve, Indiana has grasped the warped cultural context in which murders and media converge."

—*The Washington Post*

"A spellbinding fusion of journalism, social commentary, and novelistic license."

—*Entertainment Weekly*

Praise for *Resentment*

"In one beautifully written passage after another, Indiana's stream of invective against American bad faith resounds with integrity and vision . . . this may be one of the decade's great novels."

—*The Times* [U.K.]

"*Resentment* is the product of a huge satirical talent...much of this, even most of it, is brilliant. One reads Mr. Indiana's new work with astonishment."

—Richard Bernstein, *The New York Times*

DEPRAVED

INDIFFERENCE

DEPRAVED
INDIFFERENCE

GARY INDIANA

 ST. MARTIN'S GRIFFIN ⚏ NEW YORK

ISBN 0-312-31641-0

First published in the United States by HarperCollins Publishers, Inc.

First St. Martin's Griffin Edition: July 2003

10 9 8 7 6 5 4 3 2 1

FOR BARBARA KRUGER

Et le printemps m'apporté l'affreux rire de l'idiot.
—Arthur Rimbaud, *Une Saison en Enfer*

DEPRAVED
INDIFFERENCE

PART ONE

WHILE I DIE

THE
GREATEST
GENERATION

WARREN

Clutching his heart outside the Wells Fargo Bank in La Jolla, Warren remembers the day he and Devin rode in this same teal Lincoln Town Car up to the Women's Federal Secure Facility a few miles out of Frontera. They were picking up Evangeline, who during her incarceration had sent no end of insane letters to what she referred to in one epic of dubious remorse as "the two great big men in my life," meaning him, Warren, and Devin, who was thirteen at the time, along with the customary avalanche of legal papers, motions to dismiss in the insurance countersuit case, appellate briefs in the pilfered chinchilla case, an elaborate medical and psychiatric demur in still another case, all of these drafted in journeywoman legalese by Evangeline for polishing by whichever attorneys had not already been stiffed for their fees. There was a civil suit pending that is still pending, bolstered by Evangeline's conviction for coercing servitude or whatever, a case where Warren took a Harry Helmsley walk (albeit a pretty steep walk, if they don't settle the civil case soon and the lawyers for the so-called abused maids take whatever money Warren hasn't already squirreled away in the Caymans and whatever property Warren hasn't signed over in deed trust or what have you to various associates, confidantes, and whatever passes with Warren for a friend), as Warren would plainly admit, if it were the practice among the Slote family ever to plainly admit anything, including their own names. There were process servers lurking all over the countryside like kudzu on a Georgia pine barren, even poor Devin had had to deal with them, and until Evangeline's run of bad luck three years earlier (a richly deserved run, in Warren's view), they had been in incessant motion like a bunch of sharks between Oahu and Vegas and Nassau and Puerto Vallarta for god knew how many years, as if by just moving around and altering a few trifles of their public presentation such as name age and Social Security number, they could evade all sorts of unpleasant legalities, which had turned out to be true.

However, the slavery charges involved virtually all these juris- dictions, which made it a federal matter, because at one time or another most of the maids had been kept in all their houses and condos, Evangeline rotated them from residence to residence, as she believed this prevented them from "getting smart," as she put it, getting rambunctious or above themselves, though she also obliged them to call her Mama and pretend they were part of the family, a family with which they had to make grueling daily efforts to get along, as they were going to be part of this family "forever." "Forever" was sometimes a whole year, even longer, but some had gotten away during lulls in Evangeline's vigilance, slipped out win- dows or carelessly unlocked doors, or been dismissed after six months or eight months, Evangeline wanted everything in her realm spotless and shiny and perfect and not every one of these Mexican girls could live up to such imperious standards. Then too, they did not especially appreciate being kicked and punched by Devin at whatever age, or Devin feeling up their skirts for pussy, or being locked into their rooms at night, or being slapped around and pummelled by Evangeline.

Warren perfectly saw their view. In fact, he had even urged

one of Evangeline's rather dim procurers, one of these titless wonders from god knew what dreary graduate schools in the midwest
that Evangeline enticed via Internet as tutors for Devin, not to
bring any new maids in from Mexico—well, actually he had urged
the young woman to bring not more than one or two, as opposed
to the five or six that Evangeline was demanding, but he had really
meant for her not to bring any. Warren fretted about Devin. He
worried that things were happening to Devin that would have an
irreversible ugly effect upon Devin. He could not oppose
Evangeline in any more important way, so decided to voice his fear
that Devin might grow up with Spanish as his first language.
Warren said that in his experience, this could have a catastrophic
impact on a child who would have to speak English all the time
later on. Naturally Warren was drunk, as Warren had to be whenever he planned to sound an unwanted note of reality or even
unreality in Evangeline's sensorium. It never got as far as
Evangeline anyway, when he sobered up the next day he advised
the girl, Janet or Christie or one of them anyway, to forget everything he'd spilled in his cups. He said if she told Evangeline about
their conversation he would deny it ever occurred, and then where
would Janet or Christie or whomever be? Mama would take Papa's
word over any of these ungrateful young hicks who were getting
the opportunity of a lifetime working for the Slotes: international
travel, gourmet cuisine and so forth, gifts of scarves and trinkets,
best of all the festive atmosphere that Mama spread around herself,
as she herself said, not unlike the legendary Auntie Mame. Mama
referred to the chaos and panic she generated everywhere as her
"zest for living."

Unfortunately, many who lacked this protean zest sooner or
later turned against her. Mama believed that everybody made up
stories to get away with something and that almost everybody who
worked for them eventually hooked up with some implacable
conspiracy fomented by Warren's ex-wife and their kids, and
Warren's aunts, and Warren's cousins, and possibly a maverick gov-

ernment agency, along with something she referred to as the
Honolulu Mob, all these accountants and lawyers and insurance
adjustors who wriggled through their ken ended up getting
bought off, paid for false depositions, menaced into perjured testimony by threats from the Honolulu Mob. According to Mama,
Warren's relatives under the auspices of the Honolulu Mob had
planted rattlesnakes in Mama's Lexus one time and another time
Warren's daughter Ritchie tried to assault her in the clubhouse at
Santa Anita Racetrack, tipped off to Evangeline's precise whereabouts by this self-same Honolulu Mob, or by the maverick government agency. It was Devin they were trying to harm,
Evangeline asseverated, they were trying to get to her by either
kidnapping Devin or maiming him with lye or making him disappear. Because people do, you know, Evangeline often said, disappear all the time, especially small children.

Evangeline knows how to paint a picture. She is painting one
this minute for a loan officer of the Wells Fargo Bank, a picture of
144 acres of untrammeled wine country real estate aching for a
developer's touch. She is also, much more importantly, painting a
picture of Evangeline Slote that the loan officer may recognize as
the kind of person Wells Fargo Bank does business with, while slipping a veritable haystack of this loan officer's business cards into
her pocketbook. Or else she went in to use the toilet. Warren has
lost track.

Warren has an extreme, searing pain running up his left arm,
and something worse going on in his chest. For some reason, he
feels detached from this ensemble of hurt, intermittently involved
with it but mainly elsewhere in his head, recalling that morning
with Devin, come to think of it they hadn't taken the Lincoln
Town Car but a leased white stretch limo Evangeline had insisted
on, "Give these slobs something to think about when they stare at
my ass for the last time," was the way she put it, a very long limo
streaking up the coast highway. He remembers having dreamt the
night before of hands that could not be made clean, red laterite of

Paraguay, black sand below the house near Diamond Head, blood spatters in a bungalow in Puerto Plata. None of it washed off, impervious to bleach or the most pungent of perfumed soaps. Hands forever dipped in fecal springs of revenue and savorless revenge, scrubbing themselves for eternity. He did not think they were his hands, but in the dream they were his responsibility, attached to his will and agents of his nature.

"We're not too far from the Mandalay," he told Devin, reminding himself to get a manicure.

Devin in Gap khakis and a blue cotton shirt and a cream linen jacket sat what seemed a mile away from Warren, chewing his thumbnail, inspecting himself for lint, dreading Evangeline's immanence and at the same time curious to see what would happen next, so it seemed to Warren, who sprawled longlimbed on the buttery leather behind the driver's partition, poking ice in his bourbon.

"Cash cow of the Inland Empire, the Mandalay. We tried running it ourselves for five, six months, but I'll tell you something, any couple operating even a halfway viable motel, the pressures are odious. *Odious*," Warren repeated, *odious* being a favorite word.

"I can imagine," said Devin, though his imagination was elsewhere.

"I mean the *people*," Warren went on, the elbow supporting his drink hand planted on the knee of his crossed leg. He flicked imaginary dust from his loafer tassels. "Hayseeds. Kiwanis Club riffraff. Fucking Knights of Pythias. And you can imagine, love complaining. Plus you're playing house in a goldfish bowl, people checking in and out twenty-four seven. We turned it over to a nice couple from, let me think, Costa Mesa. Ran it for us for ten years without a problem, can't think of their names."

"The Richters." Devin supplied the name as Warren slopped Jim Beam into his glass. Besides liquor, the limo smelled of gardenia perfume: Warren's idea.

"Richter, of course. You've heard this ad nauseam I suspect."

"It sticks in my mind because Richter—"

"Snuffed Mrs. Richter," Warren recalled with satisfaction. There was one cunt that would never spill. Rotten way to go, though. "Used something like a weed whacker, which gave it a certain cachet in the local media. She was fucking our linen supplier, Samoan named Kendall. Now it comes back. Same week JFK bought the farm. Wiped it off the front pages for a while, but it came back. We brought in a management company after that. Had them take over the High Hat in Monterey and all the stuff in Palm Springs and Nevada. Plus the flagship property in Anaheim. Less headaches all the way around."

If any region could be called Warren Country (and in the private lingo of their family, it was), it would be the littoral of theme motels and glacier-molded hills and inlets unfurling then along that highway, and though the smoky windows rendered it as inky blobs in a dense gray fog, Warren sensed his exact location like a bird picking up the earth's magnetism.

"The Mandalay was one of the first, no, *the* first project where Zena and I handled all the financing and retained ownership after completion."

Warren couldn't help himself. He relished the vernacular of swift-moving deals, the patois of roving capital. "Up until then we were selling our equity off to various investor syndicates and taking back the operating leases and then selling those to the operators. Tell you what that Rotary Club fric and frac loved about motels. No tipping required. *Odious* bunch."

Bourbon wet his David Niven mustache. In the limo's crepuscular plush, the slightly pornographic blue neon glowing in the ceiling, Warren told himself he was still handsome in a raffish, late 1940s, David Nivenish sort of way. In bright daylight, people who remembered the younger him sometimes remarked on his alarming pallor. But such people were rare in his life by that time.

Devin slouched. He kneaded his cheek with fossicking fingers. His fingers were long and blunt, his skin chalky, like Warren's.

Devin looked like Warren. A lot. He had heard all about the Mandalay before, but it relieved Warren's nerves to tell it.

The road sliced along grass-spattered dunes and four-mile beaches, hugging cliffs held in check here and there by aprons of steel mesh. Sometimes it whorled inland through coppery hills, spilled down into glassy valleys full of sprinkler grids spraying thousands of legume and lettuce acres. The farms were Warren Country too. He could recall several crapulous seasons of pea-picking and melon-plucking right in that fertile vicinity, 1936, 1937, moving up and down the central valley with the harvests, thirty fucking cents an hour, tops. Pick until you dropped, squash, corn, you name it. Warren occasionally pictured himself torpedoing out of those sorry years like a majestic orca shattering the ocean's surface and tossing off great plumes of foaming spray.

What did he secretly know, he wonders now: just how many things did he habitually ignore to spare himself the misery of seeing them without the filter of Evangeline or Jack Daniel's? Did he perceive then, for example, what he now sees: how quickly Devin, who was so scarily younger than he should have been in certain ways, scarily older in others, clocked a recent trend on Warren's part to dwell excessively in the past? Nostalgia had not normally been one of Warren's characteristics. At least not the kind, plangent with rue over vanished joys, that he had lately expelled after a few breakfast cocktails. Warren knew that he wouldn't have shuffled Zena, his ex-wife, into previous tales of his trailblazing era in motel construction. Devin had probably never heard Zena's name at all until a year earlier, unless Warren happened to be talking on the phone with a particular lawyer—not any lawyer, Warren spent much of his waking life talking with lawyers on telephones, but a specific lawyer named Katz with whom Warren went, as he always remarked after such a call, way back.

"Poor Zena just doesn't know her way around a courthouse," was the type of thing Devin might have overheard, if Warren were on the phone with Katz. "Well, fuck her. Fuck all of them."

That day, that time, they had begun drifting into Warren's reveries, if not his actual life, the cashiered relations, including the ones Evangeline rudely referred to as "Warren's former children." They would get a surprise once he'd cooled, he thought, one that would reveal the true state of things and explain, as if they didn't know, how formidable Evangeline had really been. Warren planned to make things good, after he was gone.

"The Mandalay," he told Devin, as if they were plotting a current deal. "Fifty-nine tasteful rooms complete with A/C and private telephones, ahead of its time in both departments. RCA television. Simmons mattresses. We did good."

Warren recalls that entire day as one that moved him a jump closer to death than most individual days did, it was one of those days that comes every ten or twenty years and knocks some further stuffing out of you, he remembers that the person driving the big white limo was Perry McDaniels, a hard type who had adjusted their insurance claim the first time the Diamond Head house had a fire. Perry McDaniels had lost his position at the insurance company for approving an initial payment of $75,000 to the Slotes, so Evangeline offered him the caretaker job in Oahu. Perry McDaniels was weak-minded and cunt crazy and would likely have done anything Evangeline asked him to, including torching the house again when she needed mad money. Warren was fairly certain that Evangeline had wrapped Perry McDaniels's sausage on more than one occasion. ("Get a big limo, get Perry McDaniels to drive you," Evangeline had fluttered over the prison pay phone.) Despite Perry losing his position, Evangeline had squeezed another fifty grand from Pacific Rim Insurance by flying to Wilmington, Delaware, and scaring the shit out of the relevant CEO by showing up at the door of his suburban home clutching a bouquet of white lilies. A child's birthday party had been in progress. Somehow the presence of small children in certain locations tended to suggest to people the kinds of things Evangeline was capable of. When she wanted to scare people, Evangeline almost always found a way.

With the maids it had usually been the threat of deportation as an alternative to Evangeline's abuse, which was ironic, because some of them had absolutely no idea what state or even perhaps what country they were in. They would either see a magnificent ocean view from the windows of whatever place they were, or the seventeenth hole of a country club where Dinah Shore sometimes played golf. Other than that, the view from a moving car, and a lot of airport interiors. Some of them who had turned out not to be right for the family actually begged to be deported, or anyway sent back. There were not many minutes in the day when any particular maid might have a word with Warren out of Evangeline's hearing, and Warren had done his best to avoid such moments by announcing a headache when he sensed a moment of that sort coming on, retiring to his bed and his collection of entomology books. But of course there were those inescapable episodes when they found him alone in some odd pocket of whichever house, and more or less threw themselves on his mercy in an access of melodrama. An unpleasant, Pontius Pilate feeling would ensue, quelled only by the plopping of a few ice cubes in an expanse of bourbon.

"Warren's old, he needs help," he once overheard Evangeline telling some recalcitrant tutor who had already had enough weirdness and was getting ready to quit. The tutor was phoning from Tijuana. She was stranded near the border crossing with a car she'd rented on her own dime and two sixteen year olds who couldn't speak English and Evangeline had calculatedly failed to meet her as promised at the Sheraton down there. "You can't just abandon us," Warren heard. "Think of your references. Well, it won't look too good no matter what you tell them, there's two sides to everything and the older person is generally the one listened to, I find, especially when they're from our class of people. Did you know that Bing Crosby is one of Devin's godfathers? *Warren* served as our Ambassador to Cameroons, and later to Nigeria. I myself was Senator Cranston's chief aide for seven years. We know the U.N. Ambassadors from Quatar and Pakistan, we know shieks and emirates, who do you know? That's correct, Julia, nobody. You will one day, if you persevere and don't abandon your responsibilities. Meanwhile listen and learn. Just put the girls in the trunk and drive the fucking car through. They won't do a thing to you if you get caught and practically no one ever *is* caught despite whatever propaganda you may have heard, no one that looks like you, young, nicely dressed, well-spoken and relaxed. Relaxed is the main thing. Cops smell tension, that's their job."

EDDY

Clark County, Nevada, Federal District Court, February 12, 1986

Please state your name for the Court.
Edward Ramsey.
What is your current address?
1293 Alta Vista Road, Verdugo Hills, California.
What is your current occupation?
I operate a company that duplicates business documents.
And are you the owner of that company?
Yes I am.
Where were you employed in the fall of 1978?
I was employed by Trans-Western Insurance Company of Los Angeles.
What was your job title, Mr. Ramsey?
I was a Claims Supervisor.
What is the nature of a claims supervisor's work?
A claim supervisor reviews claims after their initial approval by a field investigator, in other words he or she audits to make sure the field investigator's findings and recommendations are in line with the company's reimbursement guidelines.

During the fall of 1978, in your capacity as claims supervisor, did you have occasion to meet the defendant Evangeline Slote?

Yes. She and her husband.

How did that meeting come about?

The Slotes had had a burglary in a house they owned in Honolulu, several items had been taken.

And Trans-Western was the insurer of that home?

Trans-Western carried the insurance on the house, yes.

And you met with the Slotes where?

I believe I met with them at the Beverly Wilshire Hotel in Beverly Hills.

Now, this first meeting was to discuss their insurance claim, is that correct?

Correct.

There had been items stolen from the home, and your job was to do what?

My job was to decide the amount they would be reimbursed by Trans-Western. Normally, I wouldn't have met with the claimants in a settlement, but the Slotes were unhappy with the figure the company had already approved, they asked for a face-to-face meeting.

What was your decision regarding the Slotes's insurance claim?

After talking with them and reviewing receipts they presented, I authorized an increase in their compensation.

In your judgment, then, the Slotes were credible.

They were very credible. I didn't just base it on them, though, we had a police report and an investigator's report, and other things.

There were no doubts that the Slotes had in fact suffered their losses in a burglary.

None whatsoever.

As far as you know, no one at Trans-Western entertained any doubt about the legitimacy of the Slotes's insurance claim.

Not to my knowledge, no.

Now, did you later have a social relationship with Mr. and Mrs. Slote?

Yes, I became friendly with them.

Can you tell us a little about that?

Well, they were a very warm and energetic couple, very outgoing, I think at some point they told me that they had a home in Las Vegas, and it came up in conversation, that I went to Las Vegas frequently. They may have said something to the effect of next time I was out there I should look them up. I think several months after their claim was settled, I had a call from Mrs. Slote, Evangeline, saying they were grateful for my help with the settlement and I should make a point of visiting them in Las Vegas. I don't recall the exact circumstances. But I did meet them for dinner some time after that, and eventually we became social friends.

And you have seen the Slotes on a social basis ever since that time, correct?

I haven't seen them as often in the past few years because I don't go to Las Vegas as often.

But between 1978, let's say, and 1984, roughly, you were often a guest in their home?

I wouldn't call it often, I saw them at their home maybe three times a year, and occasionally joined them for dinner when they came to Los Angeles.

Did you visit Mr. and Mrs. Slote at their condo in Puerto Vallarta, Mexico?

On one occasion, I don't recall what year, yes.

And did you visit the Slotes at their home in Honolulu?

I was there on two occasions when I happened to be in Hawaii.

Now, when you visited Mr. and Mrs. Slote in their various homes, did you witness interactions between Mrs. Slote and the people she employed in the house?

Yes, I would say almost every time, because usually a maid would answer the door, and there were often maids working in the room where we were, or, you know, bringing things out to the lanai, sometimes they were serving food, if we were having a meal, or cleaning—

Did you ever witness Mrs. Slote striking any of the maids?

No sir, I did not.

Did you ever witness Mrs. Slote speaking to the maids in a harsh manner?

No, in fact they always seemed to be in a happy mood, and Mrs. Slote laughed and joked with them to my recollection.

She spoke to them in Spanish, correct?

Yes, sir, but I speak Spanish so I know the kinds of things she said to them.

You never heard Mrs. Slote call any of her maids "a little bitch" or "a little slut"?

Not ever.

"A sneaky little whore," "a filthy wetback"?

Absolutely not.

You never saw Mrs. Slote burn a maid with a red hot iron?

No, never. Far from it.

Did you ever see Mrs. Slote strike a maid with coat hangers?

No sir. Again, far from it.

Throw boiling water on a maid?

No, nothing like that. There wasn't anything like the kind of hostile atmosphere where any of that would have occurred.

Would you say there was a pleasant atmosphere in the Slotes's homes?

Yes, very pleasant, very relaxed.

And did the maids seem relaxed to you in that atmosphere?

It certainly appeared that way to me.

They didn't strike you as terrified and fearful?

Not to me.

Did you ever sleep at any of the Slotes's homes? In other words were you ever an overnight guest?

Yes I was, twice I believe, once in Las Vegas and I stayed overnight at their place in Puerto Vallarta. It got very late and we'd all had a few drinks, and Evangeline, Mrs. Slote, didn't want me to drive back to where I was staying.

When you stayed overnight did you have occasion to witness Mrs. Slote locking her maids up in their bedrooms?

I never saw that, no.

You never saw Mrs. Slote lock a maid in the closet in her own bedroom?

No sir.

Did you ever see anything to suggest that the maids were being kept in the house against their will?

No absolutely not, the doors were all open, sometimes they were working outside, washing the car, or gardening, there weren't any walls keeping them in.

Did any of the Slotes's maids ever beg you to help her escape from the house?

No, again, there was always a pleasant easygoing situation. You could see they worked hard but they were smiling and normal.

What was your reaction Mr. Ramsey when you learned of these charges being brought against Mrs. Slote?

I thought it was just outrageous. I know these people. I can't conceive of them doing anything like that. My first thought was, these are wealthy individuals, this has got to be about money. I thought there had to be some mistake.

Thank you Mr. Ramsey. No more questions Your Honor.

Mr. Ramsey this is Mr. Steinberg one of the prosecuting attorneys, he's going to be asking you questions, if anything is unclear or you don't know how to answer a question, tell me and I will have the question rephrased or explained to you.

Good afternoon Mr. Ramsey.

Good afternoon.

Mr. Ramsey, when did your employment at Trans-Western Insurance Company come to an end?

I left at the beginning of 1980—let me think, it was either at the end of '79 or right at the beginning of 1980.

So you were still employed at Trans-Western in 1979, correct?

Correct.

Now, do you recall being asked by Mr. Hennessey about any questions arising at Trans-Western about the legitimacy of the Slotes's insurance claims?

Your Honor, objection—

Your Honor, Mr. Hennessey opened the door.

I asked about a claim, singular—

He asked about talk at Trans-Western Insurance, Your Honor.

The objection is overruled, witness may answer.

Isn't it a fact, Mr. Ramsey, that after you met Mr. and Mrs. Slote concerning their burglary claim in 1978, the Slotes filed two more claims with Trans-Western, one in June, 1979 concerning another so-called burglary at the same house in Honolulu, and another in October of that same year for a fire that damaged that house?

I couldn't testify to the exact dates but I believe so yes.

And isn't it also a fact that Trans-Western denied both of these subsequent claims on the grounds that the property claimed in the second robbery didn't exist, and the fire was determined to be an arson fire?

I didn't handle these other claims, I never saw the paperwork—

Your Honor, I'd like to introduce this document into evidence as People's Exhibit 62, and show it to the witness—

Okay, this will be People's 62, and that is—

It's a Denial of Claim Affidavit, would the witness kindly have a look at this document and tell the Court if this is a form familiar to you.

This is a form we used as an internal document, to record why a particular insured's claim was rejected.

It's different than an adjustment affidavit in what way?

An adjustment affidavit would go into reasons why the company intended to compensate less than the amount claimed by the insured. A denial of claim is what it says, the company denies liability.

Would you read Mr. Ramsey the portions of this affidavit that I have highlighted there in yellow marker?

". . . given that the door locks recovered show no evidence of tampering, and a trained arson dog indicated the presence of accelerants in four separate locations on the property at 9600 Thalia Massie Drive, the fire is assumed to be of malicious origin by persons with normal access to the property and therefore claim is denied."

Now. When this insurance claim was turned down, is it not the case, Mr. Ramsey, that your prior approval of a claim by the Slotes was the subject of an internal investigation?

The prior approval was reviewed. I wouldn't call it an investigation.

What in your mind Mr. Ramsey is the difference between a review and an investigation in this context?

The difference is that there was never any suggestion that I deliberately approved an illegitimate claim, only that I had made an error.

And didn't you leave Trans-Western shortly after the results of that investigation, I mean that review, questioned your judgment as to the disposition of the Slotes's initial claim?

That isn't why I left—

But you did leave, shortly after the so-called review was concluded, correct?

Well, yeah, correct.

I have no further questions.

WARREN

O h Mother of God that war, Warren used to tell the pretty
ladies in his life. For many years after that war it had never
been necessary or even welcome to talk about that war, everybody had been through it and everybody had lost something
important and nobody much cared to think about it, but like
millions of other people all over the world, when Warren got
hammered, he had to talk it up. Going through the war in one
piece had energized him into a state of nervous ambition and
patriotic mendacity, he wanted money and he wanted kids and
he wanted to grab the whole fucking enchilada in the greatest
nation the world had ever known, he saw that a transplanted
Okie with a contractor's license could live like a Roman emperor
if he played his hand right and the war had taught him exactly
how.

He talked about it to Zena down in Austin one night when
they were both trashed on Pisco sours, Zena not especially
prompting him to entertain her with it but smiling her unreadable
smile the way certain women who knew their pussies were the target of all conversation smiled. Zena had flame red hair that fell
straight the way Veronica Lake's did, a slash of orange lipstick on
her long, thin lips, and quick green eyes slightly too big for her
face. Zena had a real aptitude for the main chance. She wanted to

get out of Texas, bad. She cooked a mean chicken fried steak and knew how to make a room look friendly.

"I bet you could make a million dollars," Zena prophecied that night, "building these roadside hotels. Seems like everybody coming back from Europe and what have you don't want to just settle down on the farm like before." That had been his eureka, all right. At least as far as Warren can recall.

Twenty years later, Warren told Evangeline his war story on the third occasion when chance or Evangeline's compulsive plotting had jostled her into his path in Palm Springs. Warren owned two motor courts that were wildly popular with, and always full of, motion picture business pansies from Los Angeles, at that time still not a completely ubiquitous feature of Palm Springs lodging establishments. There too Warren was ahead of his time. He knew from a friend of his sister Tammy Ann, that Evelyn, as she called herself then, had been checking him out through the usual circuit of afternoon boozers in places where Warren was fond of drinking. The first time he saw her she wore some sort of Indian sari and teardrop earrings adorned with fake emeralds and she looked a lot like Liz Taylor in *BUtterfield 8*. The second time she wore a white dress cut below the shoulders. The third time it looked like the same white dress with more cleavage showing and a cloud of gardenia perfume choking off the air around it. Her hair was wrapped in a white turban. She drank Wild Turkey neat. She laughed at Warren's jokes. They were in a bar full of neon beer ads that had a dance floor and a mariachi band.

By the time of this third encounter with Evelyn Carson, Warren had studied a rap sheet Styles Janowski had dug up for him, Styles being a retired Oceanside investigator who owed Warren many favors and creamed his pants sniffing into other people's business. Styles had the creased face of an old iguana and drove around the desert in a white Cadillac with steer horns jutting from the front grille. He wore a black suit and a string tie at all times, looking like a cowboy undertaker. His voice had been wrecked by throat cancer surgery, he had a nasty scar like a translucent centipede running up his throat, words came out of him wrapped in crackling mucus. Warren thought Styles said something about a "colorful past" as he knocked back the Cuba Libre Warren bought him, though it might have been "color fast" or "crooked ass," Warren never could understand a word Styles Janowski ever said. Luckily, Styles knew how to type.

So that third time, when he danced with Evelyn Carson, Warren knew, for example, that Evelyn Carson worked as a lobbyist for a slightly fishy managed health care company in Irvine. He also knew that Evangeline Annamapu Thurlow Slater Carson, a.k.a. a surprising number of other things on various warrants and indictments had been had up on grand larceny in Palm Springs for charging a mink coat and a set of diamond earrings to another Evelyn Carson's I. Magnin account on the strength of a receipt with the other Evelyn Carson's charge number on it. The interesting part was that the other Evelyn Carson shopped at the Santa Barbara I. Magnin, and the receipt was from there. Somehow the case got dropped, because the charging of the mink and the earrings had been approved by the store credit manager. Lucky or ingenious, either way it was all good.

Warren further knew that Evelyn or Evangeline or whatever her real name was had been arrested for shoplifting in 1961 in Sacramento, booked but never tried for grand theft in Long Beach in 1965, tried and convicted and given probation for auto theft that same year for taking a Glendale dealership car on a permanent test drive, arraigned but released on a plea arrangement for credit card forgery in Santa Ana in 1968. She had never done time. This history intrigued Warren as no other woman's ever had. Warren had not, in fact, ever been much of a student of women's histories unless, among male friends, the history of a particular woman's vagina happened to be under discussion. Knowing these things about Evangeline ratcheted up her already potent allure. She had initiative and mobility, things Warren prized.

And he knew she would listen to him. Warren sensed from the beginning precisely what Evelyn Carson wanted from him and that she would let him do anything he wanted to her and he knew he could tell her all he'd been through, Up There. She liked hearing him talk about the war. She recognized that mortal time was hard to get through even when it was good, and it usually wasn't. Evelyn Carson knew some things about time, she knew for example how long she could be Evelyn Carson in Palm Springs and when that would have to end, it was something feral about self-preservation and her instincts in this area were both delusional and impeccable.

It was always sunset and it was always gray, he told her that third night, gazing at her snug torpedo breasts as they danced. They'd roll out these steel mat runways, the B-17s coming into Umnak would bounce thirty feet the second the landing gear kissed the matting. Motor oil congealed like sheep fat. We had to heat the plane engines with fire pots. Men came back from the shithouse with their buttocks frozen black. What you were really fighting up there was the weather.

That Attu battle, Warren told her. The Navy and Army brass were at war with each other more than the Japs. They were having themselves one great big pissing contest in the middle of the Arctic Ocean. First they laid out this amphibious assault on Kiska, then they decided to leapfrog over Kiska and take out Attu. The guy who invented that strategy really won us the Pacific war but up there it was just a pain in the ass, the whole idea of it. Then the Japs got wind of the invasion. From Walter Fucking Winchell, blabbing to Mr. and Mrs. America and all the ships at sea to keep their eyes on the Aleutians. They went ahead with the invasion anyway. Night before the landing was scheduled a williwaw socked everybody in for three days and left this fog as thick as plaster behind it so the destroyer *Macdonough* rams this other destroyer and has to tow it three hundred miles back to Adak. We're out two destroyers, and the enemy knows we're coming. Brilliant. Even with that fuckup they went ahead.

All the artillery got stuck in the permafrost about ten yards from shore. Talk about a clinical strike, half our casualties bought it from foot rot and frostbite.

Warren could conjure the battle of Attu in each of its particulars for at least three hours. It was the longest story Warren ever told. He often condensed it to get to the beauty part, the two years at base camp after the Japs were driven out, when Warren became mess sergeant for two hundred and eleven grunts. Through meticulous pilferage of surplus fatigues and damaged weapons and things like soft-lead ammunition that they didn't use—you needed armor-piercing bullets up there to shoot through the ice—Warren contrived a prodigious trade with the laconic, primitive Aleuts for salmon and caribou steaks. Warren often claimed to have been the best-loved mess sergeant of the entire war.

Warren also finessed permission to amplify morale by setting up a poker game in a spare Quonset hut, an aluminum igloo that quickly became a full-fledged, gamy-smelling casino. The poker turned into blackjack. They even got a roulette table shipped in from Anchorage. Warren was a cautious gambler, a shrewd gambler. Then too, though he always left this out of the story, he cheated a lot. He came out of the Army carrying a sweet little stake, next thing you knew Slote Construction was born.

He did not tell Evelyn Carson so very much about Zena, except that his daughter Ritchie and his son Mike would necessarily be in the picture, if any picture happened to develop. They had left the nest and all that but they depended on him. Ritchie managed the Driftwood in Laguna at that point in time, and Mike was a foreman for Slote Construction. Warren expected to provide for them when he passed, and he had other obligations too, his mother Ruth for one, his aunt Velma for another, two widows who had never turned a dime on their own and were basically homeless, shifting back and forth between houses owned by Warren or houses owned by his brother Cleve, an oral surgeon in Petaluma. There was also his sister, Tammy Ann, who was subject to spells of narcolepsy and thus had never led what anyone could call a full life, if anybody deserved a full life it was Tammy Ann, but the Lord or whatever worked in mysterious ways, narcolepsy being one of them, Tammy Ann also lived with Warren when she wasn't living with Cleve, or with Velma and Ruth in one of Warren's houses, or one of Cleve's houses, this tribe of dependent ladies migrated seasonally from house to house, motel to motel, much to Warren's amusement, because by God he did have a soft spot for them, call him crazy if you would. Evangeline aped enchantment at these long-term but probably rectifiable problems.

He did not mention that Zena had been the management brains behind the motel ventures, or that Zena had nailed up Sheetrock and laid in floors and mixed cement and worked twelve hours a day the same as Warren had when they were just building the places instead of running them, Warren didn't need that type of person in his life anymore, and he didn't expect Evelyn to play that type of role, what would have been the point of discussing all that, rehashing all the charges and countercharges in that endless divorce suit, possibly justifying himself in some lame-ass way, when Evelyn seemed eager to accept Warren's ex-wife as the insane lazy greedy slut he implied she was.

Warren enjoyed the advantage of knowing that Evangeline had been named correspondant, in divorce papers filed by the wife of Evangeline's then-husband's employer, in one of the nastiest divorce cases ever to hit the *Sacramento Bee*. Warren happened to know this employer, a developer named Newhall, who put up subdivisions, including this Gracious Acres deal with ranch houses on half-acre lots. Evangeline had been working some kind of California Welcome Wagon grift, while Mr. Carson held contracts for two or three Gracious Acres properties. Mrs. Newhall's PI had numerous tasty snapshots of Evangeline and Newhall, unfortunately not included in Styles Janowski's dossier, in flagrante up the ass in Carson's office, or so the legend went. During the epic Newhall divorce, Evangeline and her husband had sued the by then former employer for defamation and nonpayment of wages and mental distress and a lot of other ingenious stuff. Evangeline had later duped Carson after an expedient reconciliation, by having him served with divorce papers when he rushed from Vegas to visit her in a California hospital, where she was supposedly recovering from a hit-and-run accident. Her timing had to do with making Carson liable for a slew of attorney's fees after their settlement with Newhall went into Evelyn's bank account.

All Evangeline offered on the subject was to say that her ex had turned out bisexual and not especially bright in business. Warren knew there was more than one former husband, and also a seven-year-old, semidetached son parked with distant relatives out in Henderson, but that had as little interest for him as Zena had for Evangeline: they'd been young, they'd been dumb, what the fuck, fuck it.

Of her first marriage, the one before Carson, this May-December thing with a Navy grunt named Slater she apparently knew in high school, the only detail that piqued Warren's interest was an unexplained fire that had ravished the couple's home a few weeks after Evangeline blew $14,000, roughly Slater's annual income, on Christmas gifts. She was able to produce receipts for these dispersed items to the insurance company as a record of personal belongings destroyed in the fire. The beauty part was, she'd gotten away with it, even hounded the carrier until they forked over several thousands more. This appealed to the side of his brain that Warren usually devoted to blackjack.

DEBBY

All the way to Cedar City, Evelyn fussed with her white mink turban and the zirconium replica of the Hope Diamond pinned to it and fiddled open vodka miniatures she kept in a zippered Petrossian bag, the kind they icepack caviar in. Debby Prio fooled with her hair and watched the wrinkled landscape wipe from desert to forest to mesa to forest to desert again as the car crossed a sliver of Arizona into the craggy wastes of Mormon Country. Devin, up front beside Warren, kept swiveling to regale Evelyn (and, presumably, herself) with limericks: *there was a young girl from Ohio, who spread 'em as wide as the sky-o*, Evelyn howled every time Devin opened his mouth. Debby couldn't get any read on Warren, whom she usually saw feeding quarters into the video poker games in the Wiggle Room, a lounge near McCarran Airport where she sang under the *nom de chanson* of Gloria Raymond.

Debby hadn't passed much quality time with Evelyn since the unfortunate point during one of Evelyn's appeal hearings when she, Debby, got subpoenaed about a so-called letter the judge in the case had received, begging for leniency on the grounds that little Devin, as he then was, cried every night for his mother and was starting to "act out" in disturbing ways. The prosecutors happened to notice the letter's signature read Deborah Pria, with an *a*, and forced her to expose the whole thing as a forgery: dumb move on Evelyn's part, especially since Debby wasn't even looking after Devin and wouldn't have been able to say, under oath or otherwise, how the kid was taking mom's incarceration. From everything she'd heard later, it was the happiest time of his life, despite the embarrassment. Warren, for one thing, put him in regular school and let him have friends over and got a pool poured for Devin's birthday practically overnight thanks to his contractor cronies, all this a far cry, in Debby's estimation, from Evelyn's customary circus of locomotion and calamity. Once Evelyn got paroled, a year shy of her sentence, the usual lunacy resumed, with even less rhyme or reason than before. Devin had had to finish high school out in the Bahamas or somewhere, at a parochial school where they pledged allegiance to the Queen of England.

She didn't think Evelyn knew that she had set her up the time Evelyn escaped from prison hospital (in Evelyn's version, by bribing some dimwit guard who quit the next day and claimed she'd been tricked into taking Evelyn's cuffs off and letting her use the toilet unattended); Evelyn had made a beeline for Debby's apartment, hiding there for a day and a half, trying on $5 acetate wigs and making herself up like a bag lady, leaving Debby exposed to some fugitive harboring rap. Evelyn really had been terrified, as if a soft six years was life imprisonment on a diet of worms. The minute she scrammed, the FBI came knocking and Debby was compelled, by her own lights anyway, to reveal Evelyn's whereabouts.

She had made the agents swear never to let Evelyn know who ratted her, like a federal agent's word meant anything. But Evelyn's mouth being what it was, probably thirty people could have told them how to find her. She was working skid row in rags but popping into her favorite bars after midnight, like a showgirl on break. Evelyn thought being a federal fugitive was just another costume change you could share with an audience. Much as Debby liked Evelyn—not all that much, when you came down to it—she resented being used like a paper towel, and Evelyn was incorrigible that way.

"There was a young girl from New Yawwk," Devin chirped, freshly inspired, "by rumor addicted to cock—"

What son says these things to his mother, Debby pondered. What mother encourages it. Devin was now a young man, handsome in a chiseled, frigid, almost corny way, like an ice sculpture at a cheesy wedding. He had many unnerving tics and peculiarities, sidelong looks and thumby hand gestures he seemed to have picked up by faintly reptilian mimesis from other college kids, a kind of smirky way of showing off his alleged intelligence. Debby had never considered the kid very bright, just overexpressive, and always in this rather phony way, like the male ingenue in a bad afternoon soap.

"—the rumors are sketchy, she loved to gulp leche, unless she was gagged with a sock!"

Evelyn exploded in mirth as if she'd been goosed with a cattle prod. Warren coughed meaningly. This cough threatened to deflate the carnival ambiance Evelyn tried to churn up in the car. Debby forced a weak giggle, but felt weird doing it.

"There was a young girl from Bilbao," Devin continued, leering at Debby. Evelyn unscrewed the cap of another liquor miniature. Debby turned to the window. "Who jammed herself onto my prow—"

Yes, there was something horrible between these two, Evelyn egging him on, as if they were the only real people in the world. Devin probably got a boner strangling kittens. The landscape made sudden transitions, from nothing to larger nothing. The car plunged into a vertiginous zone of foreboding geology, the road threading along the base of huge rock formations packed with hard black shadows.

". . . ten inches of meat, was happy to greet, that buxom young girl from Bilbao!"

"That's enough of that," Warren said quietly. Surprise fluttered across Devin's face.

"Oh, Warren, such a prude," Evelyn laughed. She sucked on her tiny bottle. Devin turned around to face the road. Warren could reel him in, Debby thought, but probably not for long. Evelyn had the kid by the nuts. Warren seemed tired as death and drained by any effort to assert his existence. Debby had seen Evelyn pumping him full of booze in the Wiggle Room, *I don't care what the doctor told you, Papa, a few drinks are good for your heart, it's been scientifically proven.*

The Cadillac-Olds place in Cedar City squatted beside the highway facing the silos of a bauxite mine, five scungy cylinders flanked by pyramids of slag the same drained color, and spiky mounds of rusting steel equipment. In lunar complement the distant mountains looked leached of any hue, dappled by livid shadows of fast-moving clouds. The dealership had about thirty cars on the lot, and others inside, behind plate glass, in a low white structure with an office at one end, and a thirty foot high neon sign, unlighted, that promised 5.6% financing. There were people in the showroom, feeling the upholstery of an immense blue vehicle.

The car dealer, Hardy Harbisher, could barely squeeze into his clothing. He wore a plaid shirt over a white t-shirt, the ends of both shirts untucked and stretched across a protruding wedge of white belly. He had fussily waved blond hair, and a face so enormous that his eyes had the unnerving sentience of a blubbery aquatic mammal, a lion seal or hippopotamus. On the trip, Warren had mentioned that Hardy Harbisher had been a popular children's ventriloquist on local TV in the early, early 1950s. Hardy's signature dummy had been named—in blatant, and as it quickly turned out unfortunate, imitation of Edgar Bergen, Joe McCarthy. Senator Joseph McCarthy became a national figure soon after Hardy's first triumphs in the golden age of television. A long decline, punctuated by a small role in an episode of *Sea Hunt*, had culminated in Harbisher's Luxury Vehicles.

Enormous as he'd become since his glory days, Hardy Harbisher still knew how to put on a show. For the Slotes—"these are my favorite customers," he asided to a spectral audience—he had an extremely tasty Coupe de Ville. He led them to it like a gang of children on a morning program. It was a Cadillac, but something more than a Cadillac. Hardy opened the driver door with an air of wild surmise. He slid his immense, ungovernable carcass behind the magnificently padded wheel. Wormlike fingers caressed the molded contours of the dashboard, its implementa recessed and beaming out data in soothing colored light. Something happened to Hardy's face. It became a souffle of contentment, as if every pore were soaking up the intoxicating perfume of the interior leather and its firm give under three hundred pounds of stress.

"Well, get in, get in, let's take her out on that big dead ponderosa out there and see what she'll do."

First Hardy drove. Then Warren drove. Then Evelyn drove. Then Devin drove. Debby felt she had gotten to know Cedar City intimately well in a very short time. She did not care to drive. Evelyn clutched her Petrossian bag with avid fingers and offered miniatures all around.

Back at the dealership Hardy studied the car they'd arrived in, one he had hated to part with a year ago, he said, and proclaimed it a masterpiece. Warren took Devin with him into the office, leaving Debby out in the sun with Evelyn. It was odd, Debby thought, for Evelyn to stay aloof from a transaction.

"Warren always buys his cars from Hardy," Evangeline told her. "Hardy's a card. All he needs is his old dummy. Wanna vodka?"

In the office, Warren tried to convey the precise flavor of Debby's, that was to say Gloria Raymond's, lounge act. For a small commission Debby laundered cash, but she was also a chanteuse. She had easily the worst vocal stylings Warren had ever heard. Hardy poured some shots of Old Kentucky.

"Friends who don't drink and drive," he snuffled, "aren't friends."

Gloria's act, Warren said, imitated the "old trouper who's seen it all and survived" routine of Liza Minnelli, and her repertoire, as well, was a piece of Liza memorabilia, including such long-ago hits as "Cabaret" and "New York, New York."

"Sounds like somebody I should get to know," Hardy said.

Evangeline, when the subject came up, said:

"You know, Debby, you could've just told them it was your handwriting."

"No, I couldn't, Eva," Debby said firmly. "First of all, you could have brought me into the picture in the first place and saved yourself a lot of grief. Second of all, how would I forget how to spell my own name? I don't make my as anything like my os, which any handwriting expert could testify. I'm sorry hon but it's you that screwed up. I don't pass judgments on people, we all gotta do what we gotta do. Whatever your thing is, live and let live, but don't blame me for your fuckup, especially when it was my signature."

Evangeline squatted down to examine her teeth in the driver side mirror of a gleaming four-door sedan.

"You just don't know what hell it was for me in there. Rats and vermin night and day."

Her teeth seemed to all be there. She rested her portable bar on the car hood.

"I admire you surviving the joint, I truly do," said Debby. "Guy I been seeing has just been scarred for life by his senior year in Atascadero, and I mean scarred. Took it up the ass from one mean nigger every night for eight months. Worst thing in his mind is, he loved every minute of it. Lucky thing he don't have AIDS."

Evangline attempted more oomph in her description.

"And regular, regular beatings, Debby. They used a phone book, so it wouldn't leave bruises."

Evelyn showed her an aghast expression, like a prom princess who'd been violated by domestic hogs and other livestock.

"That's a new one on me. Phone book, huh? I bet Evelyn they used the Yellow Pages. The Yellow Pages are a whole lot thicker than the white ones in Vegas. Course you were up Frontera way so maybe it's not the same, those little prison towns. You know something hon? I bet you'd adore and more my new hair stylist. Randolfo he calls himself, gay as Halloween and boy does that queen know hair. He does my boyfriend's hair as well. I notice Devin could use a little trim."

"You know," Evangeline persisted somewhat obsessively, "this one pregnant woman in there, no older than a girl really, she was being sodomized every night with a mop handle by two chapter heads of the Daughters of Bilitis—"

"Now what is that, Evangeline, Daughters of Bilitis, biker gang?"

"No, it's dykes, Debby, I was being sarcastic, that's what they called them in my day."

"Oh honey your day ain't over, stop actin' so tragic. Dyker gang, gotcha. I never turned to another woman's love but given what's out there in terms of men, it's crossed my mind plenty."

"Well," said Evangeline with rue, "if any dyke came on to me I'd bite off one of her fingers."

Debby had to laugh.

"Only one, Eva?" She changed her mind about a miniature and fished one from the Petrossian bag. "I'll bet house odds you could handle more than one finger. You know something hon sometimes I think you're trying to shock me. Let me tell you, you are one tough lady and I admire your grit but plenty of people have experience in this life. Sometimes Evelyn you take other people for a fool."

This wasn't going at all the way Evangeline had pictured. She yanked off her turban. A ganglion of black spit curls spilled out.

"Look here Debby it was hard up in Frontera."

"Hon I'm sure it was, I'm sure it was. And I sincerely sympathize with all you been through, but Frontera's a federal joint and I know plenty of women gone through there and there's plenty worse places, count your blessings for a change. I did a little time myself, and it wasn't no federal spa. Remember what Pat Nixon told you."

"I don't recall ever mentioning that to you," Evelyn said perplexedly.

"But you did, sweetie. That time you jumped the joint. Now, let's get straight what's going on here. I love a ride in the country and Interstate 15 is just about the prettiest ride you can take, but I have an idea you need something, to put up with my poor company all afternoon."

Warren told Hardy about the night he won a thousand dollars after the radio went dead up in Dutch Harbor.

"Warren adores you," Evangeline told Debby, changing horses.

"Hold on there," Debby said, putting her hand out like a stop sign.

"No, I just mean, we both love your company. Warren thinks you're a firecracker. There *is* something Warren needs to do, but don't think we only asked you out with us to do a favor. I'm not like that and neither is he. It's no big deal, it's temporary, we have these court judgments pending. We're optimistic but we're not stupid, if you follow me."

"I'd guess I'm slightly ahead of you," Debby said, "but go on. This more of the same thing with those maids or what?"

"Punitive damages and I don't even know what all. They're trying to fleece Warren dry for everything he's got."

"You can fight those type of things for decades before you ever pay a dime."

"I know that, but we're also being sued for attorney fees and that's been in the pipeline a long time, Warren's gonna have to cough up."

"So what is it Warren needs me to do?"

"Warren needs to sign some property over to a friend. That friend would sign a quit claim so the property has to go back to Warren next time it changes hands, at some point in the future when we're not facing a judgment."

"You need a cutout," Debby said. It was not such an unusual request.

"I'd call it a friend," said Evelyn, as warmly as she could. "Then if the friend gets uncomfortable or there's any mickey mouse that comes up, we sign it over to somebody else."

It was Debby Prio's sense that all reality was a pyramid scheme or a food chain. She did like to put things into play, just for the practice of it.

"Let me get back to you on it, Eva. I got to talk to someone first."

"Don't! There are people spying on us. Spying on our friends too, if past history's anything to go by."

"Spy meaning who, FBI?"

"Warren's relatives. They watch our every move. It's really become a witch hunt as bad as the McCarthy era. That Ritchie Slote, I swear to you, has hated me from day one. She'd send her own father up the river just to get back at me."

"If this thing is halfway legal I'll consider it," Debby said after a thoughtful swig from the teeny bottle. "If it's legal, though, I'll bet anything that deed's gotta have a correct date on it. I think sometimes they look and see if somebody's signed something over with a judgment pending. If I remember my law."

"I tell you though it's temporary. We sign it from you to a corporation once we get the papers filed."

"Like I said Evelyn I'll have to talk to somebody. Not mentioning names, of course."

"But you'll let me know as soon as you talk to them I hope?"

Debby nodded and emptied her miniature. Plastic blue and yellow pennants on staked diagonal wires flapped in the hot breeze.

"How's your other son doing, Eva?"

"He's out of the hospital, anyway."

"I heard they cleared him on that charge up in Ely. That must make you feel good."

Evangeline's heavily mascara'd eyes narrowed.

"Winnemucca," she said pedantically. "It was Winnemucca. They proved he was in Ely when they claimed he was in

Winnemucca. The ridiculous part of it is, Darren wouldn't have the wits to pull anything like that off."

"What, shoot a cop?"

Evangeline made a skeptical face.

"I think there was a whole lot more going on there than shooting a cop," she said. "Some drug thing gone sour. They had a meth lab in that trailer. I heard the cop was seen over there plenty before this so-called shooting. You have to learn to question authority in this life. Just because the papers say one thing."

"Well, so he's doing okay."

"The cop is *dead*, Debby. DOA at Ely Memorial."

"I meant Darren."

"Darren, huh, he's fine, sure, fine with his vacuum cleaners and whatnot. His daughter's seven now. Still with Milly, plus ça change. He absolutely had to marry a slut, you know. Completes the image he has of himself."

"I met Milly one time. She isn't bad. She's sort of nice, I thought."

"Milly is nothing but trash," Evangeline said vehemently.

Hardy pulled a plastic dummy out of his bottom desk drawer. The dummy wore a tuxedo.

"Joe McCarthy memorabilia," he was explaining to Warren and Devin. "This is just a prototype. 'Hello, boys and girls!' "

DARREN

Darren, the seven-year-old, was a dropsical bedwetting brat whose rearing Evelyn approached as a desultory science experiment, kenneling him for long periods with her estranged ex over in Henderson, alternately with her otherwise estranged foster parents up in Reno, in fits of maternal avidity enrolling him in a sequence of orphanagelike institutions of lower learning and yanking him out at arbitrary intervals in favor of Nevada public schools (which had been good enough for her, she harrumphed, peeved at the expense of pseudosteiner and cryptomontessori alternatives), with one nanny after another clearing Evelyn's calendar for the full-blooded pursuit of her consuming dream, i.e., "influence" among the more easily purchased members of Congress whose interests extended to the ripening neoplasm of Managed Care, and, concurrently, Warren's metamorphosis from generic tycoon to hyperpatriot and public figure.

As he had played no role in Darren's primogeniture, Warren assumed a neutral policy with regard to his upbringing. From the outset, Darren apprehended Warren with a sullen indifference that ripened over time into mild resentment, mingled with a sort of pitying, laconic friendliness. Warren did not hate the child. Warren was not a hateful person, in fact. He simply didn't see the point of him.

It did not help that Evelyn fed Darren bitter stories about Warren's relatives, with whom Evelyn herself maintained, during those first years, an honorary civility. Evelyn welcomed them in her various homes with unguinous familiarity, but the boy remained mute and rebarbative in their presence. They were country people, or anyway from country stock, and what they lacked in urbanity made up for in peasant cunning. They knew the difference between a shy child and a brainwashed one. They noticed things missing from their houses whenever Evelyn had visited with the incubus in tow, their pocketbooks looted when left unattended in Evelyn's houses. The boy's few remarks to them were invariably rude, obscene, and mistrustful, and obviously reflected what Evelyn herself would have said had she not nourished some fugacious hope of winning them over to her own exalted view of herself.

Evelyn tutored this brooding, silent, pudgy creature in casual pilferage from retail stores and the homes of neighbors. She drew him maps of the houses, stuffed his clothes with grocery items and cosmetics in the stores. To deflect an immanent bust in a Nordstrom's franchise, she once punched his face hard enough to draw blood, then screamed for the store to call an ambulance. After receiving an F in math, Darren learned from Evelyn how to distribute accelerant over school linoleum and chalkboards and set an entire classroom ablaze with a single match, crawling after midnight through a window he'd furtively unlatched in the afternoon. She also whacked the daylights out of him for failing math in the first place. *"What do you think MONEY is, you moron, it's NUMBERS!"* She regularly edited his selection of friends, never a numerous group to begin with, declaring to parents of the disqualified that Darren was "on the fast track" to an Ivy League university and could not consort with their mentally inferior offspring. Impervious to any notion of tact or even a rough sense of what a normal childhood might be, Evelyn made Darren anathema at every primary school in Las Vegas. Parents at these schools referred to Evelyn as *that lowlife bitch from hell*, to Darren as *that lowlife bitch from hell's little bastard*, their children heard this so naturally Darren heard it too. By age ten he had a citywide reputation as a thief and liar, as well as a budding pyromaniac, and though Evangeline compelled him to study up to four hours every evening, Darren was a dull, frumpy lad, shapeless in mind and body, torpid of affect, even deficient in criminal energy. He lacked the improvisational panache to deny that shoplifted objects discovered on his person had been deliberately pocketed, or to blame friends for little larcenies he was suspected of at school. Because he so readily confessed his transgressions, authority figures imagined him remorseful and worthy of a guidance counselor's bland behavioral tinkerings. He wasn't violent, as far as anyone could tell. Neither was he the worst student at any of these schools. He did averagely well in subjects requiring no imagination. There just wasn't any point to him, as Warren said. Even Evangeline wearied of him every few months and shipped him back to Henderson or Reno via Greyhound bus with the vague wish that Darren would "develop into something" by the time she saw him again. Warren predicted trade school rather than Harvard as Darren's likely alma mater. Among his own people, Warren referred to him as *the lump*.

They, naturally or unnaturally, delighted at Warren's indifference to the lump, and were heartened by his refusal to refer to it, ever, as his stepson. Among themselves, Darren was known as *devil spawn, evil junior,* and *Rosemary's Baby.* They prayed he would be the extent of Evangeline's vermination, that she would conjure no teratoid issue from Slote DNA. They predicted Darren's early incarceration in juvie, precocious heroin addiction, decapitation in a joy-riding auto wreck. All but the decapitation eventually came true. Still, their Christian faith, such as it was, obliged Ruth and Velma and Tammy Ann, and to a lesser extent Warren's brother Cleve, to periodically attempt some improving influence on the lump, which did not so much grow as expand as it aged, and to concede that it was much too witless to qualify as the anti-Christ, a role in any case amply filled by its mother.

VARLENE

Varlene Swales sniffed up a pebbled worm of crank, chopped fine on a smudged pink-framed mirror on the scarred dining table of her trailer. Bobby Ray dozed in the single armchair in the so-called living room, the TV rolling images across his eyelids: a Vincent Price lookalike with puffy lips and copious white hair demonstrated a boxlike cooking device as an avid woman in a dirndl marveled at each of its features as if they were giving her multiple orgasms.

Bobby Ray, Varelene considered, not for the first time, looked as adorable as Brad Pitt, if Brad Pitt put on fifty pounds of beer gut and lost a lot of hair. He was sprawled in a pair of white boxer shorts with red hearts on them and sweat socks, his red parking valet uniform balled up on the sofa. Passed out drunk as usual, but at least he wasn't passed out on top of her. One of Bobby Ray's recent problems was an inability to complete the act of love as he understood it, a relief to Varlene, really, though she tried hard not to say so when Bobby Ray flung himself on her in a vain attempt. Bobby Ray was quick even when he functioned, but packed a lot of action into a short time, much of it too raunchy for Varlene's taste.

Varlene often told herself that things would be good again, and sometimes she believed it. But the clear path she occasionally saw in her mind from points A to B invariably muddied up and disappeared, eclipsed by a congenital confusion which Varlene, over seven sessions she'd had with a clinical psychologist named Potter Phlegg, had uncovered as her Main Problem in Life.

Varlene had won the trailer in a private poker game when she was still dealing blackjack at the Nugget and living in a Motel 6. It was emphatically nothing special. A bedroom in back and a living room in front and a kitchen and toilet in between, a view of other trailers and mountains far away that wobbled in the heat. She'd added some touches, the afghan on the sofa an aunt of hers had crotcheted back in Topeka and quilts, quilts were a big item in Varlene's family, plus the table from Pier 1 Imports that got scorched the one time Bobby Ray tried to cook something and a little painting of a sailboat she'd paid twenty dollars for at a side-walk fair in Phoenix. She had also planted a little cactus bed beside the entry steps and fenced it off with small white crosses of the type found in cemeteries where people are buried by the County.

She reeled from the crank for a scary moment, then pulled the room into focus: a bowl of bruised peaches on the table, the sofa, the tv, the snoring man in the chair, the chipping rust-colored polish on her nails. The louvered window slats framed the propane cannisters of a trailer across the unpaved lane. Things would be good again, but probably not with Bobby Ray. Besides his parking gig, Bobby Ray had a part time weekend thing with this plastic surgeon who had a ranch out Moapa way, Bobby Ray was vague about the details but Varlene surmised it as untrained and unquali-fied surgical assistance. Ever since he'd started working for this Dr. Waldo, Bobby Ray had been lobbying for Varlene to get a tit job, supposedly at a huge mark down. Varlene considered her bosoms already too ample, and anyway she'd read all kinds of horror stories about burst implants and silicone traveling into people's facial nerves, and the bottom line was, Bobby Ray wasn't worth having any type of augmentation for. He worked hard, true, but then he pissed everything away on craps and liquor, just like the losers you'd see in the bus station any Sunday evening on their way home to blue collar hell in L.A. and San Diego, trying to lose the rest of it on slots before their buses pulled out. She lit a Marlboro and stood up, walked down the little hall and into the bathroom, which was roughly the size of an airplane lavatory, and began brushing her long straight brown hair and making speed faces at herself.

She was a short, slightly chunky woman of vaguely Amerindian, penguinoid visage, not at all pretty as she perfectly well knew, but genial-looking, as puffy-faced people sometimes are. She laid down her brush and did what she could with her face in the way of makeup, which tended to float on her reddish skin like leaves in a swimming pool instead of blending. She had a hard time leaving the bathroom. The drug made her want to scrub every visible surface with a toothbrush. Varlene resisted. She found a dark green sweater in the bedroom and pulled it over her t-shirt and changed out of her russet corduroy slacks into a pair of jeans. She briefly obsessed on a small moth hole in the sweater. She thought about leaving a grocery list for Bobby Ray and this reminded her that Bobby Ray was absolutely no good at shopping. His idea of a balanced meal was a tub of KFC wings, a six pack and a bag of chips.

She took the Mustang, noticed new speckles of rust near the door handle. She would have to bring it in, get some primer slapped on. She would have to buy food and beer and call the propane company and find a decent apartment somewhere and get rid of Bobby Ray and schedule a mammogram and re-enroll in her speech course because her "*w*'s" were coming back every time she got stressed. She called Warren "Wawwen" half the time lately. You disgust me, she told her reflection in the rearview. You never stick to anything, you keep getting waylaid.

It had been Dr. Phlegg's idea that Varlene should move into his place in North Vegas and get the full benefits of therapy while working as his housekeeper. Even Varlene had had enough sense to nix that arrangement. But without the full benefits of therapy she had just drifted into this Bobby Ray thing, one sozzled night of rough dinky dunkin' and all of a sudden he was living there, laundry and all.

When there was no calamity in her life, Varlene felt weirdly bereft and resourceless. At such times the bleached landscape with its thinned-out signs of life looked like an inescapable dead end, a place where people got trapped in the mountains and ate each other, where it was all just her and the rocks and the aging process. Out here in the ass end of town the billboards of Sigfried and Roy and the other big faces of the day looked especially robotic and scary, towering over the dust and mesquite. She knew why she'd left Kansas, but she no longer understood why she'd ended up here, where everything went way beyond phony, into a tawdry dream world of drizzling neon and funny money.

She turned up Tecumseh Drive and steered past the golf course entrance and several big houses, pulled into the curved drive of the Slotes' place. The guy who answered the door was this Roland O'Higgins character Evelyn claimed to have found through an ad she tacked up on a Salvation Army bulletin board. Tall, twitchy, muscular in a skanky way, kind of hawk-faced and ravaged, he reminded Varlene of the type of guy who'd got Agent Oranged over in Nam.

"Hiya there, Wowand," she greeted, attempting to brush past him. Roland blocked her, looking her over as he might some roadkill crawling with maggots. Yet he didn't really see her, Varlene could tell.

"It's Varween, Wowand," she said, waving a hand in front of his eyes. "The bookkeeper." She supposed she could act pissed off, but Roland became so abject and cringing in the face of any harshness that she didn't have the stomach for it.

Roland squinted. He tugged at his nostrils with grimy fingers. He seemed to emerge from a world of private care long enough to grimace at her and wave her inside.

She found Warren and Evangeline in the dining/living room,

a hacienda-style cavern centered around a huge fieldstone fireplace and full of shiny wooden furniture that tried for some species of high tastefulness. Varlene did not know from taste, but she did know most of the Slote house had fallen off a truck one time or another, the stuff that hadn't stood out. Teakwood screens pillaged from Tibetan monasteries and that kind of thing. They were drinking with their rabbity new lawyer.

"Varlene, Varlene," Evangeline sang out. She wore a weird chiffon Christian Lacroix knockoff, with a lace chamisette that made her neck and head look oddly prim, like Miss Jean Brodie trapped on the body of a fat Kim Novak. She waggled a martini glass at the lawyer on the sofa. "Otis you met before, haven't you?"

Otis Lemming, Varlene thought, looked like a man who'd already burnt up all his lifetimes, and like many such people inhabited Outer Vegas as a kind of wavering ectoplasm. He would go through several wives and get prostate cancer, if he was lucky. His watery features seemed to dissolve behind a scrawny mustache, which was going gray. His thin mouth appeared hard and determined but he was, somehow obviously, easily and repeatedly steamrollered by his own existence. Like Bobby Ray, actually. Varlene knew all the signs.

The only great thing about drinking on speed, it took vast quantities of alcohol to become slightly less than coherent. Speed organized everything in the brain into something bright and manageable. It was one in the afternoon. Not the cocktail hour for Varlene, but Evelyn always insisted.

For Otis, who'd recently taken on the precipitous drama of Evangeline's appeal in a civil suit her former maids had won against her, as well as her litigation against the insurance companies that had failed to indemnify her against damages in the same suit, the cocktail hour couldn't come too quickly. He had worked for eccentrics in the past. He knew that with these people he was perilously out of his depth. They thrived on litigation. Otis thought they probably dreamed up lawsuits in their sleep. If he were a younger man, with a staff of twenty, he supposed he could be in shyster heaven. But I am only Otis, he told his mirror every morning. Believe it, the mirror told him. He'd answered an ad in the *Nevada Law Journal* and even though he was not actually licensed to practice law in Nevada, or anywhere else at the moment, Otis had been a halfway good attorney in his heyday. A company lawyer, though, a lawyer for a bank, nothing like this. On the other hand, the law was pretty much the law no matter what you applied it to. The trouble was, the situation here had moved way outside the law in record time, and Otis found himself carried along like a cork in a whirlpool.

"We're getting ready to travel again," Evelyn announced. She presented Varlene with a Bloody Mary, a drink she had for some reason decided was Varlene's favorite. "Nice and spicy the way you like it."

"Where you goin'?" Varlene just hated the taste of tomato juice first thing in the day.

"I never know just where we'll end up," said Evangeline, going for a frothy Rosalind Russell effect. "But I do know I'm gonna need a notarized thing again saying who I am."

Warren cleared his throat. He seemed about to speak. He apparently changed his mind. Otis got up to fix himself another drink. He obviously couldn't wait for it. His hands shook. Warren and Evangeline watched Otis make his drink. They watched his hands shake. Evangeline took off her large harlequin-style eyeglasses and laid them on the glass coffee table. The clear surface was supported by a monstrous chunk of driftwood that always gave Varlene the creeps. That Otis, she thought, is one scared motherfucker.

"I lost the one you gave me. So I'd like you I guess to just make one up and put your stamp on and leave the lines blank for me to sign later."

Artificial logs crackled in the fireplace, a useless intrusion on the powerful air conditioning. Varlene felt things sliding, as she often did here, into areas where she had a certain degree of hapless equivocation. Hapless because whatever qualms she felt working for the Slotes, she could not resist Evangeline's implacable confidence that Varlene would do anything she asked her to.

"Face it," Bobby Ray told her whenever she voiced her trepidations. "You're a spineless tool for anybody says they love you. I should know."

At first Evangeline had showered her with presents, dresses, hats, a lace brassiere, novelty items of a type found in casino gift shops. She declared that they were true sisters, soulmates even, and when Devin was home from college, he too paid her elaborate compliments, kissed her on the cheek and gave her hugs, called her "one of the family." Only Warren maintained a measure of formality in their dealings. Warren had hidden depths, Varlene believed.

"I'll need it toot sweet," Evangeline told her. "Roland's picking up the mail while we're gone, you don't need to bother. You should just come on Friday and write checks for the phone and electric. DO NOT pay that garage, they're trying to rob us blind."

One day Evangeline began depositing thousands into Varlene's checking account so that all her bills would be paid in Varlene's name. Varlene felt a vertiginous thrill, as if she were being hurled off a cliff. Accountants did, of course, often pay people's bills for them, but this was something else, some manner of cleaning job. Varlene had notarized a fair amount of blank paper before it occurred to her that Evangeline routinely lost the documents Varlene notarized for her and had to have stamped duplicates lacking any signatures. But it did occur to her eventually. She had never worked a laundry thing before, well, she had, but a different kind of laundry thing. If she ever got Otis alone she planned to grill him about her potential tax liabilities and RICO status.

Evangeline had told her some story in the middle past about why she didn't use her U.S. passport to travel in and out of Mexico and the Bahamas. It made as much sense as anything else, so Varlene let it go. Pieces of paper, how meaningless could anything be. Otis was drinking too much. Anybody could see that. A Type A personality, sure to keel over in middle age.

"We really need to pop in on our beachfront in P.V.," Evangeline said in her Gracious Hostess manner. Something bawdy and potentially nasty lay coiled up behind it, a hint of demonic exuberance that Varlene thought of as Evelyn putting on the Liz. "Warren loves it down there."

"Horse shit," Warren said. Evangeline ignored him.

"He's always adored that funky little town," she added.

"Horse shit," Warren again stated, lurching forward to stare into Otis's eyes. The zeal of liquor burned in his face. "Are you with it and for it, Otis? Is America the greatest democracy the world has ever known or what?"

Otis looked alarmed. Warren sank back. His face creased benevolently.

"Famous last words of Pat Nixon," Warren cackled, toasting Otis with his empty martini glass.

"Warren, do me a favor, go to hell," said Evangeline.

EDDY

The white hotel in Encinitas was a crumbling many-gabled wedding cake popular in bygone years with Del Mar punters and adulterers en route to Tijuana. Erroll Flynn was said to have played "Chopsticks" on the second floor bar's ornamental Steinway, once upon a time, with his balls. During the '60s, it had been a favorite rendezvous for rock stars and their heroin dealers.

The tennis courts had not been resurfaced in many years. The swimming pool, shaped like a giant lung, emitted excessive chlorine fumes. The clientele had thinned out, but Warren still enjoyed the big low-ceilinged lounge downstairs, with its plate glass vista of the roiling Pacific. He liked the carved panels of dark wood, the thick figured carpet, the fiberglass models of World Cup sailboats mounted on the walls. He had thought about buying the place, decades ago, after spending a weekend there with Maisie Richter. He had discovered a hammock spider nesting in the shower curtain: a good augury, he thought. But somehow that deal had traveled south, nothing to lose sleep over, yet Warren often imagined certain parts of his life turning out a different way if one or another small element in the past were altered: a fuck here, a deal there, you really couldn't ever know.

He munched from a bowl of tiny pretzels and sipped bourbon on the rocks at a round table beside the window. It was the waning part of the day, the clouds at sea turning pink along their edges. The hotel stood on a cliff. The sea began past an outcrop of laterite that had been collapsing in stages since the 1930s.

"Such, such were the joys," a hearty voice intoned, breaking into Warren's contemplation of a cargo tanker in the blue distance.

He surveyed the figure in tennis whites jogging in place at his elbow. A stubby, tough-looking man with his sweater arms knotted at his sternum. Beside him, in a pleated tennis skirt ending an inch or so below her pussy, stood a ponytailed woman of round, pointlessly grinning features, who appeared to be about sixteen.

"They still have a bottle with your name on it over the bar, Lester," Warren said pleasantly. He noted Lester's leathery dermis, his pendulant jowls with satisfaction. "Take a pew."

Lester declined, though he did stop jogging, giving his companion's arm a proprietary squeeze.

"Trish and I are going to play a few sets, thanks anyway. You're looking hale, Warren." Lester did not bother introducing Trish.

"As the end draws near," Warren sighed, with a droll look, "a feeling of peace seems to smooth the ravages of time."

Both men laughed tinny laughs. Trish flashed an impatient smile at Lester.

"How's Evelyn?"

"Oh, Evelyn goes from strength to strength, Lester, she always has."

"All that court business cleared up now?"

Warren tongued his teeth for pretzel debris before replying.

"Well, Lester, you know that whole business was all about money. Cocksucking lawyers put them up to filing charges in the first place."

"I heard one of your attorneys on that thing had his office firebombed."

Warren shrugged. "What can I tell you, those people play dirty."

Lester was enjoying himself, Warren felt certain.

"I hear that last guy you had kind of dropped out of view," Lester persisted.

"Not sure I follow you," Warren said, tossing a pretzel into his mouth. "Which guy."

"That Lemming character," Lester elucidated. Warren tracked the note of insinuation and wondered what combination of words would make Lester go away. Lester's date rubbed her twat against his tennis shorts, purring her eagerness to hit the courts. That should do it without words, Warren thought.

"That fella had problems of his own, as it turned out," Warren offered. "He's probably down in the Caribbean somewhere slurping up the Mai Tais. Incidentally, Lester, I heard they were extending the statute of limitations on fraud in the state of Maryland from seven to twelve years, where do you come down on that, philosophically speaking?"

Lester didn't miss a beat.

"I think I come down on the happy side of that, actually," he laughed. Trish laughed with him, involved for a moment. "As the end draws near the time goes quicker, I guess I don't need to tell you."

"Glad to hear it, Lester. Best of luck. And best of luck to you too, is it Trish? I thought I caught the name. Short term memory's still intact. Doesn't go back twelve years, but twelve minutes I can manage."

Warren made a shit-eating grin into a quotation of itself.

"Best to you too Warren," Lester said with excessive warmth. Warren barely bothered to get up and let Lester pump his hand from a somewhat meaching altitude. "Give my best to Evelyn."

"She'll be thrilled that I saw you," Warren said. He saluted the departing Lester with his empty glass. When Lester was completely gone, Warren gave him the finger. He gestured at the bar for a refill, turning to see Edward Ramsey arrive, in jeans and a crewneck sweater with no shirt under it, carrying a Rite Aid bag. Warren imagined the Rite Aid bag was full of condoms and toothpaste. Eddy must have been pushing sixty but looked, to Warren, like a merely middle-aged Ryan O'Neal. He rose fully from his seat to shake Eddy's hand. Eddy's hand darted out of Warren's like a nervous little cootie. The contact was decidedly pro forma, not the firm hearty grip of yesteryear. Warren had reason to notice such things.

"Did I just see Lester Ryman?" Eddy sounded doubtful.

"Certainly did."

"Haven't seen Lester in God must be seven eight years." Eddy said this as if he felt he'd been lucky.

"Used to see him all the time when he was fucking my wife," Warren said evenly. "Since then I haven't had the pleasure of his company at all until this afternoon."

Eddy didn't know what to do with his face.

"Anyway," Warren said, "I asked you here because I need a favor. I'm not the type to lead up to it."

"I know that, Warren." Eddy had been helped on the interest rate of a small-business loan by various friends of Warren's in the middle past. Of course he might have thought that marker already called in, given his testimony in the slavery trial. Warren gathered his wits, such as they were.

Eddy's drink arrived. He drank it quickly and ordered another. Warren also got a refill.

"Basically, here's the problem. I signed a house over to someone, and I need to move it to a third party. This I'll be frank is to shield assets. You're a lawyer, I wouldn't ask you to take it on faith that it's legal."

"Technically speaking," Eddy said, "whether it's legal or not depends on a number of different things."

"I'm talking about Nevada," Warren said.

"I don't know the statutes in Nevada," said Eddy. "This is a house you're living in?"

"One of them, yes," Warren said. "On paper it's a motel, or rather property of Slote Motels, it's listed as a corporate office.

Deeded to somebody else as I say, but there's a quit claim reverting it to me."

"And if I asked, you'd file the quit claim?"

"Absolutely. Why don't we get out of here and go sit by the pool."

They paid up and went to the pool and ordered more. No one else was in the pool area. The light had fallen. The hotel's spotlights diffused into DNA helixes under the water.

"This pool used to be full of people," Warren said. He sat on the leg hinge of a chaise, with a leg of his own on either side. Eddy walked around the edge of the pool. Stars appeared between clouds, but were hard to see through the crisscrossed spotlights.

"Can you remember a moment in your life when you thought, 'California, this is it, end of the road.' " Eddy spoke from across the little motes of steam running off the water. They caught the light and made Eddy look like an x-ray.

"The end of the road is the end of the road," Warren said. "Wherever you happen to be."

Eddy nodded. He could tell Warren couldn't see him. He walked around the far end of the pool and back to where Warren was.

"Thing about Lester," he said, squatting on his haunches near the water. "One part of him wants to be the biggest prick in Orange County, the other part wants to bake cookies for a long-shoreman."

Warren cracked up. "Lester's a fag? I always thought so." He had never thought so, but instantly warmed to the idea.

"I just say he has a submissive side. A little-girly side. Look who he goes with. They're always nuts."

"Evangeline's nuts," Warren blurted.

"No shit, Evangeline's nuts." Eddy instantly perceived that this was not the moment to second Warren's opinion. "I mean, we're all nuts, Warren, who isn't nuts? Evelyn's fun-nuts, compared with these neurotic bitches Lester finds. Or used to find, anyway. I really haven't kept up with the Lester saga."

Some people they couldn't make out too well had come out and were settling on furniture across the pool.

"Plastic Bertram, X-Ray Spex," a woman's voice said. The voice was young, theatrically jeering. She was giving the answer to a pointless quiz.

"I need to transfer this thing as soon as possible," Warren said.

"Yeah," said a man's voice rising from the mist. "and then it's all, 'Bunny made me go, Bunny got me to take the keys out.' "

"All right," Eddy said. Warren heard his reluctance, in some way sympathized with it. He had a sad feeling of remoteness from Eddy, who had once been a close friend.

"Muchas gracias," Warren said. "I'll have the paper work messengered on Monday." Something still prickled. "With a Xerox of the quit-claim," he added.

"Yeah, right, exactly, like she should just wish," brayed one of the dark specks beyond the pool steam.

Eddy rattled cubes in his glass. He would not tell Warren that his word was good enough. They both knew it wasn't.

"You still haven't said if you ever had that California moment."

Warren thought about it.

"I've had a whole lifetime of fucking California moments," he said. He felt stoned. "I'm thinking of this as a California moment."

If silence could be a piece of gristle shunted to the margin of a dinner plate, the moment that followed would have been like that. And a venomous nasal shrill poked through it a moment later, from the murky group of golden youth ranged in darkness across the pool:

"I hope she's scarfing down a whole cow up there in Mendocino. Fucking bulimic bitch."

EVANGELINE

No part of Evangeline's later plans included Warren having friends of his own, run-of-the-mill golf buddies maybe but not intimates she didn't know or cotton to, in whom Warren confided. Evangeline wanted people to experience them as a couple. A couple of what changed from week to week, but the important thing was togetherness, unity, a sense of cohesion, for if one other being mirrored for her whatever odd thing Evangeline suddenly decided she was, no power on earth could declare her anything else.

She didn't want any part of his life closed to her. She was all he would ever need, and he was more or less all she needed to get everything else she wanted. The same deal he'd had with Zena, with the roles turned around. Warren was less uncomfortable about it than he thought he should be, except when he had to jettison friendships he already had. He let them go with great anguish he could only share with a decanter. Those days went very dark for Warren, and he sometimes washed down a pill with whatever he was drinking. Anybody would.

He had been really fond of Trudi, extremely fond, he could chitchat with Trudi about insects and other things that interested him, things that made Evelyn shudder and accuse him of morbidity, *Oh honeycakes why do you dwell so much on bugs? It isn't healthy,* he enjoyed getting Trudi a little tanked and talkative, just a friendly thing, nothing to get twisted about.

"Tell me again about the icknu—what was it?" Trudi implored him that last working day, genuinely curious.

Warren's office, the northern dead end of the mazelike house on Tecumseh Drive, was a long comfy rectangle brightened by a slanted skylight of pebbled glass. It contained two Ikea work stations, two desktop Macs, six five-drawer file cabinets, a small wheeled oak-veneer bar, and a decrepit black leather sofa. It had tall standing lamps of undistinguished design and some framed pictures on the walls: Warren and Eva in the White House with Mrs. Nixon, Warren and Eva meeting the Fords on a reception line, Warren and Eva with an itty bitty black man in a large white headdress from the U.N., Warren by himself, looking very dashing indeed, holding a framed Flags of the Fifty States poster.

"Ichneumon," he told Trudi. He gathered breath to regale her. "A parasite wasp. I've told you all about the orb-weaver spiders. One of nature's true marvels."

Warren had his long legs up, ankles crossed beside his computer. Trudi had put her computer to sleep and taken him up on his offer of a nightcap, though it was only three in the afternoon. That day she wore blue jeans, a wrinkled seagreen crepe blouse, and a scuffed pair of Nike running shoes. She lay on her back, svelte legs draped over the couch arm, her head on a shoulder bag in soiled rainbow colors she always carried, stuffed with her gym sweats, keys, bills, notebooks, snacks, everything you'd need for a month in the country.

"They spin a perfect web," Trudi recalled.

"As round," Warren said, "as a compact disc. The wasp is the orb-weaver's mortal enemy. If she can, she stings the spider's abdomen and emits a kind of curare that induces temporary paralysis."

"Egad," said Trudi. Her feet squirmed in their running shoes. "I read that Serpent and the Rainbow stuff about how they turn people into zombies down in Haiti. It's the same bad mojo."

"For the spider, it's worse than zombie-ism," Warren assured her, as if zombies were a normal feature of his day. "After she recovers, she spins her web in the normal way for up to two weeks. But the wasp has already laid its egg, which adheres to the orb-weaver's stomach. And now the larva feeds on the juices dripping from the little punctures." Warren shook his head. "It's a damned shitty way to go," he said.

"Nature can be so sick," Trudi said. "I mean that is so ugly."

Warren shrugged. In the spider kingdom he had seen it all.

"It's evolution," he said. "You think people are horrible, look what insects do. Eat their own kind, suck the guts out of still-living prey, you name it. Now, the ingenious thing is, the night before the larva actually finishes off this unfortunate orb-weaver, something in its chemicals, the scientists still have no idea what, causes the spider to create an entirely different kind of web than its usual disc of perfect symmetry. Instead, it now spins something that looks like tangled macramé. And once this stronger, less elegant web is complete, the larva kills its spider host and secretes its cocoon on the ugly macramé."

Trudi shuddered. She drank the last of her Campari and soda. She stood up, flung her bag strap around her shoulder.

"That larva reminds me of somebody," she said.

Warren smoothed his mustache with a fingertip. His mouth crinkled in a curdled smile.

"Me too," he said. "Quite a few people, really."

"Gotta go," Trudi told him. "See you next week."

"May your nest be free of parasitic wasps," Warren told her.

But he didn't see her the following week. Evangeline shit-canned her that weekend over the telephone when Trudi refused, for the third or fourth time, to give her specifics about Warren's stock holdings. The irony being that Warren had little wealth tied up in securities. He mostly owned land, and buildings, and kept bank accounts that Evangeline knew all about anyway, at least at that point in time. The further irony was that after the Trudi

episode, Warren began sequestering his assets even from the subsequent bookkeeper's scrutiny. Poor Trudi. Well, not poor Trudi,
Trudi would manage, poor him. Warren had driven over to
Montecito for a couple days for a zoning board hearing and a
piece of ass, when he came back to Vegas Evelyn told him she had
been "forced to let Trudi go."

"You see Warren don't you that if *I* am to feel that someone
regularly comes into the place where *I* live, and darling this is not
about privacy I *respect* your privacy you know I do, but someone
who actively *dislikes* me, because I swear to you on my Catholic
faith Warren I *never* asked Trudi to divulge anything relating to
your business that was none of my business, and how am *I* to feel
safe in *our house*—"

Her voice was an astonishing instrument, raspy yet melodic, bell
clear yet pillow soft, spongy in fact, as if straining through layers of
muffling gauze, versed in all the artless cadences of reasonableness,
clogging, when all her beneficent intentions had met with the
implacable malignant forces ranged against her God knew why, with
the choked tapering scrape of incipient tears welling in her throat; her
voice barely paused, audibly overcame the kind of outrage and hurt
that would leave ordinary mortals speechless and sobbing, and struck
instead a munificent world-embracing note. She was trying, in the
manner of a much-abused but undeterrable clinician, to get to the
bottom of the latest assault on her sensibilities.

Not everyone hearing this voice might entirely credit its sin-
cerity, or find it plausible that Evangline's major problem in life
was, as she believed, *always trusting the wrong people*. This swearing
on her Catholic faith malarkey when she didn't even know the
Our Father—not that Warren, a convert, knew it all the way
through himself—really was pushing things, but she had clasped his
head and plunged his face between her gigantic breasts all cloudy
with jasmine talc, and from this enveloping, primal vantage point
he had to concede that there might be "some truth" to what she
alleged.

They were in the kitchen, at night, her tits, her, Warren, the windows open on the sepulchral quiet and bluish nacre of the golf course and the cooling breezes of the desert night, the appliances threading the silence with faint theramin-like vibrations. They had recently installed tiny halogen fixtures on mauve-colored aluminum stalks that sprayed out of the ceiling like spider legs, casting small puddles of lighting drama on a marble cooking island and a bowl of guavas on the breakfast nook table. The contractor who installed the lights was suing them for nonpayment, Warren recalled. Well, it wasn't exactly what they'd had in mind, the guavas looked hepatic, the whole setup made the kitchen cold and morgue-like, full of feathery shadows. Evelyn sat on his lap. She loosened his tie. She caressed his remaining hair. She painted his scalp with pink lipstick kisses, cooing terms of endearment like bird calls, *honeybunch, sweet thing, why can't everyone be as happy together as we are, am I your woman Warren tell me I am promise me I am and always will be.*

"You know you are," Warren awkwardly whispered. He had no aptitude for love talk. Her breasts shifted massively in their white silk cocoon. He cleared his throat. Her tits were taking over his mind. "Trudi is a goddam good bookkeeper," he said, fighting them off. "I can't keep everything in that office straight. I don't know where I can find anybody who can."

"*I* know how much you relied on Trudi, Warren, I only *wish* we could've kept her on, but when someone actually *threatens* you—it hurts to have to tell you, but she did, she made threats, she let it slip she's been in contact with Ritchie and Cleve and spreading stories about *me*—"

"Are you *sure* that's what she said, sweetheart? Are you one hundred percent *certain* you heard her right?"

Warren's voice gently chided his sweet chuck, as it were, approximating her birdlike coos. At such moments Warren felt very much like Joan Crawford in *What Ever Happened to Baby Jane?*, an unmanly feeling that promised nothing good.

It was quite impossible and pointless to accuse Evangeline of lying, for to do so was to unleash a tsunami of hysteria no sane person, having ever witnessed it, would ever wish to see again. Evelyn did not lie. Could not lie. Reality, rather, assumed a different form in her mind than it did in anyone else's. Evelyn believed that anything she said was true and real, even when it had no conceivable relation to the world where other people lived. Lying, as an effort of will, didn't enter into it. Evelyn lied as the bird sings, as the spider spins its web. She simply was not aware of this instinct in herself, and never could become so.

When Warren contemplated this fact, he felt incredibly protective of her, as though she were a fantastic, threatened species of orchid dealt him in the card hand of fate. It was a test of his obduracy, even his virility, to shield this night-blooming exotic against the withering daylight. The best he could ever attempt in the way of reality testing was to suggest, as a very obscure possibility, that Evelyn had misheard, or misinterpreted, whatever it was that no one at all had said or done in the first place.

"I'm far from being deaf or dense, Warren, Trudi stood *right there*"—Evangeline pointed at empty space behind him—"and told me she'd get me, get both of us if she had to, she said she was going to your relatives and tell them I made false claims on our insurance company, she talked about *tax evasion*, and writing a letter to the IRS, she said I was *evil incarnate*, that I didn't *deserve* a man like you."

Warren sank into familiar confusion. Was it possible? Just a tiny bit possible? Trudi was no saint, Warren wasn't foolish enough to hire any saints to do his taxes. He could, with some effort, visualize Trudi standing in the kitchen, carried away, perhaps, by some half-conscious infatuation with himself, certainly she did admire him, and level-headed as Trudi seemed, emotions raged in women because of hormones and what have you. He recalled, suddenly, a night in the Aleutians, with Mavis, the Red-Haired Whore of Dutch Harbor, him getting out of bed to take a leak and coming back to find Mavis's eyes fixed on his privates in a murderous glaze. There had been a knife lying on a table in the room, a long knife for cutting tall grasses the Aleuts fashioned their folkloric baskets from, some blubber-chawing aborigine had traded it with her for a little jiggy-jiggy, no doubt, something like a machete, he remembered Mavis's eyes and his eyes drifting in unison across the blade for a long time, and then she'd tossed her flame red hair back and reached for a cigarette and lit it and coughed and smoked and motioned for Warren to bring his dick closer to her face.

"Well, the good news is, I have found a woman who is twenty times, a hundred times the bookkeeper Trudi could ever hope to be," Evangeline serenely announced, her fingers now busy inside Warren's fly. Mavis dissolved in flakes of cerebral confetti. "You are going to adore her, Warren. She works at the Sands three to eleven in reservations, she holds a very high job there, I tell you Warren when I met this woman the thought jumped right into my head, 'This is my kid sister. The kid sister I never had.' It truly did. Full of fun, and smart as a whip. Her name is Varlene and you're just going to love her."

TAMMY ANN

Evangeline's boudoir stares into Maunalua Bay from a godlike elevation. Far below its seven windows and their view of trellised bougainvillea, spiny giant aloes, hibiscus, glossy anthurium, and candlenut trees full of chattering mynah birds, a footpath zigzags down a thicket-encrusted slope to a private beach. The beach is invisible to her, but the broad swerve of the bay, and the blunt mass of the island's prize volcano, give an awesome sense of her enviable domain.

The room awash in frilly beige and ivory accents, the bed covered in mango silk and fat decorative pillows, canopied by gauzy curtains on a trestle of hooped CorTen. Lamps and decanters and family pictures in frames, on tables covered in the same mango silk. A Japanese maple reaches to the ceiling, rooted in an embossed clay tub. A mossy scent from the garden and Evangeline's ever-present gardenia perfume hang in the air, which is humid enough to rinse laundry in.

Evangeline reposes in a chenille armchair, her feet in furry bunny slippers resting on a tufted beige ottoman. All, here, is beige, or peach, or pistachio, or mango. She considers these her "safe" colors, colors that evoke a sense of relaxed control over her environment. The blue of the sea, the cotton clouds, all of that. Her lap supports a large oval tray of painted tin with a portrait of Britain's

Queen Mother waving from it. On the tray, a phone with the speaker switched on, a prescription bottle, two miso soup bowls, a two-pound bag of Gold Medal flour, a coke spoon, and a stack of paper napkins from Burger King.

"Boys enjoying themselves?" Warren wants to know. Warren is in California, many time zones away. Evangeline selects a gelatine spansule from a pile in one of the lacquered bowls. She carefully twists it open and pours the tiny pellets inside into the other lacquered bowl. She places the short end of the empty lozenge on the topmost paper napkin and packs the long end with flour using the coke spoon.

"Darren took Devin to the beach," Evangeline says in a loud, hearty voice. "He's going back to Henderson tomorrow, thanks be to Jesus. Can you believe he's got that trailer park Lolita knocked up already?"

Warren can well believe it, but really doesn't care. Evangeline's first-born has receded from their lives to a condition of sporadically pestering revenant.

She taps the two chambers of the spansule together, wipes a fleck of escaping flour with a napkin, drops the completed pill into the prescription bottle. She wets a fingertip and dabs it in the mulch of varicolored pellets, licks off whatever sticks, dries her finger on a fresh napkin, plucks a new capsule from the bowl.

"What about Tammy Ann?" Warren asks.

"Oh, you know, Warren, she wants to bake a *pie* for you when you get home, it's all she can talk about. She's had pie on the brain ever since you left."

"Bless her heart," says Warren. "Has she started that new medication yet?"

"She certainly has," Evangeline says, tapping flour from the spoon into the new capsule. "And I'll tell you, I'm already witnessing an improvement. Miss me?"

"Like a frog misses the pond," says Warren.

"Since when am I a pond, lover."

"Like a crane misses Lake Titicaca," Warren amends.

In California, he wiggles his long, bony toes. His long, bony toes are embedded in the pubis of one of Sheik Ubu El-Ketami's houris. She squats on a plump pillow demonstrating, on his right foot, an ingenious form of massage therapy that a second love-gal is performing on his left. A cloying incense mixes with a faint but burgeoning gamy odor. This fantasia from the bawdy underbelly of Islam has been improvised by Sheik Ubu, who sprawls on a Moorish divan matching the one Warren's sinking into, enjoying similar attentions from two other transient concubines. His raking mustache and jutting, hornlike beard are speckled with white powder.

Sheik Ubu, scion of a limitless oil fortune and, in some sectors of Islam, a direct descendant of the Prophet, is a young man, not yet thirty, tennis trim, handsome in a Levantine way despite the pitted dark skin so common among even wealthy Saudi males, who thinks of himself as a Byronic figure. Like Warren, he wears a terrycloth pool robe, fresh from a perfumed idyll of underwater fucking. In America and Europe, the Sheik devotes himself to the "swinger" lifestyle, which, though harder to ferret out these days than in decades past, keeps the saturnalia of the '70s alive in secret little enclaves (few of them as lavish as the Sheik's $4.7 million mansion), its acolytes signaling each other in the classified ads in *Screw* and similar publications.

The Sheik scandalized his Beverly Hills neighbors a year ago, by installing numerous statues of his naked female hirelings, or whatever they are, on the lawn of his estate, in full view of Sunset Boulevard. The statues were painted flesh tone and resembled plastic love dolls, bearing similarly astonished, oral-receptive expressions. After months of nuisance complaints, the statuary was crated back to The Kingdom, where it now graces one of Sheik Ubu's many palaces.

"Ah yes squeezing the manly foot with the very moist cunt," the Sheik groans encouragingly. "And you," he says, mussing the hair of his easiest to reach date, "chew upon her rosy nipple!" The Sheik has English as a third language. Despite his evident satiety, his face is a mask of contempt. He likes to say women are like insects. He knows about Warren's fondness for insects, so the remark has a bifurcated edge.

"Where are you, Warren?" Evangeline counts the remaining pills in the bowl.

"In the lobby at the Marmont," Warren tells her. "I'm supposed to be meeting Eddy Ramsey for a drink, but I don't see him."

"It's early here." The emptying and filling of pills has assumed an assembly line rhythm. "I may join the boys down at the beach."

"I'll be back on Thursday," says Warren. He can hardly keep his place in the conversation. "Ready for that pie. If I know Tammy Ann it'll be cherry. I wonder—oh, I think I see Eddy now. Looks like his blue blazer."

"Eddy's there? Let me say hi!"

"You know what, Evelyn, he's stopped to talk to somebody over by the desk, I'll have to say hi for you."

"You give Eddy a great big hug. Tell him to have a kir royale on you know who. You have fun, don't let him keep you out too late!"

Sheik Ubu glided into Warren's radar in the Vegas past, at a baccarat game in Circus Circus, incarnating in that unsurprising way that Vegas people do a satorial and ethnic stereotype of what Varlene Swales likes to call "the high wowwers." The Sheik's overheated comeliness, his aura of unimaginable wealth appealed to Warren, who normally thinks of himself as not having a single homo bone in his body. Not that he wanted to *do* anything with Sheik Ubu, he just found him strangely attractive. His uninhibited facial expressions, especially a certain look of incredulity when anyone had the temerity to bore him, his elegant, decisive gestures on the baize. Slightly larger than life, like a well-drawn cartoon with a ton of money. And the sheik, whose sexual and financial extravagances have always had a certain Mephistophelean object aside from quelling his implacable libido, "took a shine" to Warren, whose curiosity he scented, primarily as a potential client of the so-called Royal Saudi Bank of the Caymans, which he happens to own. And he sensed in Warren the yearning of a pussywhipped hick for the kind of kinky thrills exotic men far richer than himself indulged as a matter of course.

The Sheik has a few esoteric tastes that Warren doesn't share. He finds it amusing to treat Warren to the occasional swinger-style *bal musette*. He's exposed Warren to his little perversities in calculated doses, always as an honored bystander free to partake or leave it alone, in this way securing a connection of intense complicity based entirely on mutual exhibitionism.

Warren has never known this sort of quirk-sharing intimacy with another man. At times, he views their relationship as peculiarly fated, an initiation into a headier knowledge of carnal nuance than most people ever acquire, useful in all sorts of ways, like Evangeline's esoteric system of type-coding. At other times Warren feels he has crossed some perilous line with this special friend, whose rampant fetishism often strikes him as grotesque. The Sheik sees their bond in religious terms. In The Kingdom, Ubu often says, a man of his sort is as a God, and each of his whims are the glory of God. For if a man does not express his nature, he says, it is the same as if he never breathed.

Ubu travels with several wives, who rummage through Chanel and Alaia boutiques wherever they go for insanely expensive clothes they will only wear for each other, at home, since they are only permitted outside heavily veiled. Along with the wives, though there is no contact between the two groups, travels a floating seraglio of nameless, infinitely pliant, big-breasted, genitally depilated women, do-anything call girls, Warren assumes, or perhaps slaves the Sheik acquires from kidnappers.

Ubu sends the women away. He calls for a cleansing footbath. Two epicene youths bearing gold basins arrive, with others carrying ornate water pitchers. As the boys rinse the men's feet, Sheik Ubu expounds on his bank, his seemingly desultory Caribbean project.

"The range of services we offer now is expanding exponentially," Ubu declares in Fortunespeak. "Say the word, we incorporate you, no need to involve third parties."

"As before," says Warren, "I would like to move something a few ticks shy of a million offshore. This is nothing I want discussed with Evelyn, by the way. She's bound to call you. Maybe not this week, or this year, but she knows we have a friendship, and Evelyn digs into things. Evelyn would like to know where every dime I own is. You know we have some entanglements. I'm more concerned than ever about getting around reporting requirements in a bulletproof way. I don't want to end up like Robert Vesco."

"This is the perennial question." The Sheik nods, his dazzling teeth appearing in an all-knowing grin like a display of bathroom tile samples. He decides not to say that Robert Vesco had quite a good run for quite a long while. He lifts a long foot from its bath. It is swiftly embraced by a towel. "If you incorporate using a fresh account, before the initial deposit, we can guarantee maximum privacy, discretion . . . invisibility, in fact."

"You can do everything with wire transfers I assume."

"Oh ho yes we can. We're not flying little Cessnas full of currency down there, Warren, if I were in the flying business I'd load them up with cocaine. No, this problem is one we have reduced to rubble for the immediate future. Because of our superior encryption technology which is jolly good. You have to stay a few steps ahead when the tracking software changes, I pay a lot of brilliant people to do that. That's enough, you little boys. The transfer goes to a European brokerage right in Beverly Hills and then with a different number it moves to the Caymans into an account only you have the number of. It's Switzerland without the ice and snow, my dear. Free checking, by the way." Ubu is always amazed at how many multimillionaires insist on free checking. "And another attractive feature,

Warren. As a Royal Bank client you never find yourself dealing with Jews. Here, when you go to a bank, you step into a virtual den of Hebes, like the ones who made me get rid of my statues. If the IRS pulled out a harmonica they'd all start singing like parakeets. My own people would swallow cyanide first."

"There you are, Tammy Ann, you slippery eel," Evangeline drawls, brandishing the prescription bottle. "Look what I found behind a sofa cushion, that we've been searching high and low for."

Warren's sister has the translucence of a china teacup. Tall like Warren, even "statuesque" in a modernist sense, brittle fright-white hair spilling negligently to her birdlike shoulders, her wan face a mask of infinite wariness and suspicion, mitigated by irresistible torpor, Tammy Ann has long thought of herself, for some reason, as an "aquiline beauty," perhaps in some dyslexic identification of herself with Eleanor of Aquitaine. Today she's pulled on a yellow sundress pleated with suitcase wrinkles, her sole attempt to dress herself in something besides a wispy nightgown in over a week. Despite the supposed efficacy of her new medication, she finds herself drifting into dreamland whenever she sits, or lies down, or even stands still for more than a minute or two, with the result that the real world has become interchangeable with timeless imaginary landscapes, the dead as palpable and talkative as the living, Hawaii a smudgy analogue of Anaheim, Long Beach, Petaluma. She has wandered into the sun-drenched entrance hall of the mansion on Thalia Massie Drive, in disorganized response to a doorbell.

Others have gravitated to the hall also. Pilar and Conchita, the current maids, who've been told never to answer the door, but range near it anyway when a guest arrives, for Mama will eventually screen the arrival by peering out the window panels in the door frame and bark permission to open, or order them to ignore it; and Roberta, Devin's latest tutor, recently arrived from the mainland, who's still adjusting to *la vida loca chez Slote.*

"I thought I heard the chimes," says Tammy Ann, lunging for the prescription bottle.

"That'll be my lunch appointment," says Evangeline, happily relinquishing the medicine while picturing Tammy Ann's continued incapacitation. "Lester's taking me to brunch. Korean barbecue. Let's hope it isn't cocker spaniel. I need some air. Now Roberta. You be in charge of the house, darling, and when the gardener gets here, you tell him I said one o'fucking clock on the button come rain or come shine, if he no comprenhay you tell him his ass is no longer welcome around here, he's got to thin out that crepe myrtle in back of the guest cottage, also, see that Darren and Devin get their lunch and remember, Pilar and Conchita are NOT TO USE THE PHONE. It's bad enough we're getting double billed on local service thanks to fucking AT&T. I'd like to rip their CEO's testicles out through his nostrils. Also, do not let anyone into the house. Pilar, Conchita, *vosotras chicas, hace falta que costura—*"

She pulls open the door, revealing a feisty, bullish, hankering Lester in aloha tropical wear on the threshold. A witticism of some stale variety appears to hover on his tongue. Evangeline intercepts it with an imperious display of eyeliner.

"No need to delight the whole house with your presence, Lester, I'm horribly peckish."

She slams the door on a tableau of female bewilderment.

"Lester Ryman," Tammy Ann clucks for Roberta's benefit. "I'd like to see what kind of air she plans on getting with him."

Roberta doesn't know what to say. Tammy Ann is given to sudden cryptic pronouncements and mysterious inward smiles.

"That bag of yours ever turn up?" Tammy Ann demands to know, almost accusingly, shaking her pill bottle in a demonstrative way, as if to say that the same agency that made it disappear whisked off Roberta's missing tote bag. Roberta suspects as much anyway, though it makes no sense to her that this rich woman she works for would pilfer her personal ID as well as her diary.

During her first few days on the job, Roberta was pelted with gifts on any occasion or nonoccasion—dresses, sun hats, bits of costume jewelry, pedicures, perms, everything was darling and sweetie and dearie, but now a note of circumspection has worked its way into Evangeline's dealings with her, Evangeline has in fact screamed at her twice for "getting familiar" with Pilar and Conchita, and since her tote bag went missing, Roberta could almost swear, eerie echoes of things she wrote in her diary have crept into Evangeline's conversation, phrases about funny money and bracero labor and Evangeline's diaphanous outfits, lately an element of feline insinuation seems always to assert itself in the way Evangeline regards her, an appraising pause before she says anything growing longer and longer. Like a cat, Roberta thinks, stalking a canary. She has, in fact, begun feeling caged, cornered, trapped in a murky realm of silences and secrets.

Roberta thinks of herself as a hick. This is her first real teaching job, and for that matter the first time she's traveled outside the Midwest. The splendor of this seaside home is quite foreign to her, Honolulu entirely outside her frame of reference, though it looks like every place else, with some beachfront added, and these people, too, who seem to inhabit the same big airy spaces without ever really interacting, except during moments of unpleasant drama, when Evangeline berates the maids for some trivial mistake, or, possibly worse, the longeurs when Evangeline decides to slobber and coo and mother Devin into a state of attention deficit, proclaiming him the handsomest and smartest little man in Hawaii, and then there's this weird somnambulistic Tammy Ann, never quite awake or in sync with the rest of the household, poking around in the fridge at four a.m. or wandering at the same spooky hour along the lanai, with waves crashing on the rocks far below, like the madwoman in Jane Eyre, or the catatonic wife in *I Walked with a Zombie*, and really, the minute that tote disappeared, Roberta had a gut feeling that Evangeline took it, yet she continues in her mind to dismiss this possibility, since her experience doesn't encompass anything like novel uses for other people's documents.

There is, though, she thinks, unquestionably, though she cannot isolate exactly what it is, something askew around here. Something hidden, something scary. Or at least something so alien that an impulse to flee grips her at odd times, usually when flight would breach her basic responsibilities: she has thought of abandoning the boy in the Aloha Tower Marketplace and heading straight for the airport on a recent afternoon. Only now with her credit card and even her license missing, she couldn't buy a ticket anyway. And if she left Devin unattended in some public place, she could probably be charged with child endangerment or who knows what.

Roberta prowls the vast house, as she does whenever the Slotes go out. The place is spread out along one floor, a sequence of cottages linked by planked oak walkways. Palms and exotic flowers thrive in every open space. Evangeline's bedroom is locked, Warren's, locked, the study where the computer is, locked. She looks in on the maids. They are running various garments under the needles of two Singer sewing machines. Besides slaving over everybody hand and foot in this place, the maids have every fallow moment taken up with sewing: stitching monograms on pillowcases and pajamas, appliqués on dress collars, fancy needlework on shirts and blouses, the sewing room smells of starch and heated cloth, and everywhere, on benches and sideboards and stuck to walls and scattered wherever clothes lie in readiness, these Post-It notes in Spanish, in Evangline's loopy lettering, green, purple, yellow Post-Its that warn Pilar and Conchita to ADJUST STITCH LENGTH FOR TOPSTITCHES ACCORDING TO WEIGHT OF THE FABRIC. USE SHORT STITCHES ON LIGHTWEIGHT FABRICS TO PREVENT PUCKERING. USE SEAM GUIDE OR QUILTING BAR TO KEEP STITCHING ROWS STRAIGHT. Exhortation is Evangeline's natural style. MAMA'S SILK DRESSES MUST BE HAND WASHED AND DRIED BY ROLLING IN A TOWEL—PRESS IMMEDIATELY WITH A <u>DRY IRON</u>. MAMA'S SCARVES MUST BE

HAND LAUNDERED!!! DRY THEM IN THE SALAD SPIN-
NER!!! PAPA'S SHIRTS MUST BE STARCHED!!! PRESS
VELVETS AND CORDUROYS <u>FACEDOWN IN VELOUR
TOWEL!!!</u> USE DISHWASHING LIQUID NOT DETER-
GENT ON WOOL ITEMS!!! WE ARE YOUR FAMILY AND
WE MUST BE PLEASED WITH YOU!!!

Pilar and Conchita do not trust Roberta. They have observed
Evangeline fawning over this new teacher and assume that she
reports any infraction of the rules, even though Roberta has made,
with both of them, many language-impaired efforts to express her
displeasure over their long hours and the crazier strictures of the
house, such as this phone thing, and answering the door, and going
for walks. As far as Roberta can tell neither girl has ever been off
the property by herself.

Pilar glances up from her humming machine. The teacher is
there in the doorway. Spying again. Pilar forces herself to smile in a
self-effacing way and turns back to her work until the teacher
leaves.

"Who is that man who came," hisses Conchita. "I did not see
him before."

"You will see him all the time now," Pilar whispers back.
"Right now he is screwing the woman like a dog. Screwing her
right up her ass."

"I, I will not be here to see him, Pilar. I am getting out of
here."

"Where can you go, without money?"

"The neighbor lady who brought me here. I will go to her. If
you have sense, Pilar, you will get out of here too."

The neighbor lady collected Conchita from an employment
agency in California, as a favor to the horrible Slote woman.
Conchita says this lady speaks Spanish and met her a few days ago
at the iron fence behind the property, Conchita says she told the
lady everything: that they are never paid, and sometimes the Slote
woman hits them and locks them in at night. The neighbor has

promised help, Conchita claims, Conchita however is legal in the country and Pilar isn't. Even so, Pilar cannot stand much more of this sewing all the time and cleaning up after these pigs twelve hours a day, if it means returning to the favela in P.V. at least she would have her family. That neighbor lady never eats anything when she visits the Slote woman. A little cottage cheese when she comes for lunch. On festive occasions, pineapple in it. What joy in life can pineapple bring?

The doorbell's cathedral chimes bong through the house. The maids ignore it. Roberta, busy ransacking a storage closet, also ignores it. She's unearthed a cache of official looking papers, not hers unfortunately: Army discharge papers of someone she's never heard of, some doctor's hospital ID, various drivers' licenses, many notebooks filled with Evangeline's handwriting. These notebooks are inscribed every which way with names, birthdates, numbers of different kinds, and lists, "to do" lists, shopping lists, lists of businesses, lists of first names linked by arrows to lists of other names, sometimes names annotated with words like "emotivity," "pushed to act by outside causes," "primary = lives in immediate present," "powerful, instinctual, excellent improviser," "ambition will go beyond personal interest." Roberta hasn't a clue what any of this signifies, but she's sure it has some bearing on the murkiness around the edges of things.

Tammy Ann, however, has opened the door, to a man who looks tremendously like an overtalkative promoter she has seen in a local infomercial, selling band-width equipment of some sort, or humane killers for home butchering, who says his name is Lance Randolph. A man in a thin wrinkled suit, holding a cheap briefcase. The briefcase has somebody else's initials engraved on the lock. That tells a tale, Tammy Ann thinks. Lance Randolph would like to know if she is a member of the household. Tammy Ann supposes that she is.

She ushers him into a sunny day room where sliding glass panels open onto the lanai, with its glorious panorama of humidity.

Down below, she imagines, surfers are being chomped in half by sharks.

"Haven't we got a pretty sky today?" Tammy Ann moves like a floating Giacometti about the room, waving her palm over various knickknacks as if putting them to sleep. Evangeline's decorating efforts have congealed in the day room into a virtual manifesto: a Mughal-era white marble bed in the center, festooned with marble lingams. A seventh-century, pre-Angkor Cambodian stone statue of Ganesh. A bronze Art Nouveau lamp, its base a delightful jade frog. A chair by Jean Prouve, next to an African monkey figure. In Evelyn's time with Warren, she has rummaged many less fortunate regions of the globe in the manner of a White Goddess, wrestling bargains from impoverished natives, piling the booty up in these shrines to consumption. In every house, The Pile. Tammy Ann, rare among the Slote tribe, has had the benefit of higher education, despite her handicap. She knows what these objects are, and guesses that Evangeline hires people to tell her which ones are "tasteful."

Mr. Randolph opens his briefcase. He says he's from some company, Tammy Ann doesn't really listen. Her mind's ear hears a distant surf, bright voices of another era. She catches bits of dialogue from her ghosts, a whole sentence here and there: *I keep remembering that lonely chicken run.* The voice of her mother, she thinks. Poor Ruth with her ovaries. Repining for Oklahoma on the afternoon they went to Disneyland. Her guest appears to be quizzing her about some rare Japanese tapestry, which becomes a watery image in her mind. An undulating saraband of ghosts and demons, giddy paper lanterns, kimonos. She has sighted ghosts and demons here, as lately as a week ago: a robed woman with the head of a fox, an Abyssian cat who speaks Portuguese. The whole area rustles with spirits.

". . . which, from what I can discover, is an extremely rare, museum-quality type of object, that they list as a, you know, eighty thousand dollar item, and we're wondering how your sister-in-law happened to acquire this item. . . ." Mr. Randolph's eyes roll over his documents like a scanner. He has fidgety, fat, childish hands, and the fatty face of a thyroidal child, a child that sells humane killers.

"Mr. Randolph," Tammy Ann says, through a fog of spirits, "I prefer not to speculate on my sister-in-law's manner of acquiring things."

Her flotation arrests itself momentarily, in a shaft of bright sunlight. In her mind, she's Vivien Leigh, confronting Marlon Brando. Only for a moment.

"Imagine my rudeness, would you care for a cup of coffee?"

"No, thank you, you were saying—"

"These priceless objects you see around you, Mr. Randolph, are the mute testimony to my sister-in-law's desire to surround herself with what she considers beautiful. Alas, once Evelyn acquires these things they seem to lose all meaning for her. She's a restless soul, Mr. Randolph, unable to find peace in contemplation."

Oh boy, thinks Randolph, a live one.

"Can you show me where she had this tapestry displayed?"

"I cannot, Mr. Randolph. Because I never saw any tapestry." *Unless you count the tapestry of lies and duplicity that woman has woven*, thinks Tammy Ann. "There may have been one," she says skeptically. "I'm rather nonvisual. I see things, but they don't always register."

"Mrs. Slote has given us a notarized bill of sale from a B. Lin Enterprises in Hong Kong—are you at all familiar with B. Lin Enterprises?"

"B. Lin doesn't ring a bell, I'm afraid."

Chill scuttles up her back. She knows before looking that when she turns she will see the child, those cold gray eyes, little Hitler. And there he is. Drinking in every word.

"Perhaps B. Lin is a purveyor of antiquities," Tammy Ann suggests. Fear overtakes the manic release that talking to anybody, even this Lance Randolph individual, brings on. If only she could hack little Devin to pieces with a machete, Rwanda style. "I know for a fact, Evelyn and Warren *have* visited Hong Kong. You know Mr. Randolph how people abroad are always showing you rugs and tapestries."

"Not usually eighty thousand dollar tapestries, I wouldn't think."

"Well, some people have eighty thousand dollars," Tammy Ann says with a trace of idle malice, suddenly bored to death and terribly, terribly sleepy, "and some people don't."

RITCHIE

On one of the scattered occasions in later days when Ritchie contrived to spend any time with her father (after that horrible thing Evangeline did to Aunt Tammy Ann, which no one afterwards could bear to speak about, contacts between Warren and his ur-family always and only occurred in Evangeline's absence, when she might be off in Washington for example, trying to palm herself off as a protégé of Senator Laxalt, or an old family friend of Joseph Califano, inserting herself into various congressional offices on behalf of Nelson P. Lezard, guru of Managed Care Innovations—that quack out in Irvine, in Warren's phrase, middle name Prick with his M.D. from Grift University), Ritchie managed to penetrate the house on Tecumseh Drive, muscle her way in really, past Rosaria or Inez or whichever underage girl they had living in at the time, Ritchie wanted to know out of Warren's own mouth why she and Mike and Uncle Cleve and several other people had received a legal letter from this firm of Quackenbush Wiltern Sonntag and Sprath advising them to have no further contact with him, Warren, and furthermore why she and Mike and these several other blood relatives were being sued for harrassment and defamation and who knew what other insane allegations, to the tune of six hundred thousand dollars.

"You don't have to even tell me this is all her idea," Ritchie fumed, lighting up a Virginia Slim with a heavy gold lighter. "I'm well aware. What I want to know is why you let these things happen. It's your life too, isn't it? And some day she'll do damage that you can't undo, if she hasn't already."

Warren felt some real emotion about it but couldn't have said precisely which emotion it was. Alcohol tended to run them together haphazardly.

"I can't control her," was what he finally said. "She lives in fear of things I don't even know about."

"Then get a divorce," Ritchie said witheringly.

"Impossible," Warren said. "We're not married." Every time Warren had told her this in the past, it had been true. Now it wasn't, as far as he knew. He did not quite remember the two-minute ceremony at the Chapel of Eternal Love on Sahara Avenue, but Evelyn had the certificate in her bank vault.

"She says you are. She uses your last name."

"Evelyn uses a lot of last names. A lot of first names, too."

"That's her business, it's your business if she uses yours."

"She's afraid of the Medellin cartel, if the truth be known."

"If the truth be known, Daddy, Evelyn could eat the Medellin cartel and the rest of Colombia for breakfast, you know as well as I do the only thing Evelyn's afraid of is she'll lose you and your money and have to go back to being Miss Welcome Wagon of Sacramento, or whatever she was."

Ritchie had, of necessity, tithed some of her auto insurance salesperson's salary to a well-recommended investigator in Santa Monica, someone she'd met through someone she knew in the CHP, to nail down a few verifiable specifics about Warren's inamorata. Warren knew this because he happened to know a Target store personnel manager who regularly binged with this investigator in Primm, thank you, that circusy shithole just over the Cal-Neva line, the guy had twice practically begged Warren to come along sometime to soak up the vibe of people who couldn't wait until Vegas to start losing their paychecks. These were the true marks, the Target store guy insisted. We could nail down a faro table franchise right there where the centrifuge sucks out the money and flushes it upstairs, was the way he put it. As far as Warren was concerned, going to Primm was like going to hell to get away from it all. Primm had something like the tallest Ferris wheel in Western Nevada, or the highest crime rate, Warren couldn't recall which, maybe both, anyway, they could have it. To each his fucking own.

He loved to play the half dollar slots in Vegas, with an endless refill of Jack Daniel's at his elbow, preferably somewhere on Fremont Street like Glitter Gulch or the Nugget so he could go outside once in a while and look at the light show, and where it looked and felt like the old Vegas, not the light show but the rest of it, the wedding chapels and pawn shops not far away, liquor stores and hole-in-the-wall Chinese joints out in the pitchblack ass end of Fremont Street, not this new Disney bullcrap, and for Christ's sake not the Luxor, or, what he dreaded most, the cocktail lounge on top of the Stratosphere, which Evelyn favored, Warren felt certain, because most people are afraid of heights and especially the downward perspective offered by that particular cocktail lounge, whereas Evelyn had as much bother about heights as a cat. In fact she loved prancing around that place in skinny high heels, the closer to the windows the better. Evelyn liked wearing minks and chinchillas in desert air conditioning and of course people did mistake her for one of the world's biggest movie stars, typically in the sundown lighting of airborne cocktail lounges, all the more so in places like Bombay or Rangoon, where no one was entirely sure what Liz Taylor was supposed to look like. A well-orchestrated sparkle of gems or, more usually, small gemlike objects completed Evelyn's masquerade. In a rush of malignity towards his absent paramour (you mean *parvenu*, Daddy, Ritchie told him the one time Warren idiotically tried the word out on her), he felt a stirring of defiance, not unlike the rousing patriotic fortitude Evangeline

had inflated him with and manufactured about him in innumer-
able press releases and speeches she'd cooked up during the Mr.
Bicentennial con. Which had, he reflected, been a sweet con from
anyone's perspective, even if it did end badly, in what Evangeline
decided to call "a storm of controversy," her tone suggesting that
any kind of controversy was essentially meaningless, and wel-
comely flattering.

Eva, the name she'd favored at the time, had a truly florid way
with words. She had painted all manner of valedictory effusions to
convey Warren's "staunch Americanism" to various Rotary and
Kiwanis clubs along the coast, for instance in describing the
numerous international children's causes for which Warren had
supposedly "been a tireless advocate." She even conjured an Oxfam
citation into his résumé. Of course the idea of donating as much as
a nickel to any type of philanthropy affected Evelyn as garlic affects
a vampire, and Warren's sentiments about such largesse were only
fractionally less phobic. There were, inevitably, functions of an
ostensibly charitable purpose that involved, say, a glamorous ball,
and the chance to rub up against celebrated individuals, Evelyn just
adored that, and Warren just hated it, unless Evelyn was lining up
her ducks for something minor and anonymous, like jewelry pilfering. That type of sly, quick action excited Warren. It gave him a
measure of tolerance for the blah blah blah those types of events
entailed. Keep it fast and simple, he always begged Evelyn, who
preferred a big store scene involving intricate planning and loads of
time. Warren got too jumpy and consequently too drunk to be of
any use on a long con. He could ride along on one, that was about
it. When they used aliases, for example, he always forgot her name
or his name or some vital element of the endeavor. He could never
support the Mr. Bicentennial trip for more than a few hours at a
go, come to that, fun though it was. They both loved clowning
around, putting one over, but really, enough was enough. The
pending chinchilla case floated into his awareness. Between that
and the slavery business, he'd had to sign the Las Vegas property

over to a cutout, Warren had seven or eight cutouts at that particular time, when his assets might easily have been frozen or forfeited
overnight, and the bitch of it was, you had to trust a cutout. They
could get out of any mess of their own that developed, by turning
you. They could also just claim your assets were their assets, and
make it stick, too. And maybe there was forfeiture simply for con-
cealing assets, probably there was, Warren really didn't know. His
swell of confidence passed like a fart.

He remembers this scene taking place in the breakfast nook
of the house on Tecumseh Drive, with the starched greenery of the
unpleasantly sloping golf course framed in the French windows,
which had a wrought iron security door bolted across them.
Evangeline insisted on telling people that their ugly house (their
"Las Vegas getaway place," she sometimes called it when meeting
new people elsewhere), with no windows on the street side and
queerly sectioned rooms and alcoves arranged like a labyrinth leading nowhere, had been "inspired by Frank Lloyd Wright," for reasons Warren could never discover, since no one with the slightest
idea of architecture could possibly believe this. On the other hand,
most people Evelyn cultivated had little close knowledge of anything besides specific sections of the penal code.

Ritchie looked thin and professional in muted separates, and
Warren thought she might surpass her mother in luck, if not in
beauty. They had the same silkfine strawberry hair and abnormally
large green eyes, the same oddly avian features, like owls harken-
ing to sounds beyond the range of normal hearing. For a Texas
girl, Zena still carried off the svelte emaciation favored by
California women of a certain milieu with brittle conviction;
Ritchie just looked skinny and bored by her own physicality,
impatient it seemed for the time by which she would have made
more money than Warren. Ritchie's self-possession in this regard
put Zena in the shade. She worked at things until she'd learned
everything about them and promptly moved along to the next
thing, with what appeared to be an exuberant love of strategy.

That year it was auto insurance. Later she opened a posh restaurant in Tiberon.

A man's fecklessness would never land her back at Square One the way Warren's had with Zena. No efficiency bungalows in Laguna Beach for Ritchie, who of course hadn't started out on any Square One in the first place, and was a lesbian anyway. Good for her, too, Warren thought, she'd never know the heartbreak of divorce, except perhaps as it pertained to testifying against her mother in one of the most protracted and unflatteringly publicized divorce proceedings in the history of Orange County. On the down side, Warren considered his daughter too highly strung and too chummy with law enforcement personnel and prey to sudden manias of a mystical nature. He offered her a glass of chablis. That brought forth a tight look, as if Warren's degeneracy were exhibiting itself in a mortifying way.

"Last month at the Beverly Center," Ritchie told him as she helped herself from a pot of Mr. Coffee, "Evangeline put me into some type of hypnotic trance for two hours."

She sniffed a container of Half & Half, then replaced it in the fridge, turning her full vulpine gaze upon Warren and his deliquescent wine glass, a tableau of obvious dissipation in the silly breakfast nook, with the harsh golf course sunlight streaming in across the Laura Ashley tablecloth. Warren pictured himself an actual bag of bones, in something like a Gladstone bag, becoming ever more dessicated in the desert air. They would find him one day, he felt sure, out in the dry wash where they used to drop gangsters, arms folded like Nosferatu, shrink-wrapped in his own mummified flesh, his parchment features preserved by atmospheric mineral salts or radioactivity. Evelyn had talked him into signing the papers and filing the suit and she had made it seem absolutely the right thing to do, the only certain way of thwarting this cabal she claimed Warren's people had churned up against her in a feeding frenzy as she put it, and it had never made any sense. Actually, for brief stretches, it had made sense, that was the insidious baffling part of it, Evelyn made sense if she absolutely thought she had to, and even sometimes made sense unwittingly. She had left the rattlesnakes out of the lawsuit, that showed you reality still had some play in there. But if it ever really went to court, of course, the rattlesnakes would slither into it from the defense side of the aisle. She had once persuaded an FBI agent neighbor of theirs in Santa Barbara to testify about the rattlesnakes, but in light of her subsequent history, any manifestation of these rattlesnakes in a court of law would guarantee victory for whomever Evangeline was suing, or for whoever was suing her.

Warren had never reckoned on facing any of these latest defendants until it was long over with, if ever. It seemed to him that suing your own children put you somewhere beyond the pale, where justifications become useless. He did not quite have the touch to explain that once you have gone too far down the road with someone like Evelyn there is only one off-ramp still available to you.

"Ritchie, I understand that you have issues with Evelyn. I know she loses control, she does things without thinking them through."

"I know she put me under hypnosis in Bed, Bath and Beyond, Daddy, and nobody can tell me any different."

As Ritchie told it, she had parked her SUV at the Beverly Connection parking structure, thinking she'd pick up some grapes and some other stuff at Ralph's, but then recalled that she wanted one of those meat hammers, those gavel things with metal cleats on the end to flatten steaks, so she went across the road to the garageway where you enter Bed, Bath and Beyond in a kind of eternal Swedish twilight, down that ramp or whatever, where there was always a security guard saying hi, like he wasn't a security guard but somebody who liked the store so much he'd decided to hang out there all day in a paramilitary outfit, anyway, Ritchie went on, she'd marched in there with this meat hammer in her mind and nothing else, her whole attention was absorbed in remembering just where the kitchen utensil area was, Ritchie could never memorize the layout of any large retail store, she recalled going through a dense area of gauzy bedroom draperies and entering a veritable force-field of Egyptian double-threaded cotton sheets, when Evangeline, caressing a mesh bag of Accent Stones she claimed she was planning to use in the master bathroom at their La Jolla place "for a stroke of color," startled the shit out of her by being there in the first place, then said she had something Ritchie really had to see—and Ritchie's gut fear of Evangeline made her somehow all the more curious to discover what kind of thing Evangeline considered something Ritchie had to see. There was the kiss of a threat in there somewhere, perhaps it would be something wildly expressive of Evelyn's loathing, anyway she was digging it out of her big fake Vuitton purse on top of an expanse of fluffy, mint-green bath towels, a little blue-black sack, it turned out, made of dyed chamois or very supple leather, or bat's wings and elephant's balls for all Ritchie knew, it had a discreet matching nylon zipper that Evelyn suggestively undid, winking luridly, parting the seam with her fingertips to reveal what looked like an aubergine, potato-shaped rock, or some type of igneous material, that had tiny white eyes embedded in it, eyes that were shells curled in on themselves the size of thumbnails, a mouth formed by a different kind of shell, a razorback clam shell possibly, and even though Ritchie couldn't testify to it in court (not long after her parents' divorce, Ritchie began referring to things she wasn't certain of as things she couldn't testify to in court, a habit she never got rid of), she believed the effigy also had a little nose.

    "This here is Oggun Slote," Ritchie claimed Evangeline told her. "See its interested eyes taking everything in? He's the protector of the Slote family. By which I mean Warren me and Devin. See kind of rippling lines around the edges of your glasses?"

    Ritchie had just endured a bout of viral conjunctivitis, so had relinquished her Accuvue contact lenses for a time. And as Evelyn spoke, she indeed began to perceive a pattern of movement on the parts of certain colors in her peripheral vision, colors that floated off stacked linens and hanging fabrics, off plastic pastel tumblers and some silver basins the purpose of which wasn't identified on their price card. These roving color bands began at the sides of Ritchie's glasses. If she looked straight ahead, things looked normal, except for the effigy sitting there, but the visual field above the top rims of the glasses also brimmed with oscillating strips of color, mainly a light greenish-blue that she followed for a while, until, she said, her eyelids became heavier and heavier, and her eyes tired from the vibrations.

She didn't know exactly what Evelyn said to her while the store's colors whirred and melted around her. It seemed like Evelyn's mouth moved without any words coming out, or that Ritchie heard words in her mind without Evelyn actually speaking them. She only remembered staring for a long time at a wall of microwaves in the decorative colors of that season, translucent melony plastics evocative of fruity tropical drinks, and when she turned her head—with great difficulty, she said, because she felt this overwhelming heaviness, an unwillingness to move her eyes from one quadrant of space to another—Evelyn had disappeared.

Ritchie began moving through the store, with nightmarish difficulty, as if slogging through an expanse of thickening psychic mud, her attention sucked from one display to another. She remembered being surrounded by candles, scented candles, candles in tubs, Animal Print Pillar candles that were zebra-striped and tiger-spotted, candles in purple glass and fleur-de-lis holders, candles emitting odors of grapefruit, mulberries, rotting pears, an overpowering nimbus of vanilla, sandalwood. These candles terrified her. They appeared to be sculpted from waxy flesh, or fat rendered at the morgue, and if she gazed at them even for a few seconds they seemed to twist and bend themselves into misshapen body parts, infant fingers, leprous wrists, a piece of cheek with some alabaster lip attached, an ear, testes.

If she stumbled upon housewares, it was really by accident, she had forgotten all about the meat hammer. Instead she saw knives, carbon steel knives, ranged in lethal rows, and cheese graters with tiny pirhana teeth, and sauté skillets balanced in a threatening way on their shipping boxes, later many bath items, cobraheaded handheld shower sprays, petrographic loofahs, azure jars of bath oil beads like eyeballs plucked from mannekins or gouged from antique dolls, and these products, all of them, were whispering to her, in gurgling demi-voices impossible to decipher at first, she had the impression they were ruminating about the best way of making themselves understood, whenever Ritchie moved away from a garrulous clan of wire whisks or Oxo Good Grips tomato sauce spatulas or hundred piece Mikasa Zena flatware services some large object, a Joyce Chen non-stick wok and its bamboo stir-fry tools, or a stainless steel fish poacher, or a Polar Ware Stainless Chafing Dish, would hiss to snare her, and she couldn't help it, she began weeping, silently, realizing all at once that the assembled contents of Bed, Bath and Beyond were not simply beckoning her, but actually crying out for help. They had become trapped in the store just as she had, prisoners of a malign will much greater than their own. *I'm just plastic*, sobbed a cherry pink wastebasket, *what can I do?*

It took her an hour to leave the place, and then she found herself wandering through Macy's Men Store holding a bunch of Hardy Amies ties in dark solid colors, like a wilted wedding bouquet. Ritchie recognized her surroundings in complete bewilderment, as she had no desire to be in Macy's Men Store now or at any other time, except to use the elevators in the rear if she had to park in the lot off Beverly, which of course she hadn't. She now believed that Evelyn may have planted so-called post-hypnotic suggestions in her mind, suggestions that resulted, for example, in a fender bender that could have been a lot worse than it was in the Whole Foods parking lot on Santa Monica, plus getting her period twice in one month, which put Ritchie into a full-blown cancer panic, and there had been a series of inexplicable mishaps involving the computer system in the SUV and Ritchie's wireless phone and the software programs in Ritchie's laptop, mishaps which taken one by one didn't necessarily point to anything so awful, but taken all together so soon after this encounter were at least, she said, cause for suspicion.

Warren found her story painful. Clearly, Ritchie was losing her mind over this lawsuit business and becoming consumed with animosity, paranoid too, the same way Evelyn was paranoid. He told her he didn't think Evelyn would really pursue the lawsuit much beyond filing it, because they were already getting dunned by the attorney she'd used and threatened with lawsuits from him, another goddam shyster like they all were, anyway you could buy those Santeria effigies in any tourist trap in the Caribbean and they didn't work, Warren thought, unless you had hair or nail clippings or a precious item belonging to the intended victim, and what did Evelyn have that was precious to Ritchie?

"She has *you*, Daddy," Ritchie told him that day, bursting at last into tears and running out of the kitchen. Warren followed her out to the driveway, watched her fish her keys from her shoulder bag and climb into her obnoxiously large car.

"I'm sorry about all this," Warren wailed after her, overcome by chablis, and by the realization that everything from long ago really was gone for him, including this child and Zena and the glory days when he had control of things, standing stupidly in the cracking, moss-crusted cement ellipse in front of their property as Ritchie backed out onto Tecumseh Drive.

"It's too late, Daddy," Ritchie sobbed from her rolled-down window. "She's going to kill you, I know she is, I saw it in her eyes at the Beverly Center, that's what I came to tell you!"

EVANGELINE

Evangeline's lusty efforts in Washington and Sacramento and Carson City (Warren had his suspicions, later confirmed, about how lusty they really were) kept her in perpetual motion. Even when she happened to be home, she spent every waking hour on the phone. For many of Darren's so-called formative years, she hadn't pulled the burgeoning evil that was Warren's family into clear focus, hadn't realized the murderous extent of their malevolence. She even tried, early on, to play stepmom to Ritchie and Mike, sponsoring disastrous family excursions to Mexico and Belize. She remembered Ruth's and Velma's birthdays, often with handsewn monogrammed blouses and kerchiefs fashioned by the first slew of illegals, endured their seasonal visits, thoughtfully consulted Cleve regarding various business ventures even though his advice was worthless. She treated Tammy Ann to facials and manicures and shopping trips, bought her marvelous hats and sundresses, even quizzed a neurologist she met in Caesar's about the narcolepsy. No good deed goes unpunished, she later said about all these efforts.

I don't know where you get all your class, she told Warren, *you certainly didn't inherit it.* These remarks "escaped" her in the beginning, as if wheezed out after a body blow of his relatives' ingratitude, and were immediately followed by analgesic verbiage of a vaguely forgiving nature. Eventually, though, she could brook no more of their antagonism. They had no appreciation, no taste, no nothing. No touch for the finer things such as classical music (Evelyn adored it!) and candlelight dinners on the lanai (what delicious memories Warren had given her in exactly that way) and the craftsmanship of the gifts she'd bestowed on them over the years. *Rosita almost went blind getting your mother's initials on that handkerchief and she hardly even says thanks, I like that.*

During their so-called honeymoon era, when Darren and his nannies and the first assortment of Mexican girls and Warren's original family circulated in and out of their domain, Evelyn commenced calling herself Eva Annamapu, reverting somewhat to her exotic heritage. Its minority ring, she said, gave her an edge at various federal agencies. When they traveled, she used other names, offering an array of life stories to people they met in transit. In lemurlike astonishment, Warren watched her lambent trumpery at work, noted the instant truckling of total strangers who spilled their most intimate secrets to this larger-than-life Sexy Lady, spellbound by her snow white turbans and see-through evening dresses, her fondness for words like "cunt" and "fuck," her high decibel demands for attention that were so like Liz in that *Virginia Woolf* thing. She animated something primal in the sensory sleet of chaotic rooms. Her assurance that she could say or do anything she pleased made people almost desperate for her approval.

If Evelyn wanted to know something, people gurgled it right out without ever wondering why she asked. And in this deft manner, she extracted a complete blueprint of a stranger's life, right down to what state his car was registered in and how much insurance he carried on his house, where he banked, how much of his mortgage was paid off, who his friends were, which schools he'd attended, what magazines he read. If it were a woman, Evelyn culled her sexual and emotional history, employment résumé, and family background, all the while chattering about twenty other subjects, sounding scatterbrained and cocktail-sloppy as she stuffed her mental file cabinet.

At the end of a night she could tell Warren close to a penny what the man she'd been talking to was worth, what kind of murky business schemes the guy would fall for, and how he could be dissuaded afterwards from taking any legal action. With women, it had more to do with what they could be talked into doing. If they worked in offices, it might involve fudging details on legal documents, or digging up confidential information, or having a real company vouch for a not-so-real company, as steps, for instance, towards a loan to be taken out in a fictitious name, or the name of a cutout who didn't know he was a cutout.

She collected future marks like lottery tickets. She operated by reflex. Any public room that she entered was a pristine harvest of human information. Not just business cards, phone numbers, fax numbers and the like, but weaknesses, quirks, character flaws, delusional ambitions, risky dreams, medical problems, shaky marriages. Everybody came equipped with a panel of invisible buttons, Eva called them elevator buttons. If you had the right touch, if you knew how to press one button lightly and another button with a bit more force, at the same time, you could make the emotional side of a person swing up and down as you wished. With carefully paced experiments—whether compressed into one or two days at a ski resort, drawn out across a week of mud baths and heavy drinking in Cozumel, or languidly stretched over months of "coincidental" encounters with a human elevator—you eventually learned to press all the buttons, with exactly the right pressures, in exactly the right sequence, to produce the desired result. The epiphany came when Evelyn, in whatever hotel room, popped the cork on a magnum of Piper-Heidsieck Cuvée Brut and announced that she could play the mark "like Chopin played the piano."

OTIS

Otis considered, in a light-headed way, what web of inane circumstance had its vibrant center in the pitchdark wooden house near Diamond Head, waddling through it with a twelve gallon plastic gas can, soaking the sisal rugs and the peach bedroom curtains and any absorbent material his eyes could make out in the grainy moonlight. Otis had overslept in his room at the Royal Hawaiian and roused to his task in panic, convinced he would forget some critical detail. He knew he had mainly to douse all four sections of the house and the walkways connecting them, that it had to be a total loss. The worst part was that he'd investigated this type of fire himself at least twenty times and knew that no insurance carrier in the world would ever pay off on a blaze this suspicious, this blatantly set. The Slotes had to know it too, but they had a fanatical obdurate bravura about end-gaming people whose losses in litigation would exceed the cost of settling out. But how did I, Otis, end up here?

What played through his head like a slide lecture were illustrations of how he got to be the incendiary schmuck of the year: bad marriage number one, which could've offered the quotidian stability leading to mortgages one two and three, steady promotions at the bank, and early retirement; bad marriage two, to a file clerk who worshipped him (as only a file clerk might) and parlayed

her subsequent disillusion into epic consumption of gin and pre-
mature cirrosis; two children not so much abandoned as forgotten
about, during his shift into private practice, which drove him to
bankruptcy faster than flushed shit; scams, many of which Otis
actually believed in until federal regulators stepped in; topping it
all, five years of playing nurse and confidential secretary to Walter
W. McCloud, magus of the now-renowed Walter W. and Janet F.
McCloud Foundation, purveyors of the so-called Brilliance Awards
to every imaginable and unimaginable third-rate performance
artist, stand-up comic, crackpot theorist and museum hack in
America.

Walter W. and Janet F. McCloud had pushed him over the
edge, making him live in the spare room of a fleapit apartment they
occupied like geriatric roaches at the wank end of Miami Beach,
billionaires in the Howard Hughes, Fu Manchu tradition, surviving
on take-out from the corner deli, the whole house reeking of pas-
trami, Walter W. dreaming up ways to "shape the cultural dis-
course" in his invalid chair, Janet F. shrinking away in an
Alzheimer's fog, as every day a sack of begging letters from the cul-
turally needy arrived.

They were both utterly sick in the head, living like the kind
of old people you read about dining on cat food to save money,
bickering incessantly over pennies, and them listed each year in the
Fortune 500. Otis had set up the Foundation exactly per their
specifications, feeling at times an onrush of noble purpose, but
mainly thinking there was something vile and reprehensible about
it, that it was just another of the million ways to confer an absurdly
arbitrary prestige on the most persistent and worthless characters.
The Brilliance Awards threw money at people who already had
plenty, and in most cases were not by any extra-McCloudian meas-
urement the sharpest tools in their respective sheds. Every year two
or three of the twenty or so recipients actually deserved the recog-
nition, and maybe one actually needed the money, but like the
Guggenheims and other less lucrative prizes the McClouds, as they

came to be known, conceived as the biggest jackpot of any largesse short of the Nobel Prize, were primarily awarded to cronies of the various board members, who got a huge social kickback from enriching the people they usually met for dinner.

Who was Otis to judge, but he could smell a con as well as the next guy, these grants for three, four, sometimes five hundred thousand bucks weren't just doled out disinterestedly, whenever he looked into it there were close personal ties between a candidate and whichever member of the board was pushing the candidate, and in a few cases, the kickback wasn't just a social one, either. Three years after the Foundation was up and running, Walter W. croaked, Janet F. having predeceased him by several months. Their money had come, on his side, from an indispensable toilet fixture. Hers had derived from the invention of the Hula-Hoop.

Leaving Otis not a dime in the will, not a crumb of the billion dollar pie. Nothing. There followed more scams, more fines, more trouble. He drove a taxi in Vegas for a while. He attempted to market a "miracle grow" kind of grass seed. Otis's nadir was a minimum wage gig as a department store Santa. Now this.

He backtracked through the house, the gas can getting lighter every few yards. The cloying fumes made him gag and his eyes stung in the dark. He knew Warren had driven away a U-Haul piled to the roof with antiques and objets d'art two days earlier, that was bound to come out in an investigation. Occasional headlights sliced across the stubby vegetation at the top of the gradient, along Thalia Massie Drive. Otis pictured an enterprising neighbor taking down his license plates as he drove away. He had been born, he thought, for better things than this, a brighter fate, something. Fumbling in slivers of moonlight for his matches, Otis sensed a wholly posthumous life opening up for him. *From here on in, you're dead meat*, was how he phrased it to himself. He dropped the match and ran for his car as a ball of bright heat swelled behind him and lit up the gravel driveway.

Otis had been dead meat for a while, really, but three nights later he was dead meat with three thousand dollars in his pocket.

The Slotes were pleased, and so in a way was Otis. He could drink. He could order single malt and think nothing of it. He could visit his favorite whore, pay his phone and electric, have his oil changed.

There was a place he liked to drive, a Mexican place up in Overton. He liked driving out there in the dark and watching the Overton lights come up on the desert. Blackness, then light. And the night heat rolling off and coming back. He liked margaritas and salsa dip.

Elliot Tunney was in there. Eating something stuffed with avocado. A halo of red and yellow chili pepper lights rained around Elliot's monkish head. A lot of young couples were eating. Eating and screaming. Elliot drank a Corona with a slice of lime in it.

Elliot Tunney was the author of "A Visitor's Guide to Roswell." He wore an Area 51 t-shirt. He had seen the glittering ships of the Visitors, many times. He knew the perfidy of the federal government in keeping the truth of our alien neighbors away from the public. Otis had doubts about the absolute secrecy of this information, as he read about it every week in the *Enquirer*. Anyway, it worked for Elliot, who took a businesslike tack to his obsessions. If there had to be aliens, it ought to be possible to turn a dollar on them, and Elliot did.

"You look like shit," he told Otis. "No offense or anything." Elliot himself looked like a svelte, intelligent insect, an impression heightened by his choppy ponytail. He had the kind of weird looks that everybody finds sexy, a come-fuck-the-geek thing going for him.

"Have another Corona," Otis told him. "I'm buying."

Elliot looked dubious. Otis let him see his new bankroll. They drank for a while and went out to Elliot's van at the end of the parking lot. Elliot dissected a cigar using a penknife on his keychain. He rolled a blunt, lit it, sucked in a huge cloud of smoke. He held it for a long time, then fastened his mouth on Otis's and blew it into his throat.

"Spill," he said.

Once he was stoned, Otis recounted the Hawaiian adventure in fabulous detail. In his telling of it the Diamond Head house became a virtual Xanadu, the fire an epic of daring, fraught at every moment with the chance of discovery or accidental inciner- ation. He mentioned the objects he'd decided were flammable, the ones he'd vetoed, his decisions informed by his early career as an arson investigator. As Otis talked, Elliot casually reached into his pants and played with himself, in an understated way. The first time Otis met Elliot, Elliot revealed that he was chipping Viagra and had to ejaculate on an hourly basis. Otis's descriptions of the burning house excited him, apparently.

"You said they were on the verge of selling this place," Elliot said breathlessly.

"Well, then they found out there was a lien on it. There's a civil judgment of a million two in the works. They jacked the price to a million nine, the buyer agreed but they figured they could clear more just burning it down. You gonna come, Elliot?"

"I fucking did, man, a whole pantload. Shit, Otis, I have got to get some pussy."

"Just open the phone book," Otis told him. "Nothin' more full of pussy than the Vegas phone directory."

"You ever do a she-male?"

"Can't say as I have."

"Chicks with dicks, nothin' like that? Tell you something, Otis, it's a real experience. You kind of get beyond the gender thing. What I keep thinking, maybe the aliens are set up that way. Big tits, and a cock. They don't all necessarily look like the ones bought it in that Roswell crash."

"Now, I heard, that was a secret weather balloon and not any kind of UFO."

"Don't get me started, Otis. Biggest cover-up in U.S. history. Christ I'm horny again."

Elliot Tunney had a horror of the federal government, but he also had a possession charge pending, and took Otis's information directly to the FBI, which laced him into an electronic corset and listened in on his next chat with Otis. Otis believed that Elliot wanted to hear all about the fire again because it helped him whack off. Which it did, almost shorting out his wire.

They came for Otis in a black unmarked Chrysler. They took him to a warehouse in North Las Vegas and put him in a mint green room. There were two agents. One looked like a feral dog, the other looked like John Wayne Gacy.

"You're up to your shitty fucking nose in shit, shitbird," the feral dog one snarled.

John Wayne Gacy nodded agreement, as if this saddened him.

"What kind of shit," asked Otis. The feral dog reached across the table and slapped him hard.

"YOU don't ask the questions around here, shitbird."

"Okay, okay."

"You don't have to rough him up," John Wayne Gacy said in an almost effeminate voice.

"Little shitbird's gonna TALK," the feral dog promised, pounding the table with his fist. "Little shitbird's gonna SING!"

"Tell us all about it, Otis," said John Wayne Gacy, in a soothing therapeutic way.

"Tell you about what?"

"YOU FUCKING KNOW FUCKING WHAT YOU SHIT-ASS COCKSUCKING SHITBIRD."

"Give you a little hint," John Wayne Gacy said quietly. "Evangeline and Warren Slote."

"Oh sweet Jesus," Otis whined. Fucking Elliot Tunney for sure.

"Jesus can't help you now," sneered Feral Dog. "Your little fuck buddy told us the whole thing."

Otis thought to say that he and Elliot had never gone beyond mutual masturbation, but realized this was now irrelevant. Agent Feral Dog expatiated on his opinion of firebugs, and what should be done about them.

"See, what I would do," he said, lurching across his side of the table to poke the air near Otis's eyelids, "I'd take a shitbird firebug like yourself and soak his balls in gasoline. I'd tie him up with his hands in the air and then I'd take a blowtorch and light his shitbird nuts for him, and let his goddam shitbird balls roast until they fell off."

"He would, too," John Wayne Gacy nodded, wide-eyed.

"Do you have any idea how many innocent kids are burnt to a cinder every year by lowlife firebugs exactly like you, trying to pull an insurance grift? Take a guess."

"A hundred?" Otis guessed wildly.

Feral Dog guffawed. He leaned back in his chair and slapped his thigh and generally aped hilarity. John Wayne Gacy flashed an indulgent grin, shaking his head in disbelief.

"A hundred, shitbird here thinks," Feral Dog said. "You think this is one big hilarious joke, don't you shitbird? What's a hundred little kids all carbonized like pork rinds when a squalid turd like yourself can make three thousand bucks burning other people's houses for them?"

"I'm sorry," Otis said, getting close to tears.

"He's sorry," Feral Dog chuckled menacingly. John Wayne Gacy sighed. "Shitbird here's sorry. Yeah. I'll bet he's as full of remorse as a seminary full of pedophiles. The only thing worse than you, Lemming, are the guys who rape and torture little kids."

"I'll do anything," Otis wailed.

"Goddam correct you'll do anything, you pointless fuck, for starters you're gonna wear a wire strapped to your sorry tits and you're gonna be all over these Slotes like a fly on shit and you're gonna *report* every move they make and you're gonna get them on tape, I want you up their assholes every minute of the livelong day, fella, and maybe, just maybe, the United States Government will let you take a walk when we lock these predators up and throw away the key."

"Oh god thank you, thank you," Otis gushed in an orgasm of abjection.

But afterwards, the days and weeks went by uneventfully. Otis drew his five hundred a week from the Slotes, and most nights stared at television in his shitty efficiency, munching microwave tortillas and chugging quarts of Rainer Ale. At times he seemed so pathetic to himself that wearing a wire became the only interesting or important thing about him, not that the Feds were getting anything useful from hours of Otis getting drunk with the Slotes. They were eagerly pressing their fire claim. The insurance company had checked its own files and discovered itself already embroiled in two different lawsuits involving the Slotes. Their homeowner division should never have insured them in the first place.

Otis told Debby Prio about the wire. Debby Prio had some obscure gripe against Evangeline, or so Otis thought, she looked at him funny when he told her, but Otis thought she seemed basically pleased to hear it. Otis told a lot of people about the wire. It brought an edge of drama to his stale routine. Otis had a regular route of five or six bars he haunted in the course of an evening, where the same tired faces greeted him and the same tired conversations ran.

Drinking made him inclined to share the Otis Lemming Experience with practically anybody. The joke of it was, Evangeline spent all day jabbering on the phone, using different voices, and Feral Dog and his child-murdering partner could've gotten far more on both Slotes by just tapping their phone. Well, maybe they did have a wiretap. The night Otis got back from Honolulu, Evangeline refused to discuss anything to do with the house and acted very surprised that it had burned down. She called him at a pay phone a few minutes later using her mobile, to say his money was under the floor mat of her car, which, to Otis's surprise, turned out to be the case.

Otis dranked and whored his way through the three thousand in two weeks. The Slotes asked him over for drinks. They announced that they were all going down to Santo Domingo—

Warren, Evelyn, Devin and himself. To look at property. Resorts were sprouting like wood lice all over the Caribbean. Warren pondered getting back in the game, Evangeline said. It always helped to have a lawyer along. Otis happened not to be wearing his wire that day and phoned the FBI from the Slotes's downstairs bathroom. He told Feral Dog he couldn't talk. He said the Slotes were on the move, that he was nervous, that he would call again later.

When he left the bathroom, the atmosphere around the field-stone fireplace seemed a degree cooler. The Slotes acted cagey. Overanimated. Otis topped up his drink. If he drank enough he could get through anything.

Varlene showed up. Perky on the outside, total mess on the inside. Otis thought she was being set up for something with a lot of lead time to it, he didn't know what.

"We're getting ready to travel again," Evangeline told Varlene. She began mixing a Bloody Mary at the wet bar.

"Where you goin'?"

"I never know just where we'll end up."

When he got home that night, Otis wrote a letter to his son Benny. His daughter would not want to hear from him. He wrote that if he didn't make contact after two weeks that Benny should notify a Feral Dog or a John Wayne Gacy at the FBI office in Vegas. He mentioned gathering evidence against a client. Otis also had to acknowledge that he had, as an estate, absolutely nothing to pass on, except his collection of colorful hats and a complete set of *Playboy* going back to 1965. Worth something, probably.

WARREN

Evangeline referred to those years of happy scams as the honey-moon era: the phrase had a double edge of fond nostalgia and the implication that the honeymoon had ended long ago, not that romance had ever flagged, but the good times had long been sullied by these plots and machinations against her; Warren, his stomach flooding with blood, remembers other names they gave things, this leads to a picture (he knows that he doesn't know if the images fluttering in his cortex represent what was ever real, so long did he and she cohabit in the ether of make-believe; surely Ritchie's visit to the house on Tecumseh Drive happened years earlier than he remembers it taking place, and maybe all the details were different, there was no Whole Foods on Santa Monica then, and Ritchie's car may have been a sensible Acura Legend instead of a tank; maybe it's not even your life that flashes in front of your eyes, but somebody else's) of strolling into The Mint in his Styles Janowski drag, better-tailored suit, naturally, but a vintage Styles steer-head string tie with glittering ruby glass eyes and a pale Stetson over his drastically thinning hair and a Cohiba clenched between his choppers, he was supposed to be, on that occasion, Fletcher Mayhew of Kansas City, Kansas, and Eva Annamapu was Fletcher Mayhew's "kid sister" Angela.

It was almost certainly The Mint, or 4 Queens, something like that. Angela/Evelyn looked hallucinatory, like some precipice

about to be fallen off, in a polyester crepe evening gown that had a
lot of open space in front, white as a new refrigerator, the region
just under her cleavage speared by a preposterous rhinestone-
encrusted, fake garnet dragonfly brooch of a color Warren associated with bone marrow biopsies.

The gurgling, pinging eructations of the slot machines wiped
away all residue of the outer world. The casino carpet's whirly
arabesques had the dry squish of something animate and vaguely
carnivorous. Evangeline looked more like Liz than Liz did anymore, the pink lipstick, the turquoise Cleopatra eyeliner, the
whorled peek-a-boo of her ink black wig fringing a signature
white turban stabbed here and there with motes of paste jewelry.
She might have been Dido, Queen of Carthage, surveying nether
regions of her Realm.

"Some people," she was saying, "need an outlet for their
mediocrity."

Warren wondered if she were speaking of him. She let him
hang on that for a second. "You know, some really tasty opportunities are in the wind."

She went on to say, not for the first time, that an enormous
amount of patriotic horse shit was about to ennervate legions of
the witless masses, and to make many clever people's fortunes, what
with America's Bicentennial coming up.

"Think of it, Warren. Our nation's 200th birthday. I love
America, but you have to admit it's a country full of morons, we
really owe it to ourselves to make some money off them."

He thought to say that he had not detected any particular fer-
vor for America's 200th Birthday blowing in the wind around
Vegas, that he had already been clever and also already had a fortune, but kept quiet because he supposed she might be on to
something.

Her plan involved him, evidently, giving public speeches
about Our American Way of Life, The Constitution, and similar
themes—she was already writing these speeches, with help from

Darren's old civics textbooks, and declaiming them as she paced the rear patio in Tecumseh Drive. *The Bicentennial bestows on us the golden opportunity to celebrate the noble values that all people the world over aspire to and that our nation single-handedly has upheld for two hundred terrific years*, the same type of thing they heard in Albania.

The plan further involved running up thousands of national heritage–oriented posters of undetermined design, for edifying display in Our Nation's Classrooms. It also involved setting up an office in Orange County and hiring this sinister bulldyke, Patty Frasier, as Evangeline's "administrative assistant." Patty had been one of Evangeline's Sacramento Welcomers, once upon a time. ("Tell you the truth, Mr. Slote, I'm not that welcome in Sacramento myself these days," Patty had recently confessed, with manly pathos. She had, she said, been booked for kiting checks in Sacramento and Independence. Eva, mixing daiquiris in the next room at the time, cackled in a strange way. She was giving herself a slug or two straight from the bottle. "Is that *all?*" she spluttered, nearly choking.)

Whole rows of slots were vacant at that hour. Their serried opalescent lights effervesced as if happy to carry on by themselves. While telling her in a placatory way that he would chew over the Bicentennial more energetically, they entered a frigid lounge where vinyl-padded stools ringed a tall oak bar that looked like the frame of a billiards table.

"Gimme a Jim Beam," Angela snarled at the lone bartender, like Liz bullying Richard Burton in her favorite Liz movie. The bartender loved it because so much of her tits were showing. His face was a map of the rougher parts of Ireland. He gaped at her cleavage as if he were about to fire his spunk into it. "Gimme *two* Jim Beams and a cigarette."

The lounge, though it had no atmosphere, felt like an oasis of as much calm as you could get in Vegas unless you got off the Strip. Warren was the kind of rare bird who felt at home in characterless, artificial settings. So was she. Evangeline smoked her cigarette, watched and waited. She made loud small talk about the planked salmon they'd just eaten.

"They don't have to *smother* the fucking fish in kiwi Fletcher do they? Who needs *kiwi slices* on a piece of salmon?" She honked her thoughts for the room at large, which was more or less empty. In a lower, more Evelynlike voice she said, "If we get lucky, Warren, you're going to be driving, so try darling not to have more than four or five of these things. Try to pace yourself."

"This shore is a nice vacation," Warren proclaimed loudly, raising his Stetson slightly. He was going for an Okie from Muskogee effect.

"Oh Warren, save it for later," she hissed. "Don't get into it unless you have to."

"I was trying to feel my character."

"That's fine, darling, but we're not doing dinner theater, it isn't that complicated. You just mumble and let me talk."

She would confide, later, the finer points of her system, which she'd outlined for him a year or so after they met. It was called the French-Dutch system, and had to do with these biologists or psychologists or something from over a hundred years ago who had people classified into types.

You could identify these types by studying faces and the shapes of heads and bodies. Ectomorphs, mesomorphs, and what have you. Within a few minutes, a type showed up. A tall, lanky, slick-haired dude three sheets to the wind whose overgrown mustache obscured his looks, if he had any. The lighting made it hard to tell.

Warren pegged him for 39 with a fair amount of bad living inscribed around his gray eyes. He wore sharply creased loden pants and a white shirt with a motif of blue palm fronds. Jumped-up jackass on a spree, was Warren's guess. Began hitting on Evelyn immediately. He seemed to hold back a fulsome repertoire of filthy suggestions, taking Warren's presence into account.

Angela was delighted to meet him, she said. They didn't know a solitary soul in Vegas, she said. It was a far cry from Kansas, she said, overdoing it, Warren thought.

"You look like a man of parts," she quipped, casting a peckish look over the parts most likely to get him going. "What is it you *do*?"

Jackass instantly warmed to the subject: he ran a Mazda dealership on a fallow stretch of 15 just inside the Barstow line, he revealed. He had been revealing this all evening, Warren sensed, on various barstools, to various women who had decided not to sleep with him. The man's voice bespoke a quizzical awe at his good fortune in the world, though it did not sound especially awesome.

You'd hardly guess, he said, that anybody would venture out to Barstow to buy a Mazda—they still had the rotary engines, if something seized up you could kiss the whole vehicle good-bye— but Rick Reebenack's reputation was such, he assured them, that Mazda enthusiasts made the pilgrimage from all over, Utah and Idaho in a couple of cases, because he dealt with people square, and he would always take what they were driving on a trade-in.

"I don't drive a Mazda, myself," he quickly appended. "Sweet little car, but why bother if you own a Cadillac?"

"I adore Cadillacs," Angela said, truthfully enough. She had stolen several, and two others had been legitimately purchased for her. "I've always driven them. Call me spoiled, I love how they handle. This is my brother Fletcher, by the way. Fletcher, this is—"

"Rick," said Rick redundantly, all handshake and cigar aficionado, suddenly. His overestimation of the incest taboo had just brightened his prospects with Evelyn. He asked Warren what "game he was in," Warren said grain futures but Rick wasn't listening. He flagged down the bartender, whose black bow tie was coming ungathered. Angela proposed a kickier beverage than the beer Rick was glugging, she felt like switching herself—a Tequila Sunrise, how about it?

Rick and Angela folded Warren, or rather Fletcher, into the conversation for a little stretch. Soon, however, they were deeply engrossed in an obvious mating dance, and Warren shunted his attention elsewhere. Rick had a big hard lump in his trousers, Warren saw that. He assumed the glaze that came over him following a great deal of alcohol, lost in thoughts of motels arrayed across the desert that were designed so that viewed from the air, the structures would appear as blocky, assertive letters. The letters would be C, U, N, T, as Warren pictured them. It would be important to landscape them for optimal foliage. At some point, Rick pushed off to find the head. Eva-Angela leaned into Warren, licked his ear.

"Fletcher, I mean Warren, that guy has *seven thousand dollars* in his room at the Gold Coast."

"Really," Warren said. "How foolish of him."

"I'll say. Now, listen, I'm going over there with him."

Evelyn's Breathless Hush was spiked with the thrilling prospect of getting money, any money, at someone else's expense. She would have noised the same thrill if she had merely pocketed whatever tip Rick left for the bartender.

"You don't need to know what I'm going to do." She paused to allow Warren's mind to clog with unsavory images. "I won't fuck him but that goes without saying. It does, doesn't it, my one and only? What that fool has in his pants is of no interest to yours truly. You wait here for five minutes, then drive over there and start playing the slots in the back. You go in from the parking lot, where the awning is, Warren, walk past the reception and around the bar there, back towards the elevators. That's the only place they post security. Go as far back as the slots go. Play in the second row, not the first row because their security guys have an unobstructed view of the first row.

"Just play, for however long. I put something in his drink but he's got to have a little more in him so I'll deal with it up there. Be prepared, Warren, I might say to you, 'go up to the concierge and tell them you're him, you want your stuff from the safe.' He checked in this morning and he's been out boozing all day so nobody on the night shift will know what he looks like."

"You know you're going to have to tell me all this again. I wait five minutes and drive to the Flamingo—"

"Jesus Christ, the Gold Coast, right next to the Rio, a forty dollar a night dump we've passed a million times, please tell me you're joking."

"I *know*, I have it all in my head, will you please stop *patronizing* me."

"I'm sorry darling. You do understand though I might not tell you anything, if I just hand you the room key and maybe his license. And if I hand you anything *really quick*, lover, just hide whatever it is. Or drop it down between the slots."

"I don't look anything like that person."

"You don't think so? When was the last time a desk clerk spent a real long time looking at an ID picture."

"They spend a lot of time doing that in this town, there's all these fugitives and card-counters and people banned from casinos. You know that."

"First of all you're practically his twin, Warren. Anyway the Gold Coast isn't exactly the pulsing heart of Las Vegas, either. They need business. A place like that, they certainly don't care who's banned from the casinos."

He would have to do it anyway and so decided she was right. I am the virtual mirror of Sammy Dave no Rick, Rick Reebenack. If she thought him the double of a guy trying to hit on her, that was a positive sign, he supposed. He liked the idea of scooping stuff out of the safe deposit, but not if they put you through a lot of rigmarole. Warren's veteran status caused him to bristle when asked for identity documents. They certainly didn't care who you really were when you were getting your ass shot off for them, was his attitude.

Of course we never see ourselves as others see us, Warren considered. He did have a mustache and so did Rick Reebenack and Warren knew from experience, a lot of times that was the only feature people registered. At his age it was silly to keep up that "debonair" thing but Rick was too young for that to be an issue.

Evelyn insisted on the mustache, to her it was distinguished. Clark Gable, that look. The Mr. Bicentennial concept she kept floating, he realized, Evelyn saw as his dignified, Clark Gablesque *aloha*, in the dictionary sense of hello and goodbye, both, since Warren was creeping up on retirement age.

He had thought it would be nice, after the tumult and triumph of his business career, to sit home in a comfy chair and read up about spiders. He had read almost nothing since *Forever Amber* back in high school, but was hooked on spiders and their surprising ways and any books he could find about them, even abstruse scientific things. But Evangeline craved this other thing, for Warren to cut a figure in a wider arena than *Motel Management Monthly*. He supposed it would make her feel grandly visible too.

Rick returned, apparently confident of his plumbing. More chit chat of a suggestive nature. Before Warren could summon another round they were up and gone, like that. Fast and cheap. And Rick goodlooking too, in a briny, lounge lizard way, Warren noted ruefully as they left.

Had she considered how long it might take him to get their car out of the lot? What if she couldn't put the guy under? Warren pictured her legs in the air, feet dangling over Rick's muscled shoulders as he plunged his fat tool into her moist quim. Warren pictured this walking to the parking lot, pictured it driving to the Gold Coast. By the time he parked and made his way through the murmurous boozy ground floor to the clattering slots, Rick's virile member had assumed zoologically significant proportions. For sure he was fucking her, what else would they do while she waited for the Mogadon or whatever to kick in?

Maybe not, though. She had already disabled Rick's libido with drugs, or so she said. These slot machines were pointless, Warren thought, though he won just as often as he lost. He didn't have the head or the stomach for roulette any more. Evangeline favored blackjack. She even liked losing at blackjack, it stimulated her to win back her stake at something riskier.

You could go to the pen for it, was how she described a desirable thing. Warren could not go to the pen, that was where Warren drew the line, that was understood. Evangeline could do time, she had plenty of years left, Warren on the other hand was nearing the home stretch as far as longevity went. She had never involved him in anything that didn't have a loophole of deniability built into it for Warren, that was their deal.

Or at least, he believed that was their deal. If he had given hard thought to how things played out that night, this deal might have appeared to him in a different light, for after he sat feeding oily quarters into the slot for an hour she materialized at his elbow in a fog of that awful gardenia perfume she carried in a spray can, insisting he come up to the room and join them for a cocktail, not in the playbook, *Rick insisted*, she brayed, holding the magnetic room key and biting her lips and like a fool he trailed after her, past security and onto the elevator, up to the seventh floor, down an endless corridor full of sharp turns to a door that seemed, somehow, not a good idea to open.

Rick sprawled facedown on the quilted comforter. Warren noticed the shiny beige ankle boots on Rick's feet. Silly boots. Average feet. As soon as the door closed Evelyn said:

"I have a feeling he might be dead."

"Oh fucking Jesus," Warren said.

"If he's dead," she said coolly, "I guess we shouldn't bother with the safe deposit. I don't see a receipt for it anywhere. But look at this."

She angled her open purse to show the fat sheaf of bills inside.

Warren walked over to the body, felt around on its throat.

"He isn't dead," he told her. The pulse seemed steady. The guy did look dead, though.

"Well, I suppose we ought to get out of here, in that case. . . ." Evelyn slipped into the bathroom and swept all the courtesy soaps and shampoos into her pocketbook. She went to the closet, rummaged in Rick's overnight bag with growing dismay. "This guy. What a rube. You wouldn't get five dollars for that watch."

Warren took the watch anyway, souvenir. Evelyn grinned, making impish dimples. She took the glasses they'd been drinking from and rinsed them under the bathroom tap.

"I feel like a steak Warren what do you feel like," she asked through the hissing of the tap. "A nice big prime rib, how about it, with a baked potato."

The thought that Evangeline had brought him to the room to place him at the scene of potential bad trouble didn't enter Warren's head in 1973, but it does now, when it truly doesn't matter, as if paperclipped to the memory.

WARREN

He doesn't see these things in all their finely webbed surrounding detail now, only pictures, tendrils of dialogue attached, fading echoes of ancient voices crowded together. He's stopped feeling pain, now it's as if a morphine enema just kicked in. He tries to snag memories as they wash through him in a blissful torrent, wanting to freeze them into legible snapshots. Instead they sleet past, tossing out the random face, fractured vistas of long-ago streets, houses and airports and tropical sailing harbors, bodies of water viewed from great distances, human bodies in wavering shapes moving in crowds in unknown places: all the data etched in memory for no reason he or anyone else could possibly give. The present snaps free of his awareness. In his mind he is six years old, and forty, and seventy-three all at once. He sees himself crumpled up like a crushed photograph, stretched like a ribbon of taffy, on an unstable mirrored surface, a lake of mercury that splits and rejoins itself as a wind or someone's breath shivers over it.

They did open that office, in a strip mall adjacent to a science park in Irvine, and Patty Frasier basically ran it while Evangeline had "lunches" and "junkets," Patty Frasier was good on the phone with Jaycees and Young Republicans, people who booked keynote speakers for patriotic events. A few days after she started working for Evangeline, Patty Frasier spelled out her position to Warren, *I'm one hundred twenty percent behind this Bicentennial thing, but if she starts screwing me around with money, Mr. Slote, I'm out of here.* Warren paid her out of the Slote Construction kitty, slush fund really, whenever Evelyn cut her a rubber check.

Most of Evangeline's lunches were eaten with Lester Ryman. She described Lester Ryman as her mentor. Lester was ten years Warren's junior. He had the build of a stubby college linebacker thickened by four decades of drinking in sports bars. A short man who followed golf and kept a twenty-foot sailboat in Newport Harbor. He had cold, trustless blue eyes in a square, hostile face. He had a condo on the beach with a LeRoy Neiman lithograph of Arnold Palmer in the living room and an array of manly fragrances ranged along the bathroom mirror.

Lester normally dated dark-haired women slightly taller and much thinner than himself who worked in offices and had mildly crippling personality disorders. He was wanted in Florida and Michigan and a few other states on something like thirty-eight charges of fraudulent conveyance. Lester had fraud in his fingertips, the way some other people have the piano.

Checking out Lester was the last marker Warren ever called in on Styles Janowski, Warren hated asking because by that time the veins in Styles's hands had been scorched black by the chemo but Hell, Styles told him, keeping busy's keeping me alive. It kept him busy for three weeks, Warren sent a wreath.

Lester knew a lot about off-shore tax shelters and laundering property through shell corporations and Evelyn's talk for a while was all Lester this Lester that, when Lester dropped out of her prattle Warren knew they were screwing. Insult to injury, Styles clocked them screwing at three Slote-owned motels. So the employees knew it, too. Warren had to turn, as the saying goes, a blind eye. Technically, Evelyn was his public relations person, if he wasn't going to marry her she had to keep her options open, though obviously Lester wasn't marrying her either, Lester couldn't even go to D.C. on her junkets because of an outstanding forgery warrant.

Darren, whose bleak existence Warren scarcely registered, had recently been held back in ninth grade, fucking imbecile, Evangeline squawked that the boy Needed A Father Figure, she wanted Warren to take the brat along on these speaking tours, give him somebody to look up to. She shouldn't have been banging Lester, it gave Warren leverage. If he needs a father figure so bad, send the little shit back to his father, he told her. Evangeline's mouth dropped open. She looked like the Liz of *Secret Ceremony* swallowing a martini down the wrong pipe. (Evangeline studied all Liz's movies whenever they played, even the stinkers, dragging Warren along. He had seen *X, Y, and Zee* four times.)

She's aging, he thought. Twenty-eight my ass. She's ten years older than that and now it's catching up. It crossed his mind that he was "falling out of love." If he could hold that feeling, he might manage to get rid of her. Yet he knew, deep down, that she had trumped him in strength. The baton of ambition had passed from him to her, and his apotheosis as Mr. Bicentennial entirely depended on her wiles. Perhaps he could dump her afterwards.

Meantime Warren gave the speeches. In hotel convention rooms, smoky VFWs, shopping mall parking lots on flag-draped flatbeds, anywhere Patty and Evangeline booked him. They were all more or less the same speech, and the merchandise that came with it, these Flags of the Fifty States on a midnight blue background, were supposed to move at ten a pop, but they were not much coveted at Warren's venues, go figure. Eva, as she then was, tried hustling them at the U.N., which did get them an audience with an Under-Under-Under Secretary General or something, skinny towelhead from Uttar Pradesh named Rajinder Randawa who later became, in Eva's mythology, a fairly close relative of hers. (She was, in fact, part-Indian, Annamapu hadn't really been her father's name but it was close enough.) She also snagged some official at the actual Bicentennial Commission, who liked the Flags well enough to arrange a little meet-and-greet in his office. Once Eva had her foot in the door, she was over there doing her Auntie

Mame impression two or three times a week, using their phones to save on long distance.

Warren realized it was a long con. He knew the object was to get HEW or the Ford Foundation or some entity like that to buy up all the Flags and donate them to schools. Eva had dreams of clearing a million three on them and Warren shared these dreams the same way he'd shared the take on ten or eleven bogus insurance claims. But during those months of eating airline meals and waiting for dry cleaning delivery in less than five star hotel rooms, he underwent an unaccustomed inner shifting of emotions and thoughts, almost as if his secret soul, long unitary in the manner of an iceberg or some massive boulder, were cracking apart into glistening chunks, the pieces strangely revivified, sparkling in celestial light, himself becoming accessible to grace and wonder.

He couldn't have articulated this change inside him to anyone, least of all Eva, and it took Warren some time to recognize that orating these speeches, in his flat homiletic Californianese, poised before the flag, mumbling his love of its fifty proud little stars and the awesome regions they symbolized, was having an almost orgasmic effect on him, resurrecting boyhood hopes and noble dreams and the uplift of righteous striving, as well as a strong somatic memory of his first apprehensions of Eros.

When he posed himself at a rostrum, angling his aging screen star profile to a gathered herd of forgotten veterans and regulation-thwarted businessmen and right-minded young people who rejected the satanic culture of permissiveness, Warren felt himself to be rediscovering America: the America he'd crossed in youth from the parched and scattered Oklahoma topsoil to the fecund Central Valley; the America whose onions and okra he'd harvested; the America whose lofty ideals he had not exactly fought for, but cooked for, Up There, the America whose motels he'd built.

In this mental America anything was possible. It was possible, for example, that Warren really *had*, by God, helped the world's needy children, and been a Will Rogers type of role model for other entrepreneurs. In his own quiet and unassuming way. What Warren had actually done in his life, and what the Irvine office said he'd done, achieved a happy confluence in his mind. He felt charisma flowing in and out of him, as if he were a conduit for invisible historical forces. Let the cynical nay-sayers (Warren had a natural feel for the apt Republican phrase) call it a scam all they pleased.

And somewhere within this nimbus of heady feeling, mixed with a sense of transcendent, rapturous belonging to a place, a land, a nation and its myriad people, Warren began to discern, hovering above, or somehow suffused through his audiences, like a particle beam, or a surge of ecstatic protons, the aura, perhaps even the physical personality, of Mavis Jenkins, the Red-Haired Whore of Dutch Harbor.

There had been several red-haired whores living in Dutch Harbor after the Aleutians campaign, all from Nome, for some reason, but Mavis Jenkins, by dint of seniority and superior allure, alone held the title as her appellation throughout the seventeen hundred mile span of that gelid, barren archipelago. Warren knew about her, impossible not to, nearly every man in his division claimed to have flung a load into Mavis's mound of love, but Warren saw her for the first time well after her legend had traveled to troops in far-off Asian jungles and the parched deserts of Africa, when she'd already become a phantasmagorically insatiable piece of ass for the unwritten chronicles of war, something more than a whore, almost a clitoral Sphinx or vaginal Houdini, and for that very reason less approachable than other whores, red-haired or otherwise. With Mavis it wasn't a question of how thoroughly she waxed your banana, but rather a test of your own battle-readiness: any man in the islands could mount her, perhaps, but how long could they stay in the saddle?

Warren's first glimpse came through a snapping curtain of hail and sleet, in the dark, just as what they simply called Weather up there was about to rip through the town's wind tunnels of aluminum and ravaged wood frame. He had just won thirty dollars in a gin game and knocked back his sixth jigger of rotgut whiskey with his seventh beer, and staggered into the incipient squall, his bladder ready to back up into his brain. Outside there was nothing but snow and slush and the black half-barrel shapes of Quonset huts and the black outlines of frozen houses. Warren weaved along with a rough idea of where the barracks were, his boots sinking through tiaga into the deadly sucking mud. Then the Weather hit. Like a wave dragged out of the frozen ocean and shattered into tiny needles, blown into swirling chaos by a hiccupping wind pushing down from the mountains.

The road ahead disappeared. The air became a soupy cauldron of fog wracked with needles of ice that splattered against his fatigues. And out of the fog, a shape, its indistinct visage haloed in a fur-trimmed hood, came lumbering like some blinded mastodon, lurching right and left just as Warren lurched, perhaps just as drunk and disoriented as he, until their faces heaved close to each other in the pelting mist, and their freezing eyes met, and in that moment of partial legibility one of hers winked and drew the corner of her mouth up obscenely. Warren reached out for her, and suddenly puked his guts up.

When he woke hours later in her room, a stark place with a kerosene stove and burlap curtains, he felt her mouth engulfing his manhood. It started then, in the frozen nothingness of Unalaska, and in some sense it never ended. Echoes of Mavis, memories of Mavis, scattered bits and pieces of Mavis had wafted through all of Warren's subsequent experience of Carnal Love, and now Mavis loomed, like a fata morgana, on the discernible horizon of his immanent Personagehood, his arrival as a public figure—as if Mavis herself, like the arctic williwaw, were steadily blowing him towards his destiny.

A puzzling feature of this destiny was how little Warren personally had to do with it. Evangeline wrote his speeches and booked them and arranged semi-public meetings with gnomish individuals "in politics," she trained on these gnomes the steely hustle she'd learned as a lobbyist, which they seemed to tolerate mainly because Evangeline was "a real character," and looked a lot like you-know-who. Anyway, any HMO from California had almost anybody's ear.

Warren drifted through the events, the meetings, the visits, like a papier-mâché statue of American Enterprise rolling along in the Rose Bowl Parade. It was a weird time in the public life of America. A weird time to move around amid the histrionic architecture of Our Nation's Capital, so unlike the sybaritic beaches and palimpsest deserts he was used to.

He repined for those desert sundowns and wished for a craps table and a pair of dice for Evelyn to blow on for luck. People in Washington spoke a clipped jargon Warren couldn't follow. It was a language of knowingness, about levels of power incarnated in people or committees or agencies, a language of gimme, gimme this, gimme that, gimme some kind of blowjob. The people Evelyn turned up had Access, or could grease the way to someone with Access. Eva and Warren picked up a lot of dinner checks, a lot of drink tabs, took in a lot of cherry blossoms from a lot of office windows. Everyone they met, in all the offices and hotel lounges, seemed profoundly small, pathetically self-involved, and full of gimme.

B-52s were bombing North Vietnam. The Senate was investigating the Watergate break-in and various people involved in covering it up. Melancholia had drifted into the daily mood. The whole country had taken a bleary turn. Evangeline's bubbly insistence on talking to people who had no idea who she was exerted a certain charm on bureaucrats who welcomed distraction from the national mess. She did all the talking for both of them. Warren had precious little small talk, though when he tried, he often, loudly, bemoaned the Calvary they were putting the President through on the Hill. His vehemence on this topic usually alarmed even Nixon's warmest supporters. Warren felt a special loathing for Sen.

Sam Ervin, as he automatically did for many Southerners. He could never understand why the Dust Bowl hit godly, fertile Oklahoma instead of the depraved South, with its gene pool of flatulent hayseeds.

He felt a mystical connectedness to Richard Nixon. He would never forget Nixon's acceptance speech at the first or second convention (he did forget which), where the lonely train whistle on the faroff prairie or whatever was evoked. By God that man had a way with a verbal image. The veteran in Warren felt that all Communism and probably most Asiatics should be wiped off the face of the earth, and therefore Nixon's Vietnam policy was the right way to go. Not the popular thing, obviously, but the line had to be drawn somewhere.

Warren occasionally dreamed of meeting Richard Nixon, or rather dreamed that he already knew him, and had been dragooned into accompanying Richard Nixon on a kind of Arthurian quest that sometimes took place in the first stucco shack the Slotes had lived in in California: this shack, in dreams, magically generated more and more rooms, dank secret tunnels, creepy passages where various figures of the Nixon Administration lay in wait, to advise or bedevil the Chief Executive. Warren had to shield Nixon from the incubi and succubi his dreams tossed into their path. Evangeline often put in a cameo, frequently frilled as a busty dairymaid, offering Nixon a free, all expenses-paid trip to Guadalajara in exchange for his Social Security card.

So it was something like a dream transition from his ever-present apprehensions of Mavis, or the spectre of Mavis, to the lipstick trace of the President himself, when Evangeline contrived this little Flags of the Fifty States meet-and-greet right there in the White House with the First Lady. It was unclear, afterwards, just how Eva got them penciled into Pat Nixon's calendar, she'd circulated some sort of memo through some White House underlings she'd befriended—fags with an Auntie Mame fetish, Warren figured—confirming a nonexistent appointment, supposedly booked through the Press Secretary or whatever, mysteriously fortified by a bread-and-butter note Warren received from the recently hospitalized President himself, thanking him for a Get Well floral arrangement Warren sent to Walter Reed.

He recalls dressing in his best suit and, smitten with nerves, gulping down way too much scotch, and Eva primping for hours before squeezing herself into something resembling a Royal gown so busy with lace it looked like cake frosting. Rolling through the White House gates in a hired limo. Security and then an intern ushering them to a bright, historic hallway.

Eva had dragged along Patty Frasier, who had to have made a wretched impression in her godawful turquoise pants suit, flitting around with a Nikon snapping pictures of everything. Warren carried a Flags of the Fifty States in a deluxe frame all ready to present to Mrs. Nixon. He was far drunker than he'd expected to be. Patty gawked at the polished marble and the chandelier and the Chinese vases full of blue hydrangeas, like some hick, there were two armed Secret Service men with walkie-talkies watching every move, and a press person, and an intern, and suddenly Mrs. Nixon emerged from between white double doors, in a gray and red-flecked wool-tweed two-piece suit.

As Warren assumed his all-purpose look of graciously aging affluence, specks of glitter whirled in the air. Fog like a cosmic breath blowing through the cold swirled in front of him. The White House seemed to breathe and expand, like a lung clogged with chandeliers and staircases. Bits of Mavis Jenkins crackled out of Warren's memory and throbbed like sunspots in the general area where Mrs. Nixon stood, seeming to assimilate parts of Mrs. Nixon, then fizzed into nothingness. Mrs. Nixon smiled a thin, noncommittal smile and scanned their little group with eyes, Warren thought, that had seen just about everything.

Although Warren did not assemble the perception at the time, Mrs. Nixon's face underwent a series of subtle but visible changes as she approached. First an automaton cordiality. Next a closer look of shrewd curiosity, as if a morbid interest were piqued by Patty's frumpiness, Eva's incongruous evening wear, and Warren's scarecrow height. Followed, Warren later realized, by the trapped expression of someone who had entered the perimeter of a noxious odor.

There came into Mrs. Nixon's large eyes a faint cadaverous wariness, as if she were so damned tired of meeting people who didn't matter that her next move would be for a bottle of Nembutal. The hollows of her cheeks deepened. Her legs became locked by contrary impulses: move closer to this fishy tableau, or run the other way?

Eva closed the distance between herself and Mrs. Nixon with the subtlety of a linebacker, her hand limply extended, a hand sporting a mammoth chunk of glass faceted to simulate the world's biggest diamond. She gushed some breathy phrases about the Bicentennial and the Secretary of Education and a "dazzling moment in America's History." She looked to Mrs. Nixon, she said, to "help kick off this noble endeavor."

Mrs. Nixon disbelievingly gaped at Evangeline's ring. Nothing quite so tacky had come that near her face without warning in many, many years. The Secret Service people ambled closer. Mrs. Nixon flashed them an imperious look. She shook her head, just slightly, holding them in readiness. She turned her attention to Warren. Her eyes moved over the Flags of the Fifty States as if they were an assortment of mounted dog turds.

Patty, meanwhile, snapped pictures. Eva stepped into tight proximity with Mrs. Nixon, and Mrs. Nixon, sizing up the situation, decisively moved her face very close to Eva's ear. Warren saw the First Lady's lips moving quickly. An indistinct, hissing susurration issued from them.

Pat Nixon backed away several paces, as if clearing a path for machine-gun fire. Eva's face remained frozen in a ceremonial smile. Before Warren could blink, they were all rushed out of the White House by the intern, the press secretary, the men with the walkie-talkies.

Some of Patty's pictures captured the strained flavor of this event. However, several conveyed a look of official sanction that such photos are meant to achieve, and proved useful on numerous occasions ever after. Warren came to believe, at least whenever he said it, that he had in fact been a close personal friend of Richard Nixon's, on the order of someone like Bebe Rebozo, and had been especially close to Mrs. Nixon. God, he would tell people, what that poor woman had to endure.

It took him years to ambush Evelyn into spilling the exact words the First Lady had whispered to her. When recounting their Washington triumphs, Evangeline invented all manner of remarks supposedly uttered on this occasion. Then, in one of her ten cock-tail, fuck-it-all moods, she cackled bitterly as she recalled the flicker of horror that passed over Mrs. Nixon's face "when she saw that gigantic rock on my finger, know what she said, Warren? She said, *'Listen here, little miss nobody from nowhere,'* this is what she said, Warren, love it or leave it, *'it's time for you and your little friends to take a hike.'* And then when I moved my head away she *dug* her nails into the back of my hand, and sort of *yanked* me back so she could finish, and she says, she says, *'Never shit a shitter, sister.'* "

Years later, however, when most of their shared memories had been revised and embellished so freely as to seem infinitely mal-leable and unreal, Eva told him that his liquor breath had driven Mrs. Nixon off. "She asked me, *'Who's the juicehead,'* Warren. She really did. *'Who's the juicehead.'* "

DEVIN

One afternoon, shin deep in the shirring eddies of a cove, on the smallest link of an island chain from which he could see, depending on the clouds, a string-thin yellow crimp on the horizon that was, his father said, the eastern coast of Nicaragua, Devin wrenched a glabrous shell from its stubborn footing in the seabed and discovered, wriggling in the pearl-smooth maw of its underside, a livid protoplasmic animal, gelatinous, monstrous, eyeless and many-limbed (if its invertebrate appendages were limbs of a kind), that threshed loose with a squirming fluster into the sand-clouded water. Devin ran up on the beach gagging, though the thing was no bigger than the heel of his little foot, and seemed insensible to his presence, absorbed in its own mindless panic.

He had scooped five shells from the tidal cuticle, all vacant except that one. Some sprouted calcified knobs like misshaped horns, pocked with tiny parasite burrows. The best ones shimmered like blown glass, streaked milky brown like daubs on an African mask. Their useless mineral beauty reminded him of music, the kind his father listened to while slouched in the wing chair in his study. Not Sinatra and the corny romantic tunes he played when he wanted to be loud—*it's witchcraft, crazy witchcraft*—but the ancient German stuff full of violins.

His father's nerves weren't good. At times, his father drifted away. When Devin lingered near the study he heard ice clinking and labored footsteps and now and then that music with so many confusing feelings in it and once or twice he heard sobbing, but those times he assured himself it was something else, some adult eructation he couldn't know the meaning of. Surely, his father never wept. Their lives weren't sad. Everything was always new, or, if not completely new, at least the scenes kept shifting until they came around again, like sets in a movie. Always the sea, and the sky. Big clouds that weren't trapped by buildings. Or a city at night exploding with lights.

Here, around the shack-like hotel of breezy clapboard bunga-lows and a thatch roofed veranda bar and restaurant, the trees filled at odd hours with dense, obstreperous flocks of red and blue par-rots. When the parrots were silent the sea made the only sound. Ordinary time had no hold on the island. Meals were served whenever the rains stopped, or the generator came back on. They would open the bar at four in the morning, if somebody wanted a drink.

That period of his father's bad nerves would pass later on. Devin would recall it as a gray smudge in his childhood, an oily fingerprint pressed deep in the soft film of time. Other parts of that same time would live inside him like a bloody Technicolor loop.

His father would like the amphibious ick that plopped out of it more than the shell itself. He probably could have told Devin what it was. He had dug up the shells for his mother, who would nuzzle him and call him her precious little man, her cavalier. And brave, if he told her about the scary whatever. Or she might let him know, it might spill out of her, that prettier and stranger shells existed (not that his weren't "gorgeous," but one saw them every-where, sold as trinkets) just over the muddy ramps of the island's easterly tentacles, between the tangled roots of knobby trees and underwater debris, in the shallow bay facing Colombia. Devin's gifts didn't always bring waves of warm approval. She pretended when her mind was elsewhere, but Devin felt it when his presence strained her reserves of mothering, when the things he'd practiced telling her in nice rounded sentences full of vocabulary reached her as the oppressive gibberish of an implacable child. A child who was everything to her at erratic moments and an utter irrelevance at others, another face mouthing at her through glass bricks.

He couldn't have said, then or even years later, why she wore thick glasses she didn't need when people she didn't like or trouble invaded her realm, but he sensed the movements of the brain behind her eyes, her eyes could betray her. She could tell the biggest lie without missing a beat, or sliding her gaze off a target, but this other thing, this furtive, bottomless indifference to the existence of other people, including him, was the only secret she felt ashamed of. She hated herself for feeling this shame and believed it rotted her insides. Devin knew this without thinking it, he felt the contours of a wound that could never close, that signaled itself uncontrollably when fatigue overtook her.

Devin was eight the year they stopped at the island, and already old enough to know she needed him and needed his father but would calmly have chopped them into stew meat if the food ran out. The effort of winning her love was a daily struggle, and usually a daily failure. Devin's only triumph was that he wasn't Darren. Not being Darren bestowed the glow of a blessing, the luck of a rabbit's foot.

His mother had Things on Her Mind, all the time, sometimes Devin figured in them, he overheard himself described in ways that suggested his active membership in a tribe of enraged marmosets or a corporation whose boardroom could have been plausibly located on Mars, but often these Things involved the tenebrous world of invisible adults, wireless voices, paper transactions of occult obscurity. They involved the frequent use of wigs when she went out, a comedian's array of voices on the telephone. He was told to explain that the wigs, if anyone happened to see them, covered the defoliant effects of chemotherapy. Her invocations of fantasy cancer planted in his mind the absence of boundaries to her emotional demands as well as her secret view of herself as a putrid organism wasting from within: fearless, protean, and gorgeous on the outside, a festering sludge of disease beneath the skin. Devin loved her for this, in a sickly way, it was bravery.

She explained, when wishing to impart some minatory wisdom about How The Real World Worked, varied threads of her current tangle: how one person in Vegas was connected to another one in Scottsdale and another somewhere else, what motives pushed these phantoms through life, the flaw in the way they were put together. So he learned at the same time that he learned to ride a bike that lawyers were mercenary douche bags, insurance companies bloodsucking leeches, process servers and police a league of alien life forms bent on destroying his mother, his father, and himself. Darren was a passive choleric personality likely to go nowhere, not that she wasn't heartbroken about it, but facts are facts, Devin could, she said, comfort himself that Darren was hardly his real brother, as far as that went. His Slote aunts and cousins and uncle were a clan of parasites who'd do them physical damage without her unwavering vigilance and might yet snatch him from his bed in the dead of night. This was why they had to keep moving, changing houses and hotels, why she and they had to be so many different people. As for the rest of the human race, most of it was genetically flawed and only useful to clean houses. She really believed these things; Devin was never sure.

He thought of the palms as spider trees, for the hotel attracted spiders, several species of them, and occasional snakes, thin pastel green snakes silvery on one side, as long as two feet, that whipped across rooms in a blink and vanished through gaps in the floorboards. The trees were thick with slumbering bats as well as parrots. It was customary for the island's small but regular scattering of visitors to sip mojitos garnished with rice paper parasols on the veranda while watching the bats launch themselves into the pink dusk.

They had gone to the island without all the people who came along everywhere, the nanny, the servants, Evelyn made them stay behind in Cartagena, at the Hilton, because, she'd told them, as if sharing a good joke, they had all begun to bore her, they couldn't do a thing right, she wanted them to reflect on their mistakes and resolve to do better. After this tirade, she hinted coquettishly that besides all that, in the private fastness of the island she and Warren would fully stoke the flame of romance that always smoldered between them like a peat fire, and rarely blazed free because of their high-powered social lives and ardent business schedules. Devin saw, though she didn't, that the help gaped at this florid recitative as if Evangeline were a raving maniac. No way could these low people understand a person like his mother, a woman of gigantic heart and wondrous personal blandishments. Forever rising above malice aimed at her by envious individuals. It did occur to him, from time to time, that she was, in fact, nuts. But her insanity was so much bigger than anything these people could imagine that their puzzled faces simply made them seem small and stupid.

He returned to the island again and again while drifting through classes at Bishop Gorman High during Evangeline's imprisonment, and the Catholic school in Nassau after she got out, and later in the dorm at UCSB. He thought up phrases for that time in Spanish. He re-created the heavy rains that fell at three every afternoon and stopped abruptly at three-thirty. He had his own spacious bungalow, a cavern really, containing a bed and a table and a wicker chair, an oil lamp for power failures, a cheap metal shower stall and a toilet. Sounds from the veranda filtering through the vegetation deflected his fear of scorpions and the tiny lizards perched along the walls.

Some Germans arrived late that afternoon, drenched from the terrifying passage in a disintegrating boat that never rose more than a couple inches above the waves. The boat shunted between the island and the reeking marina next to the Cartagena Yacht Club. The fun of that trip was that you really put your life at risk, a different flavor of risk than the one you took by being in Cartagena in the first place. The boat leaked and carried no flotation devices and the engine spat out bees' nests of slimy smoke, and the weather always shifted midway through the twenty mile trip. If you survived, as people always did, you had a story to tell. On their own crossing Devin had puked all the way out, and even his dad turned green. His mother had a mysterious arrangement with mortality that made her indifferent to danger. She poured martinis from a Conrans thermos as they bounced on the choppy sea, spreading her arms out in ecstasy whenever a wave hit her in the face.

The restaurant had a small nightly orchestra, a hapless ensemble of five ugly Ecuadorians hired for the season. They played "Siboney" and other Caribbean standards, in three unvarying sets, between ten p.m. and whatever hour turned out to be closing. Between flubbed chords and screeching cello passages, the voices of the Germans carried, entangled with his mother's and father's, down the plank walkway behind the restaurant and into the trees, the gurgle and throbbing of the forest thinned them into shouted phrases, *Well I'll be damned*, and *Try the chicken if you're so tired of fish*, and his mother, he thought, had made herself interesting to the beefy krauts, her voice pitched higher as the other voices dropped to a ruminative mulch. He heard: *legal brothels*. He heard: *gaming commission, you've got golf, you've got broads, chemin de fer, you name it, we've got it*. He knew this Viva Las Vegas mantra as the family's travel anthem. And in fact, these people they met by chance and had nothing in common with frequently did show up at their house, or phoned to say they were at the Sahara or the MGM Grand and fired up to party hearty. It was part of the occult transactions of grownups, this strange enthusiasm for each other's company in places that weren't, in Devin's mind anyway, connected, except the way slides are connected in a projector carousel.

He slept. He dreamt about a Rottweiler dog hooked up to machines. He opened his eyes. The oil lamp was lit. A kerosene smell hovered near his nose. The shadows of the ceiling fan sliced along the walls. She was there in a nightgown.

"Salt ruins your skin," his mother said.

"Hi mom."

"Never let your skin go to hell," she said. "Bad skin looks worse on a woman, but it doesn't look good on anybody."

Devin sat up under the sheet.

"Can we see the witch tomorrow?"

There were two plantations on the island on a flat piece of land high above the hotel. Sisal farms abandoned to their share-croppers after World War II, when the sisal market collapsed. The smaller plantation had a resident witch, a woman rumored to be 120 years old, who never stirred from her rocking chair. She was known for casting spells in a squawking patois that resembled the shrieking of slaughtered birds.

His mother glided closer to the bed. She pushed up her ruffled sleeves. Her perfume mixed unpleasantly with the lamp fumes. The light caught her face at an angle that hardened her makeup lines.

"Well, we might have to skip it," she rasped. "These people who showed up today, that Hugo and Otto pair, I think they know your Uncle Cleve."

It was strange to fear his uncle. Whatever satanic capacities he might aspire to, Uncle Cleve was really just a dentist. He heard his father laughing with Hugo and Otto, fat and harmless-looking men. His mother waved her hand as if dispersing their minatory odor.

"Papa knows how to handle them," she said. "He fought those Nazi murderers in World War II." She ran a finger under Devin's nose. "We need to get you freshened up, sugar beet."

"I took a shower." Devin thought his father had fought the Japanese. But maybe there were Nazis up in Attu.

Evelyn licked her finger.

"I still taste salt," she clucked. "Come on, I have some coconut soap, it protects."

She had always bathed him, in bathtubs. Now there was the cold water stall with a round rusted drain in the bottom.

"I'll have to get in with you," she said, tugging off his pajama bottoms. She took the soap from her pocket and pulled the nightgown over her head.

She was the only person he had ever seen like that, everything showing. The fleecy triangle down there, and her breasts hanging like patted mounds of pancake batter, nipples like ray guns pointing in opposite directions. She had fed him there a long time ago, and some fuzzy image of that drifted through his head. Now he stood level with her nipples. She steered him into the stall under the cool stuttering spray. She stepped in behind him. Devin kept his back turned. He felt her breasts against his hair, her stomach against his back.

She soaped his curls, which had grown down over his ears since his last haircut. She lathered her hands, slid them up and down his arms and chest, then his shoulders, his back, his buttocks. He felt the soap foam buttering his penis, her fingers pressing it lightly, fingertips rolling his testicles.

For a moment he believed she was introducing him to some hygienic nuance, but she continued, and the pressure of her wet skin underwent a little shift, as if her blood warmed the trickle of the shower, and slowly this thing that had happened before in his sleep was happening here, stiffening, then really hard, pointing up. Her hand slithered across his shoulder, kneaded a gout of muscle. She pirouetted him around facing her, lubricating his penis with her other hand, squinching it up and down.

Heat spread over his body. His breath quickened, like breathing in hot mustard, and his mouth fastened on her nipple, sucking. He tasted coconut and a bosky taste like smoked meat, a trace of rust from the water sluicing around his mouth. She went on kneading his balls, pumping his organ. Fingers brought his hand to the wrinkled slit at the bottom of the triangle, pressed his fingers into a sinewy place sticky with something like jelly, pulled them slowly out, and pushed them in again. Finally his entire hand sank into her hole, and nervously he tugged it out and pressed it in again without help. She made a noise with her throat, more and more insistently. He felt an intense tingling, a nerve explosion in his balls, that wiped aside his consciousness, and when the feeling left he felt abruptly horrified by the picture he saw of them together. At that instant he felt his mother's cunt shudder. Some kind of hot goo slathered itself on his fingers.

It began like that and went on like that, not exactly the same way again, not in bathrooms and showers, and never predictably, never at his instigation, even though there were moments later on when the thought of it aroused him, sick as it might seem to some narrow minds around him. Long periods elapsed when he came to believe they had finished this lick of his education. Gradually he understood that the island and its heavy veils of silence and dark- ness marked the shift, the segue, when Devin became, in unre- marked and barely discernible stages, *the man of the family*, a juvenile reincarnation of his still-living father, sporadic conjugal privileges transpiring unsuspected by anyone despite the untoward symbiotic intimacy remarked upon by almost everybody, during the gypsy years between the mess with the chinchilla jacket and his mother's sentencing, when Evelyn hired and fired an impossible number of itinerant tutors and screened out all but a few malleable and unlikely friends for him: Myra the fat girl, for instance, who lived fifty miles from them on Oahu, fetched and returned by livery car for intensely supervised and hence rather drab Saturday play dates. Inevitably, Devin found other children, in Hawaii and Vegas, who lived in their neighborhoods, with whom some clandestine approximation of childhood became occasionally possible, even though sooner or later Evelyn always put a stop to it. It was entirely clear to him that *that* was more secret than any other secret he'd been trained to keep since the time he learned to talk. That she didn't trust him with it only made itself felt in the unreasoning vigilance she maintained, about who came in contact with him. He confused her intent with her fear of this kidnapping threat.

For the most part, Devin felt part of the team. The Slote team. A special team with special rules, secrecy foremost. He knew she stole things, his father also, he knew their last name wasn't Evans or Parillo or the other ones they registered under in hotels, he knew there had never been a laptop computer stolen from the garage, but unlike his passive choleric stepbrother, Devin was a great decoy on shoplifting excursions and always remembered he was Devin Evins, Devin Parillo, Devin Whatever, he could describe every symbol on the keyboard of that mythical computer for the insurance man. Until Evelyn got sent up, Devin's object in life was to keep her happy with him, if he could not avoid her fanatical attentions. If this included what she pet-named their bedtime jiggy-jiggy, Devin took it on as best he could, but he certainly wasn't going to advertise it. He knew it was something he could never talk about, it had some nuclear trigger built into it that would blow their lives into lethal neutrons the second he opened his mouth.

Only after the slavery uproar, when Evelyn took up clamorous residence at Club Fed in Frontera, and Warren enrolled him in Bishop Gorman, did Devin perceive how repellently odd and different his life had been from that of anyone he met. Evelyn had ripped out a lot of wiring needed to connect with other people. She had drilled him in good manners, but under that skin he knew nothing of how or why deeper affinities formed between people, what they talked about when they "really" talked, what understandings lay behind certain intimacies. He stuffed the empty spaces in his personality with clichés, like newspapers wadded into drafty windows. His emotions had been hijacked at a delicate age and left to stagnate. The rest of the world was a deep mystery to him. Devin coasted amid its blurred forms, mimicking its most banal and accessible features.

Her jail term humiliated him. He told people who knew better she was in the hospital (he knew they knew, the case had been headlines for months, it was a fiction people swallowed out of kindness and laughed about behind his back). But he felt unshackled, too. His father let him do anything: fill the house with his friends, make a mess, play baseball in the back yard. And not just because he was drunk. Quite often, in those years, he wasn't. They were happy times for Warren too. He took an interest in his businesses again, he went golfing. He fired the servants. He did all the cooking at home, proud of his planked salmon and baby back ribs. Warren had a flourish with food. He listened when Devin talked about his homework. He even went to PTA meetings and softball games. If he didn't keep the house as sterile as an operating room the way she did, that didn't ruin Devin's day.

He entertained a hope that he was only slightly mutilated. Maybe the damaged tissues of his soul would grow back without scarring. On the other hand, they both knew Evelyn would be coming back, and that neither of them could resist her will. They never discussed it, or her, unless they absolutely had to. When the fat FedEx envelopes arrived full of legal papers and lists of things they were supposed to do for her. Her endless letters dripping with platitudes and self-pity, and chilling promises that *when I get home I'm going to make up for all the years you've been without your mother.*

Even in hell, she would have managed unlimited access to a phone, so the calls, too, opened hairline fractures in the calm of a given week. Sometimes Warren simply winked across the dinner table, and they went on eating while the phone rang.

The visits were the wrenching parts. You couldn't get the taste out afterwards. The forced regression to the primal schema, Mama Papa Baby. Devin always wished they were separated by thick glass panels like in the movies. Instead she could feel him and smell him and mark him with touches the way a dog marks a hydrant with pee. Prison didn't dent her manias, every time they took that long sullen drive to Frontera she was anxious to complain about her ovaries, blurry vision, earaches, sinus pains, vaginal itching, migraines, problems with her kidneys, constipation, possible bowel cancer. She had convinced herself that the hit-and-run in Washington had left her concussed and subsequently brain-damaged and balance-impaired, never mind that Warren and Devin knew perfectly well she'd never been hit by any laundry truck or whatever she claimed it had been, for her that accident and these snowballing symptoms of decomposition were more real than her husband and son, and the worst of it, for him, was that he not only still loved her and felt he had to protect her somehow, but also, at these moments, desired her, *that way*.

She had foisted an ersatz puberty on his childhood, and now that puberty had actually arrived, his only lubricious thoughts were of her, of pounding her absurd flesh until she screamed, making her do filthy things, making that dumb bitch grovel for her boy's man-size woody. Every vision of this stripe curdled into loathing as it broke the surface of his thoughts. He wanted to slice her out of his brain with a serrated knife and throw the bloody gob in her face. And his father, who'd come a little more alive every week she was gone, turned to oatmeal in the visiting room, Devin watched him shrink as the will drained out of him, until his dad became a piece of lint on his mother's orange prison shift. Months before her release, Warren started drinking, as if it would take months to get numb enough not to kill himself, or her.

When she came home it was like poison, a few drops a day. A slow-acting neurotoxin. The sound of her voice made him physically ill. It never stopped. It yakked at everything and everybody at the same time. It pleaded and cooed and declaimed into telephones and snarled demands at the new staff. It interrogated, it sniffed, it ripped sympathy out of people's throats with a palsied tremolo. It waxed nasty as any CIA torturer, it climbed to a fruity falsetto in the face of any accusation, it issued a ceaseless ukase that covered everything from the decoration of a room to the color of Devin's socks, it filled space and time like rising water seeking every dry submersible corner of the universe.

Drastic changes happened overnight, without warning. She transferred his high school and only told him as she handed him his lunch bag at breakfast. The friends he'd made were embargoed one by one, first from the house, then from his life, then she pulled him out of school, hired a tutor, and forced them to move, claiming her notoriety in Vegas made normal life impossible. For a while they rented a ranch house in Henderson and somehow Evelyn and his father connived to scam it out from under the owners, using a forged stipulation in the lease. This led to a new whirlwind of suits and countersuits, and even a fraud investigation by the Nevada Attorney General, since the name Slote had become synonymous within the state's legal system with a particularly flagrant type of chicanery.

Devin ran away, several times. He slept on sofas offered by other kids' parents. He craved the ordinary stupid life of any family besides his. He tried to be the perfect adopted son of strangers.

These families liked him. He smiled a lot and made himself useful, cleaning out garages and mowing lawns. During his four year reprieve from Evangeline, he had learned what a normal teenager of that cultural moment was like. Although he couldn't actually become one, he did a highly credible impersonation. It was still half his wish to blend in, but it could never be more than half. The other half of him was her. He knew if he stayed anywhere too long, she would track him down and make his new friends targets of bad things they couldn't possibly imagine or cope with. He was too old to be ordered home but invariably slunk back, because he worried about Warren.

Warren meanwhile resumed his interrupted decline, his heart wasn't fit, his mind wandered, he relapsed into bourbon miasmas. The long Hawaii flights took a visible toll on his stamina, likewise Devin's war with Evangeline, which escalated for a year before they actually hit each other. Warren thought every argument was a small, self-contained misunderstanding rather than the latest skirmish in a mounting conflagration.

The fight was over in five minutes: Devin slapped her, she punched him, he punched back, next they clawed and pounded each other on the floor, trying to smash the thing they hated in each other with elbows and fists. Devin thought, *I am going to stop your goddam clock once and for all*. He felt her teeth sink into his shoulder, yanked her hair to pull her mouth off him. Her wig slid off in his hand. He stared at the fake black curls between his fingers and then at her real hair, a greasy mat of thinning sausages that had gone gray and silver in prison.

He rolled off his mother. Her wig had defeated him. Evangeline scuttled away on strangely twisted limbs, as if changing into a crab or lobster. She angled into a corner and crouched with her arms folded across her breasts. She rocked back and forth. Her breathing belonged to some animal in a cave. Mascara smudged around her eyes gave her the look of a mauled raccoon. She stared at a broiler oven inches from her face. After arranging herself in an abject heap she began to cry. Devin got to his feet, feeling gutted and sewn up with some parts missing, reeled through the house to his bedroom.

The house went still and dark and heavy. Hours later, he heard Warren's taxi drop him home from the airport. There was a blind spot in Devin's memory of the next day, he recalled sitting with her in the back yard and spilling everything that made him crazy, and she must have had the words ready to draw him back. A neighbor was running logs through a wood chipper. The machine splintered their conversation into weird non sequitors, his memory was that the wood chipper brought them together more decisively than anything they said. In the days and weeks that followed an inexplicable peace settled in, as if the air were suffused with lithium.

We have traveled far, we have traveled fast, he heard an English tourist singing to his wife in the hardware store on Calle Separación in Puerto Plata. Devin's fugue of recollection broke up as the man and his English accent passed near him in the pest control section, an ill-arranged compost of aerosol cans and plastic bottles in a dusty alcove. They were an old-young couple, a skinny nebbish in crumpled khakis, his clear-eyed face pinched and disap-

pointed behind a walnut beard, the woman dissembling extra holiday pounds under a loose frock she'd bought at the beach, putting
on a show of light-heartedness for each other. She had actressy features, vivid from a distance, that turned flatter and surprisingly
coarse in close-up. If they had traveled far and fast, Devin thought,
they had taken all their baggage with them: the voices, the faces,
the stale dialogue. He could tell what they were like at a glance,
not strictly according to Evangeline's system, but rather by con-
torting it slightly with his own intuitions.

The man worked in a laboratory, Devin guessed. Sensitive
hands, but not as careful of themselves as a surgeon's or a pianist's.
Maybe a marine biology lab. There was, come to think of it, a
peculiar modern building in a narrow valley between forest hills, a
blob of poured concrete suggesting both a mosque and a radar
installation, off the road running west from Puerto Plata. It could
be a laboratory, it had cyclone fencing topped with razor wire and
a certain military je ne sais quoi. But he felt certain these were
vacationers. A lab in England, then, busy with fetal tissue research,
or pig cloning. His other guess would be something in software
development.

Devin had done a lot of solitary driving in the white Nissan
they'd rented on arriving three days earlier, following dirt roads
and barely navigable car tracks veering inland off the coast road
(which did not, in fact, run near the actual shore, but afforded
brief, blinding views of its ongoing rape by developers), into the
rain forest, or tracking along cane fields where Haitian migrant
workers hacked the crop and slept in tin shanties, cooking on open
fires fed with gasoline. Some tar roads, all of them disintegrating,
wound through eerie green silences where cottages of a tropical
gingerbread tendency stood flush with the roadbed, bright yellow
and green houses with blocky Santeria carvings on porch rails and
window shutters, here and there a ranch with horses roaming in
pens, the houses spaced at quarter mile intervals. He'd also found a
road of packed mud running straight between hardwood trees

beside a mangrove swamp, the canopy so dense that passing under it turned the day dark and cool. The road had one inhabited spot, where a black-skinned family whiled the day in hammocks and folding chairs, drinking rum from plastic tumblers and listening to static on a prehistoric radio. Children swung from a fraying rope to fling themselves into the swamp. Their house, like the road, was wedged between tall trees, thrown together with waste board and debris from the stalled construction sites, west of town, where several gargantuan resorts had passed into receivership while still in a skeletal state, like exterminated hives. The swamp family waved without interest when he passed on his way to the end of the road, and waved with the same indifference when they saw him coming back. The road ended after a mile, in a cul-de-sac of impassible bamboo.

Yes, the man was someone who put tiny things between microscope slides, plankton or dolphin liver scrapings or what not, and looked for anomalies or variations. The woman did something creative. Painted, or designed clothes, or took photographs, and believed herself very good at whatever it was, because people told her she was. Perhaps people paid for the things she made.

They would be open to meeting new people, but unlikely to let these new people draw close to them quickly. You couldn't "do" that kind of tourist. The kind you could easily "do" were the ones who acted out some dewy romantic script in an exotic setting. Couples who, if left on their own, would probably discover in a few days how little they actually liked each other, and who also felt slightly threatened by their surroundings. There was a promising assortment of deluded North Americans and crass, credulous Euroscum wandering the streets, but Puerto Plata had nothing menacing going for it, no unnerving downside to attract the jumpy to a family of more seasoned travelers. In places like South Asia and India, the sheer density of the human mass was alarming enough for such people to bond instantly with their own Western kind. Puerto Plata was only unfamiliar for the quantity of dark skin. Underpopulated, if anything. It was a sleepy, slummy Caribbean town sloping down to a fabulous beach. In season it probably swelled into carnival hideousness, but they had not arrived in season.

". . . a crash pad in Brixton, and tiny waffles," the woman said as she held up a can of insect repellant.

"They actually *mailed her the tits* in a sterile container," said the man.

"Bloody fuck," said the woman, "this stuff contains DDT."

Devin pressed the little collar button speakers of his Walkman into his ears. Op Ivy, "Gonna Find You" obliterated ambient sound. The tourist voices didn't bother him. But he wanted overpowering theme music to cast these minutes as a shot or scene in a movie he was acting in, he wanted the hardware store and its provender to take on a fictional dreaminess. The store was close and cluttered and motes of dust swam in light streaming through the street window. Without the music, the store had the forensic look of dampened sawdust, or metal shavings. . . .

His eyes passed over an array of shovels projecting from pegboards. The store had a puzzlingly large selection. Long-handled shovels, short-handled shovels, shovels with end grips, shovels without end grips, straight-bladed, V-bladed, shovels for light soils, trowel-tipped shovels for gardening, shovels for digging clay and heavy soils. And the shovel display itself showed a considerably larger effort, aesthetically speaking, than the rest of the dull emporium, in the matter of spacing one style of shovel apart from another, and whether the individual shovel type offered the concave or convex side of its blade to the customer's eye, and if it hung from its bracket by the blade, pointing upward, or by the end grip, if it had an end grip, pointing down, and some attention had been paid to the eye's progression from rounded-tip shovel blades to flat-ended ones, from lighter finishes to darker ones, some shovels loomed, their baked black enameling cowled like the hoods of a satanic order, some seemed to fold shyly in on themselves, self-effacing as a shelf of spermacides, there were bold, masculine shovels and shovels of a quiet, more elegant strength, plain jane shovels that would just get the job done and delicately balanced shovels that would spare you as many blisters as they could, fey shovels too short for anything arduous, a shovel or two with real swagger in its heft, *Don't step in the water till you know you can swim*, sang Op Ivy.

He picked out a shovel of medium length that had a sportif accent of green paint on the end grip. It weighed, by the feel of it, two pounds, it had a round point blade of tempered steel and a fiberglass handle, it was easy to carry, and it looked all of a piece with Devin's Walkman, Devin's bone white shorts, Devin's red shirt open to the waist, Devin's Thalo-green Jellies. He added the shovel to a fourteen-inch faceted steel crowbar, a hundred-foot-roll of ⅜-inch polypropylene cordage, a heavy-duty box cutter in a yellow plastic slide grip, and a twenty-by-thirty-foot blue multipurpose polytarp he had already piled on the counter. He paid the sleepy mulatto clerk, a slack-faced boy with silver rings in his eyebrows and some kind of Moorish crown molding tatooed on his left wrist. The boy bagged the smaller items and stapled the receipt to the bag.

In the dead midday street Devin loaded the trunk of the Nissan. He drove east along Avenida Gral. G. Luperon. He stopped at a flower stall on his way out of town and bought a paper horn full of pink and yellow blossoms. He went on to the Sea Breeze Hotel in Sosua and ate an omelette in the dining room.

After the omelette he phoned his mother from the lobby. She answered her mobile at a seafood grille on Chiquita Beach, a place of fishnets and plastic lobster ornaments. Warren and Otis had practically driven to Haiti with some dubious business contact that morning. They had looked at a ten-acre parcel outside Monte Cristi that had the ruins of a sugar mill on it as a point of charm. But no ocean view and bad highway access, so now they were unspooling at the bar.

"Frankly," Devin told her, "I think the floating capital floated up to Florida about two years ago."

"No shit, Sherlock. Otis is clueless. He saw that Omni down on the water and said by the looks of things we got here just in time. He's playing pinball with some twelve-year-old queer. He says he wants to go waterskiing. I mean, can you see Otis on a pair of water skis?"

"Only if they were up his ass," Devin said. "But you know, this whole strip here might turn around in ten years, Otis does have a point."

"A useless point," said Evangeline. "In ten years I'll be sixty-seven. Santa Rosa's the only gold mine this keester's gonna sit on *that* long."

"So fine, mom, fuck the Dominican Republic, it's too full of niggers anyway. What's dad doing?"

Evangeline heaved a theatrical sigh.

"What he's always doing," she said. "For once, it's a blessing."

"Have you said anything? About Las Palmas Freneticas?"

"What an idiotic name for a place."

"Well, have you?"

"I'm picking my moment," she said.

Las Palmas Freneticas was a brace of rental cabins and a large al fresco bar on a road forking off from the Cabarete highway. The supporting pylons of the bar's conical roof were veined with Christmas lights that at nightfall gave a sinister gaiety to the unpopular, underlit bar and its many tables, empty and in deep shadow, that suggested Las Palmas Freneticas at least occasionally functioned as a restaurant. Devin drove there directly from the Sea Breeze and confirmed the reservations he'd made for three cabins. It was obviously unnecessary to make such reservations, and the bartender indicated his amusement by pouring Devin a shot glass of rum, on the house. The bartender was Venezuelan. He was heavily scarred around the mouth and eyes, and had the restless physicality of a person who had done hard time in ugly places.

"I want the three on the side road," Devin reminded him. "I don't want to park out front here."

"Movements in and out of here are of no interest to the management," the bartender said, meaning himself. "You can bring whoever you like here. If you want company, I can manage that for you. *Los chicos* or *las chicas,* whatever you prefer."

Devin left it at that. He put two U.S. twenties on the bar. The bartender took them. He introduced himself as Luis. He strode off to a small office, returning a while later with a scrawled receipt and a set of keys. Devin drove the Nissan onto the side road and backed up beside one of the cabins.

Thirty minutes later he drove to the Cementerio de Santa Rosa de Lima, a hilly sprawl of waist-high Houses of the Dead and grave markers of wildly varied expense, though mostly shabby. It was on an especially bad road strewn with large rocks and potholes. The path winding through the cemetery was reverting to crab grass.

Two shirtless men wearing straw hats labored in a hole near a thick grove of white cedars. Their spades flung dirt on a growing mound. They stared at the Nissan without pausing. Devin parked a few yards away. He got out of the car holding the paper cone of flowers. He walked in among the headstones, up a grassy hill, with a searching look. He stopped at a stone marked PEDRO MONASTERIO ALONSO, 1-6-1989.

He assumed a posture of relieved discovery, solemnly placing the bouquet where he supposed Pedro Monasterio Alonso's crotch would be nourishing various larvae a few feet below. *There was a young girl from Hong Kong,* he whispered piously, his head bowed, *whose cootch was too tight for my dong. I couldn't go south, so just fucked her mouth, that six year old bitch from Hong Kong.* Devin thought that was long enough for a prayer. He crossed himself, then ambled down the hill. He strolled over to the gravediggers as if he'd just noticed them. They were both the color of acorns. One middle-aged and out of shape, with a bulbous face. The other lean and handsome, around twenty, with shrewd brown eyes and a thin scar from a basted harelip.

"*Ustedes trabajan bien duro,*" Devin greeted. "Is hard work."

"*Sí,*" said the older one. "In the sun . . . *pero, estamos acostum-brados.*"

"You have a loved one here?" the younger one asked. His face was skeptical. He took in Devin's shorts, his bright shirt, his sock-less Jellies.

"*Un amigo de la familia,*" Devin said sadly. "Taken from us when he least expected."

"*Un accidente?*" asked the older one.

"*Sí, sí, algo se cayó en su cabeza* . . . something fell on his head," Devin improvised.

"*En Sosua?*"

"*Ah, no, sucedió en otro país.* In America. He's brought back to bury here. *Sus restos fueron retornados aquí.* To make the hole, *cuantas horas?*"

"One hour," the younger man shrugged.

"I like to get out of here before dark," the older one said. He made a comic face and crossed himself.

"*Es supersticioso,*" the young man laughed.

"*Nadie en esta isla vendría pour aquí en la oscuridad,*" the older one told Devin seriously. He put his hand on the younger man's arm. "*Used ha visto cosas por aquí igual que yo.*"

The young digger crossed his hands on his shovel handle and rested his chin there. "He has seen things. He says I see them too, *es cierto.* Sometimes a child in a blue dress. She rolls a hoop with a stick, I have seen her over there." He flung out his arm and ges-tured at the white cedars. "And a lady all in white, in the trees. They do not know they are dead," he explained.

Devin nodded.

"And this dead one?"

"Old," the older man put in.

"Old, and suffering a long time," said the young one. "His mind had gone from him as well. *También había perdido la razón.*"

"When he died?"

"This morning."

"*¿Y el funeral?*"

"*Mañana bien temprano.*"

"*Eso es rápido.*"

"We must bury them quickly, if you wait they will stink."

The older man understood.

"*Sí, sí,* if you keep them they smell."

Evangeline met him in the airy travertine lobby of the Sea Breeze. She wore an uncharacteristically glum gray pants suit that featured her big ass, and a pale scarf tied negligently around her neck.

"Your father feels queasy," she said. "I gave him a Demerol."

On the brief drive to Las Palmas Freneticas, she said she had decided not to propose a whole night away from the hotel.

"Because then, even just overnight they'd both want to bring a bag, and whatnot."

"I spent a long time on this," Devin said peevishly.

"Things are just going to happen," she said.

Devin pointed out the fork in the highway, the side road where the cabins were.

"You and dad in that one, me there, Otis there."

"All right darling, I get the picture."

"Well, *fuck*, at least let me show you the stuff." Devin nearly whined. Her whole attitude.

"I'm so proud of you," she told him, after she saw the stuff, riding back to the Sea Breeze. "You know Devin you're a born problem-solver. And you really have an artist's eye for detail."

"Aw, mom."

"Well you do! I have to marvel," she said in her most trilling voice. She waved at the Sea Breeze doorman, who had offered to fuck her earlier in the day.

"Ten o'clock, no later," Devin told her.

"Darling they don't eat down here until ten. That dump is open all night, isn't it?"

"Okay, eleven. Promise me something, okay?"

"Anything, dearest."

"Bring me a fucking doggie bag? So I can eat?"

In his room, Devin showered away the day. His body looked good in the steamed-up mirror: abs still washboard, hard pecs, quite a hunk if he said so himself. The nose job in Fresno six months earlier had not worked out, but he thought they could fix it. He dressed in black jeans, a black t-shirt, and white socks. He packed his Jellies and two sets of clothes in the plastic bag from the hardware store. He ordered a chicken club from room service. He read part of a Tom Clancy novel until the sandwich arrived, then selected a movie, *Anal Vixens of the S.S.*, from the hotel pay-per-view.

When the light went down on the water he laced on a pair of Timberlands and rode the elevator to the lobby. The atmosphere had shifted from siesta torpor to the meretricious quickening of evening. A ceremonial tackiness prevailed among the staff, trumped by the bulbous gold jewelry and billowy designer knockoffs sported by American and German couples arriving for dinner. A short, perky valet, who had offered to fuck Devin a few days earlier, fetched the Nissan from the bowels of the car park.

Resentment pestered him as he drove to the cemetery. He knew she'd be telling them some tale about him going into Puerto Plata to get laid, the very thing that being around her all the time prevented him from doing. Not just being around her, either. When he came close to anything like that at UCSB, some basic element of the procedure failed to materialize. Either the girl said something that wilted him, or he came in his pants without getting hard, or very bad things came into his mind, and he had to stop himself from doing them.

No cars on the cemetery road, no houses along there either. But all manner of persons lived outdoors in these regions, in shacks buried in the woods, in cardboard boxes, mole people with empty white eyes. He could not avoid the feeling of being watched, thinking that the squeaking lurch of the car as it moved between ruts and rocks and fallen tree limbs was alerting the whole countryside to his movements. The moon inside the cemetery was bright enough for him to inch along without the headlights, but he imagined the churring engine noise fanning through miles of darkness, drawing these dead living silent people like voodoo drums. When he found the grave and turned the car off, the air filled with owl cries and vegetal rustling, twittering nocturnal insects.

He tossed the shovel in the hole and leaped in after it. The soil was packed tight, but broke apart easily. The only hard thing was the scraping sound as he stomped the blade in, and the dirt smutching on the pile above. The sound seemed as public as a cannon.

It was sweaty, filthy work, but Devin enjoyed physical effort. He lost himself in it, he liked the burn on his palms from the shovel grip, the heft of soil on the blade, his stolid footing on the pliant earth. The sky was smeared with stars, and cloudy spirals of the cosmos. People were all such pathetic strings of drool in the universe, he thought, himself included. So why was he digging a hole, under a carpet of stars, in a hole already dug, somewhere on the northern coast of the Dominican Republic? The only answer that came to him was, *Because nobody else is doing it*. It was his thing, this digging, in a Catholic cemetery where people who didn't know they were dead were feared by the local population. *I'm digging a doorway to hell*, he thought. He thought of hell as a Macao casino he had read about in a James Bond novel, and as a place he would like to go. There would be suicides at the roulette table, an aging chanteuse with a feathered headdress, and Mother Gin-Sling planning her Chinese New Year party.

"There was a girl named Whiskey Soda," Ona Munson told Gene Tierney. "And another called Miss Martini . . ."

He would have to rent that movie again when he got back to school. And *Spetters*, that one had practically changed his life. Dead Kennedys, *Spetters*, and—*done*. It would have to be done, he couldn't see how deep it was and either it worked or it didn't. He dropped the shovel behind the dirt pile. He sat down on grass, mopped sweat from his face with his shirt tail.

"Fuck a whore," he yelled. He got up and picked up the shovel and tossed it into the Nissan. He left the cemetery with the headlights blazing and made for Las Palmas Freneticas, singing a Dead Kennedys song. *Now I'm seeing colors, I'm getting higher, I think I'll start a forest fire.*

He drove past the Christmas lights, noting white shapes at the bar. An unexpected posse of cars on the gravel and along the road. He drove around back and parked on the road several yards from the cabins.

He let himself into the middle cabin and found his way in the dark to the bathroom switch. He tore off his clothes and scrubbed himself under the shower with a courtesy cake of pink soap. He dressed in the fresh clothes he'd brought and double-checked things in the other cabin and then crossed the rear courtyard behind the platform where the tables were, into a soup of voices and clinking glasses and Afro-Cuban salsa.

The bar had a karaoke thing going on. A Brunehilde blonde in a white jumpsuit mouthed Spanish lyrics into a cordless mike, gliding clumsily between tables, egged on by a trio of Japanese men in identical tourist shirts. A party of drunk Americans filled three pushed-together tables, whooping like brazen stereotypes. There were couples, solitary drinkers, parties of four, a real crowd, nothing like what he'd expected. But this was better, in a way. He saw his father leaning on the bar, gaunt and brittle-looking, soused to the trained eye, ordering something from Luis. It wasn't Luis, though. It was another short, excitable person who looked like a convict, or an underwear model. Devin moved towards him and caught his foot on a chair leg. Evangeline was sitting in the chair. She craned backwards and gaped into his face.

"Quite a crush!" she screamed, her mouth a rictus of sarcasm.

Oh fuck you.

Otis slouched in his seat, rapping his fingers on the tablecloth, following his own inner beat. His eyes were wider than usual. He had ferret eyes that punctured his face like taxidermical prostheses, but now they really saw things. Otis, overall, looked more alive and alert to noise and color and light than Devin had ever seen him. And, at the same time, oblivious. Devin sat down. The music was ridiculously loud. Evelyn brought her mouth to his ear and told him she'd sprinkled speed into Otis's drinks. Otis was so far gone that she could scream this news without attracting his attention. He was transfixed by the karaoke, the Christmas lights. Some hungry inner thing. What an asshole. Evelyn dug an aluminum foil lump from her bag.

"Shrimp!" she yodeled. "Breaded in yucca!"

Warren launched himself from the bar, clutching several drinks in tall plastic cups. He was, Devin saw, extravagantly smashed, in a blackout zone, shedding whole realms of coordination. Yet he landed in his white plastic chair in breathless triumph, having spilled very little. Come morning, he wouldn't even recall being here.

Otis had also liquefied much of his logical process, but his verbal one was amphetamine-propelled, along with rapping fingers and feet, shimmying shoulders, and an alarming array of grimaces and toothy smiles. Otis had awful teeth. Devin ate the shrimp with his fingers while Warren tried to explain something. Devin only caught bits of it, something about drug dealers and remote control devices that turned on your car ignition from several yards away. You could trigger detonators inside banks or supermarkets, using the same remote.

One of the Japanese men who looked like triplets carried the microphone around the room like a cocktail shaker, singing "Fiesta de la Rumba." He attempted lithe movements in a stiff but determined way.

"Point and click," Warren told him for the fifth time. "Ralph's, Chase Manhattan Bank, point and click, kaboom!"

WARREN

. . . the week the whole shithouse blew up, Warren thinks, *November May no June '74 maybe earlier no somewhere after June, Devin's birth-day's April,* Warren's organ systems are shutting down and now he has all the time in the world (a few seconds) to say goodbye to all the bygone puzzle pieces, *Cleve tracked us down I guess Varlene must've spilled, after all it was urgent They're at the Hotel Madison in Washington, don't say you heard it from me, Eva grabbed the phone that sour paranoid face on her face It's that jackass brother of yours, Ruth had had some type of collapse staying with Ritchie out in the Valley and Cedar Sinai ran an MRI or whatever they had then some mass around her ovaries and Cleve says Warren no matter what you think about the rest of us Ma needs you now they scheduled a procedure for Thursday I said I can't promise Cleve I wish I could but we're completely upsy daisy out here Well I figured he says I'm sure if she doesn't pull through that troglodyte you live with will get you to skip the funeral too, I knew Evelyn had big plans for Thursday and what could I tell him, what would an oral surgeon know about the kind of networking we had to do trying to nail down these poster contracts and this was a question of key timing Who's performing the surgery, a Dr. Braden, they'd never believe I took a firm hand with Evangeline that day and made her go shopping and five ten calls to get this Braden I tell him I'm Ruth Slote's son and I'm out of state and I'm clos-ing an important deal and naturally worried sick about this situation but a*

million dollars could go south if I miss this Thursday meeting and cold as
this maybe sounds I need a realistic prognosis it's tragic but unless he really
thinks she'll flatline I need to stay in D.C., Oh he says I'm fairly confident she'll get through the procedure, the danger is how much metastasis we
uncover and whether we can deal with that, whether we'll have to put her
through more later in terms of invasive procedures as opposed to radiation
or chemo, I could never make Cleve or Ritchie or any of them understand
that Evvy has a mental illness just as crippling in its way as muscular dys-
trophy or polio that she can't control it a lot of things she does she has no
control over they never got to know her know the good parts the funloving
side even the court psychiatrists will tell you she has no reality testing for
instance that business with Tammy Ann you can't tell me a mentally well
person could even think of anything like that and then on the other side of
it, if Evelyn was always the way they said she was would she have invited
Tammy Ann for that whole month I had to be in Florida working out that
stuff in Orlando and then parking money with the sheik if she out and out
hated Tammy she'd never have asked her in the first place she thought a
month in the islands would cheer her up she only stopped giving her food
when the depression came over her and the fear, Eva was hardly eating anything herself, fear of poisoning by the maids or something, and why didn't
Ritchie fly out there sooner when they hadn't heard anything for three
weeks if they were so concerned That woman is a homicidal maniac, she
says, she's been starving Tammy Ann and Tammy Ann's all dehydrated and
the doctors here think her heart's been weakened She gets ideas I tell her
Evelyn gets these ideas she's sick she hears voices she gets these ideas Oh
goddam it how can you fucking defend her, you want to hear the ideas she's
been getting recently? Do you? When they gave Tammy Ann her initial
workup you know what they found? Your precious Evangeline sewed up
Aunt Tammy's vagina Ritchie what did you say I didn't quite Her cunt,
daddy, your wife sewed up your sister's cunt with embroidering thread, Oh
Ritchie I refuse to believe she did any such thing Well don't believe it, ask
the doctor who examined her, which I would have if Tammy Ann hadn't
passed that weekend Tammy Ann had some strange ideas of her own and I
would have asked her too for all I knew she sewed up her own cunt but

how likely is that with Ruth yes she went too far that Thursday because for one thing Evvy said we had this invitation to Blair House and all these embassy parties, she said the Bicentennial Commission had put our names on all these guest lists and wanted us to mingle with the hoi-poloi to give the Bicentennial more exposure I remember passing under that green awning thinking all those months of sucking up to nobodies had finally paid off finally, Eva overdid it stylewise as usual the white fox turban the gown like something you'd find in a vitrine and the diamond glued right into her ear, she marches us right past the Secret Service up to Gerry and Betty Ford on the receiving line with the photographers snapping away and then whirling through these bigshots when it was white tie and Evelyn had told me black tie and grabbing a scotch out of embarrassment mistake number one while everybody stared at us and Evelyn carrying on about she's East Indian royalty and her father's a prince and the diamond is customary and who blew the whistle I don't know but there was a definite buzz, like they were all smelling the same massive fart and zeroing in on the source of it and we had to scram out of there and then it was the Belgian Embassy some cocktail thing full of stiffs from the best Belgian families, all these diamond heirs and pommes frites *heiresses and lo and behold we're not on any list for that thing either and she pretends it's all a mixup we're on our way to the Dutch Embassy and could Mr. Slote just say a few words about the upcoming Bicentennial, no Mr. Slote just couldn't, the Ambassador though lends us his limo all the same thinking this is all on the up and up a slight confusion on our parts and the Dutch Embassy's dark and the doorman tells us the party's at the Ambassador's private residence way the fuck out in Georgetown and Evelyn has the limo driver take us all the way out there the Dutch Ambassador greets us thinking we're friends of his wife shrimp canapes and a couple glasses of champagne and then the hostess comes over This is a private party but feel free to stay for a cocktail, in other words kicking us out before dinner and Ev keeps introducing me as Our Bicentennial Ambassador which I certainly wasn't in any official sense but that's how the papers figured out who we were, and then at the Madison she acts like we've had this thrilling glamorous evening while I'm ordering a ham sandwich from room service, when everyplace we went we were* treated like pariahs and I said Christ shit I forgot I've got to call Cleve I've got to phone the hospital Ruth went under the knife this afternoon and she says Warren honey I have some bad news Ruth didn't make it Evelyn what are you telling me how do you know this Warren baby Cleve called to tell you when you were in the shower getting ready Ruth never came out of the anesthesia at that age you know it's 50-50 just going under, I knew it would wreck your evening and this was a big opportunity to meet the Vice-President and Mrs. Ford, My mother is dead you fucking insane cunt and you stand there telling me you've known about this since five hours ago Well, would you rather be grief-stricken before you got to meet the Vice-President and Mrs. Ford You cunt you cunt you psychotic fucking cunt my mother's dead and all you can think about is the Vice-President Look she says Maybe I made the wrong call Warren but since you mention it that isn't all I can think about I have something quite important to think about your mother yes I'm sorry I am truly deeply sorry and sad about Ruth regardless of the fact that she hated me and undermined me for the past twenty years but telling you at six o'clock instead of ten minutes ago wasn't going to bring her back and I have to tell you something Warren Oh Jesus H. Christ Evangeline what more could you possibly have to tell me, I'm pregnant, What, I'm pregnant, I've been pregnant for three months and don't look at me like that it isn't Lester's it's yours, I happen to know, and I have waited as long as I can to say anything because it's almost the second trimester and if you aren't going to marry me Warren I'm having an abortion it's as simple as that, You say it isn't Lester's, Evelyn I know you were seeing him three months ago, I'm still seeing him Warren but no way no how is this baby Lester's baby Tell me why not If I tell you it's just going to upset you My God Evelyn how the fuck could I possibly be more upset than I am right now Oh believe me Warren you will be Well, I don't care, Lester has never done anything that could make me pregnant Oh please Evelyn do you take me for a complete imbecile On the contrary Warren I worship you if you'd only realize that, that's part of the reason by the way This is too much all at once I've always wanted us to have a child Evelyn but I have to know in my own mind that it's my kid and not yours and Lester's All right Warren my God it's so strange to have to say this at this

moment with your mother dead and all you must be feeling inside but
Lester and I have never had normal intercourse Well in that case what have
you been having Warren, since you feel you have to know, Lester has only
ever fucked me in the ass, don't ask me why but that's how he prefers it and
I've always let him do it that way because that way the only man who
really possesses me completely is you. I love you Warren I have never felt
anything like real love for Lester Ryman I've needed his advice at times
and needed him, strange as it may sound, as a kind of father figure Forgive
me Evelyn but that does sound strange considering what you just told me
Oh Warren I've always found life so impossibly strange and mysterious and
most of all these entanglements between people who may not completely
love each other but need things in Lester's case it's always been that I would
have something, somebody to hold on to if you got tired of me a man of
your wealth and prestige can have any woman he wants and what if you
went out tomorrow and found someone younger and prettier than I am
You're a beautiful woman Evelyn you know that yourself I've never been
tempted, in all the time we've been together, not seriously anyway of course
one looks at all sorts of people We're straying from the question here Warren
I can't have a child out of wedlock I won't I know it's the fashionable thing
these days but I want this baby to have a name, I want it to have your
name because you are its father and I want a family I never had a real family Jesus what a night and then the papers the next morning, BIGGEST
CRASH SINCE '29, pictures of me, pictures of her, pictures of me and
her with Betty Ford, a long article on page one about these shady people
these upstart jumped-up social climbers and why wasn't the Secret Service
on the ball and having to defend myself and give interviews and everything
I said taken out of context and made to look like I crawled out from under
a rotten log and the both of us made out to be con artists and then the FBI
gets in on the act interviewing Cleve and Ritchie and everybody else they
can dig up as if we were also terrorists or subversives, when the whole point
of the Bicentennial thing was Americanism first last and always plus
unloading those flags on the public school system and then the
Washington Post prints the courtesy letter Richard Nixon sent me
thanking me for the floral arrangement and claims the salutation was tam-

pered with and it had been tampered with, Evelyn had put Wite-Out and typed in Honorary Bicentennial Ambassador without even telling me, the typefaces didn't even match that's the other thing Eva always thinks she's so slick at that kind of thing but she fucks up critical details she thinks I don't know she signed my name on a transfer deed on the Santa Rosa property when Ritchie gets the letter I left with Katz Evelyn's going to be in shit up to her ears but she asked for it she went too far using some hare-brained patsy in a title office up in Santa Barbara and getting me roped into the chinchilla deal making me swipe that cashmere coat that didn't even fit me luckily the owner died before the case came up but a reprimand anyway and then ordering me into rehab, they never checked I promised to do the rehab in Honolulu and never heard another thing about it thank Christ I got our cases severed because we both could have gone up for five years Evangeline could've gotten ten if she hadn't waltzed out of there before the jury came in and then claims some guy in a laundry truck ran her over and she had amnesia which is why she fled to Nevada, for medical treatment, and then forges all the doctor letters for years and years claiming her life's at risk if she travels back to Washington I don't see what the fuss was in the first place she only did it as a joke, first she made a scene at the coat check claiming she'd checked a mink herself, they couldn't locate it and actually she breaks down in tears and gets all these witnesses to say she's been traumatized by the assistant hotel manager and then we went into that Lamplighter Lounge or whatever it's called it was pretty rowdy for a bunch of businessmen all trying to sing along with the piano and making tacky requests like When Irish Eyes Are Smiling and Alexander's Ragtime Band and all these maudlin hits of yesteryear that none of them even knows the words to and Evelyn makes a beeline for that table next to the Verlinger woman who'd draped her chinchilla over the empty chair and then we got talking to the Verlingers and this couple they had with them Evangeline sliding off her own mink onto the banquette the place was really packed I remember and Verlinger is rehashing the whole Watergate brouhaha which at that point was ancient history, saying what a lucky thing in '72 that the case landed with a sympathetic judge I said Sirica didn't strike me as any sympathetic judge Well says Verlinger look at it this way he managed to put off opening the whole can of worms until after the election didn't he because of his alleged back problems what if it had blown up right before the election we'd be sitting here in George McGovern's second term I feel like I'm sitting here in his first term can you see Nixon taking any shit from some sand nigger ayatollah over this hostage situation I didn't really notice Evelyn slipping the chinchilla off the chair a few pelts at a time, but I guess a bunch of people at the bar did although they were too surprised to say anything the Verlinger people were so wrapped up in Watergate it went right past them and next thing she's got Mrs. Verlinger's chinchilla jacket on and her mink over it and steers me out of the Lamplighter Lounge and up to the suite where she rips the lining out with a box cutter she just happens to have in her makeup bag and stuffs it out the window, they had louver things that only opened about four inches I'd carried that cashmere number out on my arm, even the people who clocked Evelyn didn't notice that, if they hadn't seen her then going back down to the bar without her coat and striking up another conversation with the Verlingers would've been a stroke of genius and leaving a half hour later before they even noticed the chinchilla gone but of course those other people had seen her and saw us coming back without stopping at the coat check so they also figured we were staying right there at the hotel I think Evelyn knew they'd spotted her because the minute we went back up she takes the chinchilla into the hall and jams it behind the ice machine, sure enough ten minutes after we've got our clothes off the cops are pounding the door in and she starts screaming assault and telling them her own coat was stolen by the coat check and then the hotel dick looks out the window and sees Mrs. Verlinger's lining flapping from a balcony three floors down, seven hours in the can and then the arraignment and Devin freaking out in the suite with the nanny the arraignment judge swallowed the whole thing about a morning meeting with the President and how we were so important and the whole thing was a ludicrous mixup swallowed it enough anyway to release on personal recognizance but she didn't drop the charges and that ended up ten years of postponements and hearings and finally the jury trial coming up after she did time on the slavery thing and Evelyn bolting the courthouse before the jury came back smartest thing she ever did although she didn't know it herself, because even though they sentenced in absentia we were out of the jurisdiction by then and that lawyer from Melrose Patterson Stankonia and Myers got the conviction reversed five years later on the grounds she wasn't present when the jury came in some circuit judge upheld this thing about her right to confront her accusers even during the verdict phase and they couldn't prove she didn't get amnesia after the laundry truck hit her, so they let her plead out on a reduced petty larcency charge by lowering the retail value of Mrs. Verlinger's chinchilla by a couple thousand dollars and Evelyn waltzed out of there like she'd just won Lotto or the Best Actress Oscar, cost a fucking fortune ten years of palaver even if we didn't pay half of the thirty attorneys she ran through now she'll ruin Devin like she ruined me and for him it's worse because I had a whole life behind me before I met her and anyway I liked being ruined by her for a long time, until it got into the papers, that blood keeps coming back to haunt me that blood in the cabin down there that night I woke up and couldn't find her and went to Devin's cabin and couldn't find him and then that crowbar and the blood spots in Otis's cabin which they must have cleaned up later I never said anything she had this elaborate story about driving Otis to the Sea Breeze early that morning that he'd checked out and said the Feds were on his ass and he was going on a long long vacation as far away from a subpoena as his savings could take him as if Otis ever had any savings but Devin backed her up and for a long time I wiped that crowbar and the blood drops out of my mind as one of those things you can't account for and might as well forget about I know there's something on the other side of this darkness they say a light comes on you follow the light you go to the light I know I'll see Mavis again it has to be true she's out there somewhere where is the light where is the light I don't see any goddam light

The last thing Warren hears, as he slumps over the steering wheel, is the car door jerking open and the sonic boom of Evangeline's screams.

PART TWO

AS YOU
DEVOUR ME

"Pourquoi les représentants du ministère de l'Instruction publique, à Phnom Penh, ont-ils sélectionné cet élève médiocre, qui n'a pas passé son baccalauréat, qui a tout raté jusqu'ici et qui a déjà vingt et un ans? Plusieurs explications ont été avancées."

As The Lady read to him of Saloth Sar, *"le bourreau du Cambodge,"* Asraboth remembered white images of Axum and its stelae, like obelisks of salt, carved with intricate reliefs of imaginary buildings. Asraboth's father had once taken him along to Axum, in an army-green Jeep, in the faraway time of the Emperor. Asraboth could not have been older than three or four. His father had shown him the church of St. Mary Zion. By chance, the priest of St. Mary Zion revealed to them the Ark of the Covenant, which, the priest explained, they sometimes took out of the modest building the Emperor had built for it, to give it a little air.

"Dix jours plus tard, les nouveaux boursiers se retrouvent à Saigon, où ils embarquent à bord du paquebot Jamaïque, affecté à la ligne d'Extrême-Orient."

The future monster Saloth Sar had sailed away, in 1949, for his studies at the Sorbonne. To Asraboth it was a kind of fairy tale, with a lethal ending. At thirty, he still often saw things as a child would see them, as a dreamer accepts the blurring venues and personae of the dream, without confusion or understanding. For his life so far had been a sequence of dreams and nightmares, a little unreal whether good or bad fortune came. To think only of how he happened to be here, in this great house, with The Lady reading to him in a language he barely understood, in her sharp yet coddling voice, as his mother had read to him in Amharic as a child: one morning, three years ago, he delivered some strawberries. The Lady tipped him twenty dollars. A week later he brought apricots and tomatoes, and again she slipped into her private rooms off the first floor hall and reappeared with a twenty-dollar tip. Some days passed. She phoned the Madison Fruiterers, asked for him by name, and offered him a job at double his delivery boy pay.

He would, she said, look after the plants and trees all over the house and the cats on the penthouse roof, monitor the chemicals and filters in the pool (where The Lady, at eighty-three, swam twenty laps each day, *un vrai miracle* as she often said), and perform other sundry jobs. There were nine apartments in the house, of varying sizes, bracketed by The Lady's private spaces (her first floor suite; the basement complex of kitchen, laundry, patio and wine cellar where Asraboth and Carmen, the weekend girl, had their own tiny bedrooms; the two-story penthouse and roof gardens), rented erratically, for huge sums, sometimes for a few days, a week, a couple months, always to famous writers and actors and singers and diplomats and surgeons and those sorts of grand people. Because The Lady viewed the tenants as guests in her home rather than impersonal people who payed money for housing, the rental units were continually breached by The Lady and her staff, the rooms redecorated, refurnished, reconfigured, she was always dabbling with fittings and fixtures, replacing cabinets and pictures, shelves and mirrors, beds and sofas, so the house led the busy life of a hotel, and had the imperiousness of a hotel, where changes occur suddenly, by fiat, not always to the complete liking of the people living there, but The Lady's arrangements were such that the force of her presence was an expected thing, an eccentricity that made the apartments all the more exclusive and desirable among a certain category of wealthy transient: among people who were opening shows, or teaching at three universities at once, or operating at five different hospitals, people negotiating long divorces, people who had left Manhattan and equivocated about moving back, people who'd sold their townhouses or condos and were sitting out endless renovations on their country estates, people conducting one season at the Philharmonic, or singing one season at the Met, or giving concerts for four nights, or flying in from Milan or Paris for Fashion Week. The Lady often invaded their privacy, but she also knew about the comfort level such people took for granted, and the kind of expensive surprise they enjoyed finding in their living quarters, the Renoir hanging in the bathroom, the Veuve Cliquot and Beluga chilling in the refrigerator. Asraboth easily learned about all this, for it was not entirely foreign to him. He quickly won The Lady's favor. He was one of only two people entrusted with bank deposits and withdrawals, and the only person allowed to walk The Lady's dog outside.

The Emperor had kept just such a dog, a beige and black toy boxer with a little ruff of white along his collarbone, who liked to pee on people's shoes. For twenty years, Asraboth's father's job had been to wipe urine from the shoes of diplomats with a figured silk cloth. It was his only duty at the Palace. The job came with its own special uniform, designed by the Emperor. When the first dog died the Emperor obtained another exactly like it, with the same urinary habits. Perhaps he had been trained by specialists to pick up where his predecessor left off. Asraboth's father's job had never been viewed in Asraboth's family as demeaning, because the Emperor had been, for all practical purposes, God. And for mopping up his little dog's pee, Asraboth's family was able to live in a style beyond the imaginings of most families in the Empire. All that had come crashing down, and everyone connected to the Emperor, even by way of his excretory functions and those of his animals, had had to flee the country.

Asraboth was to call her Baby, The Lady told him, because everybody called her Baby. Her full name was Wanda Koukoulas Claymore. She had been named after Wanda Landowska. Baby

Claymore took such facts about herself very seriously. During the holiday seasons a great deal of recorded harpsichord music was played in the house. At times Asraboth thought of her as Mrs. Claymore, at other times as Wanda, at still other times as Baby, but he called her The Lady in his thoughts when he was, as today, enfolded in a feeling of maternal safety by their "quiet time" together.

Other people working in the house referred to her now and then as The Lady too, though with a slightly different connotation, to sound a respectful but slightly annoyed inflection of class distance, usually when some urgent job needed doing that would further only The Lady's pleasures and not their collective contentment, in other words at times when The Lady's tone reminded them that she was, in addition to being their friend and benefactress, their employer. Baby never went so far as to indicate that she could fire anyone with impunity, though certainly she could. Baby wasn't that way. She didn't threaten, she didn't turn against. She liked to feel that the people around her really were her family, for at her great age, she had no other. (On the other hand, one of Baby's favorite bedside books was Jonathan Swift's *Directions to Servants*, which Norma had dipped into during one of Baby's rare trips to the eye doctor, supposing it to be an old-fashioned training manual. Norma skimmed enough of it to feel vaguely offended by it. Servants were not the same then as now, of course, but still.) So the thought was occasionally present to some of the staff, perhaps to all the staff except him: Asraboth lacked confidence in many areas of life, but he felt absolutely certain that The Lady would look after him all her days and even afterwards, when the house and everything in it became part of the Foundation. The others had adult cares that Asraboth had avoided: marriages, children. They worried about security, because their real lives were elsewhere. Asraboth's life was here, with Baby. He had a sister in the Bronx, unhappily but dutifully married, pregnant for the third time; his father was vegetating in Djibouti after five bitter years of selling cigarettes and Lotto tickets in an Egyptian grocery on Ditmars Boulevard in Brooklyn. His mother was dead.

Baby set her book down. *"Je voudrais aller me baigner, je crois,"* she sighed. "But perhaps, Asra, later on . . . we could read a few poems. I already feel *defiled* by Saloth Sar."

Baby and Asraboth were educating each other. These were the favorite parts of the day. She read to him in French, he read to her in English, from books written during the same historical period, or about the same subject. Saloth Sar was a little diversion related to Baby's ongoing interest in the war crimes of Henry Kissinger. Baby hoped that she would one day have the opportunity to reject a rental application from an associate of Henry Kissinger. Owing to her increasingly housebound condition, she was slowly abandoning her dream of insulting Henry Kissinger to his face at some public function.

"Hope springs eternal," Baby still said of this dream, "but somehow I doubt it will happen in my lifetime. Perhaps when I meet him in Hell."

Damnation of various kinds fascinated both of them. Saloth Sar aside, they were currently immersed in the darker literature of the late 19th century. Asraboth had been disturbed to learn that Saloth Sar's favorite poet was Paul Verlaine.

They were in the kitchen, downstairs. Ratty was curled up in Baby's lap. She fingered the dog's ear like a piece of fine silk, her eyes twinkling. Baby had something wrong with her tear ducts, her eyes needed an operation. Asraboth stood up and stepped away from the long table.

"Ratty," he called in a soft voice. Ratty snorted, opening his black eyes, which bulged roundly in his crumpled face. He leaped off Baby, stubby legs churning her nightgown. He commenced climbing in place against Asraboth's shin.

"I'll just get into my suit," said Baby, springing up from her chair like a woman of forty and moving towards the elevator. "Now should Ratty have a little treat?"

They both looked at the dog, then at each other.

"*Mais oui*, Baby," Asraboth laughed. "*Bien sûr!*"

✝

If you have any compassion, any medical ethics, please, please, I am begging you, put him on a respirator, at least keep his brain alive until I can get a specialist, we have money, my husband is a personal friend of the Surgeon General—Evelyn had pleaded for an hour with the hospital staff, the young surgeon who kept telling her that Warren's massive internal bleeding was not something they could have fixed by putting him on "life support," which she apparently believed could preserve the brain in all its cogitative glory even when a person's organs had cooled, the nurses fluttering around with clipboards and blood pressure monitors, the candy striper at the desk with the long pensive face of a dairy cow chewing hay.

She claimed that Warren had been conscious and talking to her in the ambulance, still hanging on. By the time they got his corpse to the hospital she was talking lawsuits, the paramedics didn't give him triage, she chanted like a mantra, "triage" and "life support" being roughly synonymous in her mind, *I waited fifteen minutes for that ambulance, my husband would still be alive if you people had given him triage,* she babbled and screeched to anyone who'd listen, but in fact no one would, no one paid the slightest attention, they were already plotting their cover stories, covering their asses, minimizing her shock and grief, she would not have been surprised to find out the surgeon was a friend of Ritchie's, or pals with one of their lawyers, maybe the name Slote rang a bell, maybe they all knew about that totally unfair slavery crap and figured this was what she deserved. When she realized they were just going to let Warren die she called Darren from a pay phone and told him where she was and to drop everything and get there as fast as he could.

She sat in the waiting room under a big ugly clock filling a notebook with lists of things she would have to do. In her purse she found several loose folded pages she tried always to have on her person. Someone gave her forms to fill out for the State and County. The pages from her purse had Warren's bank account numbers and information about deeds and titles, and a Social Security number belonging to a Warren Jefferson Slote, no kin at all to her husband, who lived in Merced. She entered this number on the forms. The man in Merced became dead to the banks and the feds and the three credit reporting agencies. *Her* Warren continued his career among the living, an active number in a world of digital existence. Evelyn smudged a few other tracks on the paper trail, date of birth, mother's maiden name, just in case. By some quirk of coincidence that she could never figure out, she and Warren had both been born in Oklahoma. The Asshole State, was how she always pictured the license plates.

The nightmare trip in the ambulance, the disgraceful negligence of the hospital, assumed a freighted narrative shape in Evelyn's mind. She was already "remembering" details to throw in the face of hospital administrators, lawyers, men from insurance companies. Horrible, unfeeling things had been said to her. It showed you how low people could sink. Doctors had practically dared her to challenge their cavalier treatment of Warren as malpractice. If she brooded long enough, far worse things would suggest themselves to her memory.

That was one way to play this particular scene, with plenty of emotions crackling in the mix—the drama of life and death, of a wronged family that wanted to know "why?"—but maybe not the ideal way. Accusations against hospitals needed publicity to stick, and as she scribbled the seeds of a game plan in her ring binder, Evelyn reconsidered her litigious impulses. Publicity was not really such a good idea. Publicity was, on second thought, a really bad idea. She had already bought a little time with the Social Security number; perhaps she could buy more.

They sent Warren down to the county morgue in San Diego. The stiff, the cadaver. Warren gone from the temple of his spirit.

They collected the forms, gave her a printout of charges for the insurance. Processing the dead had the same bland, digitized texture as a grocery scan. Evelyn stayed in the emergency room, waiting for Darren. She did not believe in God. It was one of her few concessions to sanity. With Warren off the premises, the emergency room took on the atmosphere of a bus depot in a small, mean city.

Hours passed. She sat under the clock feeling old. She got a Pepsi from a vending machine but didn't open it. She put her reading glasses on, wrote some notes, took her reading glasses off. She walked around the room, picked up a magazine, blew her nose, sat down on her reading glasses. Gone. Warren was gone. She went out through a set of automatic sliding doors and stood under a cement portico and smoked a cigarette. Warren no longer saw anything: this parking lot, the blue-black sky. She had known for some time that Warren could go at any minute, but all she'd done to arm herself against that minute was to ransack his office looking for the goddam will with no luck, and to find another Warren Slote through a friend at the DMV. She stepped on the cigarette and went back inside. She had not fully pictured a moment in which Warren wouldn't be there. No one to talk to any more, no one to drive home with. Alone in a whole new way.

She went up to a nurse making notes behind the plastic partition.

"Excuse me, can I talk to you?"

"Yes, Mrs. Slote?" The nurse looked at the clock, looked at her watch. She held her pen poised, her face arranged itself in a tableau of professional compassion. "Still waiting for your son?"

"Yes, and I wanted to apologize for making a scene earlier. I know everybody did all they could. It was all happening so fast. I didn't believe it somehow. I still can't believe it."

"Don't think about it, Mrs. Slote. You've suffered a terrible shock. People say all kinds of things. . . ." The nurse's voice trailed off.

"I wanted to apologize to the doctor too."

"Well, Dr. Slotnick's gone for the day. I can mention it if you like."

"Would you?" Evelyn looked at her own hands, her fingers pink and swollen that day around her rings, as if she were retaining water. She looked around the room. There were two families, a Hispanic couple with a tragic-looking old woman, another group of Hispanics surrounding a cute teenager with his leg in a cast. Evelyn's gaze rested on the teenager's shiny basketball shorts, a massive prick discernible through the fabric. "We were together for twenty-five years," she heard herself telling the nurse. "And just a year ago, we lost two of our children in a boating accident."

The nurse took this in with nods of perfunctory sympathy, all the while entering notes in a patient's chart.

"Do you have a friend in the area who could take you home? I can tell your son when he gets here."

"No, I—I'm going to wait for him here." Another nurse, seated at a little window, murmured into a telephone. "I left the car in front of the bank," Evelyn added for no reason. "I'm going to sit down over there and wait. I have my magazine to read."

She would have to talk to Lester. Lester had walked her through the paperwork of this Canadian incorporation thing, it was ready to go, except for submitting the names of the corporate officers. She had Warren's signature, a pretty foolproof rendition of Warren's signature, on the Santa Rosa transfer deed, "in consideration of love and affection." As far as she was concerned, it was Warren's signature. With the Cayman bank and the affiliate bank in the Bahamas she would have to test the waters, and she supposed it was time to get out of La Jolla. Don't let the grass grow under your feet, was Evelyn's motto.

She did not recognize Darren until she noticed the little girl beside him, a black-haired child with haunted eyes. Wearing plaid coveralls and a little Russian peasant blouse. Darren looked surprisingly fit, a tall man in a long brown leather coat with a fairly good shirt and pressed slacks underneath, expensive shoes, not at all what she expected. His black hair was an inch long and he wore John Lennon–type glasses and he had, she had to admit, turned rather handsome and hip-looking in his late twenties, almost a James Caan type, with that air of caution and guarded optimism typical of people in recovery.

"Hey, Mom."

"Oh Darren is that Polly? She's so big. Come give grandma a hug, Polly."

Polly hesitated. She looked at Darren to see if she had to.

"Go give grandma a kiss." Darren wasn't wild about the idea either. "Polly's shy," he explained. But the child stepped up to her with an almost friendly expression, let herself be hugged and kissed. She had something delicate and aloof in her bearing, and very dramatic, Victorian features, like a miniature adult. Strange, considering.

"My heavens you're practically grown up, Polly," Evelyn grandmothered in her best Mother Goose. "What grade is she in?" she asked Darren, with what she hoped looked a brave smile.

"She's in second grade." Darren struggled against an habitual disgust in Evangeline's presence: she saw it, it would always be there, there was nothing much she could do about it. Darren had Turned His Life Around, no thanks to her. He had accepted the 12-Step Program as the only thing between him and annihilation. From Evelyn's years in the joint she recognized this as the most tenacious kind of American makeover besides Islam, but she would just have to work with it.

On the way to the morgue, she explained why Warren's passing would have to be kept quiet. She banked on the fact that Darren still hated the Slotes even more than he hated her.

"As soon as they get wind of this, they'll be going through everything with an army of lawyers and your poor mother will be out on the street on her keister," she said. "I need at least a month or two to figure out what my position is legally. Before they get the jump."

Darren did not have a problem with that. He had no contact with the Slotes, anyway. He would draw the line, she knew, at personal involvement in any active scheme, but she could rely on his indifference, his passivity.

"How is Devin taking it?" he wanted to know.

"Oh, darling, that's the other thing. Devin's not to hear about this. Not now. Not until the end of his semester."

"Ma, that's just wrong. Warren's his father."

Evelyn let it sit there.

"If it was me," Darren said, with diminishing concern, "I'd tell him."

"He's got finals. This would devastate him. He worships his dad. He hasn't been having an easy time at that school, you know."

Devin's year at UCSB had not been brilliant. He had been kicked out of campus housing after a bloody fist-fight just before mid-terms. Then he moved into a Goleta apartment with three friends, and got into a money dispute with the girlfriend of one of his roommates. The dispute escalated into physical threats and mutual restraining orders and all kinds of unpleasantness Evelyn had her hands full sorting out. Now she and Devin were being accused of forging his roommates' signatures on notarized affidavits.

"Always something," she said, almost bitterly.

"Understatement of the year," said Darren. Her self-pity left him gelid. "He'll really hate you if you keep this from him."

Darren spoke as if referring to a distant acquaintance. Darren's entire contact with Devin consisted of a yearly exchange of Christmas cards.

"He won't, though. When I explain it. He'll see it was for his own good."

"Your call." Darren shrugged. Warren had always treated him like the invisible man, now he could return the favor.

She would never get anywhere with Darren by arguing. He was a non-emotive, non-active, sentimental type, what her French-Dutch system called "apathetic," without a sensitive interior life—on the plus side, tied to habit, uninterested in rocking the boat. As long as she left him a way to detach himself, he would let her do as she pleased. Calling him had been exactly the right move. Evelyn had to marvel at her own instincts in a crisis. She could still size up the marks, Warren or no Warren.

When she introduced herself as Mrs. Slote, Darren as "my son," the coroner (sixtyish, impatient, self-absorbed, apparently comfortable only with the dead, wearing thick glasses and a mustard stain on his lab smock) assumed that Darren was Warren's son as well; Darren said nothing to alter the impression. Evelyn vetoed a full autopsy on the grounds that "the family" opposed it, keeping things carefully vague, so Darren could consider himself unincluded, a supportive friend who happened to be there. The coroner could open the stomach just to verify cause of death. No sectioning of the brain or the spine or whatever. And no, they would not care to view the body, not with Polly standing right there.

Darren turned out very useful, Polly too, in leaving the impression that Warren's whole family had signed off on Evelyn's decisions. She made arrangements for a local mortuary to pick Warren up after the partial autopsy and do a cremation the following day. She would swing by the mortuary after the weekend and pick up the cremains, as they were called. She told the coroner to send his report to the mortuary. She told the mortuary to send it on to her in an unmarked envelope.

✝

Carmen Lopez manicures Baby Claymore's little fingers in the first floor suite of the house on East 65th Street. The emory board scrapes dead ivory shavings from Baby's nails, gigantic under a round magnifying lamp. Baby hums, taps her velvet slippers, chews a sugared almond. A fire spits and crackles in the biscuit-colored marble hearth (logs from Gristedes, wrought-iron screen from Restoration Hardware). A Spode pearlware vase stuffed with purple Mexican orchids and thirty teardrop bulbs in a tôle peinte rococo chandelier give the room an over-ornamented gaiety, as if it were a holiday.

Baby's hands are fine-boned as a finch's claws, wormy-veined and age-puckered, dappled with a few garnet liver spots. Carmen's are plump, mannish, their skin a fine diamond-weave canvas, moisturized smooth with plain old Jergen's cold cream every night while she watches movies on the VCR.

Baby likes her nails "Jungle Red," to match her eyeglass frames. She dyes her faded hair clown orange. Baby's personal colors are insistently cheerful. Red shoes, often. Bright flower-pattern house dresses—yellow tulips on bright green stalks, jonquils tipped in crimson, clusters of periwinkle—with huge lace-edged pockets stitched at the sides, for keys and glasses and paraphernalia she carries around with her.

On the CD player, one of Baby's favorite operas, by Janáček. Baby sings along, atonally, with scattered passages. Carmen finds this opera excessively strident, with a recurring fanfare that sounds like the climax whenever the coloratura makes an entrance. Beautiful, yes, but in a harsh, modern, unmelodic way, like Stravinsky, or the other Russian composer Baby likes, Carmen has the name hovering somewhere near her tongue, Shostasomething.

The Janáček work concerns a lawsuit that has dragged on for almost a century ("like *Jarndyce vs. Jarndyce*, in Dickens's *Bleak House*," Baby has imparted on more than one occasion) and a glamorous, cold-tempered, imperious woman, an opera singer, who, thanks to a mysterious formula, has lived to be three hundred years old. Living so long has drained her life of any meaning or pleasure. Baby plays the opera often, as if to convince herself that leaving the planet isn't such a bad idea.

Carmen, who takes psychology among other City College classes during the week, knows that Baby thinks about death more than anything else, and dreads it, despite what is often said about the aging process making people more accepting of their end. Baby does not expect to see the people and places that are gone in any type of afterlife, and this makes it harder. Carmen doesn't anticipate any posthumous surprises either, but she has decades longer to think about this than Baby does. She cannot imagine reaching Baby's age with fantasies of immortality intact. Yet people do, and Carmen thinks that Baby's gentle but palpable decline would be ameliorated if Baby did, too.

"Oh I was so scared, Miss Marty," Baby warbles in a thin voice. In Czech, no less. Carmen has scanned the libretto on enough occasions to recognize key bits of dialogue. *"Mr. Prus's servant is here, and he wants to go up to your room, and the man is so upset he can't even talk."*

Instead: restlessness, insomnia, a capricious fussiness about food, fear of going outside after slipping on the sidewalk two years ago, worries. Extravagant daily effort to confirm her continued existence in the world, much of it expended on the Foundation (which is a kind of planning for the afterlife, all the same), and sprucing up the house, changing things around all the time.

"You're pulling my hair out, you stupid girl! Show me that comb! Look here at the hair you pulled!"

This incessant revision of space is the opposite of what Carmen likes: her five-room apartment, far up the Hudson River near the Cloisters, in a Dominican neighborhood full of yellow-lit snack counters, bodegas, coin laundries, *panaderías* and OTB offices, fits her like an old shoe. Its little changes have been gradual, organic, almost imperceptible. The sameness of her kitchen table, her bathroom fixtures, her bedside lamp, of all her little things, comprises a comfort zone that protects her against anguish and depression.

Carmen is thirty-four. Much of the time, immune to boredom, unmoved by the insecurities generic to unmarried women of her age, class, and ethnic background. She has a boyfriend she likes and doesn't plan to marry, an unusual job, reasonable hopes for a degree. Her life suits her, for now. In a more general sense, she's aware that life has an entropic, negative tendency. That things run awry. That something tireless that might as well be called evil or wickedness continually intrudes into human affairs, is perhaps an integral feature of human affairs, and that it's unreasonable to want very much without expecting a lot of bad to come with it.

Carmen thinks about this, at times, specifically in relation to Baby Claymore, who listens to the opera with her eyes closed, a dreamy expression on her winsome, slightly sunken features. Carmen sometimes wonders if Baby, who grew up in grinding poverty, got rescued from it so long ago that a touch of hubris has settled into her dealings with the world at large.

"People are always killing themselves."

Baby's is a true rags-to-riches saga: born in New Orleans to newly immigrant working-class parents, father a Greek longshore-man who deserted the family when Baby was about four, mother an Italian seamstress. After the father leaves, moves with her mother to New York; mother becomes a master sewer for Chanel, Vionnet, all the big couture houses.

"Look what I've done: Matilda's jewels. Matilda is my wife, but she is old, and it is so ugly to be old. . . ."

But poor, dirt poor. Master sewers of the 1930s are paid only slightly better than migrant farm workers. Baby is considered a special child. This adds pathos to pennilessness. Annabelle, her mother, works her fingers to the bone so Baby will know life's finer side. Baby trains in classical ballet from an early age, studies with Fokine (Annabelle pays for the lessons by sewing costumes), is discovered dancing in the corps de ballet at Radio City (at that time, New York's only corps de ballet) by a Hollywood talent scout. While still a teenager, enticed out to L.A., with Annabelle in tow. Becomes an "aquabat" in Esther Williams movies of the 1940s. The great star herself teaches diminutive Wanda synchronized swimming, in her Bel Air pool. Even so, unless you are Esther Williams, being an aquabat is chump change.

Baby gets lucky. She catches the attention of Randy Claymore, a flourishing real estate operative for MGM: the pool-side equivalent of a stage door Johnny. Randy falls deeply, desperately in love with Baby, who has had her eyes peeled for exactly this kind of windfall for years. She's about to give in and kiss the swimming tank at Metro goodbye when the unthinkable happens at Pearl Harbor.

Randy signs up in '41. Pines for Baby through a long messy chunk of the Pacific war. Baby splashes her way through *Bathing Beauty* and *Thrill of a Romance*. Randy gets discharged in '45, resumes romancing Baby through the rest of the '40s while she does glorified extra work on *This Time for Keeps, On an Island with You, Neptune's Daughter* and *Pagan Love Song*. Various complications delay the wedding until 1949.

Baby, Randy, and Annabelle relocate in New York, *en famille*. The idea of Baby and Annabelle living apart has never entered Baby's head. Randy accepts this state of affairs. He often feels extraneous, even unwelcome at home, but he is seldom at home. He becomes the mortgage broker for NYU, among other corporate octopi, sucking up whole Manhattan neighborhoods to expand the university. All Randy needs to pillage a city block is a telephone, a pencil, and a piece of paper. Randy and Baby grow richer and richer throughout the economic miracle years.

Randy buys the mansion on East 65th Street, thinking it's a bad investment, on Baby's insistence. After being in the water all those years, Baby wants to become a swan. She makes the house a showplace for Randy's clients and their wives. She learns about food, about wines, and of course the seven arts, transforming herself into a society hostess and legendary madcap, often referred to as "a real-life Auntie Mame," or "an Auntie Mame type," the free-spending, blithe foil to Randy's button-down thriftiness.

Carmen came to work for Baby shortly before Randy died in 1985. She does not remember much about Baby's husband, who was old and extremely medicated at the time. It is an odd fact that Annabelle outlived the much younger Randy by three years. It was during those three years, in Carmen's view, that things began running awry.

Back then, the house had only five apartments: Randy, Baby, and Annabelle had lived in the penthouse; each floor below had a single rental unit. The house wasn't big enough to qualify for rent stabilization, and soon after Randy's death, Baby tripled the rents, predictably driving out the long-term tenants.

Baby had the basement remodeled for her own use. She also took over the first floor, installing Annabelle in what is now Apartment 1B, herself in 1A, meanwhile chopping the upper floors into smaller apartments, as many as three to a floor where she thought they would fit, squeezing in teeny kitchenettes and hotel-style bathrooms. Some were designated "studios," the larger ones "one bedrooms."

Baby did the units up in luxury style, with her own antiques and tapestries and whatnot, and they really do look soigné, in the Continental manner. Carmen was astonished, all the same, by Baby's cutthroat attitude toward the people who'd lived there for years on the friendliest terms with Baby, who were now gone. Baby had always called her long-term tenants "family," just like the staff.

The renovations were, besides, completely illegal—the building was only zoned for five rentals. After Annabelle died, Baby revealed her grand scheme: a crafts foundation that would celebrate the art of needlework and preserve the myriad wonders her mother had fashioned over the decades, not just the Vionnet gowns and Chanel suits, the muslin toiles and dress forms made for famous clients, but countless embroidered chairbacks and throw pillows and dozens of Annabelle's tapestry renditions of famous paintings. The Madame Koukou Foundation, as it was called (after Annabelle's affectionate nickname in the needle trade), would need a substantial fortune to maintain itelf. Baby considered it worth breaking the house into these jumped-up hotel rooms for the extra income.

Carmen thinks an element of carelessness has slipped into the operation, a certain royal disregard. Baby derives an almost silly enchantment from the fact that so many of her new "guests" are fabulously famous, rich, "creative," and so forth, while the earlier lot were only moderately so. The rents are often paid in cash, and Carmen suspects that the cash isn't being reported on Baby's income tax. Eighty-four or no eighty-four, that can come back on you.

"Oh Carmen off in dreamland again," says Baby, inspecting her lacquered paw through the magnifier. "It's so peaceful here on the weekends, one would think we were all dead."

"Another sleepy Sunday," Carmen yawns. "You getting hungry?"

"Let's go down and make sandwiches," Baby says, as if this were a delightfully risqué idea. "As soon as Krista burns the Makropulos secret."

"Okay." Carmen would prefer something nice from one of the gourmet shops, but she really doesn't care.

"Delicious bacon, lettuce, and tomato sandwiches, on sourdough baguette."

"All right." Baby is no waster of food, that's for sure: that baguette came in on Friday, and Baby's bound to water it and turn it into toast.

"With tarragon mayonnaise."

Elina Makropulos is three hundred and thirty seven years old. She has outlived countless lovers, friends, children and grandchildren, survived two dozens wars, seen empires born and die. All for what, really. A BLT.

"And we'll have some bubbly with the sandwiches, and then go up to the fifth floor and check my tomato plants."

"Sounds good to me."

"And later, Carmen, if it isn't too boring for you, I'd like to watch the first reel of *Pagan Love Song*. Asra found it at the video store. Howard Keel, what a heartbreaker."

†

Time and tide. In the so-called Monet Rooms of the Bellagio Hotel, several hundred vendors have assembled tables and booths in the erratic layout of a funfair, displaying cornucopias of "longevity products," from antioxidant vitamin pills to wrinkle-banishing creams and lotions, brochures for restorative spas, electronic devices to stimulate age-fighting accupressure points, "anti-aging" board games, flash cards, and t-shirts, home cholesterol monitors, on-the-spot blood tests to measure protein cross-linking levels and detect early-onset diabetes, facial wraps, facial clays, "floracide" exfoliants and enzyme skin peels, instructional videotapes in tantric yoga and other exercise regimens thought to slow, arrest, or even reverse the aging process, "secret formula" tablets and tonics, energizing necklaces and youthifying headdresses, bracelets and rings of a supposedly Aztec or Egyptian derivation, there are spangled banners promising FOR-EVER YOUNG and OLD AS U WANT 2 B, charts and posters and graphs and video displays, a veritable shopping mall of strategies and buyables for the chronologically dissatisfied.

Crowds of mainly very old people shuffle the gamut of these displays, sampling tinctures and oils and elixirs, eager to thwart all the evils flesh is heir to, hopeful that a simple fix to the tribulations of their complicated insides exists here somewhere, that a magic ointment or lucky jewelry item will send nasty Mr. Cancer and his oxidating ilk to the next-door neighbor's house instead of theirs: the same people, Evangeline thinks, who really believe they have won a vacation in Costa Rica when a stranger calls, bulk buyers of lottery tickets, people who blow their life savings on magazine subscription scams and ponzi schemes.

There is a simple, elegant justice in relieving these people of their mingy assets. And so Evangeline has created Princess Shah Shah International ("Longevity-Health-Wisdom"), a "worldwide consortium" which consists primarily of a box of business cards, a cell phone with a Bahamanian area code, and many crates of Princess Shah Shah's Inca Formula, a foul-tasting infusion of bamboo stalks, gypsum, pinellia tuber, dianthus leaves, rhubarb, and some other stuff Devin orders over the Internet from a Chinese herb supplier in San Francisco.

The beauty part is that these herbs or what have you probably do Princess Shah Shah's clientele a modicum of healthful good, they are said to have cleansing or detoxifying properties and hence, in all likelihood, don't actually *accelerate* the aging process, and from a certain view, anything that isn't actively bad for you probably helps you live longer, though why these stiffs waddling through the Bellagio with their wens and goiters and rheumatisms want to stay on earth so much as an extra day is a mystery to Evangeline, who murmurs to Patty Frasier that if she ever deteriorated half as bad as these longevity freaks she'd put a bullet through her own forehead or lock herself in the garage with the engine running.

Patty has drifted back into Evangeline's orbit following a hurtful break-up with her former life-partner Sandra, with whom she was, until very recently, raising show dogs and Shetland ponies on a ranch in North Carolina. She currently "shares her life" (as she likes to describe it) with Dominique, a gamin of a decidedly post–Audrey Hepburn stripe whose twenty-year-old hard body has beaucoup tattoos and piercings that serve as a map, of sorts, of where she has been, quite a number of wiggy places for someone so young.

At the moment, Dominique and Patty are sharing Patty's apartment off Decatur Boulevard with Evangeline and Devin, who are avoiding, as far as Patty can figure, having papers served on them at the Tecumseh Drive address, which has been in vacant limbo for more than a year, gathering cobwebs while the Slotes dissemble themselves in Cuba, Paradise Island, Cancun and Florida.

Devin has become a computer maven since dropping out of college, night and day on the Internet, he has big plans for importing Cohiba cigars from Havana, shipping them through a third country. Evangeline says Cuba is Wide Open for Foreign Investment. She envisions resorts, import-export opportunities, etcetera etcetera. Besides Princess Shah Shah International, she has this other Canadian setup, Kubla Khan Limited, to sign paper and clean money, and presumably to import Devin's cigars.

Having the Slotes around has placed a degree of stress on Patty's special friendship with Dominique, who works peculiar hours for an escort service. For one thing, there are herbs smelling like gym socks boiling on the stove around the clock, the manufacture of Princess Shah Shah's Inca Formula has taken over the whole kitchen, plastic bottles and funnels and sheets of labels run off on the computer printer covering every level surface, for another thing Evangeline has weird individuals in and out at all hours, people from shelters or off the street by the looks of them, hired to run obscure errands and perform odd jobs, wash the car, fetch orders for Princess Shah Shah products from Evangeline's several mail drops, plus, the place is festooned with notebooks and gun magazines and Evangeline's underwear and make-up bags and wigs and whatever, everything spilling all over the place, furthermore Dominique doesn't like Evangeline Slote, and the feeling is mutual, Evangeline makes no secret of her unfavorable opinion of call girls, or lesbians for that matter, in Patty's view Evangeline fears that Devin's been sprouting a woody, fat chance, around Dominique, who really is a cunning little vixen, and on Dominique's side, Dominique has loudly proclaimed her conviction that "something terrible" is going on between Evangeline and Devin, since mother and son share the guest room bed. Patty takes a broader view of the parent-child continuum, but she does feel lucky to have another girlfriend so soon after the last one and really wants Evangeline to leave. Devin she can take, but these days they come as a package. Happily for Patty, the Slotes have announced their plans, right after the longevity convention, for some R&R in the Caymans.

"Our herbs are hand gathered," Evangeline tells a sun-bronzed couple, wrinkled like elephants, who wear matching sky blue jogging outfits and large ormolu amulets stamped in the image of some death-defying god around their necks, "on the slopes of Machu Picchu."

"Do Incas live as long as Sherpas?" the wife wants to know, fingering her amulet.

"The Incas no longer exist," Evangeline informs her with grinning asperity. "But their longevity secret lives on."

Evangeline is Putting On The Liz big-time lately. Her current hairdresser, Ramu of Kush, whose salon is in the same strip mall as the Liberace Museum, has replicated Liz's do from *Ash Wednesday*. She's been fitted with contact lenses that turn her hazel eyes violet. To keep Patty on her good side, she's even splurged, with Liz-and-Dick abandon, on a room in the Bellagio to use on their breaks, though Evangeline uses it more than Patty does, also availing herself of the hotel's many massage and hydrotherapy services. She's become especially keen on the so-called Thalassobath, a seaweed and algae wrap designed to stimulate circulation.

To the old couple, she confesses that she's seventy-two.

"So I guess I'm living proof," she says, Tayloresquely beaming. "And Patty here, the President of Princess Shah Shah International, incredible as it may sound, is fifty-five. We've both been using Inca Formula for years."

Thank you, cunt, thinks Patty, who only turned forty-six months ago. As in bygone days of the Sacramento Welcome Wagon and the Bicentennial Office, Evangline leaves Patty holding the fort for hours at a time, flitting around the convention to "network." She always returns from these peregrinations breathless, with a purse stuffed with business cards, and announces that she's "tuckered out" and needs a Thalassobath, or a Kiwi Body Buff, or a Moor Mud Wrap, or a little nibble of pasta or sushi at Aqua or Shintaro to tide her over till dinnertime. All her weight goes right to her ass, but if Evelyn were chowing down as often as she claims to be, her ass wouldn't fit in the Monet Room. Patty suspects that Evelyn is getting her cootchie tore up on a daily, maybe even an hourly basis, up in the room, by conventioneers she sees as useful contacts. Evelyn has always told Patty rather bluntly that the quickest way to a man's wallet is through his cock, a philosophy that never failed with Warren according to her. Evelyn says Warren's in Honolulu, recovering from a stroke. But Patty's overheard Evelyn on the phone, telling people that Warren is in Japan opening a hotel, in Switzerland getting monkey gland treatments, in Brunei attending seminars on Global Development. Patty has the funny feeling Warren's languishing in some shady dry-out clinic or a rest home, mainly because Devin glazes over and goes all silent and pensive whenever Warren's name comes up. At the very least, there's more going on than what Evelyn tells her, but this is nothing new to Patty.

†

APRIL 1996

Norma	Mon–Wed	10–8
	Wed–Fri	2–8
Leon	M Tues Sat	11–7
Vic	on call	
Asra	Mon–Fri	8–7
Carmen	Fri Sat Sun	9–7
Tara	Tues Thursday	8–7
Reece	M Wed Fri	8–7
Fay	M Wed Fri	9–8
Cora	Mon–Fri	8–7

"These look like long hours," Norma tells the new girl, "but everything's very flexible. You won't find many days when you're busy all day. The busiest times are when tenants are checking in, or something special is going on."

Norma writes "Celestine" at the bottom of the list.

"I'll start you on Tuesdays and Thursdays, so you'll work with Tara for a few weeks."

Norma presses a button on a large phone on the wall.

"Tara?"

Several seconds pass.

"Yes?"

"Tara where are you?"

"I'm on five."

"That's the penthouse," Norma tells Celestine. "Nobody lives in the penthouse, Mrs. Claymore uses it. The cats are up there. And the pool. Tara, I'd like you to come down when you finish up there, we have a new girl starting today."

"Ten minutes," Tara says. The intercom goes dead.

"This goes everywhere in the house," Norma says, pointing out the intercom. "And this"—she points to a milky black-and-white image on a small television monitor beside the phone— "shows the lobby and each of the various hallways. Mrs. Claymore has the intercom upstairs also, but this is the only monitor. Well, there's actually another one in 1B but that was for Mrs. Claymore's mother, she's passed away. When people have guests, we have to know who comes in and out. One of the staff always answers the door. So, if a guest comes, you check them out here, and phone the tenant to say they've arrived, they can either come down and let the people in, or we escort them to whichever apartment they're visiting. The main thing is they have to be identified. We've never had any trouble this way. Never had any trouble, and also we don't want any trouble. Never, ever just buzz people in. Also—even the tenants shouldn't be wandering around the house. They're supposed to stay on their own floor, in other words come in and go to their apartment and not poke around the rest of the place showing the house to people. People we rent to we screen very carefully, but we don't know who knows them, and to give you an idea, Celestine, this little thing here"—Norma gives the frame of a small Barbizon School drawing of a tree stump beside a Regency mahogany whatnot a ginger tap—"is worth twelve thousand dollars." Norma winks. "Fit right in someone's pocketbook.

"Never clean anything," Norma tells the now fully attentive Celestine, "until Tara tells you what to clean it with. This house is full of art objects, a lot of the furniture is antique, we use special things on them. Now, you'll have a list of which apartments are occupied and who is in them, always keep that up to date, those are cleaned daily, and Mondays we do a really thorough cleaning because there's no maid service on the weekends. By the time you come in on Tuesday, it's mostly light housekeeping, but say someone moves out on Monday, we have to go through, clean every corner, and Mrs. Claymore usually likes to put different things in the rooms, it gives her a lot of fun."

Norma has been running the house on East 65th Street for eight years. She is a birdlike Argentinian somewhere in her midthirties. The new girl, as she automatically thinks of Celestine, already has enough to mull over. The chemistry of the Claymore house is a delicate thing. Norma tunes it as carefully as she can. When a wrong element gets mixed in, the people already there start wobbling out of alignment. Normas's learned not to hit new people with everything all at once, because even the brightest ones are so anxious to make a good impression that they don't really listen. Either people pick it up or they don't. She likes to start them off in the basement kitchen, with a cup of coffee, and show them the place one floor at a time. The kitchen's the most casual place, a mixture of tony appliances like the AGA stove and the massive Viking refrigerator, and rustic items like the plain oak table and chairs, the antique hoosiers and whatnots, it's where Baby reads her five morning papers and plays with the dog and gets her old bones into gear, where she serves dinner for company and spends the most time with the staff, and of course the basement's where all the useful things are, the laundry and the wine cellar and the handyman's workroom, cleaning supplies and what have you.

"You're French, 'Celestine.' " Norma is mainly Italian, by way of Buenos Aires. "Pretty name."

"Norma is a nice name, too. An operatic name."

The whoosh of the elevator descending.

Tara is laughing as she steps off the elevator.

"Ratty made caca next to the swimming pool," she tells Norma. Norma laughs. She has a throaty "infectious" laugh.

"What did Baby say?"

"Ha ha, Baby was swimming her laps, and Asra was feeding the orchids, you know how Baby sticks her head up, 'This is how we had to swim in the Aquacades so people could see our faces,' all the time Ratty is running beside the pool to look at her and stopping here, and here, like this, all along the pool making poop."

Norma laughs again. She can't help it. Ratty's bowel movements turn up all over the house, sometimes to the intense consternation of their "guests." Norma wouldn't say so to a new employee, but one of the nice things is that every day has its class war–type amusements, especially at the expense of the tenants, who tend to be rather full of themselves. Thankfully, since The Great Purge (as Vic, the Romanian building superintendent, refers to the last renovation), tenants have never been very numerous at any given moment, though the ones they get now, at monstrously inflated prices, are considerably more full of themselves than the previous lot. Less work, all the same. Currently there are only three: Wilson Farmhole, the gay novelist, in 3RW, the pop singer Mica It in 4F, and, in 2E, the futurologist Rhonda Corn and her lover, Morgan Talbot, an editor at Condé Nast. All these people are temporary, having their places redecorated or whatever. None is especially troublesome. Baby has taken a shine to Wilson Farmhole and has gone as far as having him downstairs for lunch. Norma thinks he's a sanctimonious turd and doesn't see the attraction, but no skin off her ass.

The staff all like each other, more or less. A real plus in the work environment. Funny things happen all the time. And one of the funny things is Baby, so nutty in a good way, and really a grand lady of the world, not troubled by little things like dog poop or the occasional plumbing catastrophe. Baby wants to squeeze as much fun out of life as she still can, and who can blame her? The sad thing is Baby's age, for what will happen to them all when Baby passes?

†

To: Khaled Abu Omar
General Manager
Tropical Belt Bank of the Bahamas

Re: Account #757608ZW842133

We hereby request and authorize the immediate transfer
of $10,000.00 from the above account to Wells Fargo
Bank 933910 Las Vegas Boulevard Nevada USA,
Account of Varlene M. Swales, #4958201234675.

(signed)

Warren E. Slote
Evangeline Carson Slote

†

They were driving below a twenty-foot-high, bright yellow
M&M, embedded in a mile-long frieze of extravagant signage
which, lighted or unlighted, had the daytime appearance of a pen-
timento scorched into the built environment by an atomic blast.
Vegas by day was never a pretty picture. The unreality of it turned
an especially harsh forensic corner in sunlight. Yet it had become
the country's fastest-growing city, the unreal place where everyone
wanted to be. Either they all wanted to come alive at night like
vampires, or thought that this repelling, metallic condition of
things was how days were supposed to look.

    Evelyn had dreamed about lobsters. Mottled green and black
lobsters in a cloudy Chinese restaurant tank. Lobsters meant they
should go to the Caymans immediately and close out Warren's
bank accounts. The Chinese restaurant had to signify good luck. Yet

there were other signs and presences in the dream that spelled danger. She was told not to put her hands in the tank, that the lobsters could change into something else.

"He kept asking where your father was," she told Devin. "Oh darling please don't light that cigarette."

Devin, driving, held an unlit cigarette between his fingers. He had been tapping it on the wheel and counting the seconds between the time he took it out of his pocket and the time she would say something.

"You smoke."

"Well I smoke because my mother smoked. Monkey see monkey do. And I wish to God she hadn't, I'll die before my time."

"Drink more Inca Formula. Who is this guy, anyway?"

"This is what I'm telling you. Why I keep wondering about those lobsters. I think they mean cash, but they could mean 'be careful.' Sheik El-Katami owns those banks, and all these questions he was asking, don't ask me how he had Patty's number because I don't even want to think about that."

"Varlene," Devin said, as if it were obvious.

"Never a peep about these wire transfers before now," she fretted.

She had spent the morning replacing Lester's name on the Kubla Khan incorporation papers with that of Rajinder Randawa, a minor diplomat she and Warren had met once in New York. She had also gone to a title company in a North Vegas mall and registered another deed transfer on the Santa Rosa acres. The property would now belong to The Hyksos Group, a new corporation.

"Did he actually say anything?"

"Nothing straight out, but my God, Devin, he's an Arab."

"Which means what?"

"They invented mathematics! You can't put anything past them! He must know something."

"How can he know anything? Nobody knows anything."

Lester, she thought, Lester knows something.

"I notice you don't bother asking what I dreamed," Devin said petulantly.

"Why are you taking that tone? Why are you being so touchy?"

They were moving seven crates of Princess Shah Shah's Inca Formula to the place on Tecumseh Drive. Inca Formula had not moved very briskly and it seemed more trouble than it was worth to actually ship the orders that had come in. But after boiling all those herbs it seemed a shame to just throw it out.

"I dreamed of me and Dominique and Patty in a three-way," Devin said, in a somewhat defiant voice. Evangeline deflated him with a lusty chuckle.

"Oh Lord, that's every man's dream. Two lezzies and his dick. I didn't know you were so conventional."

Devin lit his cigarette to spite her.

"Okay, what I actually dreamed, there was this polar bear. On one of those ice floes. And the polar bear dived into the water, see, and came up with a huge salmon in his mouth. I figure the salmon is money, okay? Maybe from cigars, the fish could be a cigar. Maybe from the Caymans. The water is freezing cold, but if you take a dive, you come out with salmon."

"See, that's what's so interesting. We both dreamed of fish. In my case lobsters, which are really underwater spiders. Who do spiders make you think of? And the polar bear, that's Warren. I mean he spent all that time in the Arctic. Water is sex, I know that much."

The house on Tecumseh Drive had succumbed to funereal desuetude. Varlene had kept the gas and electric turned on but the phone didn't work and everything looked like sad debris from a former life. Last year's ashes were heaped in the fireplace. Sheets lay draped over the furniture and the air had a stale dry smell of dust. Evelyn went down to Warren's office and combed the files for usable data. Devin rummaged in his bedroom for clothes that weren't too out of date.

"I miss this place," Evelyn told him as they left. "I don't think there's any reason we can't move back here. You know it's based on a Frank Lloyd Wright design."

†

The tropical Cattleya hybrids in 1B were prey to all manner of orchid peril: spider mites, root rot, sooty mold, Botrytis cinerea, all had had their epoch in the microgreenhouse extruding from the wall above the basement patio. From down below, where Baby often hostessed her intimate dinners in balmy months, these vegetal catastrophies passed unseen; only tendrils and specks of color flashed in the flamelight of Baby's wicker tiki torches. In 1B they occupied a zone of isolated eminence, in a whitish vapor of fructifying mist. Some propagated on cork rafts, or in plastic pots ranged on plastic shelves. Others cascaded from dangling baskets of hardwood hooked to the ceiling. From a distance they looked like fleshy lumps of blown glass, electric yellow, phosphorescent red, streaked and speckled like wings of exotic moths or innards of rare amphibians.

They required a nighttime temperature above 59°F and a semi-humid 86°F during the day. Climate changes sent them into shock. Asraboth had nursed their damaged roots with fungicide, scalpeled off their dry bracts and spent flower stems, fed them an exactly balanced 18-18-18 fertilizer formula every seven days, first spritzing the roots clear of mineral salts. He had rescued them from aphid infestations. He had watched, helplessly, a whole meticulously tended year's worth of blooms destroyed overnight in a viral epidemic. He was always aware of them, sensitive to the smallest anomaly in their biosphere. His dreams were peppered with orchid disasters: plagues of insects, lethal innundations, rampant bacteria.

The orchids were alive in a different way than the plants and flowers and potted trees on the penthouse terraces and even a bit differently animate than the orchids growing up there, perhaps because in 1B, under the Gro-Lux tubes that compensated for the

rear apartment's sparse sunlight, they lived apart from other vegetation, each in its private clump of bark or spagnum, like laboratory
specimens rather than parts of a garden. The fact that 1B was seldom rented out, and only erratically visited by Baby or anyone
else, made their struggles to endure and flourish cruelly poignant,
like homeless kittens in a humane shelter. They had a terrible
fragility that Asraboth half-consciously associated with Baby, who
astonished him at times, on the Moorish tiles beside the pool, or
on the iron stairway in the penthouse, by suddenly executing a *bal-
lonné sur la pointe* or *grand jeté pas de chat*, flinging an ancient leg and
perfectly curved foot into space at the level of her hipbone, or
doing a split. Her placid, evenly paced Australian crawl was a similar wonder of limber grace, and made it almost possible to believe,
as Baby did, that she would live to a hundred, but in fact these
demonstrations made him uncomfortably aware of her mortality.

Like the orchids, Baby survived by a delicate equilibrium of
things in her environment. Missing a nap, or a meal, could throw
her completely out of whack and make her more susceptible to
colds, to backaches, to blurry vision, sometimes to a ringing in her
ears or a tightness in her chest, pins and needles, numbness in fingertips and toes. She was subject to inexplicable swellings that had
to be shrunk with prednisone; cold wine drunk with hot food
brought ghastly attacks of reflux. Any minor twist in Baby's routine
could activate a plethora of physiological miseries. While she
refused to eschew her beloved splits of champagne and her favorite
rich foods, she no longer went to the opera, or the theater, or
movies, or parties. "If people want to see me," Baby grandly
declared, "they have to come here." The outer world was too
fraught with mischance for Baby ever to venture beyond the splen-
did walls of her mansion, except to see doctors.

Asraboth was occasionally troubled to realize that he himself
was thought by most of the household to be unnaturally delicate. He
pondered what it meant, "to be delicate." It seemed to mean that he
existed less palpably than other people, that his hold on life was less

assured, less robust. That he could slip out of the world without much fanfare. He was a small-boned man of five foot four, with a slight, wiry body and petite, elegant hands and feet. His vividly etched face, clouded by reserve or gravity that deflected any quick guess about his sexuality, inhabited a taut oval the color of charcoal below a skull that looked thin and brittle as an eggshell. His hair was a very short, curly, anthracitic fleece. In the ethnic paella of Manhattan, he did not possess the charged physicality of African-American men, or the gangling academic air of dark-skinned East Indians, but rather the toylike comeliness, self-effacing gait, and archetypally masklike face of an obscure unpopulous tribe, an irrelevant oddity.

He was physically much stronger than he looked, and more worldly than his somewhat spiritual face indicated, but his meek approach to daily circumstance excited the protective instincts of everyone around him. His refined looks, too, mobilized a general wish to guard him from . . . well, no one would have said exactly what, but the same sorts of things one wants to spare a sexually magnetic twelve-year-old. During his years as a delivery boy, Asra had become familiar with the carnal cravings of many upper-middle-class men and women who believed that a black delivery boy, particularly one from Africa, would have no fastidiousness or hesitation about pulling out a godlike phallus upon request. Some had been very aggressive about it, and some, of course, Asra had accommodated for the fun of it, but that era of his life seemed as long ago and half imaginary as Ethiopia.

Dracula erythrochaete needed repotting. Its compost was absorbing too much water. The triangular flower looked like the face of a space monster Asra had seen in an Arnold Schwarzenegger film called *Predator*, with red and yellow eyelike things where the petals converged—cream-white petals, rust red splotches stippled all over them like tiny pen strokes—and a spadeshaped protrusion dead center resembling an omnivorous tongue. This was the puzzling thing about the orchids in 1B: they had a paralyzing, paranormal beauty, the beauty of desert minarets and Romanseque cathedrals, of water surging over Victoria Falls or the Matisse still life hanging in Baby's sitting room. An enthralling loveliness so rich and complete that it made you ache for a better world. But when you stared into their depths for a long time, and emptied your mind of everything except their awesome visual quiddity, they all looked like space monsters.

†

Shreve Kelly couldn't talk because they told him not to. He had been crashing at St. Jude shelter for a month, mowing lawns during the day, panhandling, moving a few glassine packets of blow, whatever. The shelter handled about three hundred men. A lot of pilfering went on, and fights. Shreve stayed out of all that. Still he was a target for things because he wasn't so young. Punks took him for granted. He didn't have the height or the weight or the muscle to argue if somebody stole his shoes. He was polite and deferential to the hard types and therefore no one respected him.

The ad on the bulletin board offered room and board in a mansion to a person who could cook and clean. The printing on the card was neat and regular, in violet ink, which made him picture a winsome grandmother in a gingham frock. He called the number. A throaty female voice told him that a Mr. Win would pick him up on the corner of Revere Street and West Bonanza Road near the 15 on-ramp. Black Cadillac, a kid. Tall kid. Nose job. "I'm Bobby Win," the kid told him. Talked the whole time about these companies he ran. Hyksos.

The house turned out to be something less than what Shreve thought a mansion was, but it was quite a lot grander than anything he was used to and he'd be getting his own room and a private bathroom. The kid's mother, who said her name was Princess Shah, "though I'm sometimes known as Elinor Carson," chewed a cold chicken drumstick off the bone as she interviewed him, pausing now and then to shake a large blue cylinder of Baleine sea salt over it. She wore a shower cap and a gold bathrobe and about two inches of makeup. Shreve couldn't take his eyes off her tits. When she noticed him looking, she winked. Did he drink, did he take drugs. Like anybody would say yes. What did he know how to cook. She would need his driver's license and Social Security card to photocopy. She gave him a form to fill out, also a typed declaration that he would work for at least six months and would be "loyal at all times."

The people were friendly enough and said they traveled a lot and much of his job would be keeping an eye on things in their absence. There were shrubs and plants that needed attention, a pool requiring the usual care. "I'll tell you right off the bat that I am fanatical about dust," Princess Shah told him, poking the stripped chicken bone in the air for emphasis. "Bobby has allergies to dust and mold and so do I."

Could he start immediately. He said he had things at the shelter and could come back the next day. She told him Bobby would drive him and wait while he picked his things up. "A guy either wants a job or he doesn't," was how she put it. Shreve had wanted to think about it overnight but there it was. Our way or the highway, people with money were all the same.

Things went odd right away, but Shreve just did his work and acted dumb. Princess Shah hardly ever left the house. She wore the shower cap all the time and three or four different house coats and spent the entire day making phone calls, writing in ring-binder notebooks as she talked. Her involvement with these notebooks was frankly passionate, and no idle endeavor. It was as if she were annotating every passing moment of the day, every scrap of datum. She would bring whatever notebook she was working in to the dinner table and lay it open beside her plate; if an idea came to her or Bobby Win made some significant remark, Princess scrawled it in.

Daytimes, she sat at the glass table in front of the fireplace with a pack of Marlboros and a large gin and tonic in easy reach, punching numbers, putting on accents and voices, making inquiries of one type or another. Sometimes she claimed to be a realtor checking about liens and mortgages on various properties. She placed a number of calls every day to people who had won, according to her, vacations in Belize or Guadalupe, and who only needed to provide her with certain personal information to confirm their identities. Princess Shah taped all of her telephone calls, using a microcassette recorder and a plug-in device from Radio Shack. She played back salient parts of these conversations for Bobby Win, if he happened to be out when they occurred.

Bobby Win had a laptop computer set up on a trestle table in a carpeted study off the living room. He had a designated line for Internet use and a Hewlett-Packard printer that took magnetic ink. He had a scanner. He spent a lot of time scanning forms and documents into the computer and altering them on the screen and printing new versions out on special paper. Bobby had materials for payroll checks and even government refund checks, and of course business cards and deed forms and birth certificates and all manner of ID, university diplomas, you name it.

They had a Mailbox USA on Tropicana Avenue and another one on South Jones Boulevard and sometimes Bobby drove Shreve to the mailboxes and had him fetch the day's harvest. They received mail for Devin Slote and Bobby Win and Richard Diamond and Kubla Khan International and Princess Shah Shah and Eileen Carson and Elinor Carson and Evelyn Slote and Evangeline Slote and Eva Annamapu and The Hyksos Group and Ellie Thurlow and Anna Mae Carson and John W. Mayhew and Jewel Barlow and Sam Barlow and many other people besides, all of whom seemed to be them, it didn't take a genius to figure that out. Great quantities of mail arrived for Warren E. Slote, many legal-looking items in long envelopes, and Shreve noticed that these things always got the Princess's close attention. The Warren thing didn't take a genius to figure, either.

She was not a Princess and Bobby Win wasn't Bobby Win, and after Shreve had lived there for a time, he stopped calling them by those names. They did take off pretty regularly, a week or two weeks at a time, he wasn't permitted to answer the phone or let anyone in the house except Varlene Swales, who did their accounts. Shreve thought of Varlene as "a cute little butterball." She had recently had bad trouble, with her cervix. She repined for some jackass she'd been living with until his incarceration for medical fraud. She visited the guy in Lovelock Correctional Center twice a month and always came back depressed.

"They've got him in Anger Management now," Varlene told him. "Unit Two. Bobby Ray was always a Unit One type of person, not a Unit Two. He wasn't angry when they sent him up. He had remorse written all over him at sentencing. What does that tell you about the prison system."

Shreve was not supposed to talk to Varlene, but inevitably they did talk. The first time Shreve said anything to her she jumped a mile.

"You're a mute," she insisted.

"If you say so," Shreve told her.

"In that case how come you never talk?"

Shreve explained that his father had been deaf, that he'd learned sign language at an early age, that Evangeline had discovered this during their employment interview and decided to make Shreve her "mute valet." If there were people in the room Evangeline would pretend to render what they said in sign language, if it happened to concern him, using a lot of inept and silly-looking motions of her hands and fingers, whereupon Shreve would reply in actual sign language. Since these replies were never of any consequence, the fact that Evangeline didn't understand them didn't matter at all.

"So what type of thing do you say to her when she wiggles her hands around like that?"

"Whatever comes into my head, you know, 'Fine with me, you cocksucking bitch.' "

Varlene howled.

"You better watch out with that one," she said. "She's the type, you'll find out one day she really does know what you're saying."

Shreve came to treasure the times when Varlene was there and the Slotes weren't. She was not a happy person but exuded amphetamine cheer, Shreve admired that. He seldom had a chance to talk to anyone else except Evangeline and Devin. Shreve was not a big talker, but he did like a little human contact. The Slotes did not regard him as human, he soon realized. They gushed compliments when he fixed them something nice for dinner, they patronized, but he knew he didn't even exist as far as they were concerned. One day when he'd put his wallet on the dresser and gone in to take a shower, the wallet disappeared. Evangeline told him Varlene might have taken it by accident, thinking it belonged to Warren or whatever. Why would Varlene be poking around his personal rooms, Shreve wanted to know but didn't ask, even if she had been on the premises at the time, which she hadn't been. When he told Varlene, she just shrugged and picked at her sweater.

"Evelyn's Evelyn," she said. "When she's not Princess Shah or what have you. You know the score, fella. She's so compulsive she grifts herself when she runs out of other people."

The wallet reappeared, magically, in the same spot where it had vanished. There hadn't been anything in it anyway. Shreve kept his papers in a much-crumpled envelope from County Services: army discharge papers, Social Security, etc. When that disappeared, Shreve actually saw Evangeline take it, but pretended to be sleeping. She just crept in at three a.m. and whisked it off the night table. The part about being a loser that always bothered Shreve was this passive acceptance of things that were blatantly unfair. He didn't hate himself so much for the things he couldn't make a call on, though he knew his defects in judgment that way had fucked his whole life up. But losing all the time, losing as a way of life, to the point where you swallowed everything you knew with certainty was wrong, that's where it really stabbed, where you knew tomorrow would be just more nothing right up to your final breath. And then you'd get dumped in a hole with nothing on top of it but weeds.

Shreve had been working there almost a year when Varlene,

combing through the mounds of records that accumulated every month in Warren's old office in the back, to keep the taxes straight, a job considerably more tangled than two hundred dollars a week would buy from anybody else, noticed that Shreve Kelly was listed as President of The Hyksos Group on an account at the Swiss American Bank of Bermuda. She assumed, correctly, that Shreve knew nothing whatever about this, and considered telling him, but figured nothing very good for him could happen if he had the information. She did tell Bobby Ray about it the next time she drove up to Lovelock. It was the first good laugh he'd had all week.

✝

"The trick of it, generally speaking, was when you hit the water," Baby told her friend Ikea. Their white wicker chairs, which had once embellished the rolling lawn of the Claymore chateau near Deauville (sold long ago, when neither Claymore cared to travel any more), faced the Olympic quadrant of the penthouse pool, its water steely under light pouring through the curved greenhouse glass overhead. Where possible, Baby had gone for a Versailles effect of vastness throughout the house when they had first renovated, but now, of course, the feeling of spatial grandeur obtained only in the two-story penthouse, its roof and terraces unsullied by commercial exigencies, where lush greenery and a family of spotted tiger cats reigned in a kind of Moorish quiet.

"This Essar Williams wassa great star?" Ikea could not have been older than twenty, the scioness of a Tokyo pachinko parlor fortune who had already met personal success with a line of daring blouses and eccentrically cut unisex apparel for small people such as Baby Claymore. Not that Ikea designed for the elderly, but the fact was, Baby could pull off a breezy satin something you would normally envision on a person fifty years her junior, it had to do with her bone structure and prodigious aquatic regimen.

"Oh, Ikea, my dear, she was Metro's biggest moneymaker all through the forties. Wet she was luminous. But you couldn't make those swimming pool musicals ad infinitum. After the war, people wanted dry. People wanted Marlon Brando."

"I see Marron Brando on a talk show, very fat Marron Brando now."

"An elephant," Baby agreed. "*I'd* still fuck him, though."

Ikea twittered with embarrassment, decided that was the wrong response, and attempted a lusty chortle. She was eager to Americanize herself as quickly as possible.

She had arrived in a white leather space outfit of her own design, with silver buttons and snaps and velcro patches that peeled off, when desired, to reveal various areas of skin. Ikea's skin was so smooth and creamily perfect that she resembled a synthetic entity designed for penetration by big, brutal men. It was a fond dream of Baby's to interest Ikea in Asraboth, and vice-versa, partly to spare Ikea the trauma of *very* large men who would inevitably hit on her but mainly to promote some kind of outside interest for Asraboth. They were the same size, and Baby could visualize them gently coupling like tender lovers in a Bollywood extravaganza. She always pictured this occurring in a bassinette, and had to remind herself that they were both adults. Unfortunately, they seemed to repel each other like identically charged magnets.

"After Esther made her dive—or before, sometimes Esther would have to land in the middle of a whole cloud of aquabats— we *glided* in like a row of bananas," Baby said, shedding her pink terrycloth robe as she rose from her seat. In her one-piece magenta bathing suit, she looked almost as small as Ikea. She strode to the edge of the pool on ballet-flattened little feet, angled herself perpendicular to the tile edge with knees pressed together, and made a sinuous curve with her upper torso, raising her arms so that her hands held an invisible volleyball above her blue rubber bathing cap.

"One, two, three, four, all the way around the pool—they

were always circular or kidney-shaped, not like this one—and being the shortest, I was always the last one in.

"*Comme ça!*" Baby cried with a startled catch in her throat as she flung herself into the water. She became a bright blob of magenta wobbling in and out of roughly human outline, arms and legs scissoring along in an impressively even line towards the shallow end. At last Baby's rubber cap broke the surface, glistening, and her harsh inhalations wafted through the air.

Ikea jumped up and applauded, really excited. The excessive quality of Ikea's enthusiasm for Baby, Baby's house, Baby's mother's tapestries, Baby's little sayings, indeed for all things Baby-related, was wonderfully charming, but perhaps the one feature of Ikea that Baby sometimes found wearying. She did not mind praise, quite the contrary, but Baby did not like people to fawn over her, it made her feel horribly old, even though Ikea would have applauded anyone for making a good dive, or baking a loaf of bread for that matter, for Ikea's avidity was hardly confined to Baby's realm. Ikea gasped over every spring collection, gushed about every movie she saw, and even found something wondrous about Cirque du Soleil.

As Baby climbed out of the pool and pondered the fact that Asraboth was practically the only thing Ikea never found "mararwus," the man himself appeared at the end of the vaulted gallery, in a smart pinstripe shirt and black trousers, black felt shoes, always neat, always groomed, as perfectly beautiful in his Shetland pony way as Ikea was in her rubber doll way, carrying Baby's chilled split of luncheon champagne in an embossed silver bucket.

"Asra," Baby said, toweling as he popped the cork and commenced to pour, "Ikea's going to that new Keanu Reeves film this afternoon, why don't you two go together?"

Ikea beamed as if it were the happiest idea she had ever heard. Baby admired the Japanese for a lot of things. Asra did almost as well in disguising his horror.

"I would love to," he told Ikea, then to Baby, "But we were going to read *Arthur* this afternoon."

Baby tasted her Veuve Cliquot with relish. She wrapped herself in terry cloth and resettled on the wicker chair that brought such lovely memories.

"Darling Asra, we can read *Arthur* when you get home, and you can tell me all about the movie." Baby put on her raciest smile. *"Et aussi, ma cherie, j'ai un petit surprise pour monsieur, après."* To Ikea: "You are the *only* person he should see this with, you know so much about the martial arts."

She felt them weakening, softening towards each other. They would go together to please her, and they would enjoy themselves because she would be unhappy if they didn't. Stale but true, she thought: you catch more flies with sugar than you do with shit. She was determined to get the poor little fucker laid, if it was the last thing she ever did.

†

"Don't *ask* me why he wants to go sailing," Evelyn brayed, swirling Merlot with an air of sophisticated amusement. "You know Warren. He *begged* me to come along. Three weeks at sea isn't my idea of *la dolce vita,* thanks but no thanks."

"Dad, for some reason, just got the boat bug all of a sudden. Never liked boats, never liked the water until about a year ago. I think it's great he's exploring new things at his age."

"But I'll tell you something," Evelyn cut in. "Unbeknowst to any of us, Warren knows his boats. He spotted this thing in the marina last time we went to Havana and to me, frankly, it looked like the Wreck of the *Hesperus.* Little did I know. The owners were divorcing and that boat, to them, was the symbol of their marriage, they just dumped it for a song. Say goodbye to all the memories."

"Hamza here can take you boating if you like," said Sheik El-Katami, indicating the squat, oily, uncomfortable man at his right. "You could take them over to Sand Bluff."

Hamza Kadmonites tried for an expressive gesture of assent involving his lumpy shoulders and his pudgy open palms. Devin noted disgustedly that the man's fingernails were filthy. He was a crumpled figure in a suit all puckered by the moist night air. He must have been fifty and actually had pimples on his nose.

"I myself am off to London in the morning," El-Katami told them. "Sotheby's auctioning a Soutine that interests me."

"I adore Soutine. Did you see the one they have at the Bellagio?"

"But of course. So beautiful against that black velvet."

"We already have a boat," Devin said. "A 232 Captiva. 350 Magnum MPI."

"You bought it down here?"

"He means in Nassau," Evelyn said. "We got a very good leasing plan."

The German couple at the end of the table were feeding each other bits of seafood and cracking each other up in German. The man looked in his forties, the woman years younger. The German's ex-wife was also there, a much older, skinny person who wore a ridiculous quantity of gold jewelry and appeared to be completely drunk. She exuded bitterness and anger at some private, sozzled array of irritations, and kept snorting coke from an amber bottle. They were all Ubu's friends or associates or clients or something. Ubu had squeezed the ex-wife's nipple through her dress when they arrived at the restaurant, as if to establish an informal mood. The younger woman, svelte and big-breasted in Capri slacks and a red halter top, was, Devin thought, squeezing the German man's penis under the table. She was an Intellectual and had already bored everyone with a mortar attack of political opinions, mainly concerning U.S. policy in Israel. She had nothing against Jews, she herself had some Jew in her distant ancestry, or so, she said, the legend went. Sheik Ubu gaped at her in disgust. She winked at him.

"Gotcha that time, Ubu."

Sheik Ubu veritably giggled with relief. For a horrible moment, the idea that he had plunged his Sword of Allah into the mouth and anus of a kike, behind the back of an infidel kraut, on three quite different occasions, had overwhelmed him with its monstrosity.

The restaurant was a narrow landing built out on a pier in a brackish inlet. A stagnant, ugly night surrounded it. The light from a string of 40 watt bulbs cast a dim lividity over the table. The mating burps of bullfrogs and the percussive din of cricket thoraxes provided dismal music to the gloom. The food was crapulous, spiced with stale cumin. It did not even seem to be a restaurant but some sort of front for a smuggling operation. Big bowls of fish stew and platters of fried fish buried under tasteless vegetables kept arriving, which nobody ate. The Germans all drank gin.

They had gone to New York to avoid meeting Ubu El-Katami in Vegas. Evelyn knew where she'd fucked up, and although it seemed barely plausible that Ubu would personally interest himself, you never knew. They spent a fortune staying at the Plaza and nothing Evelyn tried panned out. New Yorkers were too busy. New Yorkers knew everything about the short con, it seemed like everywhere they went antennas shot up. The mortgage idea hadn't worked either. It hadn't worked at Fleet Bank and it hadn't worked at Chase and it hadn't worked at Greenpoint Mortgage. You can't do this kind of third party transaction in New York State, they told her. Then she had the brainstorm about Eddy Ramsey, but Eddy's signatures and the forms to replace corporate officers were somewhere in the house in Vegas. Varlene's mother was dying out in Topeka and Roland O'Higgins had attacked some imaginary Viet Cong in a Laundromat and was doing four months in County. So they got on a flight to Grand Cayman. And there was Ubu and his entourage right next to them in first class.

Even Devin had drunk too much. He caught Hamza staring at him several times. Fag? Supposedly all these Arabs took it up the ass. No, the guy's son was getting married in two weeks in Peshawar. Fag with a family, maybe. Hamza was too quiet. He

spent a lot of effort removing bones from his fish under the
grainy light. The German ex-marrieds had a lot of angry things
to throw at each other along the table, thankfully Devin couldn't
understand a word of it. Everybody talked at once. Devin
dropped his paper napkin. Bending to pick it up, he saw that his
mother had slid off her espadrilles and had a foot planted in
Ubu's crotch.

"He doesn't know anything," she told Devin the following
morning at breakfast. "He just wants to talk some shit with your
father."

I hate you, Devin thought. He was learning how to keep his
feelings off his face to thwart her. How could you fuck him. How
could you.

"He used to *pimp* for your father," Evelyn hissed through her
teeth, still able to read his mind. She had ordered up breakfast, to
his room. Devin sat eating in his gray Calvin Klein briefs. His
morning erection wouldn't subside. He shifted in the chair to display it: contempt, desire.

"You don't think they're going to think it's *weird* if you start
asking for wire transfers without the other signature? After you put
it on all this time?"

"I said *he* doesn't know anything. *Ubu*."

Devin swallowed some scrambled egg.

"Okay. I see where this is going."

"We have to take care of it. I said we'd have lunch at the guy's
hotel. I mean *I* would have lunch. He's over at the Radisson. I
don't want you involved in this."

"What the *fuck* were those Germans doing there."

Evelyn shook her head as if it had been too much even
for her.

"That's Ubu's idea of a dinner party. Rolf Seitz, who you nor I
nor anybody else should ever be seen with, is one of the chief depos-
itors at Royal Saudi. Probably their main one. And he's got to be off
Grand Cayman by tomorrow because he can't stay anywhere more

than three days. They don't even let him in Cuba. He lives on his boat. He's persona non grata in just about every country you can get a boat into. That's why that lush Greta owns the house here, she's also got a twenty room place in Manhattan he can't even visit unless he travels in black, or whatever the phrase is."

"Lucky guy, she's a complete cunt."

"She's a complete cunt holding three billion dollars of his money, if you wanna call that luck. He has to keep everything in her name. He can't own anything. *She* collects *art*."

"You can clean a lot of money with art."

"Well, there's the irony, junior, she has really bad taste, what I hear her collection's worthless. Just a lot of third-rate junk that looks like a bad imitation of something valuable. You notice *she* isn't off to London to bid on any Soutine. She gets *personally involved* with the artists. She's *lonely*. If we lived in New York like we've talked about, we could toss her salad big time and it wouldn't take but a month or two. Just keep feeding her the Beefeaters on top of her nose candy."

"The way she was pouring it down last night, she's probably face down in that shit stinking harbor this minute." Devin rubbed his prick through his briefs. Evelyn spread strawberry jam on a croissant. "Oh wait though," he said. "Rolf Seitz, Dad used to talk about him. That's who that is."

"Pirate Rolfi," said Evelyn, biting into her croissant. "Used to come to Vegas. Can't any more, boo hoo."

"That's the man who sold plutonium to Saddam Hussein."

Evelyn nodded, chewing.

"Anthrax, too," she said. "C4, sarin, everything in the tool box. I guess he *does* get to spend more than three days in Tripoli when he visits, but otherwise his vacations tend to be on the quick side. Ubu says he's shopping for fuel rods in Belarus these days."

"Jesus."

"Hey, he's a player. More than you can say for Jesus. Now what should I wear for that greasy sand nigger?"

✝

Hamza didn't want his fingerprints on any aspects of the deal, he told her over lunch at the Radisson. As a preliminary thing she would transfer two hundred thousand dollars to a numbered account in Zurich. Once that transfer showed up on Hamza's computer, an associate of his would authorize the release of everything in Warren's Royal Saudi account. She would then fax another authorization to the Tropical Belt subsidiary to transfer another two hundred thousand to a different numbered Zurich account, same deal.

She would have to think it over, she told him. He said there was nothing to think about. Hamza had done his homework. He had the dated coroner's report from San Diego and a sworn affidavit from the very much alive Warren *Jefferson* Slote who lived in Merced, photostats of all her faxes and signatures, she could take the deal or take a total loss.

He'd give her a week, he said. He would come to Nassau on regular auditing business in exactly seven days, and they would meet for dinner, and she could tell him yes or no.

You see the dilemma, she told Devin later on that day. We make any move between now and then he blows the whistle. You add up the balances, we play it his way, this little prick is walking off with eighty percent.

The fuck he is, Devin said.

✝

Evangeline later deemed their dinner with Hamza a smashing success, one of those brilliant evenings when good food in tasteful surroundings is complemented by the successful conclusion of a tangled piece of business. Hamza had checked into the so-called Atlantis on Paradise Island, a resort of truly breathtaking splendor that featured, among other blandishments, a lifesize Hydrostone simulacrum of a Mayan pyramid with water slides running down its surfaces. Hamza had reserved a table for three in Fathoms, the ne plus ultra of Carribean dining, sunk below sea level with glass walls through which diners could observe sharks and other marine creatures devouring one another.

Evangeline *adored* Fathoms but insisted, at the last minute, that Hamza accompany them to the so-called Ocean Club instead. The Ocean Club was even more Exclusive than Atlantis, she asseverated, it was a private club which only members and their guests could visit, passing first through a locked gate by entering a security code. It was also a mere five or six hundred yards from the triplex condominium the Slotes maintained on Paradise Island, and Evangeline wanted Hamza to see their place, get a fresh eye on their ongoing renovation, and offer Hamza "some ol' fashion Bahamanian hospitality" in the form of an after-dinner drink and a toothsome view of Nassau from across the canal.

Hamza took a cab to the Ocean Club, where the Slotes, as promised, waited at the gate, appearing to bask in the languid restfulness of their surroundings. They walked past the smallish lounging pools and patio tables and their festive parasols, up to the terraced dining area, which resembled the long veranda of a plantation. They were presented instantly with menus by a refreshingly obsequious Colored Person and asked if they would care for any drinks before dinner. Evelyn pondered good-humoredly, declared she was in the mood for "something silly," and ordered a banana daiquiri. Devin chose a hearty local ale. Hamza, though a strict Muslim when it came to pork, confessed that he did allow himself alcohol "in moderation," and asked for a dark rum and Coca-Cola with plenty of ice.

Evelyn had gussied up with her customary flair. She wore a fishnet white blouse through which her implacable mammaries appeared to ooze in fatty squares, with a satin white blouse thrown over it, primarily to cover her nipples. And she had obtained, at some flea market in Greater Nassau, a pair of vintage '60s psychedelic bell-bottoms commodious enough to contain her ever-burgeoning hindquarters. Around her neck glittered a brace of zircons anchored to a large square-cut emerald that had been part of a Tanqueray bottle in a previous existence. Devin, more casual, wore white chinos and a yellow tourist-shirt depicting the glories of Cable Beach.

Hamza, plodding bank auditor that he was, wore a sports jacket over a starchy-looking white shirt, but had made some concession to casual in the form of stiff, newly purchased Levi's. Sullen and po-faced at their previous dinner, terse and unyielding at his lunch with Evelyn, Hamza strove on this particular occasion to display a more amiable facet of his admittedly small-faceted personality. He was, after all, shaking these odd, disreputable, but fairly engaging and friendly people down for four hundred thousand dollars, and felt that the least he could do was to make them feel it was nothing personal. He could not reveal to them how fortunate they really were in getting any money at all out of Warren's accounts—that Hamza and certain associates, including Sheik Ubu, the putative and soon-to-be-former owner, had been looting the Royal Saudi Bank of the Caymans and the Tropical Belt Bank of the Bahamas for many years, and that after liberating their deposits and tying up a few loose ends, his associates and himself would be assuming new identities in several very secret places in South America while Ubu sold the banks to a mark he'd been setting up for three years, soon after which it was a dead certainty that all remaining assets in both banks would be frozen and, since neither bank was covered by deposit insurance, would then pass into liquidation without compensation to their customers. He could, however, and did, suggest that he was in a position to greatly amplify the mingy amounts they would be receiving on this particular deal, by means of certain other irons he currently had in the fire, as he put it. He also indicated his willingness to invest at least 50K in the internet start-up Devin had mentioned at dinner on Grand Cayman, cigarbiz.com. This, Hamza felt, put a brighter face on the business at hand, and soon they were laughing and chattering like old accomplices. Hamza even allowed himself a second rum and Coca-Cola when Evangeline urged him to "loosen up and let his hair down."

When dinner concluded and they walked down the road to the row of condos tucked against the canal behind a curving drive, Evangeline remarked that she considered Hamza "a keeper," someone who seemed pretty icy at first but turned out to be her kind of firecracker. He had, over dinner, related several hilarious vignettes of his early years in Pakistan, and a few rather off-color tales out of school concerning the erotic exploits of his boss, Sheik Ubu.

"We've had this place on our hands for I don't know how many years," Evangeline told him as they approached the house, "and I cannot make up my mind about the first floor. And try getting reliable people in. I had the guy down here mixing cement for the terrace and they got half of it on, took the whole eight hours today doing something Warren could have done himself in two hours, and left this ridiculous mess, I have to apologize for the way it looks."

Evangeline unlocked the door and stepped into the hallway.

"Really, Hamza, it usually isn't this messy."

Hamza stepped over the threshold and Devin walked in behind him and closed the door. A narrow staircase led up to the second floor. On the left of the staircase stood a long metal trough half full of wet cement.

"Just look at this," Evangeline tsk-tsked as Devin attacked Hamza's skull with a ball peen hammer. They both pushed Hamza's collapsing form, a geyser of blood spraying from its forehead, into the cement bath, face-down. They had a lot of trouble getting the squeaky-wheeled trough out to the wharf and onto the boat without disturbing the neighbors, who were rather intemperately noise-conscious, but they managed. By the time the cement hardened they were far out on the open water and able to dump the whole thing overboard without capsizing. There was a lot of damage to the upholstery and some nicks and gouges in the fiberglass deck, luckily the lease came with insurance, and in the condo a fair amount of blood spatter that Evangeline attacked repeatedly throughout the ensuing week with Clorox and various industrial solvents. It seemed like a lot of work at the time, but Evangeline later observed that it would have been twice as much bother if they'd had to drug him at Fathoms instead of the Ocean Club.

✝

Shortly after leaving the Bahamas, Evangeline replaced Shreve Kelly as the chief corporate officer of The Hyksos Group with Edward Ramsey, filing the necessary paperwork using photocopies of a bogus California driver's license and a Social Security card manufactured by Devin which did, however, bear Edward Ramsey's actual Social Security number, these documents were FedExed from Fort Lauderdale to Varlene Swales in Las Vegas and notarized by Varlene Swales, who then FedExed them to the appropriate trust company in Toronto. During this period, the Slotes acquired an RV from a dealership in Baton Rouge using a check drawn on a closed Bank of America account belonging to a Richard W. Harrison, a purveyor of restorative tonics Evangeline had drugged with Mogadon before assisting him to his room at the Bellagio six months previously. The Slotes moved around northern Florida in the RV for several weeks and then abandoned the RV in the parking area of Clover Ranch in Alachua, a breed and show facility for Arabian horses, apparently with some idea of recovering it later. . . .

. . . from the Beach Ball Motel in Lauderdale, Evangeline sent numerous faxes to the Royal Saudi Bank of the Caymans and the Tropical Belt Bank of the Bahamas, demanding further money transfers into Varlene Swales's Las Vegas bank account, unaware that the Tropical Belt Bank had passed into liquidation, as had the Royal Saudi Bank of the Caymans, that all funds in both banks had been impounded by State auditors. . . .

. . . at around this time, a store detective at a Federal

Discount outlet in downtown Miami noticed Evangeline ripping
Revlon lipsticks out of their packages and stuffing them into her
purse, when the detective attempted to search her outside the store
Evangeline kicked him in the nuts and tossed her pocketbook to
Devin, who sprinted into a Woolworth's down the block, unfortunately dropping his wallet, Evangeline meanwhile vanished into
the midday crowd. . . .

. . . Devin was charged with felonious assault and resisting
arrest and obstructing an arrest, all felony charges that a lenient
judge let him plead out on, "withholding adjudication" if Devin
avoided further trouble in the state of Florida for ten years. . . .

. . . during the same period Evangeline attempted to train a
homeless woman named Sarah Jane Smith to impersonate Varlene
Swales by obtaining a passport with Varlene's birth certificate, in
the belief that Sarah Jane Smith could present herself at the
Tropical Belt Bank in Nassau and obtain through power of attorney the remainder of Warren's deposits. However, Sarah Jane Smith
was arrested at the Passport Center in Miami for attempted fraud,
and was persuaded to lead two federal agents to Evangeline's room
at the Beach Ball Motel in Fort Lauderdale. . . .

. . . however, Evangeline's instincts had told her to leave the
room at the Beach Ball Motel that very morning, having received a
FedEx envelope containing the revised incorporation papers for The
Hyksos Group by way of Varlene Swales, along with samples of
Edward Ramsey's holograph signature from Warren's old files.
Evangeline's instincts further led her to the Oxtiern Mortgage
Company on Biscayne Boulevard in Miami, where Devin, incarnat-
ing Edward Ramsey, applied for a $300,000 mortgage at 9½ percent
interest on the property at 9300 Tecumseh Drive in Las Vegas. . . .

. . . the Slotes then returned to Las Vegas, where Evangeline
cleared the loan check through Varlene's Wells Fargo account, then
deposited the bulk of the proceeds in the Swiss American Bank of
Bermuda, meanwhile filing a quit claim which flipped the property at 9300 Tecumseh Drive from Edward Ramsey to Shreve

Kelly, who had, unbeknownst to himself, become the president of Kubla Khan International, and therefore head of the corporation formerly known as Slote Construction, the corporation to which the property deeded to Edward Ramsey had to revert according to the quit-claim. . . .

. . . Shreve Kelly then, under Evangeline's tutelage, purchased a $700,000 nonassessable homeowner policy from Metzenger Tatum Insurance of America. . . .

. . . in January, Wilbur Sumac delivered a large pizza with anchovies to the house on Tecumseh Drive. A rather tubby woman in a shower cap answered the door and told Wilbur to carry the pizza into the kitchen, paid him ten dollars in quarters she had stacked on the cooking island, and offered him another three dollars in quarters if he would carry a large package in from her car. This package weighed almost a hundred pounds and smelled faintly of gasoline and she wanted it placed in an ornamental gazebo beside the swimming pool. Wilbur remarked on the beauty of her home. She said it had been built by a world-renowned architect, a close personal friend who had unfortunately Passed On. Later, when Wilbur counted the quarters, he saw that she'd stiffed him seventy-five cents.

A few nights later, Wilbur was sent to the same address with a medium pizza without anchovies. The woman now introduced herself as Ellen Jane Smith and asked if Wilbur ever did any odd jobs. Wilbur considered most of the jobs he did odd and answered in the affirmative. Ellen Jane Smith and her son were planning to move to Los Angeles and needed people to pack up their belongings. Wilbur said he would be interested. The woman did not order pizza again, and after a few weeks Wilbur forgot all about her.

Wilbur Sumac lived in a small ranch house off Break Point Drive. The house had belonged to his mother, who died a few years earlier in a freakish electrical mishap. In his youth, Wilbur had been a handsome man, though his features had always been weak, and his face had now thickened, along with his body, into an ami-

able but forgettable plainness. His hair had retreated entirely from
his scalp and had the color of cigarette ash. In palmier times, when
he worked as a key grip in the motion picture business, he had
dated the actress Judy Canova. He had also been married, briefly, to
a prostitute named Lucille Cartland. Subsequent decades had not
been kind. Wilbur had aptitude but no push in any remunerative
direction. TV repair, shoe salesman, vending supplier, Wilbur had
trudged the gamut of punitive employment over the years, with
little to console or distract him besides his weekends of game
hunting and nights of abandon with a whiskey bottle. He preferred
brown liquor to clear, an inherited taste.

✝

On January 23rd, the same day he received the first payment
coupon from Oxtiern Mortgage Company in Miami for a
$2522.56 mortgage installment, Edward Ramsey got a phone call
from Ritchie Slote, Warren's daughter, whom Eddy hadn't seen in
over a decade and barely remembered, and since he had just idly
torn open the envelope from Oxtiern Mortgage Company thinking it was a piece of junk mail, registered the contents with alarm,
then anger, as he made the inductive hop, skip, and jump from the
bill in his fingers to the property Warren was supposed to have taken
Eddy's name off years ago. Eddy's first thought was that Ritchie's
call was some kind of preemptive explanation, that Ritchie still
worked for her father and this was some type of over-the-top
Warren Slote mickey mouse, but far from it, as Eddy liked to say, far
from it, Ritchie sounded frantic and pissed off and then, zealously,
convinced that they needed to meet somewhere to discuss what she
described as "the latest shoe to drop in a never-ending saga."

Eddy first phoned the 800 customer service number of Oxtiern
Mortgage Company and punched the loan number into their auto-
mated service system "to help us serve you more effectively," help us
downsize and waste your time instead of our money in other words,

Eddy thought, he was then presented with a so-called menu of options which eventually connected him to a so-called customer service representative, Eddy then asked for the specific loan officer in charge of the mortgage, after some minutes he was connected to someone identifying himself as Herb Baker, Eddy then told Herb Baker, if that really was his name, flat out, that Oxtiern Mortgage Company had been defrauded, that he Edward Ramsey hadn't applied for taken out or received any $300,000 mortgage loan and furthermore had nothing to do with the house on Tecumseh Drive in Las Vegas, this so-called Herb Baker told Eddy that the check had already been cut and mailed out to the address on Tecumseh Drive, and Eddy advised this so-called Herb Baker to contact the local fraud squad, which Herb Baker expressed his reluctance to do, unless compelled that way by legitimate law enforcement personnel, not that he didn't believe Edward Ramsey, this alleged Herb Baker said with robotic indifference, but objectively how did he know it wasn't Eddy trying to pull some kind of ingenious rip-off. Eddy then called the Miami-Dade Sheriff's Department and spent a half hour getting the runaround and finally spoke with a Detective Whale, a drawling Good Old Boy with an apparent IQ of 4 whom Eddy visualized as whalelike in form, immobilized behind a massive jewel box of Krusty Kreme donuts, however Detective Whale did "take down" Eddy's information, after that Eddy called his close friend Richard Escher, a P.I. in Inglewood, formerly LAPD, told the story again, and of course as Eddy told it, the whole thing rapidly jelled in his mind. Richard Escher promised to locate Evangeline and Warren Slote and get back to him.

By the time Eddy met up with Ritchie at Yuca's on Hillhurst he had put the thing together enough to figure Warren was either dead or incapacitated and Ritchie, who was climbing out of her new white Miata as Eddy pulled into the parking lot in his black BMW, confirmed this surmise, Ritchie had in fact ascertained that Warren had Passed On in 1994, actually "croaked" was the word Ritchie used, no Cordelia she, Eddy thought, had ascertained this quite recently by hiring her own P.I., and was now engaged in the intricate and baffling task of tracking down the whereabouts and disposition of all of Warren's assets, she was in fact attempting through various attorneys to prod the Las Vegas police into obtaining and executing a search warrant for the property on Tecumseh Drive, and through other attorneys to seal Warren's condo in Puerto Vallarta and another condo on Paradise Island in the Bahamas, so that whatever records Warren left behind could not be destroyed or tampered with by *that monster*, as Ritchie called her, though Ritchie considered it highly likely that any such records had already been destroyed or tampered with by *that monster*, that in fact Warren's assets had in all probability been looted long ago by *that monster*, in which case Ritchie and her brother were prepared for years of costly and infuriating litigation, assuming there was anything left to litigate over. The only bright spot happened to be that a will bearing Warren's valid signature dating from 1964 had turned up in a court-opened safe deposit box in Santa Barbara, a will leaving all of Warren's earthly goods to Ritchie and her brother, furthermore an attorney named Katz had forwarded personal letters from Warren to Ritchie and her brother indicating an illegitimate transfer of property in Santa Rosa effected by *that monster* via deed forgery, a class A felony in California, this would at least result in forfeiture and ideally in forfeiture and incarceration, though Evelyn had escaped from prison once and could probably chew through any bars or metal gates you put between her and the civilized world, Ritchie said, Ritchie's P.I. had also turned up information about this Hyksos Corporation or Hyksos Organization as well as some d/b/a for Slote Construction called Kubla Khan and Eddy's name had come into it, Eddy's name had also come into the illegitimate transfer of the Santa Rosa property, in connection with a substitution of attorney form or some such item relating to a lawsuit brought by unpaid land surveyors, and that, Ritchie said, was why she had called Eddy in the first place, though of course it was also very nice to see him again.

"You look like you're in good health, doing well," Eddy told her, bizarrely groping for a normal conversational tone. Ritchie's exhaustive recitation had occurred in full hearing of everyone eating lunch at Yuca's, which was a simple taco stand with tables in the parking lot.

"I'm doing just fine, Eddy, I just sold a very going business for a million five up in Tiberon *so I have lots of money to waste on lawyers.*" Her voice was exasperated and faintly accusatory.

"Look, Ritchie, we don't know each other well, but you have to take my word for it, I've got nothing to do with any fucking Hyksos or Kubla Khan or properties belonging to your father, as a matter of fact, thanks to your insane stepmother—"

"Stepmother of fucking *Beelzebub* maybe, please spare me any connection to *her.*"

"I'm sorry, I don't know all the internecine details of your family or Warren's arrangements with Evelyn—"

"She murdered him," Ritchie hissed. "That's the long and short of Warren's arrangements with Evelyn, as far as I'm concerned."

And then, unaccountably, she laughed, a high, bright laugh, the laugh of a self-possessed, rather stunning woman who always landed on her feet, Eddy thought. He regretted that she clearly regarded him as a relic of a generation that had thwarted her.

"Let's have some *pollo asado* for old times, Eddy," Ritchie said, imitating Humphrey Bogart, as if folding her hand and pocketing the deck. "This place has the best damned *pollo asado* in town."

Eddy's blood pressure dropped considerably over lunch, but after Ritchie drove away, promising to keep in touch, he began to feel rage and fear taking over again, rage at the Slotes, fear of the mortgage outfit in Florida, he had read all about identity theft, "the growth crime of the '90s," and the utter havoc it could wreak on the lives of completely innocent individuals, people who'd had their credit ruined, people arrested for crimes they knew nothing about, committed all over the country by other people using their Social Security number, all they needed was the number and any piece of ID fake or otherwise to open phone accounts and rent apartments and apply for jobs and basically start a whole new existence in your name, Eddy had read enough about this so-called growth crime of the '90s to know that there were ridiculously few mechanisms in place to clear people. Victims of identity theft found themselves in an interminable nightmare, if they got stopped for a broken tail-light police computers would tag them as wanted felons in states they'd never even been to, a lot of law enforcement agencies knew practically nothing about this phenomenon and basically once you'd been targeted, you were fucked.

Eddy thought about Evangeline Slote. He hadn't seen her since 1989, as far as he could recall. He had read her as a moderately loose cannon for most of the years he'd known the Slotes, a bit of a handful but basically a good-time gal who liked to drink and fuck around behind Warren's back, and Eddy'd always bought Warren's story that the slavery thing was a trumped-up canard invented by greedy lawyers on behalf of a bunch of ignorant domestics. Of course he knew Warren's businesses had murky angles, he'd never especially trusted either one of them and didn't really like her, but felt immune from their machinations because supposedly they were all friends. He'd kept them both at tong's length after the Tecumseh Drive transaction, because they'd asked him to file a burglary insurance claim a few months after Warren signed the place to Eddy, and Eddy refused, and combing through his memory Eddy figured he'd probably spoken to Warren twice on the phone after that, and then there had been some flurry of later calls from Evangeline concerning some vague business Eddy had no intention of getting into, and after that he just stopped picking up, Eddy screened.

The mortgage thing ate away at him. Richard Escher, his P.I. buddy, tried to calm him about it, they could prove whatever signatures were put on the loan papers weren't Eddy's, and besides, Rich said, it turned out these Slote people had some heavy heat blowing their way, he mentioned charges in Louisiana and some other trouble in Florida and some ongoing arson investigations and a missing persons thing down in the Bahamas.

"You mean her, she's in trouble," Eddy said.

"The both of them, they're in all this shit together."

"The husband's dead," Eddy pointed out.

"Dead as fuck," Rich agreed. "I'm not referring to the husband."

Eddy still didn't get it. Lester Ryman?

"The kid," Rich told him. "The younger son. Turns out the bitch and her kid are a team."

"Jesus H. Christ, Rich, I just finished paying off the mortgage on this place, I'm getting ready to retire, I'm going to be ruined. You should've heard the shithead at the place they took this loan out, I'm going to be spending the rest of my fucking life with this sewage on my hands, I'm fucking *ruined*."

"You're not *ruined*, Eddy, these people have scammed a loan institution, it's an everyday crime you've got nothing to do with, we'll sort it out. I'm making some calls as we speak. Take a deep breath. Go to the gym. Try to relax."

It was not in Eddy Ramsey's character to panic, but throughout the subsequent weeks he became obsessed by this phantom mortgage, by fantasies of being hounded by creditors, and by a more inchoate fear of invisible forces unraveling his careful life. In fact, from the moment he opened the envelope from the mortgage company on January 23rd, something changed in Eddy, a switch had been thrown somewhere, perhaps some incipient unconscious terror that the comfortable orderly way his industry and moderation had produced a world of reliable things—favorite restaurants, nice cars, casual lovers who remained friends even when the romance ended, an attractive home, a pleasurable daily agenda of experiences—had always had built into it an overlooked kink or flaw or something akin to a computer virus that had lain malevolently dormant, waiting for the salient moment of weakness when everything could be devoured and laid waste in a matter of days or weeks.

Eddy concealed this panic from his girlfriend, though he told her about the mortgage, for he did not like to impose his problems and negative mental states on women he dated. Most women found Eddy a relief for precisely that reason. He underplayed his distress to his daughter, who lived in West Adams and visited once a week, because she'd just gone through a nasty divorce and had a three year old to deal with. After his first onrush of paranoia, he even pretended to Rich Escher that he'd settled into a mirthful view of the affair and felt sanguine about its eventual resolution. Eddy was like that. However, the feeling of having been raped, violated, menaced, endangered, whatever, began to destroy his equilibrium. He misplaced things, things like his address book or his fountain pen or his wallet or his house keys, ransacked the house for objects lying in plain sight. He forgot familiar routes while driving place to place, got lost in Coldwater Canyon and Benedict Canyon and Malibu Canyon, on roads he knew intimately well. If he drove to Albertson's specifically for paper towels, he wandered the aisles in an anguished daze, filled a shopping cart and checked out with everything but.

On February 3rd, two investigators from Metzenger Tatum Insurance showed up at Eddy's house to question him about a claim filed by a person named Shreve Kelly. Metzenger Tatum Insurance had examined the deed Mr. Kelly presented with his claim and noted that Eddy's name and signature appeared on the deed as the previous owner of a house at 9300 Tecumseh Drive in Las Vegas. This house had burned to the ground on January 31st in a blaze of suspicious origin. Eddy suggested that the investigators return with a lawyer and a stenographer the following day, which they did, at which time Eddy deposed that he did not know an individual named Shreve Kelly and had no personal knowledge of a corporation called Kubla Khan International and that his signatures on the Tecumseh Drive quit-claim deed and the incorporation papers of Kubla Khan International were not authentic. He provided signature samples. He further deposed that he had signed an earlier quit-claim deed on 9300 Tecumseh Drive which was supposed to have been filed in 1987. He provided a photostat of this quit-claim deed and showed that the signatures on the two deeds clearly didn't match.

Despite what appeared to be an exculpatory disentanglement evolving, Eddy did not feel any better when the investigators left, thanking him for his candor and grimly assuring him that the quicksand he was sinking into had a hard bottom somewhere.

†

In mid-February, Ellen called to say that they were moving soon, that she would pay Wilbur two hundred dollars to help pack the house and drive a U-Haul to a Bekins Storage facility in Los Angeles. Wilbur went over there in his rusted Pinto and met the son, a preppy type, and this Boris Karloff number they talked to in sign language, everybody in the living room assembling storage boxes. The work went on for days. Sometimes a short, perky woman, obviously on speed, showed up to help. Ellen thought that moving was great fun, especially when she came across a thirty-piece set of dishware she said she'd always hated. She hauled the dishes into the living room and skimmed the plates into the field-stone fireplace like Frisbees.

"Your ma certainly is . . . *spirited*," Wilbur observed the day he and Devin drove over to the U-Haul on West Flamingo Road.

"There's nobody like her," Devin said. "She's my guiding light. Mom's the type of person who lights up a room when she walks in. She's always been there for me no matter what. She's a unique individual."

"Looks like rain," Wilbur said to change the subject.

And it did rain, torrentially, the minute they drove the truck off the lot, rained the whole time while they piled the furniture and boxes and every other damned thing in the back, Devin Wilbur and Shreve, stuff was getting soaked but that didn't seem to bother the Smiths, or Slotes, whichever they were, Ellen said she'd thrown her back out, couldn't lift a thing besides the tumbler of scotch she was drinking as she paced all the rooms of the emptying house, it was really kind of incredible how much household fit into the truck and how many breakable objects Ellen had smashed in fits of scary elation, leaving a debris field of glass and porcelain shards like a coral island around the fireplace. Wilbur mentioned his plans to go pheasant hunting when he got back from L.A., this led to a discussion about guns, Devin wanted to know if Wilbur owned any guns, Wilbur said he did own a few, Devin wondered if he could have a look at them before they all took off. Wilbur would be driving the U-Haul to California by himself, the rest of them were going in the Cadillac. However, Ellen refused to let Devin take the Cadillac to Wilbur's place so they ended up driving the packed-up U-Haul all the way out to Break Point Drive, leaving Shreve to gas up the car and fetch whatever mail remained in their various drops.

Wilbur did not own a few guns. Wilbur owned a substantial arsenal of revolvers, pistols, assault rifles, shotguns, sound suppressors, precision scopes, air pistols, carbines, SMGs, tactical illuminators, scattergun upgrades, crates of gun oil, cleaning rods, copper solvents, bore brushes, bookcases crammed with ammunition boxes, he also owned a fairly impressive assortment of knives, crossbows, machetes and swords. Wilbur's living room, in fact, resembled the headquarters of a klavern in Idaho.

"I see you have a rich inner life," Ellen remarked as she looked around.

"It's all legal," Wilbur said, somewhat defensively.

He showed them a 9mm Smith & Wessen and a Beretta .380 and a Royal Hong Kong Police .38 Special and two Jennings Saturday Night Specials, he explained that to buy guns in Las Vegas you gave your driver's license to the gun dealer who ran it through a background check with the Las Vegas Police Department, and if you came up with no convictions, the Las Vegas Police Department issued you a blue card. Wilbur had the Beretta and the Smith & Wessen registered in a concealed weapons program, that meant he could carry them around and not show them.

"See, you go to an administrative school, police school, they give you instances of laws about concealed weapons, they give you shooting practice, when you pass all the tests they give you a permit."

Wilbur showed them the permit, with his picture on it. He showed Devin how to dry-fire the Beretta, the Smith & Wessen.

"We'll buy these from you," Devin said.

"That's peachy, friendo, but I can't sell them. Not with that concealed weapons registration. Felony in Nevada."

"What about something not a felony? Something light-weight, but has real hitting power?" Ellen wanted to know.

"You give me a thousand bucks, I can get you any gun you want."

"What about this thing?" Ellen picked up an Autauga Arms Mark II .32 pistol and pointed it at Wilbur's head.

"You don't want that," Wilbur said without blinking.

"It's a neat gun," said Devin, grabbing it from his mother. He pointed it at her forehead.

"It's a neat gun that only fires hollowpoints," said Wilbur. "You load that thing with ball ammo, you void the warranty."

"Well, I guess we can discuss this later," Ellen said, slapping at the gun in Devin's hand. "It's not polite to point, mister, even with that little thing."

Wilbur went into his bedroom and packed an overnight bag. Ellen slipped a Glock 27 into her pocketbook.

Several hours later they all met up at Bekins Storage off Santa Monica Boulevard. They unloaded the truck and Wilbur dropped it at the U-Haul on Western and then they drove him to this neighborhood in a heavily wooded area, a group of houses with its own gate. The place they were renting was a toney sort of western-flavor house on stilts, with exterior patios looking down at the San Fernando Valley and its swarming human mess. There was a jumpy woman named Fran Something babbling on the phone in the kitchen, she waved at them impatiently as they passed through. They carried a few boxes into a cramped bedroom and Ellen signaled for Shreve to make himself scarce. Shreve signed back that she could kiss his ass and went to his bedroom.

"I like that little Beretta," she told him, handing Wilbur two hundred dollars in twenties. He wanted to count it but decided not to.

"What we want," Devin said, "is one of those Glock 19s and a Glock 9."

"And the Beretta," Ellen said. "In fact, just the Beretta and the Glock 9. Let's not go hog wild."

"You planning to shoot up a bank?" Wilbur asked, he thought comically.

"I wouldn't ask so many questions if I were you," Ellen told him. "You could end up dead."

"We'll call you," Devin said. "We'll call you and wire the money."

"Shreve will drive you to the airport," Ellen added.

Wilbur had been expecting dinner, or at least a sandwich, but getting nothing never really surprised him. He knew she'd palmed the Glock 27 and he'd known all along they wouldn't give him anything extra for the flight back to Vegas, but Ellen Smith or whoever she was had the type of personality Wilbur could never quite stand up to. He was back in Vegas by eleven o'clock, took a cab from McCarran to Fremont Street, hit a few slots, hit a few bars. Then he went home and cleaned an HK .223 he was planning to trade for a new set of radial tires.

✝

Franny Frisani wasn't stupid. She knew she was getting screwed by Teeny Harrington back in New York. Teeny Harrington was undermining her at every turn. Teeny Harrington had hired her as West Coast editor of *Soigné* at a supposed salary of ninety grand,

but she had also started Franny before the lawyers completed the
contract and now three months had passed with no contract and
Franny Frisani had gotten only two checks in all that time,
nowhere in the ballpark of her supposed salary but drawn on
"emergency expenses." Plus several features Franny Frisani had
commissioned had been shot down by Teeny Harrington, shot
down with crude rejection letters and less than the agreed-on kill
fees, which wrecked Franny's relations with the writers, the worst
of it was she'd signed a sublet on a fancy house behind Bel Air, and
had been reduced to listing the place with Home Hunters and
putting up a roommate ad at the Beachwood Café.

Franny had been besotted by Teeny Harrington back in New
York, because of her inexhaustible energy. Teeny could put in
twelve-hour days and never tire. Teeny's enthusiasm for the magazine was boundless, and talk about perfectionism, if she got a
brainstorm she'd rip a finished issue to shreds and make them lay
every page out differently the night before it went to the printer.
When she worked in the New York office, Franny had been a
Teeny loyalist, defending her to an ever-growing number of col-
leagues who thought Teeny's head should be sliced off with a chain
saw and mounted on a pike on the Park Avenue meridian. When
Teeny offered her the L.A. office, Franny thought it was a reward
for those months of fierce partisanship and what she'd imagined to
be a genuine friendship. But now she realized everything everyone
said about Teeny was true. Teeny was a squat, ugly, bitter lesbian,
who pretended to be humble and self-effacing and ingenuous, a
back-stabbing bitch, who sucked up to everybody more important
than she was and betrayed everybody down below.

Franny's hatred of Teeny propelled her to the office off
Franklin Avenue each morning, determined to assert her control
over the advertising reps and the secretaries and the staff writers
passing in and out of town, she would find ways to bring a little
hell into Teeny's day with various acts of subtle sabotage. Teeny
knew how to get Franny, but Franny knew how to get Teeny a lit-

tle bit, too, or so she believed. Teeny would force her out, and soon, but first Franny would poison Teeny's already poisonous reputation among people its poisonousness hadn't yet reached, in this little way she would do the world a good turn and possibly diminish her intake of Valium.

Franny Frisani believed that truth and justice were powerful levers in the workings of the world. Nothing in her experience had ever really fortified this belief, and serial disappointments in this regard had given her the reputation of a chronic whiner. She could have guessed that Teeny Harrington rolled her eyes in comic horror whenever Franny Frisani's name was mentioned. She did not have a clue that even Teeny Harrington's worst enemies did likewise after suffering through one of Franny's epic recitations of her martyrdom at Teeny's hands. Perhaps the important aspect of Franny's rage against Teeny was that it had made her feel desperate, and because she felt desperate, she rented the two extra bedrooms in the house on Olvidados Drive to the first people who answered the ad she put up at the Beachwood Café. These were a mother and son named Ellen and Bruce Walker who had, of all things, a private servant called Russell, who couldn't speak and talked to them in sign language. Ellen's husband was in Paris, working on some global business deal. Bruce was enrolled at UCLA. A colorful bunch.

Ellen was an exuberant old party who paid Franny eight thousand dollars for the six-month rental, with a check signed by someone named Swales. The check cleared with no problem and the Walkers started moving in boxes and filling the house with their aura. Their aura was one of perpetual activity involving phones and computers and trips in and out of the house. Franny was far too fixated on Teeny Harrington's betrayal to notice, at first, that the Walkers never got a phone installed and only used their mobiles. She did notice that they got a locksmith in and put dead bolts on their bedroom doors, that caused her a little tweak of discomfort, and she wondered why they always parked outside the gate of their cul-de-sac, around the corner, when they had a parking space beside the house. But these things registered in Franny's periphery, her vigilance down at the office and the toney dinners and parties her position still entitled her to reduced the menage on Olvidados Drive to a slightly unsettling smudge.

When she did spend an evening at home, Franny attempted to interest Ellen Walker in her travails vis-à-vis Teeny Harrington. Ellen listened for about an hour with an expression of knowing sympathy and then suggested, in a sweet voice, that Franny should hire someone to have Teeny killed. Ellen said she might even know someone willing to do it for less than the price of a used Camry. It was at this point that Franny's mania about Teeny Harrington began to diminish as the cynosure of her attention.

✝

Hardy Harbisher tugged the purple satin ribbon loose from a box containing the tuxedo he would wear that night at the Bar G Chuckwagon, a country and western venue near Zion National Park. The Bar G had never presented a ventriloquist before, and Hardy felt a trifle *agité* and out of practice, but the show business bug had been biting his ass for years, and except for the lunchtime distraction of banging Myra Headley, his recently hired transmission specialist, in a small camper he maintained behind the dealership, the luxury auto game had been sluggish and depressing lately, and when Jimmy Joe Oglethorpe, a regular client and the impressario of Bar G, encouraged Hardy's return to the boards—in the Bar G, they really were just boards, stomped vigorously every night by a succession of shit-kicking jug bands and cowboy guitarists— Hardy promptly excavated his original Joe McCarthy doll from its decorative cedar coffin down in the bomb shelter, drove up to Salt Lake, and had himself fitted for a tux.

The '50s nostalgia thing had not worked out vis-à-vis a plastic children's toy. It ought to have crossed Hardy's mind that small children aren't subject to nostalgia. Hardy lost a bundle on it. Hoping to avoid that taint of yesteryear, his act was now billed as Uncle Hardy and Jolly Jack McCarthy. Hardy had devised a whole new personality for Jolly Jack—still a wiseacre, as any lap dummy had to be, but with more contemporary material and a savvier world view. The old Joe McCarthy dummy had one lazy eye, that had been part of the sight gag, so Hardy made Jolly Jack a cynical, black-humored drug addict who held up liquor stores with comedic incompetence, and had to rouse himself off the nod to deliver his zingers. Since people went to Bar G for live music, Hardy had also written a veritable cycle of rap songs for Jolly Jack to sing between segments of repartee. Hardy considered his best effort a number called "Crack Whore":

> *Some skanky bitch come up to me she want some*
> > *Crack*
> *I tell her bitch you got it spread that cootchie in my*
> > *Sack*
> *She thinks I'm just a dummy but the wood's for*
> > *Real it's*
> *way up the fuck inside her where she can*
> > *Feel it*
> *We suck a lot of freebase and we lose*
> > *Control*
> *She says oh baby do me in the other*
> > *Hole*
> *Bitch I don't want your shit all over my*
> > *Dick*
> *She promises to lick it off I say that's*
> > *Sick*
> *But what can you expect from any stank ass*
> > *Ho*
> *No matter how much dope you give they all want*
> > *Mo*

Hardy was practicing throwing the words to "Crack Whore" so they would seem to emanate from the customer chair in the dealership office as he gingerly lifted the tux from its tissue wrappings when the phone rang. A voice he couldn't quite place greeted him with raucous gusto.

"Hardy honey is that you? It's Evelyn. Evelyn Slote."

"Well hey there Evelyn long time no hear. How the hell are you?"

"Oh Hardy I couldn't be better, and how about you?"

"Well, Evelyn, believe it or not, I've got a show opening tonight."

"You're joking! Why didn't you let us know! You know we'd love to be there!"

"It's just a local little gig. But hey, you never know where things will lead."

"I always said, Hardy, you were the best thing they ever had on *Sea Hunt*."

"Mighty nice of you to say so, Evelyn."

"You stole that episode right out from under Lloyd Bridges, if you ask me."

"Well how the hell is Warren, Evelyn, haven't seen either one of you in a coon's age."

"Hardy, that husband of mine lives life like there's no tomorrow. Right now he's over in Yemen doing some consulting work. He will be so pleased to hear you're performing again."

"It's just the old dummy routine," Hardy said. "Spiced it up a smudge for today's generation."

"Well anyway Hardy I'm calling because Warren thinks we need a new car."

"That Coupe de Ville giving you problems?"

"As far as I'm concerned that car still performs like we got it yesterday, not a scratch on it and you know we treat them like members of the family, but you know Warren, likes to impress the clients, has to have an upgrade every time he turns around. Right now he's got his heart set on a Lincoln Town Car. Doesn't have to be new, just a little more recent. Something in teal."

"I've got a teal LTC right here on the lot, just came in."

"Must be karma, Hardy."

"It's twenty-seven nine, actually," Hardy ribbed.

"Take the de Ville on a trade-in?"

"Surely will, I've had three clients asking for the '93 de Ville since November. Let me look in the book and work out the math a minute."

"Oh, another thing, we're not staying down in Vegas these days, we're over in Bel Air, I hope you can deliver it, because things are just madness here at the moment, I'm not sure we can get out to Cedar City any time before April and Warren really wants the car now."

Hardy completed his calculations on a piece of scratch paper.

"How does fifteen thousand two hundred seventy dollars and fifty cents sound?"

"Wine silky, Kemo Sabe. Warren always says 'getting cars from Hardy's just like stealing them.' "

"It's really just book value, Evelyn, but if you think you're stealing it, I guess we're all happy. I can't deliver that Lincoln myself, I'm gonna have to send Junior. You just give him the check and the keys to the de Ville, he'll have all the paperwork with him. Now, what day were you thinking?"

"Well like I say, Warren wants it right away. He's back from the Middle East on Saturday, and I would love if it was sitting there waiting for him."

"That's cutting it mighty fine, but sure, Evelyn, we've always been grateful for your patronage, if I can get the lead out of Junior's ass, I can have it over there on Thursday. Got a number we can reach you?"

"I better give you my cell, Hardy, these days I'm out running around so much we could miss each other. Junior's your oldest, isn't he?"

"Oldest pain in the ass, but he's the middle child, you know what they say."

"Go on, I bet he's a charmer just like his dad, Hardy."

"You want to cover that bet with ten grand," Hardy said, "I'll send him over there with an '83 Toyota instead of the Town Car."

†

"Just *calm down*, honey, Darla's here, Darla's going to take care of everything."

Darla Conway smoothed Franny's thin glossy hair and hugged her bony shoulders closer on the Naugahyde love seat in the "conversation area" outside the kitchen. This was an outdoor area, a tad nippy in February, made of rugged pine planks painted russet with gaps between them disclosing vertiginous peeks of a fifty-foot drop, spider plants and aloes in jute holders dangling from overhead beams, Franny's Huffy bike jammed like a reproach in one messy corner along with some sacks of planting soil and long-abandoned gardening tools.

Fran wore a thin black H&M turtleneck and Yamomoto beige slacks, an ensemble that heightened her gawkiness. To Darla's eye, Franny's face would have been perfect for its type, diluted Italian, if the little red bulb at the end of her nose were lopped off by the very expensive and competent surgeon who'd executed Darla's breast reduction. A little quality time at the gym wouldn't hurt, either. But still. That wounded bird thing turned Darla on every time.

Darla looked invincibly tough in a leather biker jacket and tight black leather pants. Her wild streaming black hair, her fiercely molded, high-cheeked, haughtily malign features, the many bits of metal skewering her tongue, eyelashes, earlobes and nostrils, and the enormous black Doberman stretched at her feet, all promised severe repercussions to anyone who fucked with her little Franny.

"But these people are so *awful*," Franny wailed, her skinny frame shuddering adorably. "What am I going to *do?*"

Darla urged another stoneware mug of chamomile tea on her distraught friend.

"Well for starters, honeybunch, me and Butch are moving in with you. We're not leaving you alone with questionable characters. Are we, Butch."

The dog lifted its large head to drool unpleasantly on Franny's foot.

"Oh Darla, I hate to disrupt your life that way."

More than I can possibly tell you, thought Franny. Darla Conway had been after Franny's culo ever since Fran's arrival in Los Angeles. They had met at a New Line Oscar party. Now, Franny realized, the thing she dreaded was sure to happen. But she dreaded her tenants even more.

"And *I* hate to see *you* terrorized by a bunch of weirdos," Darla asseverated violently. Franny pictured herself being penetrated, on her black Pratesi sheets with the red stitched borders, by Darla's balled fist. She wiped the image away fast. "I think you need to start eviction proceedings pronto, I've got an attorney if you haven't."

"That's the *thing*, they paid in *advance*, and if that scurrilous unethical bitch Teeny Harrington wasn't holding up my salary I could give them a refund, but it's all *spent*, Darla, they've got my *signed receipt*, I have *car payments*."

"Let's calm down," Darla reiterated with a soothing lilt, "let's go through this methodically. They lock their doors. They've got strange people coming in and out. They're keeping secrets. Something in the state of Denmark isn't kosher, I'll bet you anything the first whiff of legal activity, they'll be out of here and into the ozone. No deposit no return."

"Oh, and I found this." Franny leapt free of Darla's embrace and padded barefoot into the kitchen, tore open a drawer, fished out something black with jumbled wires snaking from it.

"This was attached to my telephone," Franny shrilled, waving the $12.50 wiretap unit before Darla's unfazed eyes. Darla raised herself languidly from the love seat and wrestled the thing from Franny's grip. She flung it over the railing, into the canyon.

"Obviously we are dealing with scum. Electronic eavesdropping, a class B felony. I know a very astute P.I.," Darla said. "Mickey Landry. He used to work for the studio." Darla worked at Universal, in finance. "At least we can check their car out."

†

Junior Harbisher delivered the Lincoln Town Car, not to the house on Olvidados Drive, which Evangeline explained was far too complicated and confusing to find among the twisting roads and cul-de-sacs of Bel Air, but to the Beverly Wilshire Hotel at the corner of Rodeo Drive and Wilshire, familiar to them from the movie *Pretty Woman,* where Junior and his girlfriend, Alice, were obliged to wait in the intimidatingly deluxe Lobby Lounge for nearly an hour before Evangeline and Devin put in an appearance.

Junior and Alice looked and felt somewhat out of place in the Lobby Lounge of the Beverly Wilshire Hotel. They had the sour appearance of people who had gone to seed in the desert, wardrobe first. Alice was a small, rabbit-faced, insistently self-effacing woman who was not fat but somehow conveyed flabbiness and insecurity in every movement and expression. She had a habit of twittering and fluttering and giggling nervously when any other human being paid attention to her. Junior was tall and thick and moon-faced, stolid as settled lard and laconic as a clamshell, and his mind moved with the sluggishness of some torpid sea-bottom scavenging fish that survived on very little oxygen. Together they exuded a vaguely depressing mixture of unreasonable hopes and chronic disappointments, of incompetence in the smallest things, of festering resentments poorly disguised as good will and guilelessness. They wore all these characteristics like overbright Kmart clothing: anyone who looked at them closely, even from across a room, perceived these dismal qualities without ever exchanging a word with them.

They were both, too, of a quickly triggered paranoid inclination, and therefore became obsessively aware that someone was, in fact, looking at them closely from across the room, a man in his late fifties with an austere set of square, morbid features. He stood for a long time in the entrance of the outer lobby, immobile, staring into the lounge, directly at them. This man did not "project" anything. Nothing in his stance or expression seemed inflected with an effort to suggest to anyone an excuse or reason for his standing there, he did not give the impression of waiting for someone, of intending to enter the lounge, or to eventually walk across the lobby, or to leave the hotel.

The Lobby Lounge had an *intime* decor of tightly clustered padded furniture and bedazzling floral arrangements and tall, heavy, roped-open curtains, carpets that absorbed any sound of movement, lacquered tables, candelabralike sconces, mahogany paneling, and a very low frequency of ambient noise. It was not the sort of room where you expected to be stared at for a long time by a stranger standing in the entrance. Junior and Alice each drank two chocolate martinis, becoming more uncomfortable with every sip, before the man went away. Unnervingly, he vanished at precisely the moment they both turned to look at a couple getting up from dinner.

Five minutes later Evangeline and Devin Slote issued into the elegant room, came directly at them in a froth of high spirits, and planted themselves in armchairs flanking the small leather sofa where Junior and Alice were ensconced. Evangeline and Devin Slote did not look out of place in the Lobby Lounge. They wore expensive, well-fitted clothes and furthermore carried themselves as if they owned controlling shares in the Lobby Lounge. They did not wait for the server to notice them. Devin hopped up from his chair a second after sitting down, walked right up to the guy and told him to bring two double J&Bs on the rocks "and two more of what our guests are drinking."

Evangeline trained her rapt attention on Junior. She began by quizzing him about his life history, his schooling, his relationship with his dad, whom of course she knew well, had known for years and years, it was like pulling teeth but she did extract, after much dulcet pulling and tugging, a bit of narrative from Junior, a ruminative admission that he had plangent and perpetually frustrated dreams of pulling up stakes someday and getting out of Cedar City, moving to a real city with interesting people in it, Junior thought it would be nice, he said, "to have some real cultural experiences and not just the day to day grind," Evangeline knew just how he felt, she said, she'd been trapped once upon a time more years ago than she could count in a bohunk town offering no stimulating options, she encouraged, she flattered, she told Junior he was lucky he was still young and had all the possibilities of life ahead of him, "but of course you've got to make the jump," she scolded in a motherly way, meanwhile Devin zeroed in on Alice, telling her how nice she looked, what a delightful laugh she had, what a funny way she had of phrasing things, drawing her out, asking about her roots, her family, her wishes and ambitions, which were as inchoate and contradictory and hopeless as Junior's, the Slotes insisted on treating them to dinner right there in the Lobby Lounge, sushi, and of course a bottle of saki, Alice didn't know how to use chopsticks, and Devin very patiently taught her, Alice fluttered and cooed and commenced squeezing Devin's arm or Devin's hand or Devin's thigh to let him know how much she liked him, before the evening was through Junior and Alice had come to think of the Slotes as the most wonderful people they had ever met, "magical," in fact, when the time came to do the paperwork on the car they whooped conspiratorially when Evangeline said she was too drunk to fill it out properly, she'd have to let Devin do it, Devin said he was so drunk he had to look at his driver's license to remember his address, finally he wrote a check on Varlene's bank account and signed the dinner bill and they all went outside while valet parking fetched the Coupe de Ville.

The Slotes wanted to see Junior and Alice again, really soon. Wanted to fly them down to Cancun for a real blow-out weekend of whoopie.

"This has been so much fun," Evangeline told them. "You two are adorable. We love you guys! And for heaven's sake, drive safely!"

"Yee Christ," Devin said when they had fetched Shreve from his perch in the lobby and were driving east on Santa Monica Boulevard in the new Town Car. "I thought she was going to fellate me right there."

"So was I, I was so amazed at how patient you were. Well, it's Hardy's son and she might as well be his daughter-in-law, it doesn't hurt to be gracious. He gave us a good deal on the car."

"The guy's okay, but her, God, little miss grab-ass."

"Where we going?" Shreve wanted to know.

"Shorty's," said Evangeline brusquely. "Like I told you three hours ago." She picked one of Alice's hairs off Devin's blazer. "What you really have to realize, Devin, is that they're the same person. Different confetti in their brains but the core stuff is the same. She's desperate for attention because he never gives her any, he comes off sweet because she absorbs all his bitterness and that comes out as her inferiority complex. He's choleric, she's melancholic. But both passive, inactive, and you motivate them with the same thing."

"What's that."

"Ridiculous amounts of praise and flattery, just like you were doing. They can't get it anywhere else, before you know it they'd rob a bank for you."

"See, this is what kills me about you. I know you're right, what you just said is brilliant, but the fact is, *we don't need them for anything.*"

"This is why I'm your mother, because this is what kills *me* about *you.* We don't need them for anything *now,* but you never know when we might need them for *something.* Learn to think long-term."

Devin dropped it and leered out the window. Shreve took LaBrea up to Franklin, went east on Franklin to Beachwood.

Shorty Christian lived in a decrepit rented house on lower Beachwood. He answered the door in piss-spotted underpants, his black eyes glassy, his skinny, acne-spotted body an ad for smack.

"Hong Kong Triad," Shorty whispered as he let them in. "What's shakin', Big Momma?"

Shorty Christian bore an uncanny resemblance to the movie star Johnny Depp, at least in the immediate aftermaths of his numerous spells in rehab, of which this was not one. Myriad defects in his wiring had prevented his extraordinary looks from ever doing him any real good. He had been used as a sex toy by his father, a highly decorated veteran of the Vietnam Conflict, between ages six and thirteen, when he was put into foster care, and as a punching bag by his mother, a follower of the evangelist Pat Robertson, from the time he was an infant until a few weeks before he was put into foster care, when his father used his mother's head to test fire a recently acquired Wilson Tactical Carbine UT-15. His first foster parents were Fundamentalist Baptists who lived in Los Feliz and beat him regularly with a braided whip they used for other things among themselves, sodomized him on a nightly basis with phallus-shaped vegetables and, on special occasions, an aluminum baseball bat. When the fun went out of that, they reported him as incorrigible, possibly suffering from Fetal Alcohol Syndrome that they hadn't been told about and couldn't be responsible for. A third placement, with a family of devout Catholics in Glendale, had pretty much finished off any residual possibility of Shorty becoming a productive member of society, or indeed any kind of member of society. By some miracle of street smarts and chance, he had only been incarcerated once, on a minor assault charge. In what for him were normal times he made an adequate living as a crank dealer on Hollywood Boulevard, but there were abnormal times in Shorty's life when, as he would put it afterwards, "shit got out of hand."

The living room of Shorty's one-bedroom house had blue Christmas lights stapled all over the walls, and furniture acquired from dump sites. Every level surface was strewn with melted candlewax, little metal pastille boxes full of dope roaches and varicolored pills, cigarette butts, plates caked with junk food residue, torn-up magazines, and other items of an arcane and indecipherable nature. The floor, which was not a level surface, had current debris organized into pushed-together piles. It was not unusual, when sitting in Shorty's living room, for opposums and other wildlife to venture into the place through holes in the walls.

The Slote party disported themselves among the less grotty pieces of furniture while Shorty rummaged frantically through garbage for some unidentified object. He gave up the search and sank onto a decomposing couch, scratching his balls and other parts of himself ceaselessly.

"I wish I had something to offer you," Shorty told them. "I know there was some grapefruit juice. Motherfuckers must of finished it all."

A long silence settled in. Shorty's penis dangled out the side of his underpants, large and useless, with a much-picked scab near the glans. He moved his head around in a disturbing way, as if discovering the trail of Christmas lights along the walls for the first time.

"Oh, wow," he said finally.

"I was thinking," Evangeline said, "you could come up to our house for a few days. Get away from all this racket and noise. We sure could use a hand with things."

The house was deadly still except for the blinking Christmas lights, but Shorty Christian's head, Evelyn knew, had its own racket and noise going on, between fixes of mineral silence.

"I'll get you some nice clothes and get you cleaned up," Evelyn said. "And buy you some decent dope and get some nourishing food in your stomach."

Shorty's chin sank to his chest. Either he was thinking about it or had forgotten they were there.

Devin felt mixed emotions about Shorty Christian. Evelyn liked to sleep with Shorty naked beside her, sometimes between herself and Devin when she and Devin shared a bed. She liked to hold and pet him like a child. It wasn't even all that much of a sexual thing because Shorty was light years from ever getting an erection and even further away from wanting one. It was something Devin didn't understand. Shorty's hands crawled all over himself in his sleep, scratching, like blinded birds stumbling under the sheets. Evelyn soothed him, whispered endearments, stroked his hair, even wiped the snot from his nose with her fingers and ate it. Over the years, Evelyn had at various times concocted a story that she'd had another child by Warren after Devin, a baby she'd had to give up for adoption in Mexico on Warren's insistence. Devin had never credited this story, Evelyn had dredged it up at parole hearings for extra pathos during her Club Fed period, and had dropped it into various scams as an item of interest, when she was Telling Her Story to soften up a mark Evelyn added and subtracted children arbitrarily, but Devin thought there were moments when Evelyn believed in this third son. Not just the way she believed her other lies, which screwed up the grift almost as often as it made it sing. Maybe she'd had an abortion somewhere along the line when she was still doing it with Warren and repined for this missing Slote. She'd nipped three of their own little monsters in the bud, brother-sons and sister-daughters Devin met in freakish dreams, before going through the Change. Devin didn't think Shorty Christian represented the lost imaginary child for her, but some areas of Evelyn's mind remained obscure to him, even after all these years.

Tears drooled down Shorty's face. Evelyn held him, Evelyn rocked him, Shorty blubbered and picked at his face with a black fingernail. Devin looked at Shreve, almost wishing he were Shreve. Shreve pretended he was somewhere else. Shreve stared into a terrarium where the skeletons of several small lizards Shorty had forgotten to feed lay on a bed of pebbles.

†

Throughout that season of troubled sleep, when dogs barking in the hills or a car alarm blasting unaccountably at three a.m. caused Eddy to wake with a jolt and a cold creeping fear ran from his scalp to his feet, he would force himself to climb out of bed and switch on the patio lights and open the sliding glass doors to the garden, step onto the redwood deck, and breathe in the eucalyptus-heavy air that held whatever traces of gardens and gasses were carried on the night winds, the dank wet smells of foraging animals and the subtler, almost metallic traces of sedimenting dry ravels, rill networks, the effluvia of insentient life as it cycled into growth and compost. He lived in an area of leapfrogging fires and seasonal mudslides where solid-seeming things were recognized as temporary, and rational structures participated in a mythos of miracle and magical thinking. Houses were "spared" as if by divine intervention, the survival of anything was declared "ironic" or "uplifting." The simplest acts of life acquired a tinge of hubristic defiance, something that spoke of nobility and madness in the same vocabulary.

What he saw and heard from his redwood deck, what the darkness brought to his senses, the cool boards beneath his bare feet, brought Eddy a semblance of equilibrium, it slowed to a manageable throbbing an otherwise frantic restiveness. For he had been taking inventory since the trouble started, not merely from fear of financial ruin, but because the trouble had awakened doubts concerning things less easily enumerated than material assets and their possible loss.

He had tried to live within the boundaries of what people generally understood as decency, to be what was generally considered "a good person." Yet since the problems began Eddy's sanguinity on this point had unraveled a bit more with every passing day. He didn't know why this unwanted bolt of introspection should hit him at the very time when he was the victim of someone else's malignity. His mind told him that he had been good, and generous, and kind, undeserving of bad trouble and ill will. But it also told him that his goodness consisted less in what he had actually done in his life than what he hadn't done: he hadn't stolen, he'd never killed anybody, and he'd tried to be as harmless as possible. He'd been generous to people from whom this generosity invariably elicited some reciprocal benefit. He'd been kind because it kept him from collecting enemies. All his virtues had been exercised within the sphere of Eddy's personal world, where getting and spending and acquiring for Eddy's personal comfort and pleasure were the prevailing imperatives. He had never sacrificed more than an hour of his time to the betterment of anyone he didn't know. Spiritually speaking, he had been trapped in Eddyworld, mistaking it for the cosmos.

Eddy had, all his life, felt strong impulses to do positive, helpful things in the world. He had daydreamed of visiting hospital wards for incurables, volunteering in refugee camps, flying medical supplies into war-ravaged hellholes. These ennobling fantasies always surged within him for a day or two, and only gradually withered away, refugee by refugee, so to speak, manifesting nothing more than a modest check to Greenpeace or Doctors Without Borders or Planned Parenthood, and the worst of it was when he caught himself in an access of self-congratulation for merely having had the wish to do something, or for writing the check.

These thoughts roiled in Eddy's mind whenever the immediate problem gave him surcease. Without meaning to, he thought, I have lived like a shit. I can change. I can find my will and change. He would retire soon. The business had brought enough money for Eddy to go anywhere that his intelligence and dedication would be useful.

However, the immediate problem worsened soon after Rich Escher assured him that it would quickly go away. Evangeline Slote began phoning him. She said that she and Warren were in Los Angeles and needed desperately to see him. He told her he did not consider that a good idea, that he'd started getting billed by the mortgage company and knew what she was up to. She implored him not to stir up trouble. She used the word "implore." It crossed Eddy's mind that he had always been skeptical about Evangeline

Slote because of her grandiose vocabulary. She never just worried, she anguished. Her troubles were never just witless fuckups but global tragedies. He remembered getting a letter from her once in which she referred to her little discomforts in Frontera as "a Holocaust."

She offered to give him the mortgage installments on a monthly basis if he would simply agree to write the checks on his own bank account. She said she could explain everything. That they had been forced to take the mortgage out because of bad trouble from Warren's family.

"Which is all this is, really," she yammered. "It's a persecution, never in this country, in the whole history of this country, has a private citizen like Warren who served in the military and done nothing but good all his life been put through this kind of injustice by his own family, we didn't know what else to do in the face of this witch hunt, Eddy, we were desperate. Desperate. The last thing on earth was any thought of harming you, our dear friend. You have to believe me. Believe us."

Eddy told her that he considered her clinically insane. He said that even if he were inclined to help her avoid a fraud prosecution, which he wasn't, it was too late anyway because he'd already talked to the mortgage company.

"You could talk to them again," Evangeline pleaded. "Tell them you made a mistake, you have all these different businesses with Warren and you got confused about some paperwork."

Eddy hung up on her. The calls kept coming, night and day. Usually Eddy let the machine pick up, but often the sound of her voice threw him into a rage and he had to scream at her.

"We're begging you, as a friend and as a lawyer with a sense of justice," she whined in her final call. "Even if you hate me, do this for Warren, Eddy, think of all he's done for you."

"Warren's dead, Evelyn, what kind of an idiot do you imagine me to be? You think you can grift a fucking lawyer, and I'm not going to find out what's behind it?" As Eddy said this it crossed his mind that Evelyn had grifted whole legions of lawyers who'd never figured out what hit them, and feared he sounded ridiculous.

"Well you must be talking to some pretty strange people if they told you Warren's dead, Eddy. Warren left here five minutes ago to buy a roll of toilet paper."

"I talked to Warren's daughter, you insidious bitch, and she's nowhere near as strange as you are. So when Warren gets back from the astral plane, tell him there isn't enough toilet paper in the world to clean up the shit that you and sonny boy are in."

As Eddy lowered the phone the blast of Evelyn's voice seemed to rattle the walls around him like a Magnitude 7 quake. She was screaming the name Ritchie.

✝

When Mickey Landry, Darla's friend, first phoned Harbisher Luxury Vehicles in Cedar City, Hardy said that he didn't recall any clients named Ellen and Bruce Walker, though the vehicle in question, which Mickey described in close detail, sounded like a Coupe de Ville he had sold several years ago to a Warren and Evangeline Slote, coincidentally enough Hardy had just negotiated repurchase of the vehicle in trade-in for a Lincoln Town Car. As far as Hardy knew, Warren and Evangeline lived in Las Vegas but traveled a lot and were currently staying at an address in Bel Air. He didn't know the exact address because the primary residence listed on the paperwork was in Las Vegas, and the car had not been delivered to their temporary residence in Bel Air, but rather to a nearby hotel. Funnily enough, this delivery had occurred the very evening before Mickey Landry's call.

Mickey Landry did some further digging. He learned that Warren Slote was a hotel developer who had died four years earlier in San Diego. On the Monday following Mickey's initial call to Hardy, one of the rare occasions when the Slote menagerie was entirely absent from the house on Olvidados Drive, Mickey Landry and Franny Frisani discovered a storage box in Franny's garage containing many crumpled clasp-type envelopes stuffed with documents, bills and receipts and personal papers and so forth, many of which bore the names Evangeline Slote, Warren Slote, the names of a lot of other people as well, and Franny wondered aloud if these people in her house, these Walker people, had done away with these other people, these Slotes and these other people, and taken over their identities.

Mickey then placed another call to Hardy Harbisher and ascertained that the people who had bought the Coupe de Ville and arranged the trade-in over the telephone were, in fact, the same people, or at least the woman was, Hardy knew her voice, Hardy didn't know however that Warren Slote was dead, and was rather shaken to learn that Warren had been deceased for four years.

Hardy did not, on the strength of this news, automatically assume that the check for $15,270.50 received from Evangeline Slote but drawn on the account of Varlene Swales, deposited the previous Friday with the week's other payments, would be returned in Wednesday's mail marked insufficient funds, with notice of a $30 fine attached, though that turned out to be how it played. The Slotes had always been plenty loaded, and there was no reason to assume that Warren being dead made any difference in that regard. In fact, the only conclusion Hardy drew from his conversation with Mickey Landry was that Evangeline Slote was even crazier than Hardy had always assumed she was. Awesome set of jugs, though.

✝

Varlene had found a dealer for pharmaceutical amphetamine, something she had promised herself to do after going back into therapy. Street crank made her impossibly grouchy at times, wreaked havoc on her digestive enzymes, and sometimes she became almost comatose in her zeal to pay attention to everything in her environment: hypnotized by her own state of high alert. The

new speed was a clinical synthetic with a downer cycled into it to
sand off the jagged edges. One hit in the a.m. gave her all the gusto
she needed until after lunch, and she could, on this new stuff, actually eat lunch, which kept the metabolic mood swings at bay.
Typically she would order a protein-rich menu from a Japanese
restaurant, emphasis on salmon and tuna, but not forgetting her
vegetables, scrumptious etamame and zucchini tempura and the
delicious vinegared cucumber that came in sunomuno. These, she
told herself, would keep her from getting cancer from the three
packs of Parliaments she was smoking every day. You just couldn't
do speed without smoking all the time.

She was en route to meet the dealer at the Pizza Hut in the
lobby plaza of the Riviera when she stopped to use the ATM at her
bank branch on West Flamingo. She slipped the magnetic card
between the warm gray metal lips of the ATM console, felt the
gratifying tug of its ingestive mechanism, entered her PIN, and
applied a firm fingertip to the $200 withdrawal band on the touch-
sensitive screen. PLEASE WAIT WHILE I WORK ON YOUR
REQUEST, said the screen. Who is this "I," Varlene silently asked
the empty air, as she did every time. She turned to watch traffic
through the 24 Hour Banking Center windows as she waited. She
did not hear the customary bill-flipping sound that prefaced the
disgorgement of cash. She looked at the screen. I'M SORRY, "I"
apologized, BUT THERE IS A PROBLEM WITH YOUR
REQUEST. Varlene was too high to feel annoyed, and waited to
snap her card free of the slot and give it another whirl. The card did
not come out. The machine had eaten her card.

She walked inside to customer service. Breathlessly she
explained her problem to the first available bank officer. A Mrs.
Brathwaithe, according to her metal name tag. Mrs. Brathwaithe
tapped some codes into a computer keyboard, scanned whatever
came up on the screen for a long time, continued tapping,
scratched her nose, telephoned an extension within the branch,
carried on a coded-sounding colloquy with some invisible author-

ity, hung up, and asked Varlene if she would mind speaking to a Mr. James, in an office cubicle behind the customer service area.

Mr. James was a young and extremely comely African-American in what Varlene would have sworn was a Helmut Lang suit, and someone she would not have minded running into under other circumstances. Even in these circumstances her speed high made the encounter seem, albeit momentarily, fraught with erotic tension. He was sorry to have to tell her that a large deposit that recently had been cleared through her checking account was now being tracked by the Frauds Units of three law enforcement agencies, and consequent to certain Nevada and Federal banking statutes which Mr. James cited in a truly regretful way, Varlene's account at the Wells Fargo Bank had been frozen and its funds impounded "until this matter can be cleared up."

Without the amphetamine, Varlene would probably have been moved to apologize, to explain to Mr. James that as the bill-paying accountant of a local family she often received checks for deposit, the source and legitimacy of which she had no means of verifying, would have tried to clear herself in his eyes before leaving the bank. In the bright world of the drug, however, no such masochistic self-justification seemed at all necessary. Varlene had already left the parking lot before she realized that she now could not meet the dealer at the Pizza Hut, did not have the cash for even a few pills, and would probably start crashing by eight o'clock that evening.

†

Make it nothing, she liked to say.

Make it into nothing and it all goes away.

They brought Shorty along for the ride. Me. Take the tit, Shorty. I have heard it all my life. Sure. I knew as it was going down what the deal was. Set up a witness if you can't do it in the dark. I read the papers and I am cooperating with everything. That's what they were gonna do with Wilbur, am I right or am I wrong. Set him up.

Guy had a green Jaguar maybe ten years old sitting in the driveway. Opens the door in his pajamas. Ellen pushes right in, the guy's babbling, what the fuck do you think you're doing here, Bruce takes the Glock out of a Von's shopping bag and puts one in the guy's ear. Brain splatter on the woodwork like somebody sneezed. Find his keys, take him out to his vehicle, stuff him in the trunk.

Drove out to LAX with Ellen behind us in the Lincoln. 747s sliding in trailing smoke and white lights. Orange dawn like the end of the world. Curtain coming down.

I'm nodding through the whole thing. Yes I helped I said so a million times. If I didn't help you might of found my remains if you got lucky.

Heavy. That's why it's called dead weight. Dropped him in a Dumpster back of a KFC. Bare foot sticking up through boxes of old chicken. Bruce thought it was a trip to put the Jag in Long Term Parking.

When I was in Foster Care they fucked me a lot, you know? And that was after all the shit with my real mom and dad, supposedly for my protection, they give me to the first people who apply. I could tell you worse. I could tell you the fucking was the easy part. Think about it. So you could say I have a little bit different view of shit than your average joe. This Ellen and Bruce scene wiped past me in twenty seconds if you put it in junk time.

They solved the problem. Make it nothing. So. Later. Fat girl name of April de Beckwith and this older woman Carla show up with Wilbur in the mobile home, RV, whatever, fiberglass thing Ellen says is crashproof, and Wilbur went back to Vegas. Then they need everything out of the house before the woman who lives there comes back. Ellen, see, she didn't like dogs. I think the only way you could ever get her to crack is put her in a room with a dog because I don't know anything else she's afraid of. That Fran had a dog for protection. My memory is vague about the girlfriend but the dog, that dog could tell you the whole story about the vibes in that house, because he fucking *commanded* the place. Interview the dog, man.

That was a big motherfucking thing to be tooling around West Hollywood or wherever. Like a fucking railroad train. I don't remember when those women split. I know we left them at the Greyhouse Bus in Pershing Square. Ellen and Bruce kept the Lincoln in some garage. This could be days, it could be weeks, I can narrow it down. I can narrow it down. It was after Kennedy got assassinated. Joke. Okay. They got freaked when the mute took off. I can narrow it down. We went to the pancake house. LaBrea and Sunset, around there. I-Hop. The mute went to the bathroom and never came back. You know, she's in the banquette on her fat ass chewing her pancakes, and then she realizes. Ellen went through a lot of changes. Scary isn't the word I'm looking for. She wanted to track him down and cancel Christmas on him. You try finding one little motherfucking deafmute when you're driving something the size of an artillery tank in the Glitter Gulch area, good luck. Vaya con fucking Dios.

I think we went to San Diego. Someplace with Navy boats. They ditched that tank in Hawthorne somewhere. We took the town car.

I know she sent April de Beckwith a bunch of money Western Union, and it was about buying guns with Wilbur.

Poor fuckin Ed Ramsey never made the papers. Let's face it he wasn't Paula Abdul.

I can testify. You clean me up, all twelve jurors will want to fuck me. Alternates, the judge, everybody. Song of experience. I'm not wanted for anything. They will say a known felon but that was four months in County and I was a juvenile. They seal the records.

Yes I did go to Vegas. Big thrill. April de Beckwith's apartment. Camino Al Norte I think. Looked like public housing and it wasn't, that's North Vegas as far as I'm concerned. Why do I remember why do you think I remember de Beckwith was the name of the people they put me with in Los Feliz. April no kin as they say in the trades, and believe me I asked. You say she's from Tonopah and works in a title office fine. God said it I believe it that settles it.

One two in the morning I'm pretty sure. Ellen was pissed off. Bruce kept pounding the walls. Shreve's gonna spill. I remember him saying it over and over.

April wanted them gone. She was fucking some Marine. Might have been her husband, fat girl like that. Screaming at Wilbur on the phone will you get the goddam merch over here and get this over with. It took him like an hour. The Marine was like, Get these fucking assholes out of here. Wilbur showed up with two guns. A long gun and another Glock. The Glock had a thing on it to attach an extra round. Ellen wanted him to look for real estate houses that were boarded up on public auction and she asked him how to make a silencer. I remember thinking she could just buy one if she wasn't so cheap. Wilbur said to just take a potato and make a hole in one end.

I bailed in Tampa. I don't know anybody named Pedro Delgado. I left the motel when they were fucking and just kept going. I am a material witness and I have immunity. You say he's from Belle Glade, all I hear is AIDS and mosquitos. I heard the name Wanda Claymore several times but I never knew the lady. Of course I know they're going to say I shot Edward Ramsey I may look like a fool to you but I guess they never put you in Foster Care. I'm dead but I'm not stupid.

"*Sur l'onde calme et noir où dorment les étoiles,*" Baby read, voice raspy. "*La blanche Ophélia flotte comme un grand lys . . .* it reminds me of the Aimé Césaire line we liked so much, how does it go, *maisons ont peur du ciel truffé de feu*, they sky *truffled* with fire."

New York rarely had real winter any more, but the frequent

swings between twenty and eighty degrees, though Baby only absorbed them when she opened her bedroom windows for air, had given her a bug, a prick of the sniffles, putting everyone, whether they knew it or not, on alert. *She's so strong, she's so amazing, she'll live forever,* they assured one another, and yet they were all keenly tuned to the dimmest signals of distress, traded anecdotal evidence that Baby's memory had either slipped a bit or sharpened up again, they argued about the condition of her lungs, her liver, her kidneys, her eyes, it was just plain unavoidable, and you had to go on in the usual way, pretend that "what will be will be" was somehow a goad to stay cheerful and untroubled about the future. Almost everyone on staff had a "plan," a slew of "plans," contingent on when and how the inevitable occurred: In six months? Six years? Slow? Fast? But you couldn't plan what your feelings would be when something you didn't control suddenly changed your life. Asra was especially sensitive to Baby's sporadic downturns, since he lived in the house and had a twenty-four-hour handle on the fluctuations of her health.

"In my country," Asra said, "we have streets named after Arthur. And plaques, like on embassies." He waved at the wall, the invisible limestone consulates along their block of 65th Street.

He had told her that, and she had heard it many times, it was funny how people repeated certain facts to one another, and with very old people, like Baby, such reiterations might set off a whole chain of familiar reflections, and it all seemed less about facts and associations than about something more elusive, some delicately unarticulated need.

Vic walked in off the elevator with Celestine. His lips arranged themselves in a cruel smile at the sight of Baby sitting there in her quilted housecoat, spoiling Asra as Vic told the others, books spread open on the table. Vic had dark Eastern European looks the women in the house found irresistible. All Asra saw were shifty suspicious eyes, one unbroken eyebrow that looked like a handlebar mustache in the wrong location, and a sinuous, mean mouth. Vic had a pair of fancy brass doorknobs in his hands. Vic was a slob, Asra thought, yet he had these long, delicate pianist's hands, you couldn't help notice them. Black hairs on the backs of his fingers. Asra hoped Vic had repulsive hair all over his back too. Vic held the doorknobs out for Baby's approval, smugly proud of his taste. He did have good taste, but Asra chalked that up to being European, it was nothing Vic had to work at. Celestine opened the refrigerator, pulled things out to fix lunch.

"Excellent," Baby said, gripping and turning one of the fixtures as Vic held it for her. "Asra, wouldn't these look spiffy in 1B?"

Asra eyeballed them dismissively. He wished she would not use words like spiffy, words that were their words, in front of Vic.

"Oh, yes. They're very beautiful."

The sarcastic note floated over Baby's giddy tangerine coif, such a thin kleenex of asperity that Vic himself wasn't positive that he was being ridiculed. Asra felt Celestine behind him. She had paused holding a bunch of celery, about to shut the fridge. The celery had the rich green of chemical treatment. It was a brand Norma had been asked not to buy. Celestine's face was blank but her eyes pierced straight through Asra's skull. She saw everything, she knew everything. Asra felt all sorts of things about Celestine. She moved with unnerving poise. She did everything with a self-contained economy and grace that intimidated him. She outclassed him. She even outclassed Baby. Asra resented her for it, feared and desired her.

"And I think I want my mother's Gauguin piece over the mantelpiece in there," Baby instructed Vic, who twirled the stems of the doorknobs between the fingers of one hand. "The one in Mr. Farmhole's room. We can switch that with the Weegee photo in the hall. I'd just as soon leave that space on the wall empty, it gets covered up when we fill those vases anyway."

Vic knew every bolt and screw and ottoman and framed postcard on the premises, and Baby found him invaluable. She had also had a major crush on him for seven years, Vic played on that, he played on his looks with everybody. Asra detested him at times.

Vic ridiculed Haile Selassie at every opportunity. Vic said they should all be shot, all the emperors and dictators, Haile Selassie according to Vic was nothing better than Ceausescu in blackface, the only hope was to shoot them all, all the corporation heads and presidents and politicians. Just take them out to the courtyards of their Regal Palaces and shoot them, Vic said. Shoot their wives and their children and everyone related to them also, so the fungus doesn't grow again. If Baby was present, Vic only said to shoot Henry Kissinger, which of course she agreed with, *but only after they try him for war crimes,* Baby said. *Shoot him, or hang him, I don't care which, but first I want to see that genocidal troglodyte convicted on Court TV.* Baby only got that vehement when Henry Kissinger came up, Vic liked to get her going on it. Vic had told Carmen he thought Asra was a fag, "a fag who doesn't know he's a fag," Carmen repeated it to Reece and Fay, Reece and Fay told Cora. Cora had the flu. That was why Celestine was making lunch.

Vic took the doorknobs down the hall to his workshop. Celestine chopped celery on the cooking island. Baby hunched around to see her. She took off her glasses and wiped them on her sleeve.

"*Flotte trés lentement, couchée en ses longs voiles,*" she resumed, "*On attend dans les bois lointains des hallalis.*"

The ringing of metal pounding metal carried from the workroom.

"*Tu compris ces lignes de poésie,* Celestine?" Baby shifted again to look at her, her voice teasing, almost mocking. "You understand?"

Celestine calmly focused Baby with a challenged look, smartly turned her wrist so the long knife she held pointed at the ceiling. She raised her chin a fraction.

"*Autant que vous, je crois,*" Celestine retorted in a viciously sweet voice, the heel of her hand pushing the knife blade into the celery: better than you do, I believe. Baby took it in, she lost a little color.

"Oh dear, I didn't mean that the way it sounded, Celestine, forgive me, you must think I'm a horrible bitch."

"Not at all."

"Well, I can be, I'm afraid."

"So can I, Mrs. Claymore," Celestine said in a pleasant way. "Don't give it a thought."

Norma came breezing off the elevator, carrying plastic Gristedes bags. Baby always told her to get paper, not plastic, but Norma said one was as bad as the other in terms of crapping up the environment. She looked windblown and determined, smiling as if she knew how together she looked, and as if something secret had just happened in the street.

"Someone named Ellen de Beckwith is going to call you this afternoon," Baby told Norma's back as she commenced sticking food in the fridge. Norma sniffled. She had a cold too. "About an apartment for her employer."

"We could give him the studio next to Mr. Farmhole," Norma said, shaking a bag of limes into the vegetable bin.

Vic stalked through the kitchen with doorknobs and tools.

"Sink's fucked up in the studio," he said in a larky voice, stepping into the elevator, looking confident that he'd just raised the collective estrogen level.

"Get *Leon* to *fix* it," Baby hollered after him. They heard some thickly muffled answer as the elevator shot up.

"Who's this lady's employer?" Norma asked, stuffing the empty bags in the trash.

"It's a friend of Vinnie's," Baby said. Vinnie Panicelli was a luxury butcher on Tenth Avenue whose meat Baby had been buying for years. "Someone named Bruce de Marco. A dress designer she said."

"That's funny, 'de Beckwith,' 'de Marco.' "

"You say potato, I say po*ta*to," Baby sang.

Celestine completed a tuna salad. Norma ate some of it standing over the bowl, wiped her fingers on a paper towel, and took a Diet Pepsi upstairs to Baby's office. Celestine ate her lunch on the patio, where she could smoke a cigarette. Baby hated to make people smoke outside, but her doctor said she had to. The staff drifted in and out of the kitchen, helping themselves to food, finally traffic tapered off and Asra commenced reading to Baby. They were in the depths of the fin de siècle. Bram Stoker, Arthur, Marcel Schwob, Verlaine, and Mayhew's endless books about London.

"Nay," Asraboth began where he'd broken off the day before, "he is even more prisoner than the slave of the galley, than the madman in his cell. He cannot go where he lists; he who is not of nature has yet to obey some of nature's laws—why we know not."

Ratty's claws came clicking along the tile floor.

"There's my Ratty," Baby exclaimed. "Ratty girl, Ratty girl, Mumma loves her Ratty girl!"

"He may not enter anywhere at first, unless there be some one of the household who bid him to come; though afterwards he can come as he please," Asra read. He wished the dog would settle down. Baby got distracted so easily sometimes. "His power ceases, as does that of all evil things, at the coming of the day. Only at certain times can he have limited freedom. If he be not at the place whither he is bound, he can only change himself at noon or at exact sunrise or sunset. These things we are told, and in this record of ours we have proof by inference. Thus, whereas he can do as he will within his limit, when he have his earth-home, his coffin-home, his hell-home, the place unhallowed—"

"Oh *Ratty* you *bad* girl, look Asra Ratty made caca, *Ratty* girl what a *bad* little girl, Mumma loves you anyway, doesn't she, Asra I'm sorry but could you clean that up?"

✝

I was working in West Palm Beach. Dishwasher. I lived in that apartment with a friend Leroy. Leroy met a man named Devin and a woman named Mama and he told them I was looking for a better job. They came to the apartment. They also came to the restau-

rant I worked in. They took down all our personal information, me
and Leroy, references phone numbers license number Social
Security all that information.

They wrote it all down in notebooks. They always had notebooks. They wanted somebody to do everything in the house.
Someone with a driver's license. They said they would pay
$350–400 a week.

They sent a guy, a friend of Leroy to come get me. They gave
him some money. We went to their apartment. I told them I had to
go back to work at 4. They didn't let me go back. So I started
working right away.

Devin spoke Spanish better than Mama. They never spoke to
me in English.

I started living with them. This was at the Palm Beach Polo
Club, that neighborhood. Ironing cooking washing the car cleaning the house. They gave me a paper to sign they said was a contract for $350–400. It was in English. I couldn't read English then.
It says "I promise to take care of the house for this
corporation/family in exchange for room and board. I promise to
protect and help my new family at all times. I am very happy to be
here. I promise to be permanent, at least for a year or much
longer." I didn't know what it said.

She said her husband died two years ago in Hawaii. She said
to wash the green Lincoln. I washed the car three or four times
when we were still in Florida.

She was always on the phone and writing in notebooks. Day
and night. All kinds of notebooks. Sometimes she put a handkerchief over the speaker part of the phone. Devin used a microcassette tape recorder, a phone, a computer, he used the computer
every day. He always had a notebook in his hand.

I went out a few times to buy food with Devin. He went to
Office Depot to send and receive faxes. Devin bought phone cards
very frequently.

They gave me $30 when I moved in with them. I cleaned the

bedroom in Florida several times. One time I saw a firearm in the bed when I made the bed. They slept together in that bed. I picked up the pillow and the gun was under it. I called them and asked them to pick it up. They picked it up and put it nearby.

We moved to another apartment near the Polo Club. Really close to the swimming pool. We only stayed there one night. The next day they said We're going to New York. They were going for a year, they said. After that they were going to Canada. They would be staying in an apartment in New York. The people couldn't see me or Mama in the apartment, because they would have to pay two thousand dollars extra, one thousand for each person. They told me that several times.

I packed up the car. Devin helped me pack everything in back and in the trunk. We packed the car even before we moved to the other apartment in Palm Beach. We left after lunch. They stopped at Office Depot to pick up faxes and picked up some letters at a hotel, there were some gun magazines in with the mail.

We went straight up 95. I did most of the driving until New Jersey. When Devin drove they both sat up front. When we got to New Jersey we looked for a hotel, because it was too late to find the apartment in New York and the hotels were too expensive. We found a motel in New Jersey for $25 a night. We all stayed in the room. Devin and Mama slept in the bed, I slept on the floor.

Devin stopped the car somewhere when I was sleeping in the back seat. He woke me up and showed me a construction site. They said "that's a perfect place to dump a body, the police will never find it there." I looked at the place and laid down again. I didn't get out of the car. Place that was deep enough to get rid of a body.

We went in through the Lincoln Tunnel. They said to each other Good luck and good business, they kissed their own fists and put them together.

We stopped near the Puerto Rican parade. She got out of the car to ask this guy to move his car so they could park. She talked to the guy and wrote something in her notebook. Devin parked and told us to go look at the parade. He was going to go find the apartment. He came back two hours later. We went to the Pierre Hotel to toast because he'd got the apartment. She talked to the waiter there and got all this information from him. She gave him her business card. Then we went to the apartment. I carried all the luggage in electronic equipment computer tape recorder, Mama didn't pick anything up.

The car had temporary plates made of paper. Utah temporary motor vehicle registration.

They said I had to check who came in and came out by the monitor inside the apartment also through the peep hole in the door all the time. All the time. I was supposed to call Devin Bruce. I always called him Devin anyway. I stood at the door twelve or fifteen times every day. They said to keep an eye who came in and out, write it all on paper and give it to Mama when they came back, they would look at what I wrote and throw it away.

They said they were going to buy the building. When that was done they were going to buy some land in Canada.

✝

"I'm sure I don't know why you keep referring to him as *Doctor* Kissinger," Baby told her friend Patsy Hardwick, a tall, angular clothes horse of sixty-five whose opinions Baby often dismissed as those of a Born Deb, though she loved her dearly. "He's not a *doctor*. I could see calling him that if we were living in the Third Reich, but this is still America, no thanks to him."

Patsy swigged at her champagne flute. She had never been lifted, and she still looked like several million dollars, Baby thought. It's all in the bones.

"I suppose it's because," Patsy said, "that's what Ted Koppel always calls him."

They milled about in the living room of 1B, examining the general effect of the decor from various perspectives, while Vic hung

Annabelle's framed tapestry of Gauguin's *Nevermore* above the curved mantel. Vic, a vision of slickhaired Balkan studliness, in a torn white t-shirt and frayed jeans, had taken his shoes off to stand on one of the padded chairs. Patsy was discreetly ogling his high-arched, white-socked feet. She adored male feet and socks. Baby knew.

"Ted Koppel," Baby snorted. She was getting over her cold, finally. "That reminds me, Patsy, we have to organize the Ass Kiss Awards soon."

It was a joke that had grown into an elaborate ritual between them and their mutual friend Sally Hobson: every year, they nominated public figures for the Ass Kiss Awards, in such categories as "Most Obsequious Television Interview," "Most Craven Magazine Profile," "Most Shameless Logroller," "Best Ass Kiss of a Movie Star by a Female Journalist," "Best Ass Kiss of a Politician by a Male Journalist," the categories were numerous, the supreme moment of the evening being "Biggest Ass Kisser of the Year." It was all in fun, and quite often the nominees were people they knew personally, whom they notified by singing telegram of their selection. Previous years' winners had included celebrity interviewer Barbara Walters, profile writer Kevin Sessums of *Vanity Fair*, and their perennial favorite for the top award, James Lipton, host of *Inside the Actor's Studio*. Winners were sent a chocolate cake from the Erotic Bakery, in the form of a pair of buttocks, with a legend in frosting written across them. KISS MY BIG BLACK ASS. Some honorees did not take the Ass Kiss Awards as the delicious jest that they were was intended to be. Columnist Cindy Adams, for example, had never acknowledged receiving her cake the year before, but many of their targets got into the spirit of the thing and sent back telegrams thanking the Ass Kiss Academy. A few had even phoned Baby with tearful acceptance speeches. "Of course, kissing the asses of famous and powerful people is something I do out of love for the craft, which is reward enough," one audibly drunk recipient had declared, "and even to be nominated in the company of people like Rosie O'Donnell and Nick Dunne is already the greatest honor I could ever receive. But to actually win one of these—all I can say is, Wow. I want to thank all five corporate owners of America's mass media, of course, for making all the magic possible, and all the celebrities who've allowed me to slobber over their shoes and degrade myself for the past year. And most of all, I want to thank the Academy. I want each and every one of you to know, from the bottom of my heart, that as long as I'm still around, I'll still be kissing your ass." This particularly loquacious winner had then held the phone near a speaker that played "The Best Is Yet to Come."

The fact that Patsy Hardwick herself had invented the Ass Kiss Awards proved to Baby that Patsy had a sense of reality rather more acute than the muddle-headed society blather she often came out with would indicate. But that was true, Baby thought, of many people To The Manor Born, a group to which Baby did not belong but had spent many years cultivating, studying, and emulating, without, however, entirely losing sight of her roots.

"I was born above a whorehouse in New Orleans," she liked to tell people. "So never piss on my hairdo and tell me it's raining."

Through the open door, they heard Norma pacing in the hall as she talked on a cordless phone.

"The studio we discussed has been rented," she was saying. "We'll have a one bedroom free in a couple days, but it's quite a bit more expensive. Six thousand."

"My mother really was an artist in her way," Baby said wistfully. "I remember all the little drawings she made for that, with colored pencils, at the Courtauld Institute in London. And all the time she spent shopping for thread that matched those colors."

"It's almost like Manet's *Olympia* with the bed turned around," Patsy said.

"But with very bosky skin," said Baby. "Her skin is almost *smoky* with that muddy green, and I love that the raven is blue and green rather than black."

"As I told you last time, Ellen, there's nine on the staff, they're not all here at the same time," Norma was saying as she wandered into 1B. She looked at Vic positioning the picture. "Daily maid service except weekends. Yes. We don't count Friday as part of the weekend." Norma made a "blabbermouth" gesture with her fingers for Baby and Patsy. "We don't offer *room service*, this isn't a hotel, but if you want tea, or something from the store, someone can usually accommodate you."

Vic stepped down from the chair and stood back to see if the tapestry hung straight.

"There aren't any 'common rooms' or lounges, Ellen, it's an apartment house. Look, is there a number I can call you back? You're in Brazil? You sound like you're right next door."

"Gauguin said that it wasn't 'The Raven' of Edgar Poe, but 'the Bird of the Devil biding its time.'"

"Maybe an inch to the right," Vic said. He climbed back on the chair, artfully pausing to kneel with one foot planted on the cushion to briefly display the bottom of his other foot to full advantage. Baby now wished she hadn't gossiped to him about Patsy's fetish in one of her looser moods. The man was just shameless, really.

"I wish we'd get rid of that security monitor," Baby said. "We certainly have no use for it in here."

The white plastic monitor and door buzzer console in the entryway, a remnant of the time when Annabelle was living, was the only ugly object in 1B. The floor had sand-colored terra-cotta tiles and a Bokara rug, and the room sported other nice, pricey things: a Louis XV armoire, two black leather chesterfields with throw pillows Annabelle had sewn, a glass Mies van der Rohe low table, and a rolltop desk by the Roentgens. Patsy always told her she was nuts to put such expensive things in her rental units.

"It's what they pay for," Baby told her. "I have to put them somewhere, anyway."

"As far as that goes," Patsy said, "I will never comprehend why you rent to people in the first place. You hardly need the money, sweetie."

"I don't care about the *money*," Baby lied. "I like the *company*. Wait until you're my age, you'll want interesting people around."

"I really can't stand interesting people most of the time," said Patsy. "Everybody with their yack yack yack."

"Yes, that's why you're out every night," Baby said.

"Well, if you want me to hold it for him, you'll have to give me a definite date," said Norma, pacing back into the hall. "Well, that's not good, it's Sunday, nobody's here on Sunday except Mrs. Claymore and she doesn't deal with this personally. Everything goes through me. He has to fill out an application, things of that nature. No, no, he can move in when he gets here, we know he's a friend of Vinnie, but we do need an application and references on file, it's standard. Monday's good. Any time after nine a.m. Very good. We'll look forward to seeing him on Monday then."

Baby and Patsy followed Norma out and took the elevator to the kitchen, where Baby poured them some more bubbly to drink on the patio. Celestine was standing at a counter, studying a cookbook. To everyone's astonishment, Baby had let go of Cora, the cook, and given Celestine her job. She had offered no explanation to the staff, but had given Cora such a generous severance that she'd been happy to leave.

"I wish Jerome and I could find someone as dependable as Vic to run the beach shack," Patsy sighed.

Patsy and her husband shuttled back and forth between their twenty-room maisonette on East 84th and a ten million dollar estate in Amagansett that Patsy, somewhat vulgarly Baby thought, persisted in referring to as their "beach shack."

"Well, you can't have him, he's mine."

"Felix is impossible," Patsy said. "I reminded him twice to lay in some Beluga for the weekend, and he bought Osetra."

"What a tragedy, Patsy," Baby clucked. "If you could hear yourself."

"Yes, I know, Baby, more than half the people in the world would sell their children for organ harvesting to have my kind of problems, we all know what a spoiled sybaritic existence I lead, and all for the teeny price of being married to Hughie." Hughie was an attorney. Which would have been fine, if he had also been Louis Auchincloss. "I know it *sounds* like a small thing, but it's *symptomatic*. God I wish I knew why, no matter how much you have, there always has to be some little thing wrong that ruins everything."

†

I met them the day of the Puerto Rican Day parade. They were trying to park their car on 64th Street and my car was taking up two spaces, see, I went to the parade with my brother we filled up a big cooler with beer and sodas and things of that nature to sell at the parade, we were setting up this table on the sidewalk, if I moved my car up a little they could park, so I moved it, the woman was all excited she introduced herself as Mama, and introduced him as Bruce, and they had a Cuban guy with them, sad sack kind of, she said What is this why are all these people in the street, I told her it was Puerto Rican day, she said how happy she was to be able to see it, they were just moving into their town house, she said she owned this house but she had never seen it before, they just arrived, I gave her a little bottle of rum, she was really excited, Bruce went off to look for the house or something, her and the Cuban stood around there watching the crowd, at some point she mentioned she needed a notary public and asked if I knew any- body I said why not look in the phone book she said she tried that but she needed someone who could come to the house, it had something to do with a relative she said was housebound, and I remembered that my mother has a friend who is a notary so I mentioned that, then Mama asked if I would look into it for her and she wrote down my phone number she also asked for my address, I gave her all that information, later they went off, this was before things got ugly, when the parade went a little weird, I saw some of that because we took our stuff down by Columbus Circle later on, it was like, all these guys, trying to tear off women's shirts and shit and throwing water on them, and all these cops standing around watching it happen and not doing a fucking thing about it, I mean some of those jerks were actually videotaping themselves molesting these girls and the cops are like, where's my fucking donuts, anyway, a few days later this Mama calls me at home, she woke me up, asks me how did my business go the other day, meaning did I make some money off the parade, she was so glad she met me first thing on coming to New York, how excited they both were to be in the Big Apple, did I talk to the notary, I had forgotten about it, you know, I said I would call the guy, I tried him but couldn't reach him. Then she called again, and asks do I think the guy would notarize something without the person present, if she pays him extra, say two three hundred dollars, I said I would ask, I did call the guy a couple times, he was never in, then every time she called she sounded a little more crazy to me, to me it's already a dead subject, anyway I figured she was bad news, I don't even know this woman and she's calling my apartment at all hours of the day and night like I'm this close friend of hers, about some fucking notary when there must be like two hundred of them in the phone book, the next time she called I kind of muffled my voice and pretended I was my brother, I told her, "My brother isn't here," after a while she gave up and stopped calling me.

†

A scratching sound: like a toenail ripping through a bedsheet, or a branch of the municipal ginkgo rising behind the stubby evergreens potted on AstroTurf between the house and sidewalk, blown across the window glass: clearer than a louder, inchoate fanfare, as of disorderly multitudes swarming in the streets, band music swelling and fading in the middle distance, police whistles, cries, horns, the ambient surge of a large interruption of the city's soughing arterial flow: she was inside a story, a story that she was the insides of, parts of which felt like stories she'd lived through before: the expression on a face she couldn't quite place, a word or phrase spoken by someone she forgot a moment later, a detail of a room, a stick of furniture, the pattern of a curtain, the color of wallpaper, part of a doorway: it was not a story, really, not a narrative at any rate that moved from A to B and C, but rather a shower of moments, all out of order, trying to cohere in some manner, trying to show her something: some lesson, or a crystallization of many things she had missed the logical connectives of: that she was herself outside this "I" the story seemed to be about: someone, or some*thing* else forced to observe it because it, whatever it was, was all there was, no person or place or world existed outside it. The château near Deauville was in it, and places she had seen in Tunisia and Italy and Spain, and features of her own house, and Annabelle still alive, tiny, hunched from bone degeneration, trembling, no longer Annabelle, a memory-less soul drifting through limbo in Annabelle's body, who pointed down a pitch-black, narrow hall to show where Annabelle "really" was; had Baby been to these places before, known these blurry people before, or was it a peculiarity of the story, the montage, to trick the mind into "remembering" things unseen and unknown until that instant?

She was conscious of the scratching sound—like a small feral creature, she thought, a rat or a squirrel or a bat, gnawing or clawing determinedly through ceiling plaster—or a nail scraped over cork board, dull but distinct—was the noise in her head, a sound of misfiring synapses?—and of Carmen in the room, and soon she apprehended that it was Sunday, her bedroom, daytime, late spring, life: yet the other world persisted like the remnants of a heavy sedative, the transition into consciousness didn't resolve with the usual clarity, the heaviness felt like a fresh infirmity that had taken up residence during sleep. Or like the hangover you had if you were still drunk when you woke. But not quite that, either: hangovers jolted her into bleary, rapid movement, a different kind of alienation from her body's altered state.

Carmen was telling her something. Baby had drifted off reading Paul Verlaine, *Comme le voix d'un mort qui chanterait / Du fond de
sa fosse*, with a feeling of spiraling down her own private rabbit
hole, she couldn't tell how many minutes or hours had passed, and
now the friend of Vinnie, Carmen said, that Bruce de Marco moving into 1B, waited out in the vestibule.

"Dammit," Baby said. Of all the importunate things life still
had to offer, what angered her most were breaches of the few easy
rules that kept the house running normally, of which the calm and
quiet of weekends were engraved in stone.

"I'm sure," Baby said, getting up, "Norma told him to come
on Monday. Told that secretary of his." She felt a prickle of irrita-
tion towards Norma, another towards Vinnie, but the secretary had
sounded like a ditz, probably it was her screw-up. Baby gathered
her housecoat around her, felt for her keys and her reading glasses
in the velvet-lined pockets sewn on the sides, worked her half-
asleep feet into her tiny slippers. She went into the hall, leaving the
door to her rooms ajar, and again the sensation of being elsewhere
flooded through her, like stepping into a freezer. She opened the
wide wooden door to a young man, twenty-two or so, on the tall
side, solidly built, dressed in a yellow linen blazer and a tailored
shirt, elegant patterned tie, and dark blue denims, oxblood
Ferragamo loafers. Black hair, in a furred cornrow kind of cut of
loose curls frosted blond at the tips.

His face had a jarring resemblance, a "bad twin" resemblance,
to a photograph she knew of the philosopher Ludwig Wittgenstein,
whose writings Baby couldn't make head nor tail of (she could,
though, when she'd concentrated closely, there had been many
parts of Wittgenstein's *Tractatus* that had made perfect sense to her,
and she loved the imaginary tribes the philosopher invented to
illustrate ideas about language and will and understanding in the
Philosophical Investigations, she'd also read Leibnitz and Spinoza
without becoming overly baffled, Baby had been pleasantly surprised, in the days when she audited classes at NYU, to discover

that she wasn't as stupid as she thought she was, academically speaking, but simply too frightened by abstract subjects to study them calmly and slowly), who had designed an austerely beautiful house Baby had once viewed from outside during an architectural tour of Vienna, a house that had changed hands many times and had finished up, not too happily it seemed, as the Bulgarian Embassy. As she thought of this, images of many houses, in many cities, flashed through memory rather like a deck of cards with their edges visible shuffled by a croupier. Maybe it was the bump on the bridge of his nose that reminded her of Wittgenstein: the rest of him reminded her of something else, she wasn't entirely sure what: it might very well have *been* a flipping deck of cards, a croupier's swift, shrewd hands, something anyway to do with gambling or card tricks or mouselike movements at the foggy edge of vision.

"Mr. de Marco. We were expecting you tomorrow." She kept her voice cordial but wanted him to know she wasn't pleased. He smiled rather stupidly, she thought, indifferent to the small trace of asperity.

The racket from somewhere down the street obscured the flavor of his reply, which sounded to her, quite incredibly, like a bored grunt. In the moments that immediately followed, Baby felt herself strangely intimidated by this de Marco's manner, which was fastidiously polite when he actually spoke, and at the same time implacably arrogant, as if he were addressing a concierge: it threw her off. Baby was used to establishing an immediate, superficial rapport with the people who came to stay in her house, however different they were from each other. The note of a shared plenum of cultural and intellectual references was almost invariably struck upon first meetings chez Baby, and though this de Marco had been recommended by her butcher rather than someone like André Previn, in Baby's world, Baby's New York, André Previn and the butcher might easily be encountered at the same museum opening or theatrical performance. It was disconcertingly unclear exactly what world this de Marco fellow came from, and none of Baby's usual conversational gambits brought it into any closer view. She had been told by his secretary that de Marco designed dresses, Baby knew plenty about that world, but when she mentioned this mutual interest, de Marco said that no, he designed websites. There was a palpable disjunction, in fact, between everything she recalled Ellen de Beckwith telling her and everything Bruce de Marco now said, Baby registered it, but it was all just fractionally off, a matter of a few degrees, the kind of discrepancy that made her wonder, often these days, if her memory had started to fail.

The discomfort she felt made Baby impatient and anxious to resume her day, to get back to Carmen and the recording of John Adams's *Nixon in China* by the Orchestra of St. Luke's that she wanted to hear, Edo De Waart conducting, she had people coming for lunch, there was something, suddenly, excessively wearying in this whole encounter. De Marco showed her that he had the rent in cash, and his face rather vulgarly conveyed that there was plenty more where that came from. Baby made a mental note to ask Vinnie about this friend of his, though she'd told Norma not to inquire, lest it seem to Vinnie that his recommendation alone weren't enough for them. Everyone, Baby thought, at one time or other, has slipped up recommending wrong people for all sorts of things. It was one of the unhappier effects of a generous nature.

She returned to her suite and went into the office and wrote out a receipt on a yellowed piece of old fax paper and got him his keys, the key to the iron door, the key to the wooden door, the two keys to 1B all looped together with a knotted green satin ribbon, each key marked with a different color nail polish, then went back out and gave him his keys and showed him which key was which and handed him the receipt and took his cash, six thousand in hundreds in a torn envelope, told him the phone number for 1B while he wrote it in a little notebook, and pointed him to the apartment, directly at the hall's end, next to the elevator. She wasn't about to waste her time showing him the place, if he didn't like it he could leave, take his money back, it was Norma's job to handle all this and Norma could deal with Bruce de Marco in the morning.

✝

But that wasn't the last of it on Sunday, for one thing Baby couldn't get her mind off this de Marco person's oddity, his insouciant attitude, the discrepancy between what Ellen de Beckwith had said on the phone and what de Marco told her in person, something in the grain of the man's voice bothered her as well, also something actorish in his facial expressions, it festered in Baby's mind as Carmen gave her a pedicure, *it all happened so fast*, she thought, as if de Marco had known precisely how to rush her through all the formalities of moving in, and then there was a little incident at lunch, when she was down in the kitchen making omelettes for Ikea and Patsy and Wilson Farmhole, the gay novelist, who was ever so amusing as he told them about his recent trip to Prague, Wilson Farmhole was polishing his current memoir of Growing Up Gay in the Deep South, parts of which he had recently read aloud to Baby over tea, Baby had been deeply moved, in any case Wilson Farmhole had paused during an extremely long but brilliantly discursive anecdote concerning a young Czech he'd encountered in the course of an evening walk, in the space of that pause they all heard footsteps coming down the L-shaped stairway that led to the basement from the first floor hall, a stairway Baby and her guests never used because it came out at the far end of the basement rather than the kitchen part, and Baby sent Carmen to see who it was, she then heard Carmen rather loudly telling someone whose voice Baby recognized as Bruce de Marco's that tenants were not allowed in the basement, that he was not to wander about the premises, a few minutes later Carmen came back fuming, *I tell him and tell him and he wants to stand there and argue*, she said, she said that de Marco said he was looking for sheets and towels, that she told him the sheets and towels in 1B had been changed just yesterday, that the maid would change his sheets and towels on a daily basis, or however often he wanted them changed, as Carmen related this Baby shivered, her fingers began to tremble, the egg mixture in her omelette pan started to scorch, *Goddam it*, she said, *What's wrong Wanda*, Patsy said, Patsy never called Baby Wanda unless she sensed something grave in the air, *Oh, Patsy*, Baby said, *I don't like the looks of that guy Vinnie sent over here, he looks like a thug.* Patsy made a clucking noise, Ikea's baby-smooth, moony face crinkled, inasmuch as it could, with obsequious worry, Wilson Farmhole looked mildly irritated that his coyly phrased epic of Central European cocksucking had been interrupted by a trivial domestic contretemps, *Well how many years have you known Vinnie, Wanda, he isn't going to send any thugs to rent your apartments, I wouldn't think,* Patsy now felt competitive with Ikea in concern for her friend's composure, having known Wanda Claymore considerably more years than this ever-grinning doodle-bug from Tokyo who barely spoke Engrish as she called it, Patsy was also immensely bored by Wilson Farmhole, whose world-weary tone sounded borrowed, rather witlessly, from Tennessee Williams, she did not like the way Wilson Farmhole insisted on making himself the center of attention just because he'd written a few novels, Patsy had sampled one of Wilson Farmhole's so-called novels after Baby told her Wilson Farmhole had rented an apartment, his so-called novel was high-tone enough and all that, full of jewellike descriptions of everything from apples to anuses, but really, Patsy thought, Wilson Farmhole wrote about himself as if he were some precious Amazonian butterfly and a conquering beauty all gay men were attracted to, not just gay ones but other people's husbands and plumbers and landscape architects and career diplomats and men from all walks of life who had never, until meeting Wilson Farmhole, ever even thought of having sexual intercourse with another man, which Patsy found incredible, even in a work of fiction, given that Wilson Farmhole's face looked like a pancake with bubble holes all over its surface, and nothing special in the body department to compensate, to read Wilson Farmhole's so-called novels you would have thought, Patsy thought, that Wilson Farmhole had the physical allure of a Robert Redford or the young Marlon Brando, that Wilson Farmhole emitted pheremones so heady as to cause fainting spells in all the world's best-looking men, in the novels of Wilson Farmhole, Patsy thought, some Adonis is always sniffing at Wilson Farmhole's thinly disguised arsehole, *I tell you Patsy he smells of jail*, said Baby, breaking into this thought, *Really, he looks like he just got out of jail*, by this time Wilson Farmhole looked truly miffed that his Tales of Uranian Prague had been shunted permanently out of the conversation, Ikea meanwhile had popped out of her chair and practically *ran* to console Baby, now aflutter amid sizzle and smoke at the Viking range top, and help rescue the omelettes, Patsy found herself thinking for the millionth time that Baby's earnest wish to preside over an artistic salon had never produced what Patsy considered very happy results, *I thought you said he was wearing a Christian Dior tie*, Patsy said, thinking surely this fact alone refuted much of what Baby was saying.

"In like Flynn," the chesty woman in the low-cut dress tells the two young men in the Café Pierre. She slumps contentedly, her arms dangling limp over the chair arms, then waves a lighted Marlboro in the air around her bosom, banishing the already dissolving specter of the day not turning out as planned. It's all ticking along like a Rolex. In striped chairs around a low table, the trio appear deliciously tuckered out, relaxed, satisfied with themselves, as if concluding a successful morning of whirlwind shopping, though there are no shopping bags in evidence. The woman and the preppier-looking man, on closer view, seem rather more exhilarated than their companion, who has the fogged look of trying to follow their conversation without luck. They address each other in English, sporadically switching to Spanish for the benefit of this man, who might be a relative or friend visiting from abroad.

Vasco Fibonacci has been a waiter at the Café Pierre for about six months. He is slender, of average height, with dramatic cheekbones and severe, queeny features, and long glossy auburn hair rubber-banded in a strident ponytail. His movements are clipped, intense, and rapid enough to qualify as swish, his serving style so practicedly graceful that it no longer conveys grace, but looks like tricks performed with mechanical panache: the placing of the champagne flutes, the snapping up of an ashtray while conjuring its pristine double in the same spot, the bibbing of the Cristal in a starched white towel without flecking off a drop of the ice water beading its surface, the deft unscrewing of the knotted cork wire and then the extraction of the cork itself with a soft vapor-trailing pock instead of a gaudy explosion: Vasco Fibonacci performs his endless, stupid duties irreproachably, his grim politeness never goes into remission, but he carries himself in a scornful narcissistic cocoon that signals a deep and perpetual anger that he has to dissemble all day in strained geniality and deference. This anger may have its source in his job, his personal relations, his financial situation, a drug habit he can't afford, the dying transmission on his ten-year-old car, it may be an anger that ranges around in search of ever-changing causes, a state of anger may simply be his fate, his character, his version of joy. Whatever it is, it offers the chesty woman in the low-cut dress an object of study and speculation as she ropes him into conversation.

"We're celebrating," she tells him. "I'm so happy, I wish you could join us."

"What's the occasion?" Vasco prepares not to hear the answer.

"Oh, we've just moved into our new house. I'm so excited. It's really our dream house and finally we got it. We just came from Florida."

"Well, congratulations."

"That's very kind of you. Cheers!" she lifts her glass to him with a two-hundred-watt grin.

"What's your name, darling?"

Vasco is so weary of hearing, often, and almost exclusively from patrons of his place of business, *Your last name wouldn't be de Gamo, would it?*, that he has worked out several absolutely innocent-sounding yet cutting ways of telling people that if they are referring to Vasco *da Gama*, famed explorer and commander of the Military Order of Christ, who voyaged from Portugal to India in 1497, then no, it wouldn't be. The much rarer bird who connected Vasco's last name to the inventor of the famous mathematical sequence fared no better: Fibonacci, Vasco would purr in an especially seductive voice, had been the *nickname* of Leonardo Pisano, 1170–1250, who also sometimes used the name Bigollo.

"Vasco."

"What a *spectacular* name! How absolutely brilliant. I imagine annoying customers ask you all kinds of stupid things when you tell them that."

"It's the name they gave me," Vasco says, a real smile breaking over his face.

"They heard about some explorer in sixth grade," the woman went on, "who they never learned anything more about, and want to show off how *educated* they are."

Vasco finds himself nodding in stunned agreement. A few days ago, Vasco got into a taxi driven by a very black African driver whose ID fixture said his name was Tom Sawyer. Vasco kept his mouth shut. He thinks this woman probably would have, too.

She's dressed sort of vulgar, expensive vulgar, a type he usually abhors among biological females. But there's something about how she wears these expensive vulgar things, like a costume thrown on to enact a little charade: an actor putting on what the moment's role requires. Vasco considers his serving clothes in exactly the same light.

Vasco spends a lot of time around drag queens who perform at La Escualita. Among them, he has the reputation of a delightfully brutal fuck, despite his femme facade. This woman reminds him of them, and of the rich contradictions of his inner life.

"This is my son Bruce, and our friend Pedro who's been

helping us move, and my name is Princess Shah. I'm a real Princess, but titles don't mean anything but dumb luck in the world of today. You can call me Mama, everybody does."

"Very nice to meet you," says Vasco, meaning it. She's too old for the stuff he likes to do, and encounters in the Café Pierre generally go nowhere. Bruce, though: Vasco can picture himself doing Bruce, or Bruce and Pedro together, with Mama watching. It could work. Pedro's kind of ugly, but sexy ugly like a lot of the Cubanos in La Escualita. "If you need anything, just give a holler."

✝

"I'm going to run one more title search tomorrow," Princess Shah tells her son. "Just to make triple sure."

Bruce shrugs, swallows champagne.

"We know there aren't any liens, how likely is it she's taken a mortgage out since the last time you checked?"

Princess Shah nods, conceding the point.

"I like to cross my t's and dot my i's," she says. She whips a notebook from her pocketbook, opens to the current page. "I also need to call that guy in Brooklyn about the notary."

In the notebook she's written the man's name, address, phone number, and the observation, "nice guy, helped us find a parking space." She's also written, in big letters on the inside cover, the words, "FINAL DYNASTY."

Delgado drinks champagne in short untasting sips. His eyes wander all over the room. The droopy tasseled curtain ties, the long ice green mirror behind the bar, engraved with an elaborate scene of trees, houses, birds, a river. The boxed X pattern of the carpet. So far, he's received a total of $30 in the ten days he's been working for Mama and Bruce. They have not evidenced any inclination to pay him the salary they promised. In his pocket he has the crumpled last check from the chicken restaurant he was working in when he met them.

"Make sure you always keep your back to that security camera," Bruce tells Mama, repeating this in Spanish for Delgado's benefit. "Walk in kind of sideways, with your head down."

"If we are gone from the room," Mama tells Delgado, "You must never let anyone inside. If they come to empty garbage or anything you tell them to wait, wait until Bruce is there." Mama's Spanish is blockier and uglier than Devin's. It is the kind of Spanish rich people learn to order their Spanish servants around.

Delgado does not believe that these people are going to buy this house they just moved into. Why would they need to hide the presence of Mama and Delgado in the apartment, if that were the case. Delgado does believe they intend to kill someone and dump the body in that place in New Jersey where they stopped the car. In Delgado's experience, normal people do not joke about such things. Delgado is not afraid of Devin. Delgado is afraid of Mama. Delgado has no intention of becoming implicated in whatever wickedness these people have planned. There would really be nothing to stop Delgado from walking out of the Pierre Hotel right now and disappearing from the lives of this mother and son who are fucking each other, a sin against God and also some kind of state or federal crime if Delgado is not mistaken, except for the fact that Delgado has less than five dollars left of the $30 they have paid him, and nowhere to cash the check from the chicken restaurant. He has never been in New York before, and the city frightens him.

When the bill comes, Devin slaps down a credit card which Vasco Fibonacci eyeballs as he carries it off to the cashier. When he returns with the slip to sign he asks Devin:

"Do I call you Bruce, or Max?"

The name on the credit card is that of Max Schreck, a retired dentist who lives in a retirement home quite close to the Polo Beach Apartments. Max Schreck has never heard of Devin and Evangeline Slote, or Bruce de Marco and Ellen de Beckwith, or Princess Shah, or Mama. Max Schreck recently tossed out, along with the rest of his daily trash, an envelope containing a preapproved Visa credit card application, which Devin retrieved and mailed in, noting a change of address on the part of Max Schreck from his retirement home in Polo Beach to a mail drop in downtown Miami.

"Oh, this is my Uncle Max's card. He's the executor of my father's estate. He takes care of our expenses."

On a bill that runs below an astronomical amount, Pierre employees are instructed not to question these kinds of little discrepancies vis-à-vis a customer's credit card. You never know how the customer will react, and a bad reaction could be disturbing to other customers.

✝

"Mr. de Marco?"

"Yes, hello."

"I'm Norma Benedetto. I handle all the rental business for Mrs. Claymore. I asked your secretary to have you move in here *today* so as not to disturb Mrs. Claymore."

"Apologize about that. Typical mix-up. Ellen's fault. Anyway I paid the rent to Mrs. Claymore."

"I know, but I need you to fill out these forms for our records, it's just information we record on all our tenants. I also need to see your driver's license or passport, some kind of identification."

"Well, as you can see, I'm just going out."

"This would only take a couple minutes."

"These look fairly detailed to me."

"It's our standard rental application. Look, you only have to fill it out in four places, it's simple."

"Um, look, I never sign anything like this until my lawyer has a look at it."

"Mr. de Marco—"

"Call me Bruce, please. Can I call you Norma?"

"Fine, Bruce, but this really doesn't require a lawyer, it's just asking for your permanent address, Social Security, it's basic information that we get from every tenant."

"I really have to run it past my lawyer. I'd love to oblige you but my lawyer insists on going over anything I sign. Anything of a contractual nature."

"All right. Fine. This is not a legal document it's an application. You do what you have to do. But please, get it back to me filled out tomorrow."

"I can't get it back to you tomorrow."

"Why is that, Bruce?"

"Well, my lawyer's out of town. He isn't due back until next Thursday."

"All right. Whatever. Another thing. Mrs. Claymore says you went into the basement yesterday. You should be very clear about the fact that the basement floor is Mrs. Claymore's private space, and you aren't permitted down there, or any other part of the house except this hall right here and your apartment."

"You're a tough cookie, aren't you?"

"No, I'm not, but if you stay here you have to follow the rules of the house. You need to see a lawyer about a simple form everybody fills out, fine, you do what you have to. But I can't have Mrs. Claymore bothered by tenants. I'm the one who deals with the tenants. Mrs. Claymore's old, she shouldn't have to check people in or have them invading her privacy."

"Okay, I heard you, Norma, I'm sorry, I was looking for sheets and towels. Now I know you deliver them, end of mystery."

"I gave your secretary all that information on the phone. Several times. It's a little surprising to me that she didn't pass it on to you."

"Ellen's a little scatterbrained. She forgets to tell me things. Look, I have a meeting you're already making me late for."

✝

"I knew he was trouble. Jailbird I just bet you."

"Well he certainly is weird. When I asked to see his license he kind of held it like this, with his thumb covering the name and most of the picture, and stuck it back in his wallet before I could even look. 'There,' he says, like he's really fed up, 'satisfied?' I tell him I need a photocopy, he says he needs the license for something, he'll make the copy. I mean quite hostile, Baby. Quite an attitude problem."

"The *minute* I opened the door to him I regretted it. Right away I thought Wanda, there's something *off* here. I feel like such a fool."

"It makes you wonder. About Vinnie."

"Should we call Vinnie, do you think?"

"I don't know. Maybe. What good would it do us now, the guy's already living here. We should have called Vinnie in the first place Wanda, you didn't want me to. Have we ever thrown anybody out of here besides the Getty kid?"

"That was different, Norma, his family came and had him taken out. They sent an ambulance from Silver Hill, remember? I've never had to *evict* anybody. I'm not sure how it's done, are you?"

"I'm not sure if we *can* evict anybody, Baby, ten units isn't even legal for this building, what if it backfires and you get fined a pile of money?"

"Oh God what a mess. What an idiot I am."

"Well, look, if you want my opinion he's a creep but he's harmless, he's paid up for a month, so let him stay, in the meantime we can find out how to get rid of him. Either legally, or . . . you have plenty of friends, frankly I know a few people, too. I mean if he doesn't leave voluntarily."

"If he stays, Norma, promise me, darling, keep him away from me. Take care of whatever he wants, but I don't want to come in contact with him."

"Don't worry about it, really. I'll take care of it. I'll see he doesn't bother you."

"Celestine saw him on the monitor coming in with these

strange people. She says they were *slinking around* so the camera couldn't show their faces. And me living on the same floor."

"We're all here for you, Baby. Me and Asra and Vic and Celestine and everybody. I'm sure we can handle a little asshole like Bruce de Marco."

"If that really is his name."

"You're going to make yourself ill if you don't put this out of your mind. I'm telling you it's nothing to worry about."

†

Devin rented a mail drop on Third Avenue near 60th Street next to a Chinese laundry, in the name of Max Schreck. He then went to a Sprint Wireless outlet near Pennsylvania Station and bought and activated a cellular phone using the identification of a Dr. Jeffrey Spiegelman, a friend of the woman they sublet the first apartment in Polo Beach from, an apartment the woman still occupied the greater part of when they moved in. This woman's friend Dr. Spiegelman and his wife Betty were passing through the Miami area on their way home to Pittsburgh from a vacation in St. Bart's and stayed the weekend while Evelyn and Devin were still moving things over and sleeping at a hotel. Dr. Spiegelman happened to leave his wallet on a kitchen counter while using the apartment complex's pool facilities, from which wallet Devin had been able to lift an easily tinkered-with Mass General Hospital physician's photo ID and a Social Security card which Dr. Jeffrey Spiegelman, who no longer worked at Mass General Hospital and seldom if ever actually had to display his Social Security card in the course of transactions requiring his Social Security number, failed to notice the absence of until several months later.

Devin then popped into a realty on 58th Street that was advertising commercial space on the fifth floor of the building opposite the Claymore mansion on East 65th Street, and attempted to fill out a rental application under the eye of a realtor named

Salvador Brickman, but faltered when asked for a taxpayer identification number, told Salvador Brickman that the corporation he
was in charge of, this so-called Hyksos Corporation, didn't pay
taxes, that it operated out of the Bahamas where there were no
taxes, this was news to Salvador Brickman, who himself had certain
assets parked in a Bahamanian brokerage and paid plenty of taxes
on them, but he let that go, he told this spurious-sounding Bruce
de Marco that in lieu of a corporate tax identification number he
would have to supply a Social Security number. Bruce de Marco
said he couldn't recall his Social Security number off the top of his
head, he suddenly told Salvador Brickman that he had to use the
bathroom, took the application with him into the bathroom,
passed several minutes in the bathroom, flushed, and reappeared
with the Social Security number magically entered on the form, all
of which raised the suspicions of Salvador Brickman, who later
said that Bruce de Marco had been personable enough, full of
charm actually, a sharp dresser and clearly a nice guy, but such an
obvious con that Salvador Brickman felt obliged to caution him
that his application would almost certainly be rejected, thinking to
save Bruce de Marco the $20 application fee.

✝

Delgado stood at the "magic eye" in the door of apartment 1B
gazing into the hall. This had to be the most ridiculous and disturbing job Delgado had ever held, and the thought that he was
not being paid for it, and the firming suspicion that he never
would be, caused his stomach acids to churn. Delgado had foraged
at the bottom of the food chain for so much of his young life that
he could easily picture himself starving to death in the streets of
this vast, indifferent, scary city. He could also picture taking one in
the helmet if he happened to still be around when whatever was
going down went down, he figured people like Mama and Bruce
were pretty meticulous about details like witnesses and people

who could spill the type of things Delgado had already heard and seen. He stood there for fifteen minutes at a go, staring, holding the pad of paper they'd given him, writing descriptions of everybody coming in or going out. Delgado's descriptive gifts were limited but had the virtue of isolating the blunt essentials. Often no one came in or went out, and Delgado just stood like an idiot staring out the fisheye peephole wondering where he could cash a check drawn on a Florida bank.

There happened to be a slight gap between the bottom door frame and the marble tiles, and whenever Asra or Vic or the other staff passed through the first floor hall on Monday they noticed these feet, the dark shape of feet standing just behind the door, it spooked them, these feet planted there so you knew someone was breathing on the other side, looking through the spyhole, motionless. They assumed these feet belonged to "the jerkoff in 1B," as he came to be known by everyone in the house within twenty-four hours of his arrival. One of the girls complained that she'd tried to get in there to wash the windows, and someone told her through the door, in Spanish, to go away.

" 'The news accounts,' " Baby read to Sally Hobson on the phone from a *Times* article she'd saved for Sally's return from Europe, " 'also raised questions that went beyond how the police handled the victims who reported the crimes, to whether the police had taken adequate steps to prevent the violence. One witness . . . said he was riding his bike on the eastern side of the park between 3 p.m. and 5 p.m., roughly two hours before the most serious attacks were reported, and saw roaming groups of men harrassing young women in plain view of the police.' "

"Our tax dollars at work," Sally said. "That must have all been going on about twenty feet from my front door."

"Or my front door," Baby said. "Right there in the park, in any case. I hate to say it, but I really don't trust the police."

"They've been unfailingly stupid every time I've had to deal with them," Sally said. "Polite, of course, but I suppose that's because I live on Madison Avenue."

"A lot of them would be criminals if they couldn't be policemen," Baby said. "I think it's the same personality type."

"That poor man they shot who was holding up his wallet," Sally said. "I saw his mother on television, I just wept."

"And you know something, it would be a miracle if a single one of them went to jail," said Baby. "This mayor has been a disaster for race relations."

"The crime rate *is* down dramatically, though," Sally said.

"I don't think that has anything to do with Mayor Giuliani, Sally."

"Give the man a little credit," Sally said. "If not him, who? The police commissioner?"

"*Roe vs. Wade*," Baby said.

"I'm afraid I don't follow you," Sally said.

"*Roe vs. Wade* was passed what year, Sally? 1974? 1975? I forget, maybe earlier. Anyway, think how old a lot of unwanted children would be right now if they hadn't been legally aborted, and the age of the average violent criminal."

"Gosh," said Sally. "I never even thought of that."

"I can't say that I thought of it either," Baby said. "I read it somewhere. But it's obviously true."

"I hate to bring up a touchy subject, but Patsy called me in London," Sally said. "She told me you were having a little problem with a tenant."

"Don't get me started," said Baby. "About two weeks ago, Asra needed to get in there to feed the orchids, and this person Vic suspects is living with the tenant wouldn't open the door. His gay lover according to Vic. And the man was speaking Spanish, he doesn't know English apparently, Leon was here fixing a sink so Asra went and got him, and Leon talked to him through the door, the man wouldn't open, he told Leon he worked for the tenant, this de Marco creature, and he'd be in big trouble if he let them in.

Leon tried to explain about the orchids, Asra was already having fits about them because a few days before that de Marco tells Norma, when she was practically begging him to let the cleaning girls in, that he'd watered the plants himself. Norma read him the riot act, you know you don't *water* rare orchids the way you would a geranium, anyway, this Hispanic gentleman just wouldn't open. And Leon said afterwards that the man wasn't hostile, but sounded scared out of his wits of de Marco and his girlfriend."

"I thought he was de Marco's gay lover," Sally said.

"That's what Vic thinks, but I've seen him on the monitor slinking in and out of the house with this woman, and the girls have seen her in the apartment too, they said a few times when they went in to clean this woman was there in the living room. De Marco *insisted* to Norma that nobody enters the place unless he's there, and when they do go in he follows them around, supervising everything, hiding papers and things lying around, they said they saw a big makeup bag in the bathroom trash can and left it there, and women's cosmetics on the shelves and so forth."

"What's this woman look like?"

"It's hard to tell on that little black and white monitor. She always zips right past it with her head down. Frankly though, she looks to me like she's old enough to be his mother."

"Maybe he's a gigolo."

"Well think about it Sally if he were a gigolo it would be her renting the apartment, don't you think? Unless they've decided to set up their love nest in my townhouse under his name. I can't say *that* would be a first, but the people who did it before weren't drawn from the criminal underworld."

"Why do you suppose the gay lover was so frightened?"

"De Marco frightens *me*, and I don't have anything to do with him, so there must be something fishy going on in there. Oh, and last week, Celestine finds him wandering about on the fourth floor, this I have to tell you really did upset me, enough so that I almost fired her, de Marco talked her into showing him the penthouse, next thing I know he tells Norma he wants to rent it for $30,000 a month."

"Jesus, Baby, *go for it!*"

"Are you serious? I'd rather go to hell. Can you imagine? He'd barricade himself up there and we'd never get rid of him. I tell you he's suspicious, I want him out the minute his rental's up. I've talked to my lawyer about it. *And*, frankly, talked to Leon about it too." Leon, Baby's plumber, had once been a prizefighter.

"You certainly are vehement about it, darling, but what has this de Marco actually done to make you so mistrustful of him?"

"If you met him once, Sally, you would never ask that question, he follows me, I swear to you, he stands at the peephole in his door. Keeping track of me. Either it's him or his girlfriend or his boyfriend or I don't know who, but there's always somebody standing there watching everything that happens in the hall. And what's worse, there's a monitor in that apartment we put in for Annabelle, I'm sure he's watching every floor. I wish to God Vic had taken that thing out, I asked him a million times to get rid of it."

"But what's the purpose? Why would anyone want to spy on you? Maybe he's just got a screw loose."

"Oh, he's got something up his sleeve. I can tell."

"Baby," Sally said, "I know you don't like leaving the house any more, but why don't you and I take in a movie or something? We could do a little shopping, or have a nice lunch somewhere."

"I know that tone," Baby said. "You think I'm paranoid."

"I think you're getting cabin fever, is what I think. When was the last time you got out of that house?"

"I happen to be very comfortable staying in. I'm not going to risk falling down somewhere and landing on my hip," Baby said. "That would suit Mr. de Marco to a T. Driving me out of my own house."

"You've been cooped up in there much too much," Sally said. "I worry about you."

"Well, *don't*," said Baby angrily. "I have all my faculties intact, thank you, and I can take care of myself."

"Don't be angry with me."

"I'm not *angry*," said Baby furiously. "But please Sally don't *patronize* me, what I've been telling you is no exaggeration."

"All right, all right, I *believe* you, darling. Now how about if I come over and see you? We can get nice and tight and forget about Mr. de Marco for one evening."

"Only if you bring some Beluga. I have a real craving for it lately."

"*Only if you bring some Beluga,*" Devin mimicked viciously, snapping off the microrecorder. Following the trail of the telephone cord to its jack in the closet on the day they arrived, he had discovered another jack nearby that fed into Baby's phone line. The next day he plugged in a Radio Shack box that activated the recorder whenever a call came in or went out. He now had a collection of something like eighteen tapes: Baby with her lawyer, Norma with her boyfriend, Asra with his sister, everyone in the household talking on the telephone.

"Baby Claymore certainly isn't *your* biggest fan," Evangeline giggled, knocking back a Stoli screwdriver as she scribbled in her current notebook. She had had a hectic day, putting the final bits of paperwork together. She had a copy of the deed, the transfer forms, the tax papers. The lawyer she'd found on West 38th Street had calculated the taxes that had to be paid upon transfer of the property, they needed to get two cashier checks made out to the New York City Finance Department, and they also needed Mrs. Claymore's Social Security number to complete the transaction. And a notary. That guy in Brooklyn had totally crapped out on her.

"Fucking bitch," Devin said, referring to Baby. "What did I ever do to her except give her six thousand dollars for this, this—"

If the truth be known, Evangeline thought, it was Devin who had cabin fever, he seemed to be crawling out of his skin lately whenever they stayed in the apartment at night instead of going out, and even when they went out, something seemed to be working his nerves.

"I can't believe she thinks Pedro's still here," Evangeline laughed. "Your gay lover."

Delgado was long gone. He had fled the day after the incident with the plumber Baby had just related to her friend. Devin had run into Delgado four days after that, on the street, and tried to persuade him back to the apartment, Delgado had been sleeping in Central Park and said he'd tried to walk to Union City, New Jersey through the Lincoln Tunnel, Tunnel authorities had stopped him and turned him around, Union City had a lot of Cubans, apparently, Delgado thought if he got to Union City on a bus he could find people who knew people who knew him and could help him get back to Florida. Devin gave up trying to wheedle him back into staying with them. Devin felt sorry for the guy and gave him $40. Which was just plain foolish, Evangeline told him, they didn't owe Delgado a penny because he broke his contract, she said. Devin then told her to shut up. He was sick of her meanness, he said. Sick of her penny-pinching cheapness.

"Didn't you learn *anything* in prison, Ma, about not paying people that work for you?"

Evangeline had only been mildly surprised at this outburst. Devin attacked her often and always had. Some little thing would set him off and she would suddenly become Satan Incarnate until he cooled off. The timing was the unpredictable part. Devin had such a hair-trigger temper.

"Pedro wouldn't have taken off if you had just fucking *paid him*," Devin fumed. "He said we treated him like a *slave*, Ma. Ring a bell? Ever *wonder* why everybody we employ ends up thinking you're a cunt?"

They had needed Delgado, Delgado had been an important element of the plan. The absence of Delgado or someone like Delgado was another hanging thread, another problem remaining to be solved, Evangeline had an idea about it, she jotted the idea

down, she got up from the couch and went into the little kitch-
enette and poured herself another screwdriver and let Devin go on
ranting at her, he would exhaust himself eventually, after he'd called
her every name in the book and thrown everything he thought
she'd ever done wrong as a mother in his face, she knew defending
herself would be like pouring gasoline on his rage, and sometimes
she did defend herself just to see how far his fury would take him,
the sex was always unbelievable after one of these explosions, but it
was plain idiotic to have any screaming fights in 1B, less than
twenty feet from Baby Claymore's bedroom, that would really put
the kabosh on it, it didn't help matters that every time Devin
played back one of Baby Claymore's phone calls he heard the
name he was using coming into the conversation in ever less flattering ways, Baby Claymore had worked up a regular grand jury
indictment of Bruce de Marco, suggesting he might be everything
from a drug dealer to a child molester, Devin got especially upside
down about the staff all thinking he was gay, since Devin fantasized
himself quite the ladies' man and expected the maids and so forth
to swoon at the sight of him, whereas Evangeline knew perfectly
well what Devin's shortcomings were in that department vis-à-vis
girls his own age and sometimes wondered if the problem was
really herself as Devin always accused or this other thing the servants were whispering, the whole idea of it made Devin boil, and
Baby repeating it to these rich bitch friends of hers, of course in
the long run Baby Claymore's chitchat getting under Devin's skin
would prove useful too. Looked at objectively, Evangeline thought,
Baby did score some valid points based on quite sketchy contact
with Devin, there were times when Devin played these tapes back
that Evangeline found herself agreeing with practically everything
Baby said about him. Of course it was wasted on Devin what a
character Baby was, how sharp the old bird could be. If he had any
sense of humor about himself, he'd see how funnily accurate her
descriptions were. He *was* suspicious. He *did* look shady. He wasn't
subtle, the whole smarty-pants college boy routine was overdrawn

and unconvincing. Worked okay in the sticks, but New Yorkers didn't buy it for a minute: look at the debacle at that realty office. Where did he think he was, Nebraska?

He was her son and her lover and she treasured him more than anything in the world, but as far as the grift went, Devin would never be able to play in Evangeline's league by himself, which was one reason she was desperate to pull off this transfer scam, get the paper all notarized and the taxes paid and hightail it up to Canada, where the Hyksos Corporation of Toronto could secure a humongous mortgage on this nine-million-dollar property and then dissolve itself up there in the tundra, it would be a big enough stake for them both to get out of the game. She knew at this point that whatever Warren had stashed in the Caymans was gone with the wind, and according to Lester, who'd been less than thrilled about looking into it for her, Ritchie Slote had the Santa Rosa properties frozen under court order. They still had part of the Eddy Ramsey mortgage trickling in from Bermuda on demand but Varlene, before deciding to screen out Evelyn's calls, had grudgingly tipped her that the feds were sniffing into that too, ergo the check they wrote to Hardy had bounced, besides which the brokerage bank in Bermuda kept hounding them every time they took money out, about their failure to send photocopied IDs for the Hyksos corporate officers, they really had to get the money to cover these tax payments out of there pronto, and on top of that nuisance Hardy sounded ripe to turn them, Evangeline had called him twenty times promising to make the check for the town car good but even Evangeline had to admit that if it were her instead of Hardy, she would've sworn out a warrant a long time ago. Not much of a window anywhere she looked, but Evangeline wasn't about to panic, panic never got a person anywhere worth going, let Devin rant and rave all he pleased, she was just going to sit here on the sofa with her cocktail and calmly, methodically, write her To Do lists and figure what calls to make and wrap up the Final Dynasty in time for a late summer holiday in Nova Scotia.

✝

Norma anticipated going to Sag Harbor for a wedding on the Friday, and bought an offwhite Donna Karan dress for it at Century 21 on Monday, there was every sort of bill to pay and receipt to file and stationery to order for the Foundation and a Foundation board meeting to schedule, and everybody's vacation was due—overdue, if you factored in all the recent weirdness and the way the summer's first heat wave brought the spring's psychic inflammations bursting to the surface, like boils, or ulcers—and it was never easy at the best of times to keep everything straight, she'd hoped Celestine would agree to stay the weekend as Asra was flying out to Atlanta on Wednesday to spend ten days with a friend, and Baby and Carmen would have to forage for themselves over the holiday, and Baby wanted to have some people in Saturday night for a Fourth of July celebration, but Celestine said she couldn't, someone in her family had a problem, she claimed, Celestine never got specific about her life outside the house, Norma wondered about it at times, she didn't mind that Celestine was aloof but really the girl could pitch in this once, they all did when the house was short-handed. On the other hand, why should she, why should they? They weren't slaves. Their hours ran too long most of the time anyway. Norma knew she had to get over her vexation with Baby at least for the present, until she made some decisions, but she really had been thinking hard about packing this in and going back to Buenos Aires, she was still a young woman, with a much palmier situation ready to hand in Argentina, where things were much better all around than when she left, and what was she doing here, really, almost ten years into what began as an emotional vacation, still catering to the whims of Baby Claymore? The Claymore house was one of those situations that was comfortable enough to fall into for years at a time, it lulled you into a false sense of security, almost into indifference about what went on beyond its walls, the stuff you walked into at the end of the day.

She had wanted to see the Great Beast el Norte close up, the place from which all funky things came. The place where the excitement and the fun never stopped because nobody cared about anything. Well, now she knew it, knew its robot streets and its grinning killer cops and its mad display of dazzling consumer products and its awesome mental engineering, and it bored her to tears, it made her despair for the future of human life, and it seemed to get uglier by the nanosecond: cleaner, richer, uglier. It wasn't just a country for white people, it was a country for *albinos*, pigmentless laboratory creatures with glossy white hair and Dracula red eyes burning through nights of designer martinis and wireless phone chatter.

She had fled the peculiar somnambulistic melancholy of Buenos Aires, the haunted '80s residue of the '70s Dirty War. She had not known a single Argentine who had not had someone close to them disappeared. Sometimes it was a lover or husband or friend or colleague pushed by men in trench coats into a gray Ford Falcon—the death squad vehicle of choice— in broad daylight, and never seen again. Others were shaken out of bed at three in the morning and dragged from their apartments in whatever they were wearing, or not wearing. If they were pregnant women they were taken to concentration camps until they gave birth. The babies were given to barren Army couples, the mothers flown out over the Río Plata and tossed from helicopters. A lot of it had come out in the years when Norma was away, but the ones who did it weren't punished. Every street in Buenos Aires teemed with ghosts, and with torturers in three-piece suits who now managed companies and brokered real estate. Norma had come to New York to escape all that sadness and quiet horror. America was a place without ghosts. She now understood that this was because it was a place without memory.

Norma had noticed that the big decisions in her life always caught her from an oblique angle. She might be thinking very hard in one direction when life spun her abruptly in a different one, without warning. One morning all the things that were full of meaning or promise that seemed to anchor her in one place turned cold and foreign to her, it had happened many times, people she thought she needed as much as oxygen might one morning turn into colorless, annoying presences, there were phone calls Norma found herself unwilling to return, and with places, too, a kind of emigration occurred inside her even if she were still there, she would stop for instance using a particular laundry or buying at a particular market, places she'd patronized for years, for no specific reason she could give, even to herself. They had simply gone gray for her, bled out, finished themselves off. Now New York had turned that way. And New York was all Norma cared to know of America: the rest of it could only be worse, judging from the television and the newspapers. Whenever Norma got in a cab lately, the voice of a loudmouthed celebrity came braying from the innards of the vehicle. *Don't be stupid*, one especially stupid, pushy voice commanded, *buckle up!* Somewhere in the white swarm of indistinct dreams, this voice had become the sound of America to Norma: stupid people ordering other stupid people not to be stupid, as if any of these stupid people could help it.

And the incident with Baby and the realtor, Norma wouldn't have foreseen such a small thing flipping the whole picture into the gray zone when so many worse things never had, but it did, Marguerite Jaffe from The Gilded Nest had rung up, she often found people for Baby's flats as she called them, and this time she had these so-called aristocrats interested in the penthouse, could she bring them around to show the place, and Baby had been so impressed that Marguerite was bringing around a viscount, an actual Italian viscount, that she insisted on showing it herself, and it happened that two minutes after the viscount and his swank bum boy arrived the dry cleaners came, with a delivery of things Norma'd sent out the week before, things for the house, the dry cleaning guys were old friends of the staff and it was usual to invite

them in for coffee and a bagel, but Baby had been standing in the
front hall, jabbering a mile a minute at these two piss-elegant fags
from Milan and Marguerite Jaffe, about her numerous travels in
Italy, dropping names of cities and paintings and people and palaz-
zos, and you could tell from the way these jumped-up catamites
were dressed and how they carried themselves that they thought
their arseholes crapped out gold, and when Norma moved to let
the dry cleaning people into the hall Baby stopped her, she said in
an imperious voice Those people can't come in right now, have
them leave the cleaning in the vestibule, and Norma caught the
expression on the men's faces, it was only there for an instant but
Norma thought, How could you, just to put on airs for a couple of
pointless arsefucking snobs, and then in the penthouse the one
whose ailing mother was apparently going to live with them said
something like Doesn't your staff wear uniforms? I don't think my
mother would live in a place where the staff goes around dressed
however they please, looking pointedly at Norma, My mother isn't
used to that, our people all wear white uniforms, at that point
Norma stepped into it and said, Well, our people don't, and they
aren't going to, at that Baby had to nod agreement, and cleared her
throat, and finally said I don't think we can accommodate you
there, and then they went on with looking at the penthouse but
the nod came just a tiny moment too slow as far as Norma was
concerned, and in that moment she saw all the powdered vanity
and social reachiness that filled so much of Baby's past: as if these
prissy fudge packers in their Valentino suits and Bacco Bucci ankle
boots had awakened for a moment Baby's sense of her exalted station, and stirred a feeling of regret that age had reduced her to frat-
ernizing with dry cleaning people and servants.

At another time Norma might have told herself that Baby
was not that way at all, that Baby had come up from hunger and
certainly didn't consider herself, deep down, superior to anybody
else, but the Bruce de Marco business had already put a strain on
Norma's patience with Baby's self-importance and her need to be

shielded at all times from any form of unpleasantness. Bruce de Marco was odd, but many odd people had inhabited Casa Claymore over the years, a lot of bizarre shit had occurred in the house that Baby hadn't the slightest idea of, for that matter, much of it involving people Baby herself had insisted on renting to, some of them personal friends of hers, they'd protected Baby from all kinds of embarrassing revelations about the people she thought so high and mighty, yet in this one instance, where Baby felt an extreme and to Norma's thinking irrational antipathy to a tenant, Baby seemed determined to blame Norma whenever his contin- ued presence entered her stream of awareness, as if Norma could do anything about it after Baby had taken six thousand dollars of the man's money. Which she'd wrapped in tissue paper to join the other thirty thousand in undeclared income she kept in her closet.

Norma had gone as far as she cared to in humoring Baby's de Marco fixation. And it was a fixation, Baby had even roughed out a pencil drawing of de Marco with arrows pointing out identifying features, like the surgical bump on his nose, his pointy chin, "in case we have to get the law after him," Baby said. Norma had even taken the unpleasant step of giving de Marco her home phone number, so he wouldn't pester Baby with his incessant complaints when Norma wasn't there. And that was how, and why, she hap- pened to be striding up Second Avenue in the thin, warm rain falling that Tuesday afternoon, de Marco had called her and said he had something very important to tell her, something urgent, and he also told her that Baby had been telling him horrible things about her, that part of it didn't surprise her, not because she thought it was true, but because de Marco said all kinds of crazy things to the staff, trying to incite discontent, he'd told Asra for instance that Mrs. Claymore was robbing him blind, that people who did all the different things Asra did in Mrs. Claymore's house were normally paid double what Asra was making, even with room and board thrown in, de Marco had tried to cozy up to Vic by offering him beers and giving him Cuban cigars, the cleaning maids were also targets of de Marco's questionable friendliness, it appeared that whenever he got into conversations with them these conversations always led to negative remarks and accusations concerning Mrs. Claymore, among other things he referred to Mrs. Claymore as "that bitch," or "that old harridan," and claimed Mrs. Claymore let herself into the apartment when de Marco was out, that his personal belongings were shifted around in his absence, it seemed to her that de Marco particularly wanted Norma's confidence, he seemed to be always stopping her in the hall to chitchat and keep her up to speed on his daily activities, restaurants he'd eaten in, movies he'd seen, invariably a lot of blather about business meetings, sweet deals he was winding up, contracts he was signing, Internet blah blah blah, it was all phony baloney familiarity, it didn't feel normal to talk to him and why she'd agreed to meet him at the Silver Star Cafe in the first place she really didn't know, she sort of hoped he'd tell her what his plans after July 6th were, or at least indicate that he had plans to be somewhere besides 41 East 65th Street. Baby had phoned Leon to come in early on the 6th "to help remove the tenant in 1B" if he didn't leave on his own steam.

✝

"Am I speaking to Mrs. Wanda Claymore?"

"Yes you are. I might add you're speaking to a very busy Mrs. Wanda Claymore dear, so what is this in reference to?"

"My name is Kathy Swales? I'm in charge of special promotions at Circus Circus casino? In Las Vegas?"

I know this voice, Baby thought. *I've heard this voice somewhere before.*

"What can I do for you, Ms. Swales."

"Actually Mrs. Claymore—may I call you Wanda? Actually Wanda I'm calling because Circus Circus wants to do something for *you,* you see every year we award a number of free trips with all expenses paid as a promotion, the winners are chosen at random and you happen to be among the twenty lucky people we've selected for a weekend of gourmet dining, a luxury suite in our hotel, an all-expense-paid trip to promote our hotel and casino complex, your name was entered in our sweepstakes by a friend of yours, apparently, and, we just held the drawing last night, and your name came up as one of our winners! I think you'll be happy to know that this prize is equivalent to five thousand dollars cash, and among the other things you get for free, the *casino supplies you with one thousand dollars* to try your luck at our gaming tables. Sound exciting?"

"Oh, exciting isn't the word." No, Baby thought, the word would be *scam*, or *bullshit*. Circus Circus, she thought, my ass.

"We have a very flexible choice of dates available for you to come here at your convenience and enjoy our deluxe hospitality, and there are no strings attached in terms of endorsements or testimonials. Our goal is to show our lucky winners the best time they've ever had. The idea is that they'll tell their friends, and their friends will tell other friends. We've found it's a wonderful way to draw business. Las Vegas, you know, is America's Number One Vacation Destination of the '90s, offering fun and relaxation for the whole family."

"Well, that sounds wonderful. If you happen to have a whole family."

"This is a vacation for two, Wanda, meaning that you're welcome to bring your husband, or a friend, a little niece or nephew, grandchild, anyone special you'd like to treat to some magical holiday enjoyment."

"This certainly sounds like my lucky day."

"We hope it will be your lucky *weekend*, if your pleasures include blackjack, roulette, poker, Keno, and the many other games of chance a short elevator ride from your suite, which offers a panoramic view of our entire city. Room service from our many fine restaurants by the way is also 'on the house.' But our winners certainly aren't obligated to gamble, many don't, there's marvelous shopping right here in the hotel, name brand boutiques like

Versace and Chanel, and four-star restaurants and all kinds of amusements for children, in other words fun for the whole family. Plus headliners like Sandra Bernhard and Shecky Greene, Wayne Newton, Phyllis Diller, Barry Manilow, Siegfried and Roy, Cirque du Soleil, Coolio, the list is endless. I don't know if you've ever visited our city, Wanda, but today's Vegas isn't the Vegas many people still think of. Today's Vegas is a city steeped in family values and wholesome entertainment, along with sophisticated adult-type nightlife. Gambling, yes. But also Ferris wheels and water slides and first-class art galleries and other cultural attractions on a par with New York and Paris."

"And a depleted aquifer, from what I understand."

"I'm sorry Wanda my phone just had a little glitch. Now for our winners to qualify, Wanda, we just need a little bit of information, to verify. You reside, it says here, at 41 East 65th Street in New York City, is that correct?"

"That's correct, dear."

"And Wanda Claymore, *C-l-a-y-m-o-r-e* is the correct spelling of your last name?"

"It is indeed."

"And Wanda is spelled like it sounds?"

"With one *W*," said Baby, still trying to place the voice squalling over the phone line.

"What we don't seem to have, because your friend forgot to put it in, and for tax purposes we have to enter it, is your Social Security number."

"I thought you said this was free."

"Oh, no, it's completely free, *you* don't incur any tax liability on a gift of this kind, but *we*, at Circus Circus, have our advertising deduction, we have to show where we've spent our budget—"

"Ms. Swales—may I call you Kathy?—it may surprise you to learn that I am eighty-four years old. I don't travel, and if I still did, an establishment called Circus Circus in Las Vegas is very possibly the last place on earth I would care to visit in the precious time I have remaining."

"We're only as old as we feel, Wanda."

"Mrs. Claymore to you, sweetheart. And being eighty-four, *Kathy*, I would think it self-evident that I wasn't born yesterday. So I suggest you direct your little operation, whatever it really is, at someone more gullible who has a lot more time to waste talking to you than I do. Don't call here again or I'll report you to the Better Business Bureau."

┼

Devin waited at a window table in view of the lobster tank. Queer for a coffeeshop to feature a lobster tank, right beside a five-tiered revolving cake saver, but the Silver Star Cafe did. On Second Avenue the thin rain skewed traffic, even though it fell so lightly that no one carried an umbrella.

He wrote in a pocket-size notebook, his mouth pensively slack. His morning had been fraught, even a little dicey, thanks to his own screwup, he'd faxed the Bermuda bank the previous day to overnight a money order payable to Bruce de Marco, and then tried to cash it at Chase Bank as Devin Slote. The Chase Bank wouldn't cash a double-endorsed financial instrument from a Bermuda bank, Bermuda banks it developed did not issue money orders anyway but a different, more complicated kind of certified check and it had been necessary to call the Bermuda bank from the Chase branch office and get the person Devin had been dealing with down there on the telephone, to make a voice identification of Devin as one of the officers of the Hyksos Corporation, authorized to cash the check. Even then, the Chase Bank would not agree to actually cash the check. The Chase Bank instead accepted it in payment for two bank checks written to the New York City Department of Finance, for the separate tax bills on the pending transfer of the house on East 65th Street. All this palaver

and confusion had almost eaten up the time Devin needed to pur-
chase a stun gun and a pair of plastic handcuffs at J&S Security
Specialists on West 27th Street, a box of thirty industrial-size plastic
garbage bags, a roll of duct tape, and thirty feet of nylon rope at a
hardware store on Seventh Avenue, and two Halloween masks from
the movie *Scream* at a novelty store near Union Square, before his
meeting with Norma at the Silver Star Cafe. Devin's sensibility was
such that he attached somewhat greater importance to finding the
Halloween masks than to clearing the certified checks or buying
the stun gun.

Devin's sensibility was also such that he enjoyed what he
thought of as the "irony" of meeting Norma in the Silver Star Cafe
while the paraphernalia he'd collected all morning lay piled in a
Bloomingdale's shopping bag under the table.

"Thanks so much for coming," he told her as she sat down.
"Let me buy you something to eat."

Norma shook her head. She didn't care to eat with Bruce de
Marco, or to let him buy her anything.

"I don't want anything, thanks anyway."

She didn't like him. He knew that from tapping the phone.
But she had also told someone on that same phone that she didn't
understand why Baby went on about him all the time. So she wasn't
one hundred percent against him, either, the way Devin saw it.

"He's a creep, but Wanda knows plenty of creeps, and she
hardly ever has to see this one," had been Norma's precise words.
Norma had also phoned Panicelli Superior Meats several times and
asked for Vinnie, evidently to question Vinnie about his strange
friend Bruce de Marco. Fortuitously, Vinnie was never reachable.
Golf holiday, business trip, for a pork butcher Vinnie was quite the
bloody sky bird, was how his mother put it. Ellen de Beckwith had
told Baby Claymore back in April that she and Bruce de Marco
had been friends with Vinnie Panicelli "since the Seventies." In her
calls to Norma, Ellen had unfailingly mentioned that she, Bruce,
and Vinnie went "way back," had even gone on holidays together.

And she named the golden places where these holidays took place, as if the flawless weather of those serendipitous times would be checking in with the new tenant.

Evangeline had, as it happened, gotten Vinnie's name from a Mutual of Omaha salesman she met at a longevity confab in Pasadena, as somebody who knew somebody who rented chic apartments in New York City, and Mrs. Claymore's name from some underling at Panicelli Superior Meats. Vinnie Panicelli had never heard of Ellen de Beckwith or Bruce de Marco or anyone else the Slotes had recently purported to be. Like the active phone jack to Baby's line in the closet of 1B, Vinnie's current hospitalization for bypass surgery was an unimaginable stroke of further luck.

"Listen, Norma, do you happen to know Mrs. Claymore's Social Security number?"

A waitress asked if she needed a menu. Norma told her she would have a cup of tea.

"No, I don't. Why?"

"Can you get it for me?"

"What do you need it for?"

"Well, frankly, she's been coming into my apartment and taking documents."

Norma kept her face neutral. She was no stranger to other people's paranoia and tended to handle it gingerly. You never knew when a raving paranoid would turn out to be right about something.

"Bruce, I've known Mrs. Claymore a very long time. I can promise you she wouldn't do that."

"But she has, Norma." Bruce nodded, as if it were hardly credible to him either, yet he knew it to be true. "And I need her Social Security number to check and find out if she's done this kind of thing before."

"What, check with who?"

"Well, the police."

Norma had to laugh.

"Wanda Claymore has never had any trouble with the police, Bruce, she's richer than God, and she's led a very clean life. Erratic, maybe, but clean."

"There could have been complaints," he said. "Complaints you never heard about."

"I don't think so. When there's a complaint in that house, believe it, I'm the first one who hears about it. But look, if you're so sure about this," Norma said, moving her chess piece with trepidation, "if you really think she's taking things from your apartment, I mean under the circumstances, if I were in your shoes, you know, I would just move somewhere else. All this antagonism isn't good for anybody, including you, obviously."

"How can I move? I paid her for three months."

This was bold enough to startle her.

"Three months? Bruce, you paid one month. Six thousand dollars, that's one month."

Baby wouldn't, Norma thought. Baby wouldn't hide something like that from her. Unless Baby—no, she just wouldn't.

"Norma, I gave that woman $18,000 the day I moved in."

But *would* Baby go into Bruce's place when he was out, rummage around looking for "incriminating evidence" of these wild things she imagined about him? Norma *wished* she couldn't picture it. Unfortunately, she could.

"Bruce, please, you paid her for one month, I keep all the records, I have her copy of your receipt, it's six thousand dollars. I'm sure she'd give you half of that back if you would just get out of her building."

"That bitch is lying to you. I paid her for three months."

Norma felt suddenly dead tired. Yes, she thought. I am going back to Buenos Aires. Soon. The decision lifted, for a moment, the weight of all these impossible individuals and their tangled psychic ganglia.

"Okay, Bruce, have it your way. You paid for three months. She lied to me about it and gave me a phony receipt. She's an awful person. She steals from people's apartments. For Christ's sake, she's eighty-four years old, why don't you just pack your crap and get out and leave her alone? Oh, and while I think of it, what is it you claim she said about me that was so bad you couldn't tell me about it over the phone?"

"I'd rather not upset you. It was so mean." Bruce's unchanged expression brought her back to the force field of everything she'd just resolved to give up. His blandness unnerved her. It was as if her reactions were beside the point. As if, in a way, she wasn't even there. The only thing that was there was the inner narrative of Bruce de Marco. Psychopath, she decided firmly. "I think you people would be very surprised to hear what Mrs. Claymore says about you all behind your backs."

The waitress laid the cup of tea in front of her. Norma opened her wallet and put two singles on the table and stood up.

"You're not leaving?" Bruce was, disgustingly, smiling.

"I am leaving. Listen. I don't know who you are, and I don't know what the game is, but if I were you, I'd watch what you say about Mrs. Claymore to the people who work in her house. What you think about her personally is your business, but don't bother me or anyone else on the staff about it any more, because we're all pretty sick of it. She's not the easiest person in the world to get along with all the time, but we know her. We care about her. We don't know you."

"I'm just trying to do you a favor."

"Something tells me that's the last thing you'd be trying to do. Like I say, Bruce, we don't know you. And we don't like you, either. Goodbye."

"I *am* going to look into this. I'm going to check into this with the police. I'm going to call you over the weekend and tell you what I find out."

"*Don't* call me," Norma said. "I don't want to hear another thing about this. Anyway, I'm going out of town."

†

Wilbur Sumac had nailed down an excellent deal. He had worked this deal out with a Clark County assistant district attorney and two federal agents in the presence of a legal aid lawyer. The deal kept his record clean and allowed him to retain his concealed weapons permits and all other legal items in the house off Break Point Drive. ATF would drop all the weapons charges emanating from the buy he made with April de Beckwith at Discount Pawn in Henderson in exchange for cooperation, a buy that was technically illegal because April de Beckwith had paid for the guns that Wilbur picked out, claiming, when asked, to be Wilbur's cousin, since Nevada law specifically stated that weapons could only be purchased by third parties if they were related by blood to the actual buyer, ATF would also bury any Wilbur involvement with the Glock 27 used in the Eddy Ramsey murder if that weapon ever turned up and proved to be one of Wilbur's guns, in exchange for Wilbur's testimony in the Ramsey case that the Los Angeles DA was putting together, Wilbur did not know what deal April de Beckwith had been offered so it came as a considerable relief that Wilbur was the one Evangeline decided to call.

She called to tell Wilbur to forget about looking for abandoned or defaulted properties coming up at public auction, and to offer him a job managing her new apartment house in New York City. The current owner, she said, was this senile ballerina who danced around the halls at night in her bathrobe, an old souse, according to Evangeline, sadly the victim of Alzheimer's, whose building was crawling with faggots and riffraff that Wilbur would have to throw out, Wilbur would also have to fire the staff, get all the faggots out, get all the riffraff out, Wilbur would have his own apartment on the ground floor and make more money than he'd ever seen, Evangeline told him to go to the Continental Airlines counter at McCarran Airport on the evening of July 4th, there would be an electronic ticket waiting for him, Evangeline told him to take his cell phone and get on the redeye and wait to hear from her the following morning, the morning of July 5th, at Kennedy. They were going to have some good times, Evangeline promised. They were going to have the time of their lives.

†

Evangeline had arranged, on the glass bedside table, an array of medicaments, pill bottles, asthma inhalers, green NyQuil cough syrup in a cloudy glass, an insulin syringe, and wads of tissue everywhere, as if an invalid had been expectorating for weeks in the close, stuffy room. The bedclothes were artfully rumpled, numerous fat pillows littered the bed in a state of shock, the lights were dimmed to a nighttime hospital hush. A small, fragile-looking writing table had been placed near the window, with a dim little tensile lamp sitting on it like a tiny crane, tilted at a peculiar angle that obscured the business end of the table's surface, with the chair behind it obliquely facing the only other chair in the room. She had been fussing with this dismal still-life for several days, ever since a notary Devin found through the Pierre Hotel had refused to stamp the documents they presented him with, on the grounds that they had already been signed before his arrival. She would, he said, have to sign them again in his presence, or at least sign another sheet of paper so he could compare the signatures.

Evangeline could execute a pretty fair simulacrum of Wanda Koukoulas Claymore's signature after long practice, working from Devin's rent receipt, but she didn't dare try it "live," so to speak, and the signatures on the deed and transfer documents really had to be done with a carbon trace anyway, because at the very least they had to pass a cursory inspection of signatures on file with the Bank of New York, in case the Canadian mortgage company decided to run a check. They were already on shaky ground there, since Devin had had to manufacture a Social Security card for Mrs. Claymore, using one of the blanks Evangeline always had on hand. The area number, 439, would be recognized as valid for Louisiana, Baby's natal state, and the group number, 88, seemed a safe bet given Baby's date of birth in 1916, but the serial number at the end was just a crap shoot, and woe to them, for sure, if the transfer documents fell under close scrutiny. They would have another chance to get the number right, though not on the papers they were going to file. There would be no chance at that point of getting a new set notarized in New York. Evangeline thought she could fast-talk a reason, up in Canada, why an entirely wrong number appeared on the papers if she had the correct number ready to hand, but there was also a problem with timing, a lot depended on how they handled Wilbur and how much confusion Wilbur could generate between the 5th of July and whatever date they got the loan approved.

Her more immediate concern was of course her wig, a curdled fringe of it extruding like a Clean 'n Vac brush roller dipped in orange paint solvent, trapped in place by a puffy shower cap's taut rubber brim, the morbid pallor she'd slathered over her already slack, chalky face with a thin application of clown white, the comically huge, thick-lensed glasses she'd lifted from a Duane Reade on Broadway, the flappy ice blue housecoat that looked like it had been tortured out of a down comforter, the bunny tail pink slippers: well, okay, she didn't look much like Wanda but she did look old and sick and unpredictable. Lighting was so important in this type of situation.

Devin had walked down to the Plaza Hotel to fetch the new notary, a Ms. Sizemore who worked in a realty, who for some reason would only agree to come to the house on the holiday, fine by Evangeline but how pathetic not to have any party plans, hopefully not such a lonely woman that she was hypervigilant about the exercise of her trivial authority as a notary, Evangeline kept pacing from the bedroom to the monitor in the entry alcove, she knew Baby had people coming because she'd heard her gabbling about it all day on the wiretap, Patsy and Ikea and Sally and the dykes from Apartment 2E, who were going off to the Hamptons next morning, and Mica It, the singer in 4F, who was likewise leaving town in the morning, all these people flying off or driving off, even Wilson Farmhole the gay novelist had plans to be elsewhere, he'd promised Baby to drop down for a cocktail before taking off, but she'd told Asra on the phone that afternoon how desolate the building would be on Sunday and oh how she wished he were there with her, she hated when it was just her and Carmen these days, and she mentioned too that she was having trouble with her phone, this clicking noise all the time, maybe the wires were messed up, she was going to call her friend Weymouth who worked for the phone company, Weymouth always came to the house on his own time to take care of Baby's telephone needs, old friend evidently, maybe an old fuck, Evangeline speculated, she could see the old bird having it off with phone repairmen and that linebacker of a plumber, horny old goat, Baby talked dirty sometimes and Evelyn got stimulated playing the tapes back, yes here was some lady coming in, with her blond hair worked up in a twist, one of those telephone voices Evangeline didn't have a face to go with until tonight no doubt, buzzed in from downstairs, she'd also heard the elevator going down a couple times and of course if she went and looked through the orchid greenhouse she could see them as well, down at the patio picnic table, their well-bred, dermatologically pampered faces bright and carefree in the soft flickering glow of the tiki torches, none of *their* lifts had ever gone tragically wrong, Evelyn bet, the way hers had by putting her face in the hands of that quack in Fresno who fucked up Devin's nose the same afternoon, Evelyn had commenced a lawsuit about it but then realized her so-called checkered past would probably get dragged into court and skipped the preliminary hearing, guy lost his license eventually anyway over something else but still, a real miscarriage of justice there. No surgical mishaps in Baby's crowd, no quacks for the likes of them. A regular hen fest from the muffled sound of it. Evangeline thought it best to stay out of that greenhouse area where there must have been a window seat or something like that once upon a time, a dormer type of thing they extended out to house the plants, it certainly hadn't been part of the original architecture, anyway you could draw a heavy curtain across it so people in the garden couldn't look up and see you, if she turned the light off completely of course she could go over there and watch them, but she had the light in the room just right, that perfect sickroom dying glow, faint as a fireplace ember, well, if she just parted the curtain a chink, just for a second, she'd been hearing about this party all afternoon, naturally she was curious to see what they all looked like. They wouldn't be so giddy the next time they all got together, that was for sure.

✝

"Hot dogs and beans," said Patsy gaily, heaping mesclun on her paper plate with a pair of scallop-edged metal tongs, "it's the perfect American meal for the Fourth."

The beans were a cold Tuscan white bean salad with garlic from Balducci's, and most of the numerous other fancy viands had been ordered in, but Baby had boiled the Oscar Mayer franks herself while Carmen toasted the hot dog rolls. There were three kinds of mustard and four kinds of relish and Baby's special ketchup and horseradish mixture, which tasted perfect on a hot beef frank, the secret was a dash of cumin. As part of the patriotic theme, Baby had dressed up as Uncle Sam, in the red, white and blue costume that curiously admonishing icon wore on Army recruitment posters, with the Stars and Stripes top hat crowning her "I Love Lucy" hairdo. She just looked adorable.

"Andy Warhol," said the futurist Rhonda Corn, a sveltely skinny crewcut gal of forty-six who favored black turtleneck t-shirts and beige Gap khakis with side pockets as both business suit and evening wear, "said that the Queen of England can't buy a better hot dog than the hot dog you and I buy at a baseball game."

"But you know something," chimed in Rhonda's lover, magazine editrix Morgan Talbot, a dramatically more ample-bottomed vision of fashion desuetude in a carefully ripped pair of Levi's and a man's flannel work shirt, "the Queen of England actually could. I mean if she wanted to."

"I certainly hope she could," Patsy said, "what with all this Mad Cow Disease they're getting over there."

"This is delish," exuded Sally, munching mesclun au vinaigrette from her fingers. They were all milling about the kitchen, helping themselves to goodies from enormous tinfoil takeout tubs, while Ikea and Mica It, having garnished their plates very sparingly with salad and a few beans, had been silly enough to get trapped at the patio picnic table listening to Wilson Farmhole, who had, Baby whispered, been the very first to arrive, and was inhaling martinis as fast as Carmen could pour them. Baby thought Something Had Upset the famed gay novelist, who was working himself up to some epic, Byzantine harangue, if his distinctive and pauseless voice drilling in from the patio were anything to judge by. He seemed to be discussing his Theory of the Novel with Ikea, who of course couldn't follow a thing he was saying, and Mica It, who was so ethereal and laconic that what she made of it no one would ever be able to guess. Mica It was a tall, blond, surprisingly soft-featured Teutonic sphinx who sang in a lugubrious basso profundo of madness and death and their many charms, on the Island label.

Les girls, as Baby and Sally and Patsy privately called Morgan Talbot and Rhonda Corn, were already arguing in a jokey-but-secretly-lethally-serious way about whom they would and wouldn't have over to the house in Sagaponick on the following evening, when Rhonda would make her famous tamales from scratch: Morgan and Rhonda were the kind of highly visible people who could ring friends or even perfect strangers in the afternoon and expect them at dinner three hours later, even if it clashed with plans already made and caused awkward fractures and fissures in the Hamptons social calendar. Morgan Talbot *was* "Interface," once upon a hard-to-remember time the ne plus ultra of celebrity chatter, which had lost about seven million a year and most of its readership and advertising under her relentless management, and which was now being kept alive by artificial respiration in the form of the billionaire owner's massive divorce settlement to Morgan's last-before-Rhonda-lover, the magazine's putative publisher, but "Interface" still enjoyed considerable cachet among the more addled species of debutante and heroin-addicted jewelry designer, and real brand loyalty among the very youngest butterflies and creepy caterpillars of the fashion world, and of course Morgan also wrote the influential "Time of the Month" column for the recent News Corporation start-up "Avarice."

Rhonda Corn, the futurologist, Morgan's short-time companion, had a slightly different but no less imperious fame as a lavishly paid consultant to numerous corporate think tanks (she was, by her own account, a regular one-woman Mensa, distantly rivaled in brains only by Marilyn Vos Savant, who could not predict the future the way Rhonda could and really only excelled at cryptograms and that sort of thing) and as author of the best-selling bible of futurology, *Absolute Corn: 21 Trends That Will Change Human Nature.* Morgan and Rhonda liked to tell people they had great *synergy* together. Morgan would lewdly wink when she said it. Rhonda wouldn't.

"They certainly are *synergistic*," Sally murmured to Baby as the couple moved out to the patio.

"Or symptomatic," Patsy giggled, plucking a boiled hot dog from the warming tray with her fingers. "Wait till Morgan finds out she's been Nominated," Patsy went on in a conspiring whisper.

"Let's not inform her until they move out," Baby said. "In case she takes it the wrong way."

"I don't see why Rhonda couldn't snag a nomination in a category or two," said Sally. "If anything, she's overdeserving."

"Maybe so," quibbled Patsy, slapping honey mustard on her hot dog, "but that *Ten Days That Shook the World* or whatever it was came out years ago." She returned a genial smile and wave Morgan aimed at her from the patio as she sampled her frank. Morgan and Rhonda had taken seats on either side of Wilson Farmhole on the picnic bench: the three were old chums from the same closet, which they'd all abandoned after the coast was clear, though not so tardily as to look like the last ones out. "I mean," Pasty said in an urgent lowered voice, *"whose ass has she kissed lately?"*

Sally bit her lower lip, which had the perfect shade of vamp crimson lipstick on it. Sally was fifty-six but she could still pass for the young Greta Scacchi, let alone for thirty-six, except in really harsh lighting. That regimen of yoga and the Alexander Technique, plus blended scotch, was working for Sally with at least as much synergistic pizzazz as anything Morgan and Rhonda had going.

"What about a Lifetime Achievement sort of thing," Sally ventured uncertainly.

Baby, biting into a frank, shook her head vigorously. She chewed up her gob of frank and swallowed with impatience.

"Those never have the magic of the real thing," she said. "I think the honoree always feels cheated. After all, there's no competition involved. And anyway, Rhonda's young. She'll get back in the ring with the best of them, you watch."

As the patio could not be avoided any longer and the others weren't staying long, the three friends carried their plates and glasses out to the moonlight and tiki torches. A fierce conversation had apparently flared up around the subject of Wilson Farmhole's last novel, which had flopped. Morgan was expatiating on the crassness of popular tastes, the encouragement of which her livelihood depended upon, of course, but she was speaking to Wilson as a Gay Person, someone who knew how the Pain of Rejection carried over into adult life, when one's best efforts were often ignored because of Homophobia.

"Oh, please," Wilson said contemptuously, staring directly into Morgan's face, "let's call a spade a spade."

"Maybe it's because you do," Rhonda interjected, "that some of your Southern material has met with a certain antipathy."

"Yes, from a bunch of deconstructionist Lefties on college campuses," Wilson fumed. "That whole cabal of theorists down at Duke would love to see me go the way of Edna Ferber. But at the end of the day, Rhonda, let's face it, Felicia Doberman killed that book, she called every magazine and reviewer in her Rolodex and made sure that *one of the finest works of American fiction in the last fifty years* got tossed in the critical toilet."

"Well," Morgan said, "it *was* all about her, I wonder if I wouldn't do the same."

"Did Edna Ferber write *The Good Earth*? That became a movie?" Sally wanted to know. Baby shushed her.

"I don't think you *would* do the same, Morgan," Wilson said, shaking his slightly lowered head of gloriously full, curly, salt-and-pepper hair, achieving a characteristic fusion of obsequiousness and pomposity that only Morgan herself ever truly surpassed him in. "I think you have far too much respect for art to put it on a level of such pettiness."

"Try the summer pasta salad with vegetables," Patsy encouraged Wilson with a heartening smile. "It's scrumptious."

"You really should eat something," Baby agreed. Wilson had already exhausted the gin and was working his way through her last fifth of Stoli. "The food's fabulous."

Carmen came out of the kitchen, carrying her own plate, and sat down beside Patsy, who smiled at her and said, "Okay, Carmen, you're *off duty*. Let these people fetch their own drinks."

Baby seconded her emotion.

Mica It lit a joint. She lit the joint, a major blunt wrapped in a cigar leaf, in a smooth, deliberate, expert motion and sucked in a prodigious quantity of smoke. Sally looked askance at Baby, who had once thrown one of the Getty kids out for doing drugs in the house. Of course those had been hard drugs. Mica passed the joint to Ikea, who reached for it automatically and froze with her fingers in the air to check Baby's attitude.

"Oh, go ahead," Baby told her. Ikea puffed happily, handed it back to Mica It, and broke into a coughing fit. It went on and on in tortured gasps until she ran for a glass of water. Patsy sighed expressively.

Just then, an unforseen event occurred. Everyone had something in her mouth and Wilson Farmhole turned silent after draining his seventh martini, and in the momentary suspension of talk, Mica It cleared her throat with the unmistakable intention of speaking. As Mica It never said anything, the entire company gaped in anticipation.

"I saw a woman up there," she said. She moved her chin a mere fraction but everyone followed its cue to the protruding greenhouse of Apartment 1B and the dark curtain blacking out the rest of the apartment.

"Not now," Mica went on. She had a deep, husky, abnormally slow voice and a thick German accent, in English she enunciated every word with a pause at both ends, as if it were a strange rock she'd found in her Prada handbag. "About an hour ago. She peeked through the curtain holding the edge of it so I wouldn't see, with a strange look on her face. Wearing a long blue nightgown, and a funny cap on her head, and some hair sticking out strangely, it was the same orange color as Baby's hair."

Sally automatically put her hand over Baby's trembling fingers.

✝

With your long blonde hair and your eyes of blue, the only thing I ever got from you was Sorrow, the David Bowie of "Pin Ups" sang in Devin's Discman ESP2 headphones, as he waited in the living room for Evangeline to finish her Academy Award performance. She was playing Camille for the benefit of Diane Sizemore, notary public, with a great deal of histrionic hacking and coughing and staggering about, *You never do what you know you ought ta, Something tells me you're the Devil's daughter, Sorrow*, Devin really couldn't watch it or listen to it through the doorway, he would have to either laugh or cry and he really wasn't sure which it would be, Diane Sizemore didn't *look* like a stupid person, she was about twenty-seven and looked pretty good, in fact, pretty there, pretty present, someone he might like to know under other circumstances, but she glazed over right away when Devin brought her into the bedroom and saw this decrepit invalid hawking her lungs out, he really had to hand it to Mom, she knew how to play every mark that fell into her lair, lurching over to the folder of papers she needed to "sign" while Diane Sizemore fidgeted in the chair across the room, unable to actually see the papers because of the angle at which Evangeline held the folder, they'd rehearsed it a half dozen times, so Devin knew.

He supposed he should feel sort of triumphant at this moment, *I can do anything right or wrong I can talk anyhow I get along I don't care anyway I never lose anyway anyhow anyway I choose*, and he did, in a way, but he also wished Evangeline would drop dead in the middle of pretending she was about to drop dead, it was one of Devin's misfortunes that memory played a much more active role in his scanning pattern than it did in hers, and indeed he had for a long time experienced these waves of fuguelike sadness related to things he wished he hadn't done or seen or heard about, Devin called it "memory poisoning" in the many thoughts he kept to himself around his mother, *Won't you tell me, where have all the good times gone?*

And it was always her, of course, who triggered these unwanted blurps of remembrance, some expression on her face or a word or phrase that had bubbled out of her a million times, tonight it was something she said when Diane Sizemore came into the bedroom after rendering a huge tuberculosis-strength cough and aping enormous difficulty in raising herself out of bed, all she said was, *Darling where have you got the papers*, and Devin went to the desk and picked up the folder for her to see, precisely as they'd planned, and said, *They're right here, Mother.* Adding, *I'll just wait in the living room.* In the living room he found that he needed quickly to pour himself a triple shot of J&B, because the day she came to pick him

up at the apartment in Goleta, the day after his midterm exams
when they drove down to LAX and flew out the same afternoon
to Oahu, had gurgled up from its hiding place, he thought he had
buried that day so securely that nothing she did however outrageous would ever compel him to recall it but suddenly here it was,
in living color, Evelyn behind the wheel of a rented red Mustang
convertible with a white Hermes scarf tied around her wig and a
pair of pink-framed Lolita sunglasses hiding her eyes, as Devin slid
into the front seat beside her and asked *Where's Dad?* as he noticed
an ornate metal cannister resting in the crack between the bucket
seats, which Evangeline patted before shifting into second and said,
He's right here.

✝

"I'd be very curious to know," said one of the federal agents as they
confiscated the bulletproof vest Wilbur had thought it prudent to
wear on his trip to New York, "what makes you think we'd let you
take a bullet. Also why you'd be expecting one. I thought you were
a friend of these individuals."

They stood outside the terminal at JFK in an obvious law
enforcement configuration and a lot of people passing in and out
were staring at them. The agents wore sharply fitted suits and death
squad sunglasses and carried walkie-talkies, and the holsters under
their jackets were not what anyone would call concealed. Wilbur had
on a clean shirt and a decent pair of seersucker trousers but he really
was dressed for Vegas and the cowboy boots, he realized, sent the
wrong kind of message about Wilbur Sumac as a federal informant.

"I just figure, you can't be too careful," he told the agents
weakly. Wilbur knew that however he dressed he looked like a
crumbling, disreputable loser at the tail end of a pointless life, you
couldn't change any of that by switching aftershave lotions or buying an Armani jacket. Still, he now thought those might have been
good ideas.

"But see, Wilbur, State of New York, a civilian wearing body armor, an offense punishable with jail time, you really can be."

"Too careful," the other agent put in.

"Think they'd plug you in the lobby of the Hilton?" the first agent, the agent in charge, quizzed with an empty smile on his lips. "That doesn't sound like the individuals we're dealing with. That sounds more like a Mark David Chapman, disgruntled loner type of individual. Indifferent to the setting, fixated mainly on obliterating his victim, basically asking to get caught. What our forensic psychologists call the suicidal cry for help."

"We see it all the time," the second agent added. "Suicide by cop is what it boils down to."

"That isn't what we're dealing with here, though," said the first agent.

Wilbur's cell phone went off in his pocket. The agent in charge nodded for him to answer it. Wilbur switched on the phone, said hello. He listened for a few minutes, switched the phone off.

"She says she's going to be late," Wilbur told them. "She says they're on the Garden State Parkway having car trouble, and to meet her at the Hilton at two o'clock instead of noon."

"Hunky dory," said the agent in charge. "Gives us a little time to grab a sandwich. So, let's go have a bite and check out the Hilton."

†

Carmen had taken Ratty upstairs for a run on the roof and said she would do the laundry while Baby napped. Baby however did not feel the slightest bit tired, on the contrary, what they'd seen out the window had energized her tremendously, namely the de Marco creep and his girlfriend moving things into a car, quite an elegant car, and they were stuffing everything into the back seat, in plastic garbage bags, instead of the trunk, just like the trash they were. It was a powerfully hot day and the street was dead the way it always was the day after Fourth of July, she supposed she ought to keep her eye on de Marco to make sure he didn't cart off her Roentgens rolltop desk, which she suspected he'd damaged, or some other valuable item, but chances were, Baby thought, de Marco wouldn't know a valuable item from a worthless one. And that fat ass girlfriend! Talk about a whole lot of junk in the trunk! Waddling back and forth with that big floppy hat pulled over her head, and she was actually wearing *capri pants*, to show off those piano legs evidently, Baby was tempted to call Patsy back and report the good news, because last night as Patsy was leaving Baby told her again how worried she was and had mentioned it yet again on the phone this morning, that de Marco would have to be *ejected* first thing Monday, now she felt ridiculous for fretting so much on the subject, Sally was right, she did spend too much time cooped up though really Baby enjoyed all her everyday habits, her swims and her manicures and reading to Asra in French, she didn't miss the outside, too much chaos out there, too many crazy people, anyway this episode had persuaded her that Patsy was right, too, there really wasn't any point in continuing to rent these apartments, the maintenance chewed up so much of the income that she'd probably make out better just investing what she had in a hedge fund or whatever, of course one did get interesting people still, not that the current lot were so interesting, Mica It intrigued her, though, and Farmhole when he was sober enough to carry on a conversation. But was it worth it, probably not, if you ran the risk of letting a de Marco in.

    She would have to scale back the staff, of course, but not too drastically, she wouldn't want the place to turn lifeless, all these floors of furniture and tapestries and objets d'art just sitting in silence gathering dust. Once the Foundation was operating, the house would become a school, students would study the intricacies of couture needlework and design there and live in the rooms but that wouldn't happen until Baby was gone, the non-profit tax structure the lawyers had worked out really didn't allow for her to be in residence and also maximize the tax break, and anyway she wouldn't want to have the place swarming with strangers while she was still around, any more than she wanted it empty.

She moved from the window to the chaise near the fireplace and popped a caramel into her mouth and opened a Penguin edition of Madame de Sévigné's letters. Baby went through cycles of reading letters, people no longer wrote them of course or no longer wrote them with ease and depth and reflection, life moved too quickly now and parts of the human heart seemed to have atrophied in the species as a whole, *My dearest Mary—I am writing not to write a letter but to do everything required to receive one,* Hannah Arendt had written Mary McCarthy. *Dearest Hannah: The next mail leaves in forty-five minutes, and I'm writing this note for purely selfish reasons: because my heart is full of emotion and I want to talk.* Were there any people left who opened themselves to each other this way? *Dearest Max, Your letter at first reading had a distinctly Berlin intonation, but by the second reading that had already faded away and it was your voice again,* Kafka to Max Brod, *Dyodyu, my golden one, I got your letters, No. 9 last night and No. 10 today. Thanks for writing a few warm words at last. I needed them badly, as I said in yesterday's postcard. I'm sorry about my bitter tone, but, my dear love, it hurt that you wrote only of business. Not a single loving word, and I was feeling rotten. I still do. You don't know why. Well, let me tell you,* Rosa Luxemburg to Leo Jogiches. *Dear Roma: Thanks for your prompt answer and kind words. When one has no self-assurance and faith oneself, someone else's is very welcome even if it doesn't quite replace one's own. What I lack is not so much faith in my own gifts but something more pervasive: trust in life, confident acquiescence in a personal destiny, faith in the ultimate benevolence of existence,* Bruno Schulz to Romana Halpern. The great letter-writers had been no more diffident in speaking of the heart than the simplest peasant. Who really spoke of it today without embarrassment, or irony, or the one emotion people seemed to display with real bravura now, contempt? *I do urge you, dear heart,* wrote Madame de Sévigné to Madame de Grignan, *to look after your eyes—as to mine, you know they must be used up in your service. You must realize, my love, that because of the way you write to me I have to cry when I read your letters. To understand something of the state I am in over you, add to the tenderness and natural feeling I have for you this little circumstance that I am quite sure you love me, and then consider my overwhelming emotion.* Baby wished above all that Asra would write her a letter in the course of his holiday. But people simply didn't do that any more, even when they really cared about you. They phoned, perhaps, or scrawled a little something on a postcard, but a real letter was something that fell out of time's obliterating rush, that tapped too affectingly into a kind of utopian longing that no one could afford and still live in this particular world.

There was a loud pounding knock at the door and something incomprehensible shouted outside, Baby dropped her book and stepped off the chaise and went to the door and opened it. She looked into the hall. There was nobody there, just the feeling that something had passed through it quickly, but the door of 1B yawned open halfway, and she noticed something odd about the floor in there, and her thought was de Marco and his consort had scrammed without surrendering the keys and probably trashed the apartment as a parting insult, you had to expect the worst from people like that. Baby sighed and scowled to herself and went down the hall to inspect the damage. When she stepped into the apartment she saw what was on the floor were sheets of black plastic, laid out like crinkled dropcloths, and then something stung her arm, she felt a jolt all through her body like when you touched an electrical fixture the wrong way and another jolt and then the room turned black as if black paint was spraying in her eyes and she felt her body falling, falling into black space with a smell of dentist's ether running through it, black on black and then a kind of midnight blue, where she began to see streaks of clouds or the smeary trails of faraway stars wheeling in infinite space, Baby floated and fell, weightless, passing through matter like a blade of light, into the Cimmerian land of darkness and whirlpools, all the way down to a drawing room at the bottom of a lake.

✝

They sang all the way out to the wastelands around Newark, songs they only knew scattered lyrics of, *Busted flat in Baton Rouge, waitin' for a train, My funny valentine, sweet funny valentine, Oh dear what can I do, Baby's in black and I'm feelin' blue,* Evelyn kept opening her bag and flipping through her trove, old passports and checkbooks and all Baby's memorabilia, ten thousand in cash that was lying on top of a dresser, best yet the genuine Social Security card, *three six nine, the goose drank wine, the monkey chewed tobacco on the streetcar line, the line broke, the monkey got choked, and they all lived together in a little rowboat.* And Devin was out of his funk, finally, the whole thing had really got his blood pumping, when it came down to an event like that Devin more than rose to the occasion, *forget your troubles, come on get happy, let's chase all the blues away,* Evelyn's own heart thumped in her throat as they crisscrossed the skeletal debris of forgotten industrial dreams, cranes and rail yards and great rusted monoliths of incomprehensible machinery, towers of tinker-toy iron rods splashed with algae green and russet scabs of oxidation, half-collapsed bridges sinking into lagoons of iridescent sludge and serpentine rivers of aubergine silt, Devin had scouted all these obscure access roads and bypasses whenever he had a spare afternoon, he hadn't inherited Warren's infallible sense of direction and took a lot of wrong turns but he knew, he said, certain landmarks, he'd recognize the location from various signs, there was a road winding through a forest, and another that ran through a town, and then a gravel pit, and a mile or so beyond the gravel pit an old cement plant where the land had been gouged out a quarter mile in every direction, and suddenly there it was, a vast lunar crater in the middle of absolutely nowhere, with massive machines squatting idle aside pylons and rudimentary concrete walls rising from deep trenches in the earth, the whole place empty and unguarded for the three-day weekend, Devin pulled the car down a service road that sheared off at a steep angle from the two-lane blacktop, they went rumbling along into an expanse of gravel and dust packed tight by the giant earthmovers, until they reached the most coherent of the burgeoning structures, where the inner supports of the building were already being placed. There were seemingly bottomless wells sunk throughout the phantom building, where steel girders would be driven into the foundations, holes the size of a city bus, and it was into one of these, around three on Sunday afternoon, that Devin dropped the black nylon duffel containing Baby Claymore in her swaddling of thirty-gallon trash bags. Baby Claymore, in a matter of a few days, would become an integral structural element of the newest and largest Home Depot outlet in the state of New Jersey.

†

"I need a drink," Evangeline announced when she finally arrived in the lobby bar at the Hilton. "We were *stuck* on the turnpike, I don't know what it is, that car goes twenty miles and poops out, Devin's taking it in as we speak, but you know what I think I'd like, besides a Long Island ice tea, is a little sporty car like an Audi to get around New York in. A big vehicle like the Lincoln, just try parking it when you're in a rush. And a lot of garages won't even let you park a car that big, I mean the underground garages, because they have to move the cars around all day, it's too much trouble for them."

Evelyn fairly gargled down the first Long Island iced tea, she ordered another immediately. She had her scarf in place and that air of normality but really she looked like hell, the slacks were wrong for a place like the Hilton bar even though the lobby looked like a Vegas lobby, all that vast slick marble and empty space, not that anybody besides Wilbur noticed that Evelyn didn't look right. He wasn't exactly sure where the agents were. They were blending in.

"Did you manage to find me a car rental?"

Evelyn had called him several times, each time to say they

were having car trouble, she wanted him to look into rental places
with reasonable rates.

"Tell you the truth, Ellen, I just got here a few hours ago, and
I'm jet-lagged as hell. At my age you don't hit the ground running
every place you land."

Sucking down another Long Island iced tea as if she were in a
competition, Evelyn nodded understandingly.

"Don't I know it. My God, Wilbur, I'll be sixty-three in
another six months. One day you're a little kid asking your mother
for candy, you blink a few times and you're ready for the rest
home. I've had a good life, though."

As Evelyn's third drink went down Wilbur considered the fact
that he would not be sitting there if he hadn't delivered a pizza to a
particular house on a particular street in Las Vegas, and wondered
whether a different delivery boy responding to the same order
would have found himself in the same shit Wilbur was in. He supposed the answer was no, and decided not to get depressed about
it. She told him a little bit about the senile ballerina and the house
full of faggots and how she would give him the keys when Devin
showed up, meanwhile he should check his suitcase right here at
the Hilton, just tell them he was checking in later and hold it for
him, which Wilbur got up and did while she continued drinking.

At the reception they took his bag and an agent, the one in
charge, Agent Nolan, asked him where the kid was. Wilbur said he
wasn't sure, and asked why they couldn't arrest Evangeline and get
the kid later.

"I see what's worrying you," Agent Nolan told him.

"No, you don't."

"You're thinking, what if the kid's on the loose and he knows
you set them up."

"I'm not thinking anything that dramatic," Wilbur said.

"Yes you are," Agent Nolan said with assurance. "And I'm
telling you, we've got you covered."

Wilbur went dutifully back to the lounge.

"This is one town that really sparkles," Evangeline told him, apropos of nothing. She was, Wilbur saw, drunk. He had, as a matter of fact, seldom seen her when she wasn't drunk. She was one of those functional drunks that developed a style around drinking when they were young and beautiful and kept the same style right through middle age and decrepitude. And because the style was so entrenched and generated so much self-assurance, it often continued to work despite the loss of everything that made it work in the first place. In Vegas you saw broads in their seventies still sporting the acrylic nails and the fuck-me hairdos and glitter tube tops vamping guys fifty years younger than they were, and the guys often paid for their drinks all night even if they didn't fuck them. People said the word *con* thinking it meant a specific bogus transaction, or that it was short for *convict*, but Wilbur knew perfectly well that the name of the game was *confidence*, in all the senses of the word that had always been missing from his character, that was why he was here and why he'd worn a vest on the flight and why he expected to take one in a vital organ before the day was finished, FBI or no FBI.

"Let's blow this joint," Evangeline said.

They went across Sixth Avenue to a restaurant attached to the Warwick Hotel, Ciao Europa, where they sat at the bar drinking wine. Wilbur could see one of the agents, the less talkative one, whose name was either Leshko or Lasker, standing in the plaza of a bank across the street. Ciao Europa had murals of a medieval, knights-in-clashing-armor theme and a lot of rich-looking people eating and the bartender looked a little bit like Dennis Hopper and Evangeline decided the house wine wasn't any good and ordered a bottle of something fresher, Château du Nord or Château de Neuf, something French and expensive anyway, and though she seemed to be making an effort at her usual avidity, Evelyn struck him as slightly torpid, a little bleary, the way that a boa constrictor is said to go sleepy after ingesting a very large mammal, for one thing she wasn't insisting, as would normally be her way, that twenty million things had to be done within the next twenty minutes, Ellen had always made Wilbur dizzy with the reach and prowess of her multidirectional energies, that night at April de Beckwith's place with the guns stuck out in his mind, you could cut the tension in that place with a meat cleaver maybe, yet none of it fazed Evangeline even slightly, she had been fearless and focused with the Marine boyfriend or husband or whatever he was screaming and throwing things in the bedroom, with April wailing about how fucked the whole situation was, Evangeline had just proceeded like the Queen of England dropping in on a family of loyal subjects for a photo op, and now with her wine and the soft tonal quality of Ciao Europa framing her still pleasant face and lilting voice and the casual observations she decorated conversation with, Evangeline seemed almost human to Wilbur, almost real, it was only the sight of Agent Leshko or Lasker through the long restaurant window that reminded him that Evelyn had become an object, as abstract in the situation as other people were to her.

She suggested they go for a walk, and paid the bill, and out on Sixth Avenue there was some sort of street fair cordoned off between 57th Street and somewhere south of the Hilton, it hadn't even registered with Wilbur when they crossed from the Hilton an hour earlier, maybe because it looked like Las Vegas did all the time, people teeming around, there were booths and tables and food concessions set up along either side of the street. Evangeline said this was what she loved about New York, that there was always something going on, she wanted to shop, she stopped every few feet to examine jewelry or t-shirts or baseball caps or what have you, the whole area smelled of broiling meats and Indian spices and whatever food they were selling here and there, fruit shakes and organic juices and scarves from Hindustan and puppies for adoption, kurdahs and Calvin Klein underwear and fragrances from exotic Brooklyn and bootleg hiphop tapes and videos of the current movies recorded with handheld digital cameras and people everywhere, all races all colors all sizes all sexes, in twos and threes and fours and sevens and solitary people lurching through the crowd like dazed travelers entering a mountain village after scaling the treacherous sheerness of the Himalayas, it was all like a movie Wilbur felt like an extra in, and all the motion and activity and objects and colors ran together like a weightless dream until they saw Devin and then the picture shifted suddenly, Wilbur felt himself being grabbed from behind and Agent Nolan pulled Evangeline out of the crowd into a space between an Italian sausage kiosk and a Mexican jewelry concession and Evelyn was screaming something about her pocketbook and yelling across the street to Wilbur how she was really sorry to get him involved and then Devin bolted, Agent Leshko had knocked him to the ground and pulled out a set of handcuffs but Devin rolled out from under him and ran, Wilbur didn't see it because the cop who cuffed him marched him over to the Hilton but later it came out that an NYPD officer working with the FBI tackled him in front of a Slurpee stand and because Devin kept squirming and kicking and trying to escape this officer wedged his baton under Devin's chin and immobilized him by means of the infamous so-called choke hold, which, unfortunately, and unavoidably according to the mayor's statement the next day, resulted in windpipe injury and accidental strangulation, despite the best efforts of New York Police to revive the suspect.

The cops let Wilbur collect his suitcase and drove him straight to the airport and more or less kicked him out of the cruiser without a word of thanks, goodbye and good luck.

✝

I'm speaking as a mother, Larry. Now, I know you are a recent father, you have two precious kids, those precious little ones, and you know what you would feel if anything happened, the bond between a parent and a child, how strong that bond is and how much it touches us, I held Devin in my arms as a little baby and my husband and I, he slept with us in our bed, my precious little boy. It's very hard for me every day, I think the worst thing that ever happens is the loss of one's child.

We have been the scapegoats of the biggest witch hunt in American history, in England they say it is the biggest miscarriage of justice in the history of this country. Who? Well, they made a documentary, on the English television, it's coming out here, and there are all kinds of questions people are beginning to ask about this case. When there is no crime, and no body, and not a single shred of evidence. When you look at the facts, Larry, and I hope that you will, I trust that you will. Will you?

I've always been a big fan of your show, because I know that you're fair. And I hope every person who's watching this will look into the case and don't believe all the lies, which starting from day one, I mean how would you feel if they put pictures of you on every street corner saying that you're guilty.

Well, I assume the city and the mayor and all the authorities, who-ever decides to do these things.

I am so glad you asked me that, Larry. If you look at the transcript, and I beg that every person in America who cares about justice will just read those transcripts, because now, you see, there's a record, before the trial was over you just had this biased judge and this district attorney—

Why us? Because we're the most convenient victims. Instead of look-ing for who would benefit by Mrs. Claymore's disappearance they landed on us because we happened to be there at the time. They never had a case, they don't have one piece of evidence—

Look at Diallo. Look at all these cases. They have federal monitors now because the police are out of control, these people murdered my son and this is going on every single day. If Americans don't wake up, because this goes straight to the Constitution, Larry, then there is no justice in America any more.

I met Wanda Claymore, let me think, in 1995, my husband had just died and I was interested in longevity, and a man at Prudential Insurance introduced us, we got to be friends.

I didn't hear from her for a long time, and then she called me and said all these people were advising her to do this or that with her money and she didn't trust these people and she asked if I would help her sell her town house, she knew I had connections, and I said sure.

She couldn't face these people, she didn't want them to know she was getting rid of them, this Asra and these other people, she had just had enough, she wanted to get rid of the place and get these people out of her life.

What did I think of her? I liked her, she was fun, she was a character. I didn't know her well, but I liked her, and she wanted to sell this apartment. This was a legitimate transaction, that's one of the things we wanted to bring out in the trial, but this biased judge, who kept me from testifying on the stand—

I can prove it, she kept me out of contact with my lawyer, she said I couldn't use the telephone, and I begged to take that stand, Larry, if the jury had heard me, if they'd been allowed to hear the truth—

I don't know what really happened to her but none of this makes sense, if you were going to buy an apartment, you need the person to be there.

A good friend. I'm only sorry I can't talk about that case because they tell me it will influence the trial. But I look forward to that trial because I think it will clear up a lot of mystery about this case in New York, when the truth comes out. That this has been the biggest frame-up, on circumstantial evidence, in the history of this country.

No, if you read the record, and this is what I'm saying, everything was planted. I did not have anything belonging to Mrs. Claymore, and the police themselves admit there is no trail of evidence, in other words there's no record of where they took these things, what happened to them afterwards—

I would never say that. Of course I've done things in my life, I think I've paid for them. But nothing like this. Yes, I stole some lipsticks, things like that. When I was a little girl on the streets of Los Angeles, I was homeless, I maybe stole something to eat, some cheese or something